THE BREAKERS

CLAUDIE GALLAY is a teacher who lives in Provence. *The Breakers* has been a runaway bestseller in France.

ALISON ANDERSON's translations include Muriel Barbery's bestselling novel *The Elegance of the Hedgehog*. She is the author of two novels: *Hidden Latitudes* and *Darwin's Wink*.

"Mystery and romantic tension nudge the narrative along, but the author's real interest lies in loss and the way it can shape a life as subtly and insistently as the sea ... This is a novel strung together from sentences as spare as its geographical backdrop, and a deft translation carries evocative echoes of the French original"   HEPHZIBAH ANDERSON, *Daily Mail*

"Everything is carefully described, yet the writing is never laboured. By drawing on the everyday, the small rituals, the uneasy exchanges, Gallay has written a slow-moving, calm, complicated and compelling novel that balances stagnation and panic, acceptance and denial, all juxtaposed with the way the past insists on shaping the present"   EILEEN BATTERSBY, *Irish Times*

"Gallay creates a wonderfully turbulent atmosphere"
                                        KATE SAUNDERS, *Saga Magazine*

"Voted book of the year when it was originally published in France, this is so atmospheric it transports you straight to the storm-lashed fishing village ... It seethes with loss, intrigue and secrets"   *U Magazine*

"The unravelling of the mystery at its core is compelling and convincing"   ALANNAH HOPKIN, *Irish Examiner*

Claudie Gallay

THE
BREAKERS

Translated from the French by
Alison Anderson

MACLEHOSE PRESS
QUERCUS · LONDON

First published in Great Britain in 2011 by MacLehose Press
This paperback edition first published in 2011 by

MacLehose Press
an imprint of Quercus
21 Bloomsbury Square
London, WC1A 2NS

First published in French as *Les Déferlantes*

This edition is supported by the French Ministry of Foreign Affairs,
as part of the Burgess programme run by the Cultural Department
of the French Embassy in London.

Liberté • Égalité • Fraternité
RÉPUBLIQUE FRANÇAISE

A CIP catalogue reference for this book is available
from the British Library

ISBN 978 1 906694 71 5

2 4 6 8 10 9 7 5 3 1

Designed and typeset in Golden Cockerel by Patty Rennie
Printed and bound in Great Britain
by Clays Ltd, St Ives plc

For Lucile

You will know me, I am
the one who passes by . . .
RENÉ-PAUL ENTREMONT

A NOTE ON PREVERT

Jacques Prévert was born on 4 February, 1900, at Neuilly-sur-Seine on the outskirts of Paris, and died of cancer at Omonville-la-Petite on 11 April, 1977. Associated with Surrealists like André Breton and Louis Aragon in the 1920s, he made his name with humorous anarchic "song-poems" about street life in Paris, collected in *Paroles* (1946), *Spectacles* (1951) and *Imaginaires* (1970). Many of his poems, such as *Les Feuilles Mortes*, were set to music and sung by French singers including Yves Montand, Juliette Gréco and Edith Piaf. He was also well known as a screen-writer, his most celebrated films being *Les Enfants du Paradis* and *Le Jour Se Lève*. He was described in 1959 as "a short, white-haired man with blue eyes, blunt expressive fingers, cigarette dangling from his lips like a corny Apache dancer". With Paul Grimault and others, he adapted fairy stories by Hans Christian Andersen as animated films, including *Le Roi et l'Oiseau*, on which he was working when he died and which was dedicated to him. At the opening night Grimault kept the seat beside him empty for Prévert.

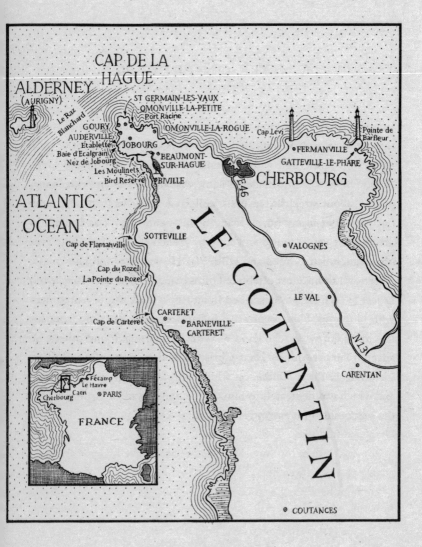

I

The first time I saw Lambert was on the day of the big storm. The sky was black, and very low, and you could already hear the waves pounding out to sea.

He got there just after me, and sat down outside, at a table in the wind. He was facing the sun, and wincing, as if he were crying.

I looked at him, not because he had taken the worst table, nor because of the face he was making. I looked at him because he was smoking the way you used to, with his eyes staring off into space, and rubbing his thumb over his lips. Dry lips, perhaps even drier than yours.

I thought he must be a journalist, a storm at equinox, you can get some pretty good photographs. Beyond the breakwater the wind was ploughing the waves, driving the currents over by the Raz Blanchard, black rivers that had come a long way, from seas to the north or from the depths of the Atlantic.

Morgane came out of the *auberge*. She saw Lambert.

"You're not from around here," she said, when she had asked him what he would like.

She was sullen, the way she could be when she had to serve the customers in bad weather.

"Are you here for the storm?"

He shook his head.

"For Prévert, then? Everyone comes here for Prévert."

"I'm looking for a bed for the night," he said.

She shrugged.

"We don't do rooms."

"Where can I find one?"

"There's a hotel in the village, opposite the church . . . or in La Rogue. Inland. My boss has a friend, an Irishwoman, who has a *pension*. Would you like her number?"

He nodded.

"And can I get something to eat?"

"It's three o'clock . . ."

"So what?"

"Well, at three, all we've got is ham sandwiches."

She pointed to the sky, to the bar of clouds rolling in. Below them, a few rays of sun filtered through. In ten minutes it would be dark as night.

"It's going to chuck it down!" she said.

"That won't change anything. Six oysters and a glass of wine?"

Morgane smiled. Lambert was on the handsome side. She felt like giving him a hard time.

"On the terrace we serve only drinks."

I was drinking a black coffee, two tables behind him. There were no other customers. Even inside it was empty.

Tiny plants with grey leaves had taken root in the cracks in the stone. With the wind, they seemed to be crawling.

Morgane sighed.

"I have to ask the *patron*."

She stopped at my table, her red fingernails drumming on the wooden edge.

"They all come here for Prévert . . . Why else would anyone come here?"

She glanced over her shoulder and then disappeared inside. I thought she might not come back, but a moment later she was there with a glass of wine, some bread on a saucer, and the oysters on a bed of seaweed, and she set it all down in front of him.

Along with the Irishwoman's telephone number.

"The *patron* said, alright for the oysters, but outside, no tablecloths . . . and you'll have to hurry because it's going to pour."

I ordered a second coffee.

He drank his wine. He held his glass awkwardly, but he was a chewer of oysters.

Morgane piled up the chairs, pushed them all against the wall, and enclosed them with a chain. She waved to me.

From where I sat, I could see the entire harbour. La Griffue, that's where we lived, Morgane with her brother Raphaël on the ground floor, and me on my own in the flat above. It was a hundred metres beyond the *auberge*, you only had to cross the quay, a house built on the edge of the road, almost in the sea. Nothing else around. When there were storms, it was absolutely deluged. The local people said you would have to be mad to live in such a place. They had given it the name La Griffue because of the fingernail sound the tamarisk branches make when they scrape against the shutters.

It used to be a hotel, before.

When was before?

In the 1970s.

It was not a big harbour. An end-of-the-world sort of place, with a handful of men and only a few boats.

La Hague.

To the west of Cherbourg.

East and west, I always mix them up.

I came here in the autumn, with the wild ducks, so I had been here a little over six months. I worked for the Centre ornithologique in Caen. I observed the birds, counted them, I had spent the two winter months studying the behaviour of cormorants on days of deep frost. Their sense of smell, their eyesight . . . Hours outdoors in the wind. When spring came, I studied the migrating birds, counted their eggs, their nests. It was repetitive work, it was what I needed. I was also trying to find out why their population was declining in the region of La Hague.

3

I was not well paid.

But I had a roof over my head.

And I had yet to see a true storm.

*   *   *

Two huge gulls came to shriek by the boats, their necks outstretched, their wings slightly spread, their whole bodies yearning towards the sky. Suddenly they fell silent. The sky grew even thicker, it got very dark, but it was not night.

It was something else.

Something ominous.

That is what silenced the birds.

I had been warned. When it starts, best not be outdoors.

The fishermen checked the moorings on their boats one last time and then they left, one after the other. A quick glance over our way.

Men are strong when the sea rises, that is what they say round here. The women make the most of such moments to cling to them. They grab them wherever they happen to be, at the back of the stables or in the hold of a boat. They let themselves be taken.

The wind was already howling. Perhaps that was what was most violent, even more than the waves. That wind, driving the men away.

Only our two tables left on the terrace, and no-one else about.

Lambert turned. He looked at me.

"Bloody weather!" he said.

Morgane came back out. "Have you finished?"

She picked up his plate, the bread, my cup.

The *patron* had got out his reinforcing rods, and was bolting the door already.

"We're in for it!" he said.

Morgane turned to me.

"Are you staying?"

"Two more minutes, yes . . ."

I wanted to see, while I still could. See, hear, feel. She shrugged. A first drop of rain splattered on to the tabletop.

"Put your chairs away when you leave!"

I nodded. Lambert didn't reply. She went off at a run, her arms wrapped around her waist, she crossed the space from the *auberge* to La Griffue, ran up to the door and disappeared inside.

A first bolt of lightning clapped somewhere above the island of Alderney, a second one closer in. And then the wind came to smash against the breakwater, a first gust, like a battering ram. Boards of wood began to rattle under the shelter where Max was repairing his boat. Somewhere a poorly closed shutter was banging.

The sea hardened, turned black as if something intolerable were knotting it up inside. The deafening howl of the wind mingled with that of the waves. It was oppressive. I pulled up my collar. I put my chair away.

Lambert had not moved. He took a packet of cigarettes from his pocket. He seemed calm, indifferent.

"Are you leaving?"

I nodded.

The winds that blow when there is a storm are like the whirlwinds of the damned. It is said they are evil souls who sweep into people's homes to take what they are owed. What we owe them, that is, we who have stayed behind, the living.

"Can you sometimes see the stars?" he asked, pointing to the sky above us.

"Sometimes, yes."

"Because in town, you can't see them any more."

The wind tore at his voice.

He had a slow voice.

"In town, it's because of the street-lamps," he explained.

He had kept his packet of cigarettes in his hand. He was turning it over and over, a mechanical gesture. His presence made the imminent arrival of the gale even more oppressive.

"But it's fairly rare, right?"

"What's rare?"

He hesitated for a few seconds, then ran his thumb over his lip. I looked at him, his face, his eyes, him.

That gesture he had just made.

It was right after that, that I heard something whistling. I had time to step back. The shadow that slapped me was red. I felt something bite my cheek. It was a sheet of metal, as big as two hands. It flew over a dozen metres then the wind slammed it to the ground. It scurried it further along. I heard it scrape over the gravel. Like teeth against sand.

I put my fingers to my face; there was blood.

"What's rare?" I heard myself say for the second time, my gaze still held by the metal sheet.

He lit his cigarette.

"The stars," he replied.

Then he repeated, "It's rare, to see stars in the sky in town . . ."

And then he pointed to my cheek. "You'd better do something about that."

In my room, later, with my palms flat against the windowpane, I saw my face, the red mark the metal sheet had left.

It was hot where it was swollen. You can die from a scratch of loose sheet metal.

Sheet metal, rust.

He had talked about cities. He had said, There are places where you no longer see the stars.

My bare feet on the floor. My fingerprints on the windowpane. I disinfected the scratch with a last drop of alcohol.

I stayed at the window. My room looked out over the waves. A big bed with a quilt. Two sagging armchairs. On the table was a box with my binoculars, my chronometer, and books about birds. Detailed maps, with photocopies, charts.

At the bottom of the box, a handful of pens. A logbook. I had been keeping the log for six months. I did not know how long I would be there. Before, I had been a biology professor at the University of Avignon. I taught ornithology. With my students we would go observing the birds in the Camargue. We would spend entire nights inside huts on piles.

After you, I applied for two years of sabbatical. I thought I would die. I came here.

The previous tenant had left everything one morning. Apparently he could no longer take the solitude. He had left tins of food in the cupboards, and packets of biscuits. Sugar in a box. Powdered milk, and coffee in little brown sachets. With a green tree on the packet, Fair Trade. Books.

An old radio. A television. There was no picture, only sound.

Two bottles beneath the sink. Undrinkable wine, the taste of plastic. And yet I did drink it, alone, one day when the weather was fine.

I went from one window to the other. I had never seen such a black sky. The clouds formed a leaden cloak above the hills. The boats were rocking. Lambert had left his table, but he was still on the quay. He had buttoned his jacket, and had his hands in his pockets. He was pacing back and forth.

It was not raining, but the rain was gathering, a frightening mass zigzagged with lightning, still above the sea, but it was coming closer. A first rumbling of thunder. Lambert took a few steps towards the breakwater, but the wind was too strong, it was impossible to go forward. I took my binoculars and focused on his face. Raindrops were lashing his cheeks.

He stayed there for a long while, then there was a crash of lightning and the rain poured down.

There were no other cars on the quay, only his. Not another living soul, only the three of us in La Griffue.

The three of us, and him there, outside.

He was in the rain.

A first wave came over the breakwater. Then others. At the same time, an ungodly roar. A bird, caught unawares by the violence of the wind, came and crashed against my window, a huge gull. He stayed there, unable to move for a few seconds, his gaze astonished, and then the wind claimed him, lifted him up, took him away.

The storm broke. Breakers crashed against the house. My face glued to the window, I tried to see outside. The street-lamps were not lit. There was no more light. In the bursts of lightning, the rocks circling the lighthouse seemed to be shattering in all directions. I had never seen it like this. I do not know if I would have liked to have been anywhere else.

When I looked down on the quay, I saw that Lambert's car was no longer there. It was heading towards the village. Tail-lights in the distance. And then nothing.

*   *   *

It lasted two hours, a terrible deluge. To the point you could no longer tell earth from water. La Griffue was reeling. I could not tell whether it was the rain that was lashing the windows or the waves that had reached this far. It made me feel sick. I stood there with my eyelashes against the windowpane, my breath burning. I clung to the walls.

In the violence, black waves were entwined like bodies. They became walls of water, propelled, driven forward, I saw them coming, fear in my gut, walls smashing against the rocks and coming to dissolve beneath my window.

These waves, the breakers.

I loved them.

They frightened me.

It was so dark. Several times I thought the wind was going to tear the roof off. I could hear the beams cracking.

I lit some candles. They melted, white wax dripping on to the wooden table. A strange burning film. In a flash of lightning I could see the quay, flooded as if the sea had risen over the land and swallowed everything. There were other flashes. Bolts of lightning like bars. I thought it would never end.

Raphaël was in his studio, a huge room just below mine. Wooden floorboards separated us. I could hear him. I could see him, too, all I had to do was lie on the floor and look through a little space between the boards, beneath the carpet, a few millimetres.

Everyone said it was impossible to live here, so close to the sea. So close, it was as if you were in the sea.

Was it daytime? Night-time? I tried to sleep. It was too warm under the quilt. Too cold without it. I closed my eyes. I saw the piece of metal. Its shadow. I heard Lambert's voice mingling with the night, the horrid scraping sound of the metal. The ticking of my watch on my wrist, it all got mixed up. I woke up, I was sweating.

The stovepipe ran through my room, heated the air and went back out through the roof. It was a tin stovepipe. The heat caused the pipe to vibrate.

Raphaël was walking, his steps like those of a wild beast in a cage, he was afraid for his sculptures. Mere plaster, clay. He said all it would take was for one window to explode and everything would be under water.

He was stuffing his stove with logs as if fire could hold back the sea.

I could hear him shouting.

"This house has held out before, it will hold out this time!"

I went and peered through the crack. He had lit huge candelabras. With the statues, it made his studio look like a church.

I looked at my wound in the light of a candle. The scratch had gone dark, almost purple.

People called me *La Griffue*, and they called me the *horsain*, the stranger, someone who was not born round here, the way they had called everyone who had come to live here before me. And all those who would follow. And they would follow.

Raphaël called me Princess.

For Lili, I was Miss.

For you, I was Blue. That name on your lips; that was what you called me. You said it was because of my eyes, everything that haunted them.

I warmed the palm of my hand by the candle flame and placed it against my wound. I planted matches in the wax.

For months I had been without you. Absence absorbed everything. It even absorbed time. Absorbed your very image. I sat there with my eyes staring at the rusty window frame. I planted more matches.

The candle, in the end, looked like a voodoo doll.

In the morning, the moorland seemed dead in the light of day. It was still raining and the wind was howling. It hurried over the surface of the water, tearing up long strips of oily foam that it splashed down again further along. Desolate packets. In the harbour, the boats struggled not to sink.

A car came down from the village then stopped. It turned around before reaching the quay.

This was the time of the turn, the moment of silence when the sea lifts up the waves and turns them over.

I slept. A few hours to catch up on my long sleepless nights. Nights gone by. Nights to come.

I drank some coffee. I rummaged in the cupboard, my arms full of piles of *Paris Match*, old issues, Grace Kelly's wedding and Jacques Brel's death. Black-and-white photographs. Old magazines. With them came dust, scraps of paper nibbled by rats. A bird skeleton. In one magazine I found a photo of Demi Moore. I put it aside to give to Raphaël.

I found a biography of Saint Teresa of Avila, and the diary of Etty Hillesum. Between the pages of a book, a postcard of a Hopper painting, a girl sitting at a table in a café. The walls painted green. I put the book away, kept the card.

I went out into the hall. The wall on the north side was damp. Wetness was seeping all along the skirting boards, on the steps. There were white streaks on the walls, salt.

The light switch on the right. The wall was peeling away. The wallpaper was coming unstuck, entire strips of it, like curtains. Other doors opened on to empty rooms. An old telephone with a grey dial was on the wall at the very bottom of the stairs. It had been out of order for a long time. When we needed to make a call, we used the telephone box on the quay, you had to have a card. Otherwise, we could go to Lili's or to the *auberge* in the port. Raphaël said that in an emergency you had to get down on your knees and pray. It made him laugh.

There was an entire row of wooden letter boxes nailed up in the entry. Raphaël's name was on one of them: *R. Delmate, Sculpteur*. There were other names, labels that had been sellotaped, peeling off. An enamel plaque: *Please close the door*. It dated back to before, to the time when the house had been a hotel.

Then it was furnished rooms, afterwards.

Everyone had left.

The labels had stayed. A stuffed dog sat enthroned on a shelf above the door. It was Raphaël's dog. His name was Diogenes. Apparently he died of fear one stormy night, a long time ago. Fear had turned his stomach inside out. It happens sometimes, with dogs.

I went downstairs, step by step cautiously, my hand on the railing.

Raphaël was in the hall. He had opened the door slightly, he wanted to look outside, to see the façade of La Griffue. It was too dark out, there was too much wind. You could not even see the courtyard.

He closed the door.

He said, "We have to wait." Then, when he saw my cheek, "What happened to you?"

I reached up with my hand.

"A flying sheet of metal . . ."

"Was it rusty?"

"A little bit . . ."

"Did you disinfect it?"

"Yes."

He looked at my wound, wincing. He had spent two years in the slums of Kolkata. From time to time he would talk about what he had seen there.

"Are your vaccinations up to date?"

"I cleaned it with alcohol."

He shrugged.

The television was on. Morgane was sleeping, curled up on the sofa, one hand closed over her mouth. With her round hips and heavy breasts she looked like a Botero sculpture. The rat was sleeping next to her, tucked against the thick folds of her belly.

Raphaël went over to his sister.

"I wonder how she can possibly sleep through such an infernal racket."

He lifted a strand of hair that was in her face and tucked it behind her ear. An infinitely tender gesture. The strand slipped down again.

He turned away.

He made some coffee.

His gestures were slow. He had time. We all did, here.

Morgane smelled the coffee and yawned. She dragged herself over to us, her eyes half closed.

"Morning, you two."

Her hair dishevelled. Her skirt too short on her big thighs. She snuggled up to her brother.

"Bit of a racket last night," she said.

"A bit, yes . . ."

I looked at them. I was just past forty. Raphaël a bit younger. Morgane was the youngest, she would turn thirty in July. A late baby, she said, the loveliest ones.

She took a sip from Raphaël's cup. She often did that. I used to do it with you, too. Before. In the morning. I would press myself against you. I needed your warmth. Afterwards, you got so cold, you could not take it any more.

*   *   *

Raphaël opened the door. We looked at each other and advanced, all three of us, strange survivors, our feet in boots. There were branches everywhere. Deep puddles. The wind was still howling, but it was not as strong. Max's boat had held up, there it was, firmly in place under its shelter, wedged on its blocks.

We went round the house.

We went into the garden. On the ocean side. It smelled of salt.

I found the broken body of the huge gull that had crashed against my window. There were pieces of beams, remnants of crates.

The waves had subsided. The shore was covered with a fringe of thick yellow foam, and wherever you looked, there were clumps of seaweed like long tresses of hair flung down in disgust.

Old Nan was on the breakwater, her arms folded across her waist. She stood there, before anyone else, motionless, her crucifix in her hand, looking out to sea. She wore her storm clothing, a long black dress of thick cloth. Those who knew her said that in the cloth you could read words sewn with black thread. A thread of words. And that the words told her story.

Nan's story.

People said too that she had had another name, but that the name had been taken away by her loved ones. Her dead, an entire family lost at sea. She was there because she believed that some day the sea would bring them back to her.

The first cars arrived. People from the village. A fisherman said that a cargo ship headed north had lost its shipment of planks, and that the wind was pushing them this way. The news spread. A tractor had parked by the side of the road, as near as possible to the beach. A few delivery vans. Max arrived. He kissed us all, because his boat had made it. He waited for the timber, next to a group of men, his hands in his pockets, his body somewhat lost in his big blue canvas jacket.

The men talked amongst themselves, never taking their eyes from the sea. I stared at the place where they were looking. The light hurt my eyes. Before, I used to live in the south. There had been too much light. My eyes were too blue. My skin too white. It burned, even in winter.

I was still burning. We all burn. From something else.

They arrived by the dozens, planks like bodies. Clear shadows lifted up on waves that were almost black, pitching shadows. Carried. Brought back, all of them, to men. Old Nan stepped forward. She was looking into the sea, into the troughs between the waves. She did not care about the planks.

The men stopped talking. Or hardly at all. A few words, just the most important things. There were a few women with them. A handful of children.

The gendarmes were there too, writing down names. Number plates.

The cargo ship had dropped anchor, you could see it in the distance, it had stopped in the very place where its cargo had slipped off. A police launch had been sent from Cherbourg. Lambert was on the quay. Alone, off to one side, in his leather jacket. I wondered what he was doing there. I focused on his face through my binoculars. Square jaw, stubble. Thick skin, with a few deep wrinkles. His trousers were rumpled. I wondered whether he had slept at the Irishwoman's place, or in his car.

On the beach the movement continued, of planks, of men. Smells of the seabed mingled with that of skin, and the stronger sweat gleaming on a horse's chest.

I followed the men.

A car arrived. We all stopped together for a moment, captured in the yellow light of the headlamps. Lambert came over. The car's headlamps lit up his face. Then the car moved on, and it was as if his face had been swallowed by the night.

I heard his voice.

He said, "This is what the end of the world must be like."

Perhaps because of the noise, and these men, almost in the sea.

"Yes, like this . . . only worse," I replied.

Old Nan turned away from the planks. She was walking from one man to another, peering at faces. Even the children's faces, that she would squeeze between her hands, her gaze greedy, desperate, until she shoved them away and moved on to another. Even Max's face. The children let her, they had been told, Don't be afraid, she's looking for someone. Here, everyone was afraid of her. Those who were not afraid avoided her.

The hem of her skirt had dragged in the water, and now it was dragging in the sand. When she saw Lambert, she forgot all the others. She grasped her heavy skirt with her hand. She came towards us, until she was right up against him. She looked at him, her eyes suddenly adrift beneath her too-white hair. With her hand she touched his face. She did it very quickly, and he did not have time to step back. She had warts on her fingers. She could have burned them off, there were a million ways to get rid of them, everyone knew them here, they called them *apples, spit, piss* . . . I think she had got used to her warts. Sometimes she would caress them. I have seen her lick them.

Lambert pushed her away.

"Fish eat eyes," she said, in her cavernous voice.

She cocked her head to one side.

"On a moonlit night, blood rises to the surface. You can hear the cries . . ."

She gave a strange smile then turned away, as she had from the others, she took a few steps and then she came back, more troubled than mad, and she stared into his face again, going over it all, his forehead, his eyes, that is what she did.

15

She opened her mouth. "Michel . . ." She smiled, a smile both very brief and very fierce. "You've come back . . ."

Around us, the men went on with their work, indifferent.

"My name is Lambert."

She gave her terrible smile again and shook her head, no, several times, a long swaying motion.

"You are Michel . . ."

She said it again, through the chalky creases of her lips.

Normally, she would cling to a face and then move on to the next one. With Lambert, it was different. A desire to touch him, a need. She caressed his cheek, again, and her smile, for a moment almost peaceful.

It was sickening to see her hand on his face, that contact, cold surely, with a stranger's skin.

Lambert pushed her away, too roughly, and the men turned round. Nan said nothing, she nodded as if there were a secret between them. She turned away.

The wrinkled texture of her dress, the hem damp with sand.

Lambert stepped back. He was embarrassed by what he had done, and also because the men had stopped and were speaking in low voices.

Nan moved away, pulling her big shawl around her shoulders. She went to the water's edge. At one point she stopped and turned round. I thought I could still see her smile.

"She's like that sometimes," I said.

"What do you mean, like what?"

"A bit mad."

Lambert did not take his eyes off her.

"Her entire family was lost at sea, a shipwreck, on a wedding day. She was seven. When there are storms, she thinks that every stranger's face is someone given back by the sea."

Lambert nodded.

He was still looking Nan's way.

"I think I know her story . . ."

He looked at me.

"I used to spend holidays here, a very long time ago . . . Can you tell me more?"

"The two families set off in a rowing boat for an outing. The weather was fine. Nan was too little to go with them. When the boat began to rock, the people who saw them from the shore thought they were messing about. First a woman fell overboard, then another. They were all seafaring people. The boat sank. Nan was on the quay, she saw everything, heard everything. Her hair turned white overnight."

"Wasn't there a dog on the boat?"

"A dog? Yes, there was."

"My mother told me that story."

He looked at the sea.

I looked at him. It was as if his features had been sketched hastily, almost at random.

Irregular lines in thick skin.

"It was a little dog," I said. "It managed to swim to a rock. It clung to it . . . After that, I don't know. They found the bridegroom's body. Not the wife's. Some say it was the other way round."

We took a few steps along the shore. He wanted to know the end of the story. I told him that the dog had held on as long as it could, and that it had eventually been swept out to sea.

He nodded his head again and said, "They rang the bells. They always ring the bells for the dead."

His face went strange when he said that.

"The sea swallowed them all, the way it swallowed the rowboat and the dog. And let them go again, one after the other . . . It lasted for weeks. There were the bodies it kept, neither the most beautiful ones nor the youngest. Others that it gave back."

We continued to walk. The wind was cold, damp with spray. Max walked by us. He was carrying a long plank. Lambert's gaze followed him for a long while, and he turned again towards the place on the shore where Nan was standing. The black of her dress merged with the black of the sea. From a distance, all you could see of her was the thick mass of her long white hair.

"Why did she call me Michel?"

"She confused you with someone. An uncle, a brother, who knows . . . ?"

He nodded. He stopped. He took a packet of cigarettes from his pocket.

"And you, are you from round here?"

"No, but everyone will tell you that story, if you hang about long enough."

He struck a match between his hands and lit his cigarette.

"Her white hair, it's because of the melanin . . ." he said, letting out a first puff. "When you've had a fright, the melanin, the colour goes away."

His hair was greying on the sides and I wondered if he had ever been frightened.

At noon, I sat at my usual table, next to the aquarium. The lobster guardian! That is what the *patron* called me the first time I came. He had seated me there. The table for loners. Not the best one. Nor the worst. I had a view on the room and on the harbour.

Because of the storm, there was no daily menu. The *patron* had put up a sign: MINIMUM SERVICE TODAY.

He showed me the meat, some lamb chops cooking on the grill in the fireplace.

The gendarmes were leaning against the bar.

"Wrecks are providential for people round here!" said the *patron*.

The gendarmes did not reply. They were accustomed, and besides they had been born round here, their sector somewhere between Cherbourg and Beaumont. They knew everyone.

The *patron* brought me a few shrimps while I waited. A glass of wine.

I looked out the window, the planks kept on coming, the men were waiting.

Lambert was still on the quay.

Old Nan had vanished.

* * *

That evening, the sea took the planks back out, and we all met up at Lili's. For a few hours, the men pressed against the bar, newcomers joining those who were already there. Kids bought handfuls of peanuts and went to eat them at the back of the room, leaning against the pinball machine. There was a smell of wool, and damp clothes steaming in the warmth.

Max was at the bar. Lili entrenched behind her counter. She was wearing her nylon dress with pink and white diamonds, and an apron tied over it.

When she saw me come in, she motioned, You alright? I nodded. I wove a way between the tables. It was full everywhere except at the back, where Old Mother sat. I made my way over there.

Lili has always said *tu* to me, even when she knew I was the woman staying at La Griffue. That I had come to observe the birds, that I had taken her father's job. She did not talk about her father.

When she heard about the wreck, she had cooked up some vegetables, an entire stewpot, with bits of bacon and sausage fat. It was something she liked, the communion of men, there in her bistro. Sharing. A particular atmosphere of warmth, when tiredness was creeping on, and the men grew drowsy and went on talking to keep from falling asleep.

"Evening, Old Mother . . ."

That was what everyone called her, Old Mother. She did not look at me. She was lapping up her soup like a famished animal, hunched over, her eyes in her plate. She was so old, to me she was ageless.

You must not ask anything complicated of Lili when the bistro is full. If you wanted soup, you got two ladlefuls. Two euros a bowl. If you did not like soup, there was mulled wine or a little green liqueur that she poured into stemless glasses. If you did not like what she had, she would show you the door.

It was crowded. It was hot. I took off my jumper.

When Lambert came in, the men looked round. A stranger in the café. Lili looked up. I saw the moment their eyes met. For a few seconds they stared at each other, then looked away almost at the same time, and I sensed that they knew one another.

Lambert made his way through the tables, he found a perch and Lili went on serving.

Conversations resumed. All anyone talked about was the wreck, this one, and others, from the past. Women who would climb to the top of the cliff in the middle of the night, lighting fires, dancing all around, their skirts swinging. Old stories with strange names – Mylène, the lovely Béatrix, names that mingled with others, I listened to them, they talked about witches and toads, in the hubbub voices ran together, I heard talk of *goublins* and fairies, marsh harriers, newts in fountains, old oaks, red maples . . .

The men told other stories, where women's skirts caused boats to founder. The children eventually fell asleep, one after the other, they drifted off with their heads in their arms, or curled up on their mother's lap. Even as they slept, their eyelids quivered. They had dreams of fire and treasures.

Old Mother dipped her spoon into her bowl. She gave me a shifty look, her mouth slightly open.

"And the old man?" she croaked.

Lili said you must not ever answer her when she mentioned Théo. I said nothing.

She insisted, "Where's the old man?"

"It's night-time . . ." I said.

I turned and pointed to the window.

"At night, old people don't go out, they're not cats."

She resumed her lapping.

The little Stork slipped among the tables and came to press up against me. She was a strange little thing, a wild child with a finger-print above her lip. A poorly operated harelip. She lived on a farm just below. She did not talk a lot. I had grown attached to her.

"Shouldn't you be in bed?"

She rummaged in her pockets and pulled out a handful of little yellow coins that she showed me, then she went to put her coins on the bar in front of Lili. Lili said a few words and the Stork nodded.

People said that the mark on her lip was the fingerprint a *goublin* had made when she was only a few days old. *Goublins* are funny little creatures, in the same family as trolls and imps. People said the one who had marked the Stork came out of the rock at Câtet one night, and he had taken advantage of the fact that her mother was away to mark the little waif in her cradle.

Children who have been marked in this way are ugly, but the fairies protect them.

I turned my head. Lambert was smoking, listening to what the men were saying. He spoke to no-one and no-one seemed to notice him. Only Lili. Several times I caught her looking at his face. A lingering look.

Here, everyone knew everyone else.

She was not looking at Lambert as if he were a stranger.

The Stork came back. She slipped between my chair and the wall. She opened her hand and showed me what she had bought, barley sugar, some boiled sweets and three little caramels wrapped in trans-parent paper.

It was almost midnight when the men went away again, one after the other, their steps slow, and they scattered throughout the village.

The Stork's father was one of the last to leave. His soles seemed heavy. I met him on the path. He was holding the horse by the bridle, an enormous beast with a broad chest, the corpulence of an ox. The horse's shoes scraped against the road.

The father's boots.

The dog, following.

And to the rear, the child, the Stork, walking with her hand on the cart. Her eyes almost closed. Staggering. On her feet, boots with laces that were too short and did not make it through all the holes.

Lambert had left, too, alone in his car. He had headed down the road towards Omonville.

I went down to La Griffue. On the way I met a man going the other way, pushing a cart, and farther along was a car, planks sticking out of its boot.

Old Nan was no longer there.

I walked along the quay. I saw the sheet of metal floating on the water, among the boats. A square of yellow light shone on the hillside, it was the kitchen window, where Théo lived.

*   *   *

There was a light still in Raphaël's studio. All I had to do was open the door. He was there, sitting at his table, his back to the wood stove. Five plaster heads were hanging from a beam just behind him by means of sturdy hemp ropes.

"Why aren't you asleep?"

He turned and looked up at me, his eyes red with fatigue. Around him the floor was strewn with rubble, bits of plaster that had been crushed beneath his feet; it looked like chalk.

He showed me the sculpture he was working on. A naked woman with a hollow torso, made more vulnerable still by the presence of a thin strip of rag which Raphaël had draped over her shoulders.

"It's just a maquette for now," he said, as if to apologize for what he had done.

The light gave the sculpture a deathly pallor. I looked away.

Everywhere on the tables there were fragments of hands, heads. Faces with gaping mouths and hands with outstretched fingers.

"Do you want some coffee?" he said.

I shook my head.

He did not give a damn about the storm and life outside. Only his work was important.

"So what happened with the storm and all?" he said eventually, all the same.

"Nothing ... The cops came. Max managed to get some planks. Old Nan was there."

I told him that there was this man hanging about at the harbour, and Nan thought she had recognized him, that he had the face of one of her loved ones.

He shrugged. "There are always men hanging about, lots of them, because of the sea."

"What are you going to do with all this paper?" I said.

"Drawings ..."

"For Hermann?"

"Yes ..." He rubbed his eyes. "He wants them by the end of the month. A series in black and white ... I'll never get them done in time."

He drank his coffee standing up, and came over to smoke, walking round his sculpture.

The night was not yet over. He was going to work some more.

"I'm going to bed," I said. I looked at him. "You should go to bed, too."

"You can sleep for me, Princess ..." He smiled. "Can you do that?"

I could sleep for two. For a long time, I slept for two. For your sleepless nights, your long nights of pain.

I went up to my room. I was cold. I had stayed too long outside, in the wind. I climbed blindly, one hand against the wall. Insects came out from the skirting boards. They were huge black beetles. I could hear them without seeing them, their legs. I could hear their shells crunching beneath my shoes.

During the night, I thought I heard someone knock on the door, footsteps echoing, I opened, there was no-one. It was the wind, haunting lamentations.

I slept for a few hours.

In the morning, the sky was white again, almost calm.

I turned on the radio. No reception for France Inter. Or for R.T.L. I managed to get a crackling news update on a local station, but though I waited, they did not talk about the cargo ship.

Max came through the door. That was what he did, he came round to the studio every morning right on nine, he came for a coffee with Raphaël.

When he saw me, he hugged me, he always did, and kissed me with a resounding smack.

Then he went to rub his hands above the wood stove. He lifted up his jumper and let the heat rise along his skin. His skin was white. A thin man's skin.

"The gendarmes said there were too many profusions of tons on the ship and the waves hit it broadside, that's why the planks went toppling, as simple as that."

With the heat, his skin turned red.

"They also warned everyone against transporting planks that still by law belong to the captain of the ship."

He slapped his stomach with the palm of his hand. He did that, and then pulled down his jumper. He went to get his cup from the shelf. It was a metal cup, full of a dark sludge, the patient accumulation of the innumerable coffees he had drunk since Raphaël had come here.

A cup that he did not wash.

He blew into it to remove the dust.

"Some day, it will be so disgusting in there that you won't be able to add a single drop," I said, pointing to the sludge.

He frowned.

"You have to wash it," I said.

He scratched at the inside of the cup with a fingernail. A dark film came away, a mixture of scale and caffeine. The sound reminded me of the sheet of metal. Raphaël watched him.

"And what did people say to that?"

Max shook his head without taking his eyes from the cup.

"They said it wasn't theft because there's no nominal proof."

"Nominal proof, is that what they called it?"

Max shrugged. He poured coffee into his cup. He said that he too had taken planks from the sea.

"I'm going to use them to reinforce the cabin and sides. And to gain in streamlining in case I need to pick up speed."

"Be careful all the same, if you make your tub too heavy, you'll sink it!" said Raphaël.

Max turned his head. He was looking towards the door. He was looking for Morgane. When it rained, she always lent him her dictionary. That was how he learned words. He would have liked to have taken the dictionary home, but she would not let him, so he would sit there reading it, on the floor, in the hall, with his back to the wall.

"Wood doesn't sink," he murmured. "It has the faculty of buoyancy."

He took his watch from his pocket, a chronometer watch with a thick face, held to his belt loop with a length of twine.

"Words are the sentence-invention of man."

Raphaël and I looked at each other. We nodded. After the nominal proofs, we were thinking that Max was off to a bright start for the day after a storm.

"It's sow-time," he said at last, putting his watch away under his handkerchief.

The sow belonged to the Stork's father, but it was Max who looked after it. He made a little money doing that, and by cleaning out the stables, too.

Max ran his hands through his hair, several times, dancing from one foot to the other, then he shook our hands.

He went out into the hall. On his way, he peered into the kitchen.

The television was on. Morgane's bare feet hung over the end of the sofa. He eyed her stomach, her heavy breasts stretching the cloth of her dress.

"'Mornin', Morg!"

She raised a hand without turning her head. "Hey there, Creature!"

Max opened his mouth, no doubt he would have like to have said something, but he hunched over and went out. He crossed the court-yard, his hands rammed deep into his pockets. On the quay, the fishermen watched him go by. One of them was pulling the metal sheet out of the water. Max paused. A sheet like that, even rusty, was something he could use on his boat.

Max liked anything beautiful, that is why he liked Morgane. He also took an interest in stones and trees. He said that he could feel the light pulsing in the body of stones. He believed that the lives taken by the sea were what made the sea alive.

His mother had loved sailors, the fishermen of Cherbourg, when they came home after months at sea. What a thirst there was in their hands! She had been a whore, and she had also worked for a stud farm inland, wanking the stallions. M. Anselme told me that. It was also what they said down in the harbour. Apparently men went crazy over her. She had thrown herself under the Cherbourg–Valognes when Max was ten.

Raphaël sat down at the table again. "It's the attachment of the depths," he said, pointing to the door.

I did not understand, so he explained.

"Max, that's what he calls it, the love he has for Morgane . . . The attachment of the depths."

At the end of the morning, I went to Cherbourg to do some shopping.

Raphaël lent me his car, an old Citroën Ami 8, that he always left up on the village square, because of the spray. There was a hole in the floor, as wide across as your hand. He put a rug over it, but when you lifted the rug, you could see the road. The door on the driver's side did

26

not lock. Raphaël did not care, he left the key on the seat. He would lend his car to anyone who asked, all you had to do was top up the petrol and change the oil when the light came on.

*　　*　　*

The village streets were still a quagmire, thanks to the muck tossed up by the storm.

I parked the car in its usual spot. I caught a glimpse of Lambert, he was standing outside the cemetery fence, with a bouquet. Flowers, an entire armful of buttercups. You could not find buttercups here, you had to go to Beaumont, or Cherbourg.

I saw him pull open the gate, go into the cemetery and walk down the path between the crosses. He went off to the left. He stopped near the wall, a plot that had been marked off by a row of flat stones and covered over with gravel. He leaned down and left his bouquet. The priest was standing outside the church. He watched Lambert. Three women were coming up the street along the pavement. They were arm in arm, close together, as if unsteady. They looked alike. They too lifted their heads and looked at Lambert. A stranger in the village, standing over a grave . . . They leaned their heads together. One of them had white eyes, and she was listening to what the other two were saying.

Lambert stayed a few more minutes, took something from his pocket, and put it down next to the bouquet. After that, he left. He crossed the road and went into the house across from Lili's place.

It was a house where the shutters were always closed. I had never seen anyone in there. The garden was overrun by weeds.

I remembered the odd look he had exchanged with Lili. I saw that it must be here that he had spent his holidays. I waited until he was out of sight, and then I went into the cemetery.

Max looked after the tombs. He would rake the gravel, and pick up the pots and jugs. Every day, except when it was raining. He also

27

cleaned up around Lili's house. He did many other things for her, I had already seen him burning brambles, replacing tiles and oiling the hinges when the doors creaked. Lili had fixed up a two-room flat for him in the lower part of her house. She did it because they were cousins.

I walked among the graves. The sun was opening the flowers in their vases. It dried the flagstones. And the gravel on the surface. Underneath, you needed only to scratch a bit with your heel, and you would find all the damp of the earth.

Next winter the snow would cover it all. It would isolate the dead. Grant them a time of silence.

Will I still be here in the winter?

I went as far as the tomb with the buttercups. It was a very simple tomb, with a white wooden cross. A rosebush had been planted in the earth, and its branches were clinging to the wall.

Two names were carved on the cross, *Béatrice and Bertrand Perack, 19 October 1967*. A plaque, *To Paul, lost at sea*. The photograph of a child on a medallion, under glass. It was the medallion that Lambert had taken from his pocket. The photograph of a very young child, scarcely two years old; he was wearing a striped polo shirt, embroidered at the top with a row of three little boats. The child was standing in front of a house, and you could just make out the clasp of a shutter behind him. He was staring at the lens. There was a shadow on the gravel, no doubt that of whoever had taken the photograph.

*   *   *

The last planks that the sea brought in were thick and water-sodden, and nobody wanted them. They stayed on the beach.

The gendarmes were still there on the quay. A journalist came from Saint-Lô. He filmed Lili. We saw her on the screen on the local evening news. She had taken off her apron, but she still held it in her hand, rolled up like an old rag. She stared at the camera and answered his questions.

When the journalist spoke to her about the men who had gone off with the timber, her face clouded over.

"The sea, giving back, in exchange for all the times it has taken away!" she said.

The journalist seemed not to have heard.

"Well, don't these planks belong to someone?"

"They belong to whoever finds them."

"Sometimes taking what you find can be stealing."

When she heard that, Lili no longer looked at the camera, but looked at the journalist, straight in the eyes.

"What are you insinuating?" she said.

The journalist was caught unawares.

"What is in the sea, belongs to the sea," Lili said. "And what belongs to the sea, belongs to man!"

She tossed her apron on the counter. A glance at the camera. "Such a kerfuffle over a pile of bloody planks!"

She left the journalist right there, and walked out of the field of vision. For a few seconds, on screen, all you could see were the bottles, the mirror, and the little blue Virgin with her holy water.

Immediately afterwards, they showed us the lighthouse with the planks floating, with some gentle music they had dug up playing in the background. It made you wonder why they had not just left the real sound of the waves.

I went to the cliffs, taking the path along the shore. On the path, on the banks, everywhere, there was the same thick mud, a mixture of sodden earth and mushy plants. Seaweed had been wrenched from the seabed in great clumps, then washed in and torn up and scattered along the beach. It would take days for all of it to dry.

I walked quickly. As it was the day after a storm, I wanted to check the nests, to see if they had held and how the birds were behaving. It was a wild place, certainly one of the most beautiful on the coast. In the summer, when the heather was in bloom, the moor would take on the colours of Ireland. I had not yet seen the summer here. Apparently there are days you can see horses in the meadows overlooking the beach at Écalgrain. Morgane said this was her beach, that it belonged to her. When she saw hikers, she would toss pebbles at them from up on the rocks.

I continued along the path in the direction of the Nez de Jobourg. Colonies of birds went there to nest and mate, in complete freedom. Access to the property was forbidden. There were fences, signs. It did not stop the hikers from squeezing under the fences.

In six months I had already chased a few of them off.

The nests had held, all but one, that of a young pair of cormorants. The nest had been poorly built, impatiently put together, and the wind had ripped it away with the three chicks that were inside.

I sat down on the top of a huge rock overlooking the sea.

A longclaw had taken up its position a few metres away. I drew it. I made note of its colours. Afterwards I lay down, my back against the rock, and closed my eyes. I had been looking at the sun too much. Spots of colour danced behind my eyelids, like fiery little sea horses.

*   *   *

Raphaël had been there for eight years. Morgane a bit less. Their parents lived over near Rennes. They were shopkeepers. Morgane told me that they sold bags, briefcases. They saw each other from time to time. Not often.

In the studio, the walls, the brick, everything was crumbling. Because of the salt. It was rising. It ate into the stone the way it ate into the trees, and the bones inside bodies.

I opened the door. "May I?"

Raphaël was working on a sculpture. A woman with long hair of stone, a Madonna's face. The pallor of plaster imposed a closed silence upon her face. For weeks he had been working on it. Every one of his sculptures had a history. This one had greatly moved me.

The day he told me the story, he said, Listen carefully, because I'll never talk to you about it again.

The story was from the time when he was living in Kolkata. One morning he left his place and came upon a woman in the street, a very beautiful woman. She was walking, one arm folded over her belly, she was carrying a dead child in her arms. A baby, a few days old, wrapped in rags. She was singing and rocking it the way she would have rocked a living child. She was begging, too. When she saw Raphaël, she pulled a breast out of her dress, went over to him and held out her hand. She was laughing. Her laugh as loud as she was beautiful. Raphaël gave her a few coins. She went into a shop and came back out with some milk. She sat down on the kerb and fed the infant the milk. It was an unbearable sight. In the evening, when she had fallen asleep, women took her child away. When they tugged at it, the child's arm came away from its body.

I stepped back and looked at the emaciated figure of the woman who seemed to be laughing, yet unsteady on her feet.

What had become of her?

Raphaël told me that in the days which followed he saw her wandering through the streets looking for her child. She tried to steal someone else's, and the neighbourhood women beat her. For a long time she walked around with a rag pressed up against her breasts, a sort of doll soaked in milk. One day he looked for her and she had disappeared.

I turned away. I looked at Raphaël's hands, the bags of plaster against the walls. All that mysterious work. It is said that a sculpture already exists in the block of marble, before the sculptor carves into it. What future sculptures were still held prisoner in all those bags?

"That woman's eyes haunt me . . ." He said this in a muffled voice.

I heard the rustling of the thick cloth of his shirt when it rubbed against the table top. The sound of a match scraping on the side of the box.

31

He never mentioned that story again. Ever. Even when he was able to cast "The Wandering Woman of the Slums" in bronze.

The weather was clear, then suddenly the fog came in, heavy slabs of it. Compact. You could no longer see the island of Alderney or even the village of La Roche, not a thing. Even the coastguard station had vanished. Along with the pebbles on the beach, the trees along the path. There was not a sound. The birds had flocked together.

The lighthouse was lit, a long blue beam piercing the fog, lighting in turn the shore, the rocks, the open sea.

I went back to La Griffue.

Raphaël had put the red stone outside his door. A stone wrapped in a thick hemp rope. When the stone was there, no-one was allowed in the studio. Not even Morgane.

Raphaël could stay shut in for days with that stone, without seeing anyone.

*   *   *

The bouquet of buttercups was on the bar. In a vase. I saw it the moment I came in. I knew that Max was in the habit of taking flowers from the graves, but never entire bouquets. They were lovely buttercups, he must have really wanted them. More than usual. Besides, it was a grave where no-one ever went. Lili must have scolded, she always scolded when he brought flowers, but she would accept them all the same.

When he found roses, Max removed the thorns and gave them to Morgane. Morgane did not want his flowers. She did not even look at them. Max placed them in the hall, outside her door. The roses would stay there for a day or two. They wilted. Over time they ended up rotting, or else they dried and the wind carried them away.

Lambert's Audi was parked a bit further down the street. Everyone had noticed his car, as well as the fact that the shutters of the house

32

were open. No-one spoke about it, or if they did, it was in a low voice.

Morgane was smoking, her elbows on the bar. Her trousers low on her hips and her rat on her shoulder. Next to her were two employees from the public works in fluorescent green overalls. Old Mother was dozing, slumped in her armchair, her hands folded over her lap. Her chin was in her neck. Woollen slippers and very thick stockings. You could hear her grinding her jaw. Apparently it was the medication that made her do that.

In the room there was a stink of stale tobacco. Lili emptied the ashtrays but the smell clung to the walls.

Lili was complaining.

The fishermen rolled their cigarettes in corn paper. Over time it made the ceiling go black. It burned their lungs and turned their teeth yellow.

It was the afternoon lull, Lili was wiping tables when Max arrived.

"The stained glass windows at the church are clean and it's not yet sow-time," he said, shaking my hand.

He sat down across from me. He had managed to repair the rudder on his boat.

"It's gestation," he explained, making a drawing to show me how he would go about doing the soldering. He scratched his head to give weight to his explanations. His boat was recycled. Rescued from the scrap yard. Two years he had been working on it.

At the table behind us, four old fellows were playing cards, some sort of *belote* with a card turned over. They called it "the turnover" or "the cow". One of them went out, every ten minutes. Some problem with his prostate. He went outside to piss against a wall. The neighbours complained. Lili scattered soda crystals. You'll see, when you're his age! That was what she would shout, brandishing her bucket.

Morgane went to press her belly against the pinball machine. Her eyes were riveted on the ball. She thrust her hips against the machine. The rat clinging to her shoulder. The old men eased up on their cards to watch her moving hips.

Max was drooling at the sight.

"Keep your mouth shut," I said, in a low voice.

I put my hand on his, "Your mouth . . ."

He wiped his face with the back of his sleeve. Max never touched Morgane. He knew it was not possible. But look at her, that he could do.

He chewed on a few peanuts, mechanically. The peanuts absorbed his drool, obliged him to swallow. He sniffed his fingers, he did that a lot. He finally forgot about Morgane and talked to me again about his boat. With his pencil he drew another diagram on the corner of the newspaper. An outline of the mast and the hull. He added a few arrows.

"This is the exact positioning for each part, to ensure the proper launch of the vessel."

He said that, then got up. It was more than he could bear, he had to go near her.

"You stink, Creature!" Morgane said, pushing him away with her hand.

He began to giggle. The smell was because of the sow. He touched it, caressed it.

Lili saw him. "Out you go, cousin . . ."

Max grumbled.

Lili did not care, she was used to it.

"At the end of the month, he'll be forty," she said, going up to Morgane.

"So what?"

"We'll have a little party. You'll join us?"

"I don't think so."

"It would make Max happy."

"It's not my business to make him happy."

Lili ran her hand through Morgane's hair.

"Don't be mean . . ." She made a face, because of the rat. "You know I don't like you coming round here with that thing!"

Morgane shrugged. She had found the rat under the sheets of metal near the boat shed. It was being attacked by three other beasts that were just as thin, but there were three of them. She put it in a box, it was not hurt but it was in bad shape. The rat would not eat or drink for two days. Morgane thought it was going to die, but one evening she heard a noise. She got up. The rat had got out of his box and was drinking from the sink, drop by drop.

Lili went back to the bar. She opened the drawer of the till. She pulled out a note, and placed it on the table in front of Morgane.

"You should go to the hairdresser's," she said. "And then you should come and live here, at least for the winter. It's too cold on your island."

"It's not an island."

The village was built at the very top of the hill. Between the village and the harbour there was a little over a kilometre, a road without houses, and yet that distance seemed like a wilderness separating two worlds.

Lili turned away.

"La Griffue is no place for a girl."

"What do you know?"

She shrugged.

Old Mother tried to sit up straight. Against her waist she clutched the little fake crocodile handbag she always kept within reach.

She was waiting for the old man. It was his time. The handbag was just in case he came for her.

Lili knew, and she tried not to pay any attention. She picked up the glasses left here and there on the tables.

"And how's your brother doing?"

"He's doing."

"We haven't seen him much these days."

". . . working."

"You'll tell him about Max's birthday, in case he'd like to come."

Morgane held the rat close.

"You bet he'll want to come."

She came back to lean against the bar.

"There's this bloke hanging about," she said.

"There have always been blokes hanging about," said Lili.

"He was at the harbour. He spoke to me."

"What did he want?"

Morgane shrugged. She fed a peanut to the rat.

"I don't know. He was looking at the sea."

With one finger she caressed the rat, the smooth fur between his eyes. "I asked him what he was doing here. I talked to him about your father."

"Why did you talk about him?"

"Because he was looking at his house."

"You just said he was looking at the sea!"

"Yes, but at one point he turned round and looked at his house. He wanted to know if the lighthouse keeper still lived there."

"And what did you say?"

"I told him he did."

Lili began drying her glasses.

"If he's a drifter, you'd best not go walking alone on the moor."

"He's not a drifter."

"How can you tell?"

"I don't know . . . He's looking round, that's all."

"They're all looking round, it's like some disease in these parts." She turned her head. She did not want to talk about it any more.

Morgane insisted. "He's not the same . . . The things he looks at, it's as if it's not the first time he's seen them."

The old men had stopped playing, and were listening.

"It's as if he were from here in some way," Morgane said.

"You're either from here or you're not."

"His name's Lambert."

Lili stood still for a moment, staring at the bar.

"You know his name already . . . ?" She paused for a moment, then said, "Maybe he's here for Prévert? You ought to tell Anselme."

36

"*Monsieur* Anselme."

We all turned our heads because M. Anselme had just come in.

"Well, talk of the devil . . ." said Lili.

*   *   *

M. Anselme made his way through the tables. With his little blue silk pocket handkerchief and his bow tie, he looked like a doctor on a house call.

"And what is it you ought to tell M. Anselme?" he said, allowing his gaze to slide over Morgane's generous curves.

"There's a tourist for you."

"The bloke with the Audi."

"Yes."

He took off his jacket and hung it carefully on the back of a chair.

"He's not a tourist and he's not here for Prévert," Morgane said.

"How can you tell?"

"An impression . . . He stares at the sea."

Lili shrugged. "Everyone stares at the sea."

"Everyone, maybe . . . but he's not everyone. May I?" he asked, pointing to the empty chair across from me.

I nodded.

The church bell began to ring. Max pulled out his watch and said it was time for him to go and look after his sow.

Morgane emptied the saucer of peanuts. She licked the salt, and put the banknote Lili had given her into her pocket. As she turned round, she bumped into Max.

"What, you still here, Creature?"

Max said nothing.

He was looking at her throat, the damp line of sweat trickling between her breasts.

At that time of day, it was tea with milk for M. Anselme. Lili knew. She took down a cup.

"Could it be the Perack boy?" M. Anselme said, his elbow against the chair.

She did not reply.

"Who's the Perack boy?" I said.

"A boy who lost his parents, and he blames the sea."

He pulled open the curtain. He pointed to the house on the other side of the street. The gate was open.

"He was there, this morning, and he's still there. The shutter is open . . . But maybe it's not him."

He leaned over to get a better view.

"His parents drowned. Have you seen the state the garden's in? Before, the road-mender used to take care of it, and he heated up the house. He died last year. A house, when there's no-one to look after it . . ."

He let the curtain fall back in place.

I told him that I had seen Lambert at the grave. I pointed to the bouquet of buttercups on the bar. He turned around, and acknowledged the fact with a nod.

"If you saw him at the grave, then it's him. His parents are buried there. I wonder what he's doing here. No-one's seen him round here for years. Perhaps the house is for sale . . . People from Paris are always looking for these tumbledown seaside places, they'll pay a fortune for them, even when they're in ruins. Have to ask Lili . . ."

He turned towards the bar. Lili was finishing his tea. M. Anselme changed his mind.

"I don't think this is the right day . . ."

He took a plastic envelope from his pocket.

"I brought you some photographs of Prévert . . ."

He had been talking to me about them for days. He set them on the table. The photographs were black and white, with old-fashioned crinkled edges. One of them had been taken in the harbour, back when La Griffue was still a hotel. The other showed Prévert with friends, sitting on the terrace of the restaurant that overlooked the harbour at Port-Racine.

"Prévert loved to have his picture taken, but here, there weren't many photographers in those days, so from time to time my father would get his camera out ... Look how elegantly he's dressed."

I looked at the photographs.

Lili came back with the milk and the tea and set everything down on the table.

"You'll never get tired of that one, will you!" she said, shrugging.

M. Anselme replied with a smile. He drank a sip of tea and carefully put the cup back on the saucer. He talked to me about the house at Le Val, the house Prévert had bought at the end of his life and where he had chosen to die.

"It's very near, in Omonville-la-Petite. From my house you can get there on foot along a charming little path." He leaned closer, as if to tell me a secret. "We could go and visit it together, I could be your guide."

I smiled.

I do not know whether M. Anselme annoyed me, but each time we met, that is how it was, he had to talk to me about Prévert. Ordinarily, Lili thought it was funny. Today, she was not in a laughing mood. She was wiping her glasses, looking out at the street.

M. Anselme picked up his photographs.

"The minute he knew he was sick, Janine didn't want people to see him any more. We'd ask for news, from the kitchen, and then when we couldn't go in the kitchen, we'd ask from the garden and in the end we had to stay behind the fence."

He pulled a brown paper envelope from his pocket.

"He's the one who gave me this collage."

He pushed the envelope over to me. Inside there was a postcard, with a little white boat stuck to it.

"When he made this collage he was already very sick. He couldn't sign it. He asked me to come back later, when he felt better." He leaned closer. "He had started to sign, though, you see, that little line with the pen ... It's the J from Jacques."

There was indeed a little line, that could have been the J from Jacques, but it could have been anything else, too.

I did not say anything.

He blushed.

"His friends, that was his whole life, you understand . . ."

I said that I understood, and I looked outside. He went on talking.

At one point, I felt his hand on mine.

"You're not listening . . ."

Lili was still behind the bar. She had no glasses left to wipe. She was waiting, leaning against the bar, her arms folded across her waist, her gaze somewhat vacant. It was rare to see her like that, motionless.

"One morning, I saw a car go by that I didn't recognize. It was the notary, he had come from Cherbourg. It was February. Prévert died in April. The idea of death saddened him above all because of Minette. Minette, his daughter . . . If we go and visit his house at Le Val, you'll be able to see some very fine photographs of her in the garden, and also of Prévert in Paris . . ."

M. Anselme sipped his tea. I looked at his hands. They were white, his nails perfectly groomed. A little gold chain was fastened round his wrist.

"You go to Cherbourg?" I said.

"Cherbourg?"

"Your hands . . ."

"Yes . . . No . . . Well, there's someone who comes to the house. A young woman from Beaumont, charming. Every Tuesday. It's very convenient having someone come to your house, you know . . . She used to be pretty . . ."

"Who are you talking about?"

"Janine, Prévert's wife. Of course, towards the end, she became dark, difficult, what she was going through was very painful, no doubt . . . Did I already tell you that Minette was anorexic? Janine had to run after her with a plate to make her eat. But that wasn't here, that was in

Saint-Paul . . . Saint-Paul-de-Vence . . . Are you listening?" He smiled a little. "Obviously not, you're not listening."

He gathered his cup and the teapot together in the middle of the table. The spoon in the cup. He turned to me.

"Are you interested in that young man?"

I did not answer. I closed the curtain.

"That house, do you think it belongs to him?"

"If he's the Perack boy, most definitely . . . I recall that the mother was very beautiful. The father was very ordinary, but she . . ."

"What happened?"

"An accident, they were on their way back from Alderney, it was night-time, their sailing boat capsized. They had a young child on board. A terribly sad story."

"And what about him, he wasn't on the sailing boat?"

"No. What do you find interesting in that young man? He's pretty ordinary, isn't he?"

This made me laugh.

He told me that the house was haunted.

Lili went over to the door, her tea towel over her shoulder.

"There are more rats than ghosts in that place!" she barked, peering through one of the panes.

M. Anselme raised his eyebrows.

"Haunted by what?" I said.

"By whom, you mean. A handsome young ship's captain, one Sir John Kepper, his boat sank off Le Blanchard. Everything on board washed up on the shore and some of the things ended up in that house."

He took me by the arm to pull me closer.

"On stormy nights, some people have seen a light shining in the window, a light like a flame. Sometimes the flame is upstairs. Other times in the skylight. People who don't believe it say that it's the reflection of the moon against the window, but on stormy nights, there is no moon . . ."

"And have you yourself ever seen the light?" Lili said.

"No, but I've heard people say they'd seen it."

"I've been living here across the street for over twenty years and I've never seen a thing!"

M. Anselme turned to me.

"They say the roof beams came from the ship. They also say there's a dresser inside with all of Sir John Kepper's dishes."

"All his dishes, that's a good one!" Lili said. "Who's ever seen a ship's captain haunt a house just for a stack of old plates!"

Old Mother was listening to us, nestled into her armchair. Her head was gently nodding. She put a hand on the table for support.

"I've seen it, that light . . ." She tried to sit up. "Several times, at night . . . A long time ago . . . The haunting was always stronger on stormy nights."

Her voice grated. Like blades. "I saw the shadow behind it, the hand holding the light." Old Mother moaned those words about the light and then fell back. M. Anselme and I looked at each other.

He ventured a smile.

"Village tales," he said.

Lili went back behind her bar and folded the tea towels. She made an irregular heap that she smoothed with the palm of her hand and then she slid them into a cupboard under the till. It was said she kept a gun there, a double-barrelled rifle. No-one had ever actually seen it, but Max said she had used it to scare off a wild boar that had strayed a bit too close, in the garden.

"By the way, Mme Lili, the Perack accident, you must remember it, don't you?"

She looked up.

"Long time ago . . ."

"Still, such an accident . . . That young man over there, in the house across the way, could that be the elder son?"

"Could be, yes."

"They had two children. One died, but the other one . . ."

"It was forty years ago, and even if it is him, how do you expect me to recognize him?"

M. Anselme nodded. "It was in 1967 . . ."

"I was young in 1967."

That's what she said: *I was young, I don't remember.*

M. Anselme turned to me.

"In those days, people said there was a problem with the lamp in the lighthouse . . . That her father . . ."

He lowered his voice, scarcely audible.

*   *   *

Théo came in. The old fellows said, "*Salut*, Théo!"

He did not reply. He never replied. The old fellows greeted him all the same.

When she saw him, Old Mother grabbed her bag. "The old man . . ." she muttered between her teeth, her belly pressed against the table. She had to repeat it ten times over for him to turn round.

"Hello there, old lady . . ."

It cost him, Théo, to say that in a hoarse voice, and the old woman said nothing more.

Lili served him the way she served everyone else. His cup on the bar. His coffee in the cup.

Mute, father and daughter.

She prepared his bag, a plastic box she had filled with rice and meat. She had pressed it down with the spoon. It had to last him two days, and no-one had better find fault if, on the way, he happened to show someone what she had given him.

She wrapped it all up, her gestures abrupt, the way you might give a dog his food when you do not care for him any more.

I stole glances at them, and I could not understand how anyone could reach such a degree of hatred. Between them even silence became an insult.

43

Théo put his cup down. Left a note next to it. He took his bag and left.

M. Anselme followed him with his gaze.

"You wonder why he goes on coming here . . ." I said.

M. Anselme said that unless you were born here, it was impossible to understand the mystery of such silence.

From the depths of her armchair, Old Mother continued to whimper beseechingly.

*　　*　　*

Théo's house was up against the hill, a large stone building, outside the village. A giant hydrangea bloomed next to the road. Théo did nothing to care for it, and it grew wild with clusters of superb flowers.

The gate was always open. There were cats in the courtyard, around their bowls. Cats under the shed, too. Those ones would growl at you, impossible to get close to them.

At the very top, an open dormer window in the roof overlooked the sea.

One of the roof gutters had a leak. The water seeped out with a cascade of fine green moss that ran all the way to the ground. In the village, people said that houses like old Théo's were home to *goublins*. They were not evil creatures, but they did have strange powers. Some of them took the form of cats, rabbits, or even hedgehogs. It was said that wherever there was a *goublin*, there was a treasure. No-one knew that the treasure was there. Only the *goublin*.

The first time I met Théo, he was outside on the porch with his cats. I stopped. I told him that I lived in the harbour, at La Griffue, that I was the one who had come to count the birds in his place. He knew who I was, and he invited me into the house. Grey curtains hung from the windows. I slipped my hands beneath the worn net curtains. The hems were hand-stitched. There were moth-holes between the rows of stitches.

We talked about the cats and only the cats that day, the ones that lived outdoors and the ones that were in the house. When I left, he shook my hand. "You'll have to come again and we'll talk about birds."

I came again.

Théo knew my habits. He had learned them. When it was my hour up at the cliffs, he would wait for me by the door. As soon as he saw me, he grabbed his cane and leaned against it. He could not stand for long, because of the cartilage that was worn away in his hips. He should have had an operation. He did not want one.

"Who's going to look after my cats if I go to Cherbourg?"

He said that all the old people who went to hospital came back between four boards.

He walked by my side. He went with me as far as La Roche. We talked about La Hague, the moor, this harsh, strong land. Man could only incline his head before such a land.

He used to work for the Centre at Caen. Everything I was doing, he had done – the reports, the egg-counting, observing the birds. Everything I saw, he had seen.

He had walked along these cliffs for more than ten years, alone.

*   *   *

The low stone walls that ran alongside the path were covered in moss. Sprouting here and there, in a tiny patch of soil, were little clusters of ferns.

Théo and I headed to the right, between the houses. We went in front of Nan's place. We always came this way to get to the path. It was not the quickest way, but Théo enjoyed taking this detour.

When we came to Nan's house, he looked at the door. He lingered a moment, his hand on the wall.

Sheets were hanging beneath the awning, beating the air like phantom sheets. The door was open, the sun shone inside. Behind one of the windowpanes, we saw the black reflection of a passing shadow, and then the shadow was framed in the sunlight of the door.

Théo gave a little wave. "You're here, she won't come."

Nan's real name was Florelle. He told me that day. Like a confession. "After her family died, she didn't want to be called that any more."

He still called her that. I pointed it out to him and he smiled.

A strange smile, like another confession. And then he turned away.

Le Blanchard was calm, there were almost no waves. A lull, before other storms.

"There are still bodies out there, bodies the sea has not returned to her."

He said this and I remembered Nan's gaze, full of pain, when she peered at Lambert's face.

"On the day of the storm, she thought she recognized someone."

He took my arm. "That happens sometimes . . . She believes that the dead return."

He lowered his gaze.

"But the dead don't return."

We took a few steps along the path, between the houses.

"She touched his face, she called him Michel."

He remained silent.

We went through the little hamlet to the last house.

He talked about her some more, about Florelle. I would have liked to talk to him about you, the way he talked about her.

After the last house, Théo stopped. There was a wide stone there, where he always sat when he came with me.

"The fields of heather, you'll see, with this southerly wind, they'll be black today."

He stared at the path I was about to take, and that he had so often taken.

"You might find some wild strawberries . . . There are a few patches after the second workman's hut, they're within reach."

He knew the rest of the path by heart. The location of every tree, every stone. The time it took to go from one rock to the next, from here to the cove at Les Moulinets, and further still, the caves and the old smugglers' hideaways.

I left him.

I continued along the path. I do not know how long he stayed there. He said he was coming along with me, that he could walk the entire path just by sitting there on the stone.

The path was narrow, winding between the sea and the moor. Beneath my feet was a mixture of slippery earth and rocks breaking the surface. I had to go as far as the Nez des Voidries. That is where the cormorants were. We were studying their ability to help each other. Their cohesion when hunting. Were they capable of driving schools of fish together? How did they cohabit when they were hunting?

It was long work. Hours of observing in the wind.

To the right, the sea was blinding with sunlight, a luminosity so fierce that I had to look away.

At the end, the light hurt you, too. We had to close the shutters. Pull the curtains. Your colossus of a body had become a little thing lost deep in a bed. Even caresses, my hands upon you, you no longer wanted them.

A rabbit sped by. It stopped for a moment, sitting up on its haunches, then disappeared between the patches of heather. Further along, in a meadow, I saw two horses, motionless. I kept on walking.

I found the patches of wild strawberries Théo had mentioned, their leaves so green that they seemed blue. The red fruit was gorged with sugar. I crushed them under my tongue, an explosion of taste. My palate saturated, I kept a handful for Théo. I went on my way.

After a while the path branched off and I was overlooking the cove at Écalgrain. Théo said that here, on summer evenings, the moor was ablaze.

There were men sitting all the way down on the beach. A dozen or so. I looked at their faces through my binoculars. Unshaven. Mostly young. Their gazes tired. They were smoking, with their knees up.

They had no baggage, did not seem to have any food. Nothing that might contain water, either. Some of the men were looking at the sea. Others were not looking at anything. Or between their feet. One of them was lying on his side. They were waiting for a boat, to get over to England.

How long had they been there? There was one girl with them, sitting off to the side. She too was looking at the sea. I observed them for a long time. I wondered what would happen to them if the boat they hoped for did not come.

After the cove, the cliffs were steeper. The heather was black. That is where the moorland goats came to graze. There were a dozen or so, living with neither tethers nor fences. Animals with long black wool. When it rained, they would huddle against the rocks or shelter by the caves.

Le Nez des Voidries was a nesting place for the peregrine falcons. I had caught sight of ravens there on occasion. It was a difficult place to get to.

I had brought a ham sandwich with me, and ate it, famished. The cormorants were fishing. I spent the day observing them. I noted down everything.

A solitary warbler kept watch by me, tucked on her nest.

Before leaving, I lay down, my belly against the earth. Short cropped moss clung to the rocks. There was a strong smell of humus, an indefinable odour that was a mixture of salt, rotting seaweed and dead fish.

I recalled how I used to lie on your body. And your body on mine. Your weight, so heavy. I loved it, your weight on me. Would I have the strength? The last day, you passed your hand over my cheek, that hand of yours so wide that it could hold all of me. You wanted to speak. You could not.

I went home at high tide. Tired, reeling. My eyes burning like those of certain old cats.

I stopped at Théo's, and on the table I left the handful of wild strawberries that I had brought back for him. He did not eat them. He said, "Later, tonight . . ."

We talked.

It began to rain, a fine rain, falling obliquely.

I headed home at a run. By the time I got there I was soaked. Cold all down my back. Animal shivers along my skin.

Max's bike was leaning against the wall at La Griffue. It was an old bike, rusted. It dated from the war. I do not know which war was meant. Max never rode it. He used it as if it were a luggage-rack, the saddlebags like two huge baskets, and he would hang bags full of fish from the handlebars.

The following night was clear, drenched with the moonlight that sometimes shone over the moorland, a pitiless light that drove out any beasts in hiding, and caused the dying ones to whimper.

II

It was the end of the month, I had my charts to fill out for the Centre ornithologique. I was late. I sat down at my table by the window and I worked. Lili was at the bar. She was leafing through a catalogue, she wanted to buy a cage with some budgerigars. To keep her company, she said. She had already had two, and they had died within one week of each other.

"Life was better, before," she said, closing her catalogue.

She was talking to the postman.

"It was cheaper, too. When I retire, I'll go to live in the south."

Old Mother raised her head.

"I won't go!" she shouted.

"Not too far from the coast," Lili said, paying no heed to the old woman's grumbles.

She did not know when that would be, her retirement. Five years, ten years . . . She had to get a nest-egg together, the south was more expensive.

When she heard that, Old Mother started sniffling, her nose level with the edge of the table. It caused her glasses to steam up, a thick fog before her eyes. Lili went on talking about the south. Eventually the postman left.

I was just finishing my charts when the door struck the bamboo tubes of the fly curtain. The door opened. I felt a draught of air. I knew it was Lambert, because of Lili's expression, and also because the old men paused in their game.

The door was still open. Lambert closed it behind him and walked up to the bar. He was wearing dark cotton trousers, a charcoal-grey jumper, and a leather jacket. He wore little boots, with a buckle on the side.

He and Lili looked at each other.

She hesitated, her gaze unsteady, then she came out from behind the bar. "Well, here you are!" she said. They kissed on the cheek, awkwardly, without touching, their arms at their sides. It was strange, this way of saying hello.

He turned and looked round. He saw me and greeted me with his eyes.

"It was like this before," he said.

"Bland yellow, I should redo it, I haven't got time. Can I offer you something to drink?"

"Please."

"What?"

"I don't know, whatever you like."

She took out two saucers and placed them on the bar.

She filled up the coffee measure.

"I knew you were here. A bloke hanging about, everyone talking about him, when I saw you in the garden and then at the grave, I knew it was you. The night of the storm, too . . ."

The tea towel was rolled up in a ball next to the buttercups.

"It was crowded, we didn't talk."

"What would we have said?"

The fact that they said *tu* to each other surprised me. A curt, abrupt informality.

She put the cups on the saucers.

"You talked to Morgane, too."

"Morgane, she's the girl with the rat?"

"That's her."

He took the cup between his hands. He looked into the cup, at the coffee. His gestures were slow.

"People have been saying you're here for Prévert?"

"Prévert . . ."

It made him smile. The spoon slipped in the cup. A light little clink.

"How long has it been since we've seen each other?"

"A long time."

"A long time, must be forty years," Lili said.

She brought out two small glasses from behind her, and put them next to the cups. She filled the glasses.

"Don't worry about it," she said.

I did not understand why she said that, whether it was because of all the time that had passed or the clear alcohol she was pouring.

It seemed to take them for ever, talking and looking at each other. To see what time had done to them.

"Are you married?" Lili said.

"No."

"Children?"

He smiled.

"No . . . And you?"

"I was married. Fisherman. He died at sea."

"I'm sorry."

"That he died? You shouldn't be."

She put the bottle back, and came over to him, her elbows on the bar.

"In the beginning, you think you're going to die, and then you don't die. You live. There are even times afterwards when you feel you've got your life back."

She swallowed her glassful.

"That might seem strange, but that's the way it is."

Lambert was staring in the mirror behind her.

"I've aged," he said.

52

"And I've aged, too, and so what?"

"Would you have recognized me?"

She shrugged.

He looked away. He stayed like that for a few seconds, his eyes on the floor. "It doesn't matter . . ."

"You didn't say, what brings you here?"

"I wanted to see La Hague again. I'm selling the house."

She nodded.

"I know, the notary is a customer. And will you stay?"

"Yes . . . for a day or two . . ."

He reached over to the peanut dispenser. He dropped in a coin, and turned the knob.

Lili followed him with her eyes.

"Where are you sleeping?"

"A room over in La Rogue."

"The Irishwoman?"

"Yes."

"She used to be a whore, did you know that?"

"It's nothing to me."

She pointed to the armchair with Old Mother in it. "That's my mother."

The old woman sat up. Her head was wobbling, she was like a broken top.

"She's not living with your father any more?"

"Would you live with that old madman? I took her in over twenty years ago."

He stared at Old Mother.

Lili looked outside.

I gathered up my things.

"We could have dinner together, if you like," she said, turning to Lambert.

"Later . . ."

"Later – when's that?"

"I don't know."

With his hand, he was caressing the smooth surface of the bar.

"I saw your father, when I went past his place. He was in the yard."

"And so what? I've been seeing him for fifty years and more, every day."

"You're not speaking?"

Lili scoffed.

"Good morning, goodnight! It's no secret. Why, is that what he said?"

"No, it was Morgane."

He looked at her, abruptly, a gaze like a stumble.

"Are you angry?"

"Angry about what? That you accused my father of killing your parents? Rest assured, I've accused him of far worse."

She had raised her voice. It was cold, brittle. "Do you still believe he put out the light? Is that why you're here?"

"Perhaps."

"That's old history, forget it."

"I can't."

"Then live with it! We've all lived with it, here!"

I was embarrassed to be there, to see them. To hear them. I got up and gently pushed in my chair. I wanted to leave without making any noise.

Lambert turned.

"What are you doing?"

"I'm going . . ."

My jacket was still on the back of the chair. I took it, and put it on.

"It's not for you to go."

He looked at Lili.

That was when he saw the flowers.

"The buttercups, was that you?"

Lili did not understand.

"What are you talking about?"

He pointed to the bouquet.

She pursed her lips. She was three steps from the flowers. She took the three steps and lifted the bouquet from the vase. The stems were wet, water dribbled on to the floor.

"I don't go round stealing from the dead, if that's what you mean!"

Water was running down her hands. She shoved the bouquet into his arms.

"How was I supposed to know they were your flowers?"

He stood there with his hands round the bouquet.

"Now get out!" Lili said.

He took a step back.

He muttered something, something I did not understand. He opened the door.

There was a plastic table on the terrace. It stayed there all year round. Even in winter. Before, there were chairs too, but one night, someone took all of them away. Since then, Lili has not put any chairs outside.

Lambert stood for a moment next to the table, the bouquet pressed to his chest. His gaze somewhat disoriented.

Finally he put the flowers on the table.

Lili went over to the window. She followed him with her gaze, while he was there on the terrace and then afterwards, when he crossed the street.

Old Mother moaned in her dead woman's voice.

"Who was that?" The hole of her mouth, gaping. "Who was it, huh?"

Lili turned round.

"Nobody . . . It was nobody . . ."

She opened the door, went out, and tossed the bouquet of flowers into the big rubbish container.

*   *   *

"You didn't put the stone . . ."

Raphaël was holding a small iron figure in his hands. He was looking at it. It was a tightrope walker. He wanted to make it balance on a plaster wire. One of its feet was already supported, but the tightrope walker would not stay on the wire. Raphaël pulled one of the arms off the body.

"Balance depends on so little . . ." With his thumb, he accentuated the curve of the back. "If I can get this one to stay, I'll do a life-size one."

With a movement of his arm, he encompassed the entire studio.

"A tightrope walker two metres high, walking straight!"

The figure's toes barely touched the wire. It seemed very light, very delicate.

"It will never stay," I said.

"It might. We manage!"

He stepped back to see how it looked.

"We don't live on a wire . . ."

He wedged a Gitane between his lips. "How can you be so sure?"

No, I was not sure. I looked at his drawings. He had not started the series yet. A few sketches, some forced, rough features.

He took a puff, then blew out a long stream of smoke in front of him.

"Hermann is waiting. He shouts at me, and says I do it on purpose! Hardly likely, that I would do it on purpose . . ."

I looked out of the window.

Morgane was in the garden, lying on a bench in the sunlight.

I went to join her.

She had the rat against her belly, curled up in a ball, asleep.

She opened her eyes because I was standing in her sunlight.

She lifted a floppy hand and pointed towards the boats.

"He's still there," she said.

I already knew. I had seen him.

A smile came over her lips.

"His name's Lambert Perack, born in 1955 in Paris in the 6th *arrondissement*. Lives in Empury, in the Le Morvan region."

"How do you know all that?"

She let her arm fall along the bench. With her fingertips she scratched the soil, plucked up the few blades of grass growing there.

"It's not my fault if he left his jacket hanging on the coat-rack with his wallet inside."

She lifted herself up on her elbow, her eyes still closed.

"I helped with the service at noon . . . he had the menu."

"You go through your customers' things now, do you?"

"I didn't take anything, just his name . . . Lambert, it's a rather strange name, don't you think? . . . Other than Lambert Wilson . . . Do you fancy him?"

"No."

"Liar."

"I'm not lying."

She lay down again.

"Do you think the sun will last?"

I looked at her, I did not understand.

"The thing shining up there that heats up our skin when we're cold?"

"It will last," I said.

The sun dropped slowly behind the house, and the bench was in the shadow.

She got up. She went into the house and came back out with a bath towel. The rat was clinging to her shoulder.

"This morning, I saw the notary from Beaumont, he was parked in front of the house across from Lili's place."

She twirled the towel from the tips of her fingers, a perfect imitation of Charlie Chaplin, the towel in place of the cane, her feet sticking out.

"Your Lambert, maybe he's buying . . ."

"He's not my Lambert," I murmured.

She went off towards the rocks. She was whistling.

"He's not buying, he's selling," I said, but she was already too far away to hear me.

The sun didn't last, the rain came down on the sea all of a sudden, and then the winds brought it lashing against the windowpanes. A cold little drizzle.

Morgane came back at a run, the towel around her head. I was in my room, I saw her across the courtyard. I banged on the window, and she looked up. It was a lovely sight, this girl running in the rain.

I sat down on the bed.

I had to clear up the apartment and use the time it was raining to paint my walls. In Hopper green, the same green as in the painting. That was what I had decided on. The card was pinned to the door. I could have gone to buy the paint, but it was raining too hard to go to Cherbourg.

I opened a bottle of Entre-deux-mers. A wine from the south, white, dry. I drank a glass. I listened to the rain. I heard the voice of Maria Callas from below. Raphaël was working. He said he always worked really well when it was raining.

There were other glasses on the shelves. Empty biscuit packets. There was a time when I used to be tidy. I would make the bed. I would put black pencil around my eyes.

There was a time, yes.

The next day, it was still raining. I had lunch at the *auberge*, sitting across from a family, a couple with children. At another table, there was also a couple. They were holding hands above the tablecloth. Their feet underneath the table, touching. This need they had for each other's skin. Each other's gaze. I envied them. At one point, the girl spoke to her boyfriend, and they turned and smiled at me. I had been like them, with you, so full of desire. Right to the end, even when your body became that shadow, I still desired you.

The Cogema bachelors were at the tables in the back. They worked at the nearby nuclear reprocessing plant. From the village you could see the tall chimneys, the lurking monster.

Two of Raphaël's drawings were hanging on the wall. Silhouettes, in grey-black tones. There was also a plaster sculpture in a little niche above the bar. Morgane was not working that day, it was the *patron* who brought me my meal.

"That still hasn't healed!" he said, pointing to my cheek.

"No, still hasn't."

He nodded.

I looked outside. The sheet of metal was still there, wedged between the wall and a rubbish container.

In the afternoon, I went to the cliffs. I counted seventeen egrets just in that very short time. I did not see any falcons or ravens, but there was a pair of very young gulls, fighting over a female.

*   *   *

Théo was leaning against the bar. On Thursdays, he always came earlier because there was a girl from the social services doing the housekeeping at his place.

Lili prepared him a coffee. That was the only time when Théo would look at her, he could see her like that, from the back. She looked at him too, her father's reflection in the mirror. Their eyes did not meet.

Théo never sat down. He could have played cards with the other old men. Chatted for a while. He could have gone to Beaumont on the coach.

He stayed there, leaning against the bar.

He drank his coffee.

Before going out, he stopped at my table. He looked at my papers.

"Are you interested in plovers?" he said.

"Plovers? I don't know . . . I haven't got any in my sector. Why do you ask?"

He turned away. His left hand was trembling slightly.

"Plovers are very fine birds, they're waders."

"I know."

"And do you know what they do when other birds come near and threaten their eggs?"

He squinted at me, I got the impression he was judging me, judging me on my ability to know what plovers did in the case of attack.

"There's a little colony on the rocks beyond the coastguard station. You should go and see them ..."

He opened the door.

"Even if it's not in your sector," he said, before going out.

One of the old men whistled.

"He's in fine form, old Théo, this morning!"

Lili came up to my table, with a bottle in her hand. She poured me a drop of her liqueur in a stem glass.

"On the house ..."

She watched me drink.

"From round here!"

I did not know what she was referring to, Théo or her liqueur. I emptied the glass without batting an eyelid. I pulled the curtain aside, but Théo was gone.

*   *   *

Morgane had gone off to Cherbourg, leaving the rat in its cardboard box. The rat had got out and had disappeared. Raphaël and I looked everywhere. We eventually found it on a shelf at the back of the studio. Standing on its hind paws, looking at us. I held out my hand, and it came up to sniff my fingers. It seemed intrigued. I do not know whether it could recognize the smell of the cats that I had stroked at Théo's place.

"They carry all kinds of diseases, those animals," Raphaël said, when he saw me pick up the rat and hold it.

"So do we."

"Then don't touch me."

"I never touch you."

He went to look for his cigarette packet. He finally found it, but it was empty. He went into the kitchen.

"The Seamstress of the Dead" cast her grey shadow on the floor. The shadow of the shroud she was stitching. Raphaël had used Nan for the sculpture, it was her, her body, her hands.

He came back.

"Théo was in love with her once," I said, pointing to the statue.

"How do you know?"

"The way he looks at her, says her name . . . Do you know her well?"

"Not so well, no . . . I sculpted her, that's all."

He tore open the carton, pulled out a packet. He threw the rest on the table.

He looked at me.

"Well, he went and married someone else, your lover boy!"

"Yes, I know. Still, it was Nan that he loved."

I walked around "The Seamstress".

"How do you explain the fact that Old Mother lives in the village with Lili and that he is up there all alone in his huge place?"

"I'm not explaining anything. The day I heard that there was an old woman in the village who sewed the shrouds of the dead, I knew I had a subject. As for the rest . . . she doesn't even know that I sculpted her."

He ran his hand over the plaster shoulder.

"If I die, I want to be left here, all alone, to rot in the middle of my sculptures. No shroud, nothing."

He went over to the door.

It was nice out. We went outside.

The cows had all gathered in the pasture near the path. They were stamping their hooves in the mud. We smoked cigarettes, watching them ruminate. A car went by.

"They shouldn't walk in their shit like that," I said.

"'Course they shouldn't."

Morgane got out of the car. She went to collect her rat and then came back to join us.

"What are you two on about?"

"We were talking about the cows ..."

"And what did you have to say?"

"That they walk in their own shit and that they shouldn't."

She nodded. A cricket was singing by our feet. Morgane bent down and looked for it in the grass.

"It's a good job Max isn't here ..."

She looked up at me.

"Max thinks that the crickets that sing when the sun is still up are bastards ... and that bastards are supposed to be bad breeders, so he squashes them."

She got up and took Raphaël's cigarette in her fingers. She cuddled up against him. It was strange for me to see this close connection they had. It was almost embarrassing at times. Was it the fact they had been born of the same womb that made them so close?

"And you, did you know that Théo had been old Nan's lover?" asked Raphaël.

Morgane shrugged. She didn't care.

She held her hand out for my binoculars.

"Can I borrow them?"

They were powerful binoculars, a gift from my colleagues when I left the university. She adjusted the lens. She scoured the space, from the coastguard station to the village and from there as far as the houses in La Roche. Then she pointed high up, in the direction of the road above La Valette.

"Open jacket, crewneck jumper ... unshaven ... he's still there."

She lowered the binoculars, just a touch, hardly at all.

"What is it you fancy about him?"

"I didn't say I fancied him."

She looked at him again.

"Full lips, rather sad eyes ... it's strange, all the same ... What do you think he's doing here? Oh, it looks as though he's seen us . . ."

"Give those back, Morgane!"

"Don't panic! He can't see us, we're too far . . . Anyway, he's looking at the sea, we're in his sightlines, that's all."

On the other side of the fence, the cows turned their heads. It was as if they too were looking in his direction.

We saw Lambert again a bit later on. He was on the shore and he was trying to grab a case that was floating on the water. It was a cello case. It had been there since morning, almost ashore. The sun grazed the sea. It was as if the crests of the waves were on fire.

Max came over.

"Do you think it's his?" he said.

Raphaël shook his head. "No."

"How do you know?"

"He'd put more vigour into it."

"What's that, *vigour*?"

"Vigour . . . passion, desire, Max!"

Desire, Max knew. He ran his fingers over his teeth and looked over at Morgane.

The case was bobbing about.

Lambert touched it, but was unable to get hold of it.

"He shouldn't do that," I said.

"Why not?"

"I don't know . . . It's odd, a case like that floating on the water . . . There might be a dead body inside."

"It's too small, a case like that . . ."

"A skull, then?"

Raphaël nodded and looked at the sky, his mouth half open.

"Yeah, maybe . . . Or bits of a corpse . . . Maybe there's even a cello!"

Max decided to go and see.

He came back with the case. "There was nothing in it!" He opened it. "The great emptiness of the things of absence," he said.

"And what are you going to do with it?"

"Put it in the sun to encourage complete evaporation of the water and restore the velvety on the inside."

"Velvet, Max . . ."

He carried the case to the house and opened it up to the sun.

"It can be a tool case for all the big utensils for the boat."

*   *   *

We were expecting flocks of scoters, formations of several hundred birds that stopped in La Hague before migrating further south.

I went to watch for them on the path between Écalgrain and La Roche. I waited. The birds did not come. I found a dead cormorant. When I got back, I called the Centre from the call box in the harbour. Someone from Caen would come to fetch the bird's corpse. I posted all my charts.

Night fell. I did not feel like going home. I spent too much time on the moors. Sometimes it got to me. I was beginning to dream of outdoor cafés, sunlight. Of the cinema.

The vet was in the yard at Théo's. He had come to look at one of the cats that was weeping tears like glue. The poor creature bumped into everything. They got hold of it, and the vet cleaned its eyes with some cotton soaked in a yellow liquid. He left a bottle. "Twice a day," he said. "If you don't want it to die blind."

M. Anselme drove by, and stopped when he drew level with me. He rolled the window down. He did not have time to talk, he had to get back to feed his tortoise.

He was already late.

His tortoise was called Chelone. He had given it the name of a young girl that Jupiter had punished. M. Anselme had often promised to tell me the story.

I leaned against the door.

"You were supposed to tell me the story, about Chelone," I said with a smile.

64

"Now?"

He looked at his watch.

His tortoise was used to being fed every evening at five o'clock sharp. If he was not back, the creature would flip over, press its head against a wall, and not move from there until the next day.

It was nearly five. But he stopped the engine all the same.

He got out of the car. He held me by the arm and we took a few steps. He was wearing a cream-coloured suit and a tartan tie. The young people who were in the little car park nudged each other when they saw him go by. They were making fun of him.

"Did you know that Jupiter married his sister Juno?"

No, I did not know that.

He went on. "In those days, marriage between brother and sister didn't bother anybody; on the contrary, it was considered good form . . . To celebrate their union, Jupiter invited everybody, gods, men, animals, anything on earth that was alive was there. Only one person refused his invitation, a young woman who answered to the gentle name of Chelone. When he found out, Jupiter was enraged, and to punish the insolent young woman, do you know what he did?"

I shook my head.

"He turned her into a tortoise."

We stopped outside Lambert's place. Smoke was coming out of the chimney. Brambles that had been cleared were piled up against the wall. There was a sign hanging from the fence, FOR SALE, with the telephone number of the notary in Beaumont painted in red. I do not know if Lambert was there. I did not want him to see us. Or to find us there. I took M. Anselme by the arm, and obliged him to turn round. We went back to his car. The young boys revved the motors on their mopeds.

"It's your suit," I said. "That's why they're making fun of you."

"They're not making fun."

"They are making fun, M. Anselme . . ."

He looked at me, astonished.

"What's wrong with my suit?"

I shrugged.

"Nothing . . . but it's a suit."

"So?"

"You are in La Hague, here."

He opened the car door. It was not the young people's laughter that had hurt him, it was me, the fact I had sided with them.

Before closing the door, he looked at me, his expression grave.

"You know, I've had a lot of tortoises, and I've called them all Chelone. And I've always worn suits. *A bove ante, ab asino retro, a sulto undique caveto!* Just tell them that, if their laughter upsets you!"

He slammed the door. He started the engine, and lowered his window.

"I like to think that one of my tortoises might have been a descendant of that same Chelone."

I went into Lili's place and ordered a hot chocolate. With a lot of sugar. I felt ill at ease because of what had happened with M. Anselme. I felt like going back out and pelting those kids, with the same rage as Morgane when she pelted the hikers.

I did not do anything. I drank my hot chocolate. At the bar, fishermen were talking about the sea. They said they had to go further and further to get the fish. Cormorants were eating the fish. They said that because I was there. These fishermen killed the cormorants. I knew that. They bought transparent nets. The fish did not see them, and were caught in them. And the cormorants, too. They killed dozens of them, beautiful birds, caught in their nets.

They said they had to make a living. Very quickly, the conversation became stifling.

I held my bowl in my hands. Warm steam. The sugar calmed my anger. My numb limbs.

I began to feel drowsy.

I swore I would ask M. Anselme to forgive me.

I looked up. Photographs had been pinned on the wall beside me, bear-leaders, fire-eaters. There were also some old postcards of La Hague, the way it used to be. Lili said that during her childhood, families of acrobats from the east used to go round the cape on their way south. They would stop on the square. The photographs were black and white. Sometimes passing tourists wanted to buy them, but Lili was not selling.

There used to be a photograph of Prévert. Someone had come and stolen it. A couple with a little girl. The little girl was drinking grenadine syrup with a straw. It was the mother who was sitting nearest to the photograph.

Lili also had a book that Prévert had signed, from the days when her grandmother ran the café. The book was put away in the drawer under the till, with the gun. M. Anselme would have liked to have bought the book, but, same thing, Lili was not selling.

The fishermen went on talking. They had got here long before I had. And would leave after me. They did not give a damn about the cormorants. Only the sea mattered, how many times they had put out to sea, ridden the waves. That is what they said, The waves, you ride them like you ride a woman! They made gestures, their obscenity made them laugh. They talked about girls, the ones they went to find in the city. Girls from the east, whose grip was not exactly innocent, that is what they said, bragging a bit. In time they ordered another round of beer.

"Alcohol helps you through the winter . . ."

"Winter is over," Lili said.

Lambert arrived shortly afterwards. He walked past my table. His features were drawn. He stopped for a moment.

"Good evening."

His hand slid over the back of the chair. I thought he was going to sit down. His jumper smelled of wood smoke. The fishermen looked at him. So did Lili. He did not sit down.

"What are you reading?" he said, pointing to the book I had open in front of me.

"Coetzee."

"Hmm . . . And what is Coetzee's story about?"

"It's the story of a professor who falls in love with one of his students. It ends badly."

He nodded. His hand was still on the chair.

"Why?"

"Because of the girl, she's not very honest, she accuses him of harassment."

He nodded again, smiled, and put the chair back in its place.

"Enjoy your reading, then."

He said that and went to sit at another table, a bit further towards the rear. I do not know what he ordered, because Lili went to sit down across from him, and after that I left.

I saw Lambert again the next day, leaning against the fence, his hands in his pockets. He was looking at the bed that had pride of place in the courtyard at the little Stork's place. It was a bed with iron bars, and an old bed base. In the summer, the dog slept on it. Curled up. In the winter, he went underneath, made it his kennel. In extreme cold, he went into the barn.

Lambert took an apple from his pocket. The sow was there, on the other side of the fence. She was following his every gesture, the knife, the apple, the skin. Right down to the pips, which he removed. He gave her one quarter, and then another, and still another, the whole apple in the end; after the last quarter, he folded up his knife, and headed down the path leading to the coastguard station.

He was walking slowly. Sometimes, he stopped, looked at the stones, the meadows. He would start walking again and stop a bit further along as if he were gathering the memories he had of the path. I followed him for a moment with my binoculars.

I thought of going to join him. To talk with him. Ask him what he remembered. I had already seen him in other places, looking about in the same way, attentive. I do not know what he would have said if I had joined him, or whether he would have been pleased about it.

I looked into the courtyard and thought that next spring, the big chestnut tree that grew there would surely have enormous blossoms.

*   *   *

Morgane stabbed the prongs of her fork into a piece of potato. She looked up. She pointed to Lambert's house. Some of the shutters were open.

"I saw him, he went to the lighthouse, by way of the coastguard station. And he's been cutting brambles in his garden."

"Are you spying on him?" I said.

She nodded her head this way and that. She had put black eye-shadow on her eyelids, a thick powder that gave her burning eyes.

"No . . . But I'm bored." She made a face. "Don't *you* get bored?"

I did get bored. I even got fed up with birds and wind. Fed up with being here, outside all the time in that perpetual noise. Fed up with counting eggs and nests.

Morgane fiddled with what she had left on her plate, holding her fork with her fingertips. Her nails were painted with red varnish. In the middle of each nail she had glued a little black pearl. When she moved her fingers, the pearls danced.

I looked at her. It was more than boredom, it was absence.

Sometimes I would scream from the top of the cliff. I screamed at you, at life. You were still too present. The sorrow had to go away. That is what I had wanted from La Hague, to help me get free of you. I do not know if it had freed me. In Avignon, our cafés, our streets, I saw you everywhere. Even in the flat. The last nights, I could not sleep there any more, I went to a hotel.

Morgane pushed back her plate.

The rat crawled down her arm, then stopped, its claws digging into her. It didn't put a single paw on the table.

Lili was setting the tables, she was expecting customers at noon. She glanced over at the rat. And then outside, because a car had just pulled up on the opposite side of the street, next to the pavement. A man and a woman got out of the car, they looked at the house and also at the very top, the roof, the dormer window. They opened the gate and went into the garden.

Lili took out a basket, the chequered napkins for regular customers. For people passing through, she used paper napkins.

A first fisherman came in, he had his billy-can with him. He ordered a carafe of wine and went to sit at a table in the back. He came in to eat where it was warm. Lili let him. She let people smoke, too. She only shouted if they did not use the ashtrays to stub out their cigarettes.

Everyone left, Morgane, the fishermen.

"A quick break," Lili said, collapsing on her chair.

She looked over at me. She was not surprised to see me still sitting here, she was used to it. I was lingering, and I did not know how long it might last.

Lili's formica table, with six legs, was pushed in the corner next to the bar. That was where she piled up her invoices, and her catalogues, from La Redoute, Les 3 Suisses . . .

She picked up a catalogue and turned the pages. Her pencil stuck between her teeth. Her head resting on the palm of her hand.

She began to fill out an order form, doing her calculations separately, the subtotal with the discounts, and then she turned some more pages.

"They all have discounts, but you can still find differences for the same item . . ."

Old Mother was dozing by the television. Gently snoring. The car was still across the road. The couple had left to walk round the village.

"Viscose, do you like viscose? Doesn't it make you sweat?"

I hadn't a clue. All my clothes were cotton.

"I don't know," I said.

I finished the newspaper.

The upstairs shutters were open. Lambert must still be inside. Maybe he was waiting for the couple to come back.

Lili had her back to me, leaning over her order, I heard her adding, thinking, for and against, trying to work out whether she would come out ahead. She really wanted everything, but wondered whether she needed it. And then she was hesitating over the colours. She crossed a lot of things off, too . . .

She ended up choosing what was cheapest, but cheapest was not what she liked best. She crossed some more things off. In the end, she could no longer work out her special offer.

She sat there turning the pages.

I could have asked her questions about Lambert, but I think she would not have answered.

Eventually I went out.

I came upon the couple a bit further up the street, taking pictures of the sea.

The next morning, I went to see the plovers Théo had told me about. I went by way of the cross for the *Vendémiaire*, which sank 1912, and to reach the coastguard station I walked along the top of the dyke, a long wall built with thousands of pebbles. On one side was the sea; on the other, sodden meadows, a sort of swampland of salt water where a few animals still managed to graze.

Walking on the meadow was not easy, the soles of my shoes slipped, my ankles turned. It was a state of permanent loss of balance, a sort of exhausting staggering. It took a long time to cross. Beneath my feet stones rubbed, knocked together. I could have taken the paved road, but for nothing on earth would I have left the sea front.

After the dyke, I was back on the path. Silence. There were no cliffs here, only flat coastland. The plovers were a bit further along, a colony of a dozen or so birds nesting in the rocks. The tide was rising. The

battery on my watch had died. I did not know the hour, only sea time.
I sat down on the beach.

No plovers had been attacked. I did not notice anything in particular.
I stayed for a bit more than an hour and then I went home.

In the evening, I heard the foghorn, the deep echo over the sea, at
regular intervals, a muted groan like a phantom knelling. Like a heartbeat. The sound grew fainter, faded, but was never entirely stifled.

The tap on the sink was dripping. The sound of water mingled with
the foghorn. Even if I turned the tap tight, the water continued dripping. I stuffed a rag in the bottom of the sink.

I curled up in bed. It was Sunday. An odd-numbered day. The 31st:
odd because of the 3 and the 1, and the next day would be the first. Two
odd numbers following one another, every other month.

I did not like Sundays. Or holidays. It went back to my childhood.
I always fell ill at Christmas, strange fevers, no doctor was ever able to
explain it to me.

In the morning, Raphaël was waiting for me by his door.

"You alright?" he said.

Because of the way I looked, no doubt, the bags under my eyes.

"I'm fine," I said. "Why?"

He did not insist.

They say here that sometimes the wind is so strong it tears the wings
from butterflies.

*   *   *

Old Mother was scratching the oilcloth with her fingernail. She had
been doing it for a while, since Lili had gone up into the attic to hang
out the laundry.

"Where's the old man, then, why isn't he here? It's his time, after all . . ."

She must have said it ten times. I glanced over at the clock. She was
right, it was his time.

"He'll be here," I said.

She went on staring at the door. She rubbed her face with her hand. Her skin was dry; it made an unpleasant sound, like paper.

"Stop rubbing like that!"

When she got annoyed, Lili would put on a tape of "Bambi" for her. I did not know where the tape had got to.

I went to sit down across from her.

"He must have found someone to have a chat with . . ."

"He doesn't have chats!"

"With me, he does . . ."

Her old eyes lit up. She was full of questions inside, of wanting me to tell her.

"The piece that Lili makes for him, I'm the one who takes it up to him," I said.

I told her about the house, the smells, the big tree with its shadow in the courtyard. All the details I could think of, I gave her. The curtains, the old wood stove, the knife marks on the kitchen table.

At one point, I no longer knew what to say. She leaned towards me.

"I remember . . ." she said.

Her eyes were shining.

She grabbed hold of my hand, and squeezed it hard. Her skin was icy.

"We had cows, we took the buckets and went to milk them. The old man was good at it! I was happy."

That is what she said, I was happy . . .

Her voice was trembling. I sat back a bit, and pulled my hand away.

"Do you still love him?"

I saw her blush beneath the dry thickness of her skin.

She grabbed her handbag, and held it up against her chest. One hand on the handle. Ready to leave. To go back there.

I wanted to hear more from her, to question her about this very particular love. Théo did not love her. Probably he had never loved her.

73

But she, on the other hand . . .

"What have you got in there?" I asked, pointing to the bag.

She looked down. Her fingers fiddled with the catch. Awkward gestures. An old woman's gestures, half-crippled, yet loving still.

Eventually she opened her bag, and spilled everything out on the table, the bottle of perfume, Parfum de Paris, still in its dark-blue box. A photograph: she showed it to me, it was her and Théo. There was a pen, a packet of tobacco, a key . . . A tin box, the shape of a matchbook, with coins rattling in it. They were francs. A lock of hair.

It was Lili's hair, she told me. The photograph had been taken outside their house.

"Those were the good days," she mumbled.

"Because you were young?"

She looked at me, suddenly agitated, trembling all over.

"Because I was with him!"

She groped about for something with her hesitant fingers. How long had it been since she had opened that handbag?

"The old man . . ." she murmured, because of her memories.

And she pushed her chair, abruptly. The back of the chair hit the wall, she was lost in this prison of legs, table legs, chair legs, the legs of the walking frame too, that she had to hold on to even to get as far as the door. She was out of breath. Out of strength. Her body could not even make it round the table.

"She's a bitch!" is what she said, her lips pursed. One hand on her heart.

She had no choice but to sit down again.

"She used to come here, at night . . ."

"Who are you talking about?"

She pointed with her finger over towards Lambert's house. Her eyes filled with tears.

"That thief . . ."

"That's the Perack son's place across the way, do you remember him? He used to come on holiday."

She wanted to scream. Even her voice had no more strength. So she began to whimper.

"She stole all the toys. She said they came from the sea, but it's not true. I know, I do, she came to take them . . ."

It was pitiful. At her most desperate, she grabbed my hand.

"She took everything from me . . . Even dogs, they don't do that."

"You're talking about Nan, is that it?"

She nodded. I could see her face a few inches from mine, I could see how she was struggling with memory, trying to summon up what she wanted to tell me.

"She did things . . . That's why she's mad, you always pay . . ."

"What things?"

She answered, a few words, her jaws clenched too tight, and then a flood of sentences, more and more incoherent, murmuring that the sea would not bring them back, that it never brought them back.

I could hear Lili's footsteps overhead. I wished she would come back down. I thought of calling to her. I put Old Mother's things back in her bag.

I got up, I put the bag on her lap, and her fingers round the handle.

Touching the handbag, she fell silent. Her gaze vacant.

I went to my usual place, further along, by the window. A moment later Lili came back down, a laundry basket under her arm.

"She's been shouting," I said, pointing to Old Mother.

She shrugged.

"She shouts all the time these days."

She went behind the bar, and plunged her hands in the soapy water. She began scrubbing.

"If we take out her dentures, she stops shouting, but then she sucks her tongue, that's no better . . ."

A smell of cooked cabbage spread through the room. A bit nauseating. I could hear the pressure cooker hissing.

"Haven't you got a machine?" I asked, pointing to the pile of laundry she had to wash.

"I do, but I don't like using it for so little. Have you got a machine, over at La Griffue?"

"Yes."

"And do you use it?"

"Of course!"

She looked at me. I was having a bad day, and it showed. I thought about what Old Mother had told me. Had Nan stolen toys from Lambert's house? Toys . . . Why should that matter?

"What was she talking about?" she said, nodding to her mother.

"Nothing . . . It was muddled, I didn't understand."

She put the "Bambi" tape on. Old Mother began to wail again, her gaze riveted on the door handle. When Lili walked by, she grabbed her sleeve.

"The old man . . ."

"What about the old man?"

"It's time for him to come . . ."

"And so what?"

"Isn't he coming?"

"No, he isn't coming."

She went back to the bar.

"You'd think he hadn't made her suffer enough already, she's asking for more!"

Old Mother was holding her stomach, she was not watching Bambi.

"I just don't get it . . ." Lili said.

She said it again, I just don't get it . . . And then she turned to me.

"She was pregnant, he was already cheating on her!"

Old Mother began to moan. For Lili, it was too much. She went back over to her, grabbed her chin, opened her mouth, and with a straightforward gesture pulled out her dentures. An abrupt jerk. I could hear the clacking of the teeth.

Old Mother had swallowed her lips.

Without her dentures the entire bottom half of her face was

nothing but a lipless chin, where a few long and surprisingly black hairs sprouted.

"I'd still rather hear her sucking her own tongue than spouting all that rubbish."

Old Mother was right, it was time for Théo to come, and he was not here.

He had fallen on his way down the path. I found out a bit later. The grass was slick, his foot slipped. The postman found him. He helped him up as best he could. A nasty injury to his leg. The doctor came, but Théo refused to go to hospital.

"Who will look after my cats if I'm not here?"

"If I see you hanging about the village, I won't give you any choice," the doctor said.

No choice, that meant Cherbourg.

And for Théo, Cherbourg meant death.

I went to see him the next day, at the end of the afternoon. He was all alone, sitting at his table, somewhat downcast. The nurse had come. She would come every morning. The table was littered with boxes of medicine, a bottle of ether. He shoved it all to one side.

He did not want to talk about his fall.

He pointed to the cat whose eyes had wept tears like glue.

"You see, its eyelids are cleaner now, it doesn't bump into everything the way it used to."

The bottle for the cat's eyes was mixed in with all the other medication.

He told me that Max had brought him some fish. And bread, too.

Lili had given me some food for him in a sealed box. I put the box on the table. He peered inside. He made a face and pushed it away with a weary gesture.

"That's not fair, Théo."

He gave a short laugh.

"What would you know? You think she does it for my sake?"

77

He shook his head.

"She just doesn't want people to go saying she's letting her father die of hunger."

He looked down.

He did not want to meet my gaze. He blushed faintly, and tapped his fingers on the table. A nervous gesture, coming from him. It was annoying. I do not know if he realized he was doing it.

*   *   *

The *auberge* in Jobourg was right up at the top of the cliff. All alone, somewhat squat, it overlooked the sea from the gigantic headland. I liked to anticipate when I would see it from afar, a sort of huge bear crouching on the hills.

I had come here often, in cold weather, in snow, at night, too. Those early weeks, when it was impossible to sleep. That was what I did in the beginning. I walked. I talked to you. When I could, I screamed. The sea is not a wall, it does not send back an echo. I stopped screaming.

This *auberge* was the refuge to reach after hours spent in the wind. At land's end, a neat wall of flat stones lined the path. The earth was soft here, covered in short grasses. The *auberge* was nearby. The path continued, afterwards, further, towards La Pointe des Becquets and Le Bec de l'Âne. I could have kept going, headed south. I had heard that down by Biville the coast was beautiful. The beach. Dunes. I could have gone to Carteret.

I did not give a damn about dunes.

I did not want to go anywhere else.

This land was like you. If I left it, it would be like losing you again. Your body was an obsession. I knew its contours, its imperfections. I knew all its strength. Every evening, I saw your face, the images, all our history playing back, yet again. Your smile, lips, eyes. Your hands. Your bloody hands, so much bigger than mine. You said, We'll part on an odd-numbered day. For a laugh, you said.

As if you already knew.

They came to get you on an odd-numbered day and, since that day, I have been walking. I came up to the *auberge* thinking about you.

It had begun to rain, and I knew I would get soaked, and it would not be for the first time.

The waitress at the *auberge* knew me. In the winter months, I came here, and I put my mittens on the radiator.

When I came in, she smiled. She saw my teeth were chattering. She poured me a glass of brandy, too strong. I drank it, looking at the sea. I ordered a crab. An enormous creature, with a red shell, I cracked its claws.

The clouds drifted by.

The sea was grey.

The seagulls had to fly backwards because there was so much wind.

* * *

I saw Lambert again the next day, at the end of the morning, he was standing on the side of the road in front of the Stork's house. A cow had just given birth in a pasture. The child's father had loaded the calf into a wheelbarrow and was bringing it down.

We met there, by chance. A birth, even that of a calf, brings people out on to their doorsteps. Makes them turn their heads.

A strange parade it was, the cow moving along with this heavy viscous pouch still dangling between her legs. Immediately after the cow came the calf in the wheelbarrow, and then the Stork's father, and then the Stork herself and finally the dog. The axle of the wheelbarrow was squeaking. Overhead the seagulls cried.

"It's a hard place, La Hague, huh?"

He said it in an odd way, and it made me laugh.

We looked at each other. The wind gave us the eyes of madmen.

"And have you sold your house?" I eventually asked.

"I've had a few visits."

I nodded.

The pouch gave way. The cow stopped, turned round to look at what had just come out of her, a pile of phlegm and blood, still steaming.

He was right, La Hague was a hard sort of place. I felt the smile return to my face.

His leather jacket squeaked.

"It hasn't healed," he said, pointing to the mark on my cheek.

I touched it.

"It always takes longer, with rust."

The cow vanished into the barn. Lambert turned to face the sea, his hands in his pockets.

"I saw you up on the cliffs . . . Max said you go there to count the birds. He said you hide inside caves to look at the sea."

"Max talks too much."

He took a few steps along the road.

"And what sort of birds are you counting?"

"I count all of them."

"Is that why you have binoculars?"

"Yes."

"And have you always done that?"

I hesitated. I was no longer used to questions. The questions people asked, and that I had to answer. The other ones, too.

"No, I used to be a biology teacher, in Avignon. I worked in partnership with the Centre ornithologique de Pont-de-Crau in the Camargue."

"Ah, yes . . . There are a lot of birds in the Camargue."

I looked at him. That way he had of expressing himself, so detached.

"There are a lot, yes."

"And you left Avignon to come to La Hague?"

I nodded.

There was no-one left on the path. The cow, the dog, the father, they had all disappeared. Then those few fragile seconds where we, too, could have left, each going our own way, as if we had merely met on the path. Two people who did not exist for one another, that is what we would have been.

"Do you count robins, too?"

"No, not robins . . ."

"Why not?"

"I'm only concerned with seabirds, migrating ones."

"Ah, so it's not all birds . . ."

He took a few more steps, slow steps.

He was waiting for me.

"Do you know why a robin has that red spot on its breast?"

I had no idea. I turned. Behind me was the village, and the street that ran down the middle.

Ahead of me was Lambert.

I took a step.

He raised his arm towards the sun. I looked at his hand, his strong wrist. The leather strap that held his watch.

I took another step.

He did not say anything more until I had come level with him. After that, he began to speak again. We went back down towards the harbour.

"This story goes back to the time when humans did not yet have fire. A bird got the idea to go and steal some from the sun, it wanted to give it to mankind, but on its way back down, its wings caught fire and it had to pass the fire on to another bird. The other bird was a robin. It took the fire to its breast, but didn't have time to reach the humans, and its feathers burned . . . That red spot they have on their breast, that's what's left. They never told you this story at school?"

"No, but I learned other things . . . For example, I know that in real life, no-one steals fire from the sun."

"So what do you suppose humans did in order to get fire?"

I looked at him. I did not know whether I found him attractive.

"They scraped stones, they rubbed sticks together. The lucky ones found flames brought by lightning."

81

He turned to me.

"How long have you been at La Hague?"

"Since September."

"When are you leaving?"

"I don't know."

"But . . . you will leave again?"

I did not answer.

That puzzled him for a moment. We had arrived at the quay, the road was coming to an end, a little bit of asphalt, the car park and the sea. We walked over by the boats.

I asked him if Le Morvan was as beautiful as here, and he said yes, that it might be even more beautiful.

And then he looked at the sea for a long moment.

"How do you know that I live in Le Morvan?"

He said that quite evenly, and I felt myself blush. There was a hint of amusement in his gaze. I could hardly tell him that Morgane had been going through his pockets. I mumbled something.

He pointed to the *auberge*.

"Shall we go for a drink?"

There was a light on inside, but the *patron* never served before eleven, it said so on the window.

I told him that.

He went up to the door.

"Shall we try, anyway?"

The *patron* was there reading his newspaper, sitting at a table. When we came in, he looked up, a quick glance, and then went on reading his article.

Lambert chose a table by the window. He took off his jacket. I was still by the door.

The *patron* did not move.

Lambert motioned to me and I went and joined him. It was warm. It felt good. Outside, it was windy. You could see the boats moving.

We talked about Le Morvan. He said that the snow there was so thick sometimes that it felt like a burying. He liked it. He also liked taking trains, never mind the destination, he liked hanging out in train stations and watching people live.

I told him I was going to redecorate my flat, green.

I took out the postcard.

"It's a special green . . . Hopper green."

We talked about snow again. And then about Paris, too. He had never been to the Louvre, he said museums bored him.

We looked outside. There was mist. Fishermen had come to cast their lines.

"I've also seen you hanging out," I said.

He nodded. He was going to add something, when the *patron* slammed his hand on the newspaper.

"Those fucking Arabs, can you believe this!"

He left his newspaper wide open on the table, and came over to us.

"Can I get you something?"

"Some wine . . . Some shrimps, bread, butter . . . Some good wine," Lambert insisted, and the *patron* said, "We serve nothing but, here."

He brought us the glasses, the shrimps, the bread, everything Lambert had asked for, and set it down on the table.

After that, he went back to his article.

Lambert filled the glasses. We drank. We started on the shrimps. They were fresh, caught that morning, the flesh firm. We peeled them. I bit into the first one. A strong taste of iodine filled my mouth.

We looked at each other. We did not say anything. We munched away on it all with bread and butter.

And washed it down with wine.

"It's really deserted here," he said.

"That's because it's not Sunday . . . on Sundays it gets lively. People come from Paris, to see the sea."

"I'll have to come on a Sunday then . . . What day is it today?"

I shook my head. I didn't know. We went on eating our shrimps.

"The sea was clearer yesterday," I said.

What a stupid thing to say.

I said things like that, from time to time. When I met you, it was on a square. I had four hours driving ahead of me, I was a bit nervous. Well, let's kiss goodbye! That is what I said to you. At the first stop sign, I pulled over. I had your address in my pocket. That night, I wrote to you.

"Because of the mist," I went on, "you can't see the surface of the water."

Lambert was looking at me. There was something of a brutal tenderness about him, an awkward charm. His gestures were slow. His eyes grey. The first time I saw them, they seemed blue.

"They're talking about you in the harbour."

"The harbour's not all that big."

A drop of wine slid down his glass. It left a spot on the tablecloth.

"In the evening this is where I have dinner, that little table over by the lobsters."

He turned, and looked at the table.

"Could I come and count the birds with you, one day?"

"Why, you're not leaving?"

He said yes, he was going to leave, soon, but between now and soon, there was a bit of time. And that he would like to use that time to go and see the birds.

The cliffs were my paths of solitude. I no longer knew how to walk there with another person.

A cork had been forgotten on the windowsill. Lambert took it in his hands and rolled it back and forth in the light.

"Do you know what I saw here one day? Some kids had caught a fish and they stuck its back with corks like this, then they put it back in the water. The fish couldn't dive any more. They thought it was funny."

He was still angry, so long afterwards, as if the kids were still there on the other side of the window, over by the rocks, up to no good.

"We ought to be able to sort through our memories, don't you think? Sort through them and only keep the best ones . . ."

He put the cork down.

I looked at him. "Is that why you're here? To find the best memories?"

He smiled. He filled our glasses.

"Could be, yes."

I liked drinking that wine, with him, that first day. We talked some more about his holidays here, and about the south.

At one point, we turned our heads because Nan was there, on the other side of the window, and she was looking at us. She had done her hair in a long thick plait. She stayed there for a minute, perhaps two. She was staring at Lambert. It lasted a very long time.

After that, she went away.

He went on peeling his shrimps. Some of them had eggs, pink clusters stuck to their middle.

"I had a little brother . . . But you know that, don't you? You must have seen his photograph? The medallion, at the cemetery . . . His name was Paul." He shook his head. "The bloody sea took him away."

He munched on a shrimp.

"The night before, we'd been to Cherbourg, my mother had bought us clothes for the rain. I remember she'd got a little polo shirt for Paul, with boats on it. Sailing boats. When we came back, my father wanted to take a photograph of us in our new clothes, and he put Paul in front of the window. The next morning they took the sailing boat and went to Alderney. I stayed here. I was fifteen, I needed my space . . . By the time I got the film developed, they were all dead."

He looked up at me. "You're not eating . . ."

I took a shrimp. I removed the head and tail. The pink shell all around, like a thick skin.

He took a sip of wine.

"That was the first time they had left me all alone. For a long time I wondered whether I had been lucky or not . . . At the end of the day, I suppose I was lucky after all."

He looked up, the shrimp between his fingers.

"Apparently they're still alive when they throw them into the boiling water . . ."

His voice was like La Hague, it had the strength of the place, and the indifference, too. I told him that, I said, "Your voice is like La Hague," and he nodded, as if he understood.

We went on eating for a moment, not speaking.

"So what are people saying about me in the harbour?"

"That your parents died in this sea . . . between here and Alderney."

"Closer to Alderney. Do they say anything else?"

"They see you hanging about . . ."

He raised his glass, as if to drink a toast to everyone who was talking about him.

The sky had cleared. The wind had managed to break through the clouds, and was already drying the road.

"It wasn't Lili who took your flowers," I said.

"I don't bloody care."

I rolled my glass between my hands. I thought back to that moment between them, the other day, at Lili's place, that very tense moment when he had implied that Théo was responsible for the shipwreck.

"The other day, at Lili's, your argument . . ."

"It wasn't an argument."

I took a sip of wine. I held the glass with its cold surface against my lips.

"Was Théo keeping the light that night?"

"Yes."

"You said he'd put the lamp out . . . Do you think he's responsible for your parents' death?"

He gave the strangest smile. "That's a nice way of putting it . . ."

He looked at his glass. The bottle, almost empty.

"Is Théo your friend?" he said.

"Yes."

86

He put his glass down next to mine. He made them touch. And chink together gently. He looked up at me.

"Théo put the light out. I don't know why, but I know that he did. I've always known."

"Is that why you came back?"

"No . . . I came to sell the house and to clear out what's inside . . . But since I've been here . . . Théo put the lamp out and I want him to tell me why."

I shook my head. "He must have known how dangerous it was, he wouldn't have done that."

"But he did." He pressed his hands together. "Their death is like a film you stop right in the middle. I'm still waiting for the rest. Forty years is a long time."

"Théo is an old man."

"That's no excuse."

There were no more shrimps. No more wine. We went out.

Nan was there, pacing back and forth along the breakwater. Insects rustled in the sand, or was it in my head, all the wine I had drunk.

Fleas by the thousands, on the brown seaweed.

He took his packet of cigarettes from his pocket. On the shore, a child with blonde hair was running to make the seagulls fly up.

He watched him as he lit his cigarette. Who was he seeing in that child? Himself, or the memory of the brother who had disappeared?

M. Anselme had told me that Lambert's mother had been very beautiful. On the medallion at the cemetery, it was the father's shadow that was cast over the gravel in the yard.

Nan stopped at the end of the breakwater, her face turned to the sea. At one point, she turned around. She was far away. Lambert did not say anything. He did not comment on her looking at us. He smoked his cigarette down to the filter, and crushed the butt.

We went further. The pebbles rattled together under the water. It was a sound from inside the sea, a muted scraping. The seagulls were searching in the water, watching for crabs. At this spot along the coast, the rocks formed a small island where sterns came to rest. The island was shaped like a nest. At high tide, it was engulfed.

Lambert went down to the beach. He went off among the rocks. On the sand there was a trace of furrows where a few rivulets drained gently away. Lambert knelt down and placed his hand against the sand. Above him, two huge gulls were playing at defying the sea. Caught in the whirlwind, they went skimming over the crest of the waves, letting out their long, strident cries.

He got up. He looked at the sea. Do people who wait always have the same obsessions?

I retraced my steps.

When I was outside the *auberge*, I looked back. Nan had gone up to him, was circling round him. She seemed very agitated.

He was a strong man, he could have chased her away. He was walking, slowly, along that beach, and Nan was following him. At times, he paused. I do not know if he did it to wait for her.

He was looking at the sea, as if his lost brother's presence in the icy waters of Le Blanchard had brought him close to the old madwoman.

*   *   *

The Stork watched me as I came over, her little child's hand wide open against the windowpane. For a long time, I had thought that Lili was her aunt or her grandmother, but Lili was nobody's aunt, and she had no children.

I went in. The Stork took a notebook out of her school bag. She laid it down flat before her. She showed me her real name on the label, written in red ink, Ila. She opened the notebook, slipped her hand into her pocket, and brought out a handful of pencils. She chose one, and began to draw her lines. Lines and circles. All over the page. Her head bent slightly against her shoulder.

Her pencils smelled of wood.

"Your pencils, you ought to put them in a case . . . That's why the leads are breaking."

In the silence, I could hear the lead scratching over the paper. Her breathing, her shoes scraping against the floor because she was swinging her legs. Her feet did not touch the ground. Only her toes.

"Circles and lines, that's not enough . . . You have to learn to make letters."

She did not know how.

I drew a model for her.

Eyes wide open, she followed what my pencil was writing. I read it to her, *Ila's dog is called Soft Spot.*

She nodded.

She looked at me. Sometimes, when she was writing, she would caress the mark she had on her lip.

Under the sentence I had written, she went on tracing her lines and her circles. I looked at her. Was she like the child that I will not have, our child, the one you will never give me? That was what I had asked you for, a child, before you go . . . You did not want to do it. You explained gently why we must not. I did not understand, at all.

I held the Stork against me. I clasped my hands round her.

"Do you want me to tell you why the robin has a spot on his breast?"

She nodded.

I told her.

At the end, she looked up at me. She wanted to know who had managed to take fire to man.

I shook my head. I did not know.

The next day was Saturday. Lambert arrived at noon. Lili was smoothing a paper tablecloth in front of me.

He said hello.

When I saw the three plates on the catalogue table, I understood that they were eating together. Old Mother came over, with her walking frame. Lili said she had a clock in her stomach.

"If you knew how many times I've had to pick her up!" she said, as if to apologize for the walking frame.

She had made mussels with rice. She served me a whole potful. I pulled over the newspaper.

They sat together, the three of them. I heard him ask whether Théo and Old Mother were still married. He must have seen the ring on her finger, that old, dull ring, still caught in her flesh.

"Divorce is for city people," Lili said.

She filled up their plates. She spooned the rice into little bowls. Old Mother's medication, a little pile next to her glass. The glass was full of water.

"The wedding ring is part of her body. Unless you cut her finger off, she'll be buried with it."

Lambert nodded.

When she saw the mussels, Old Mother plunged her fingers into the shells, then scraped at them with her gums. She threw the empty shells into the bowl. When she missed the bowl, the shell fell on the ground with a little noise.

"Mussels are her favourite. That, and dipping sponge fingers."

Lili bustled about.

"She's not difficult. As long as I can, I'll keep her with me. You can talk to her! Tell her who you are . . ."

"Who I am?"

"Why not, who you are!"

"I can't."

"You can't?"

"No."

Lili shrugged. She glanced over my way to see if everything was alright. At last she sat down. I could see him from behind. Leaning over her slightly. I had not expected to see him back here.

In the village, on the quay, in the bistro, the men were talking about him. Without saying his name. With their eyes. Or in a low voice. It was gossip.

Nobody can get away from gossip.

"Your mother used to make us cakes . . . Brioches covered with icing sugar, we loved that . . . We would go and eat them on the rocks. We wouldn't even wait for them to get cold. It made our tummies swell up," said Lily.

"We would run all along the seashore, and catch crabs. Once, we climbed up on the roof to look at the sea," said Lambert.

They talked about their childhood. Lili said, "You should have let us know . . ."

"Let you know what?"

"That you were coming back."

He shook his head.

"Have you been to Alderney?" she said.

"No."

"Are you going to go?"

"I don't know . . . Perhaps."

"If you decide to go, I know a fellow who has a boat, he can take you over."

I was eating my mussels and reading the newspaper. I was listening to them, too.

"What have you been doing all this time?"

"Not much . . . I live in Le Morvan. My grandparents were from there, they're the ones who took me in."

"Is it nice there, Le Morvan?"

"Yes, it's a good place, a bit like here, with meadows, cows, quiet little roads."

"Except out there, you haven't got the sea."

This made him laugh.

"No, we haven't got the sea . . . And we haven't got a nuclear power plant either," he said, referring to the Cogema.

Lili shrugged.

She went to get a facecloth from the kitchen, and scrubbed her mother's hands.

"And now, what are you doing?"

"Nothing."

"That's it?"

"That's it."

She glanced over at my table. When she saw I had finished, she put down the flannel.

She brought me a slice of strawberry tart.

Old Mother got her sponge finger.

"Why don't you give her some tart?" he said.

"Strawberries? They make her break out . . . You want her to die?"

"You don't die from a rash . . ."

"You can die from whatever!" Lili said, clearing the plates.

The television was on, the midday game shows.

The television without the volume, the picture showing a wheel turning.

"All these years, I thought I would see you again . . . Why didn't you ever come back?"

"I did come back."

"Yes, at the beginning . . . And afterwards?"

"Afterwards, I couldn't."

"And now, all of a sudden, you can?"

"Yes."

He hesitated before going on.

"My father was forty when he died. Now I'm older than he was. That's also why I came back."

"Because now you're older than he was?"

He nodded.

Lili cut him a slice of tart. She slid it on to a plate.

"I remember him, he was tall."

"He wasn't that tall . . ."

"Seemed tall to me."

Lambert looked at her.

"Do you remember when he found the hedgehog's nest? It was

right there, behind the wall. He called us over . . . He made us swear not to touch anything. We all swore, hand against hand, in the garden. Do you remember whether my mother was there?"

"I don't know."

"The hedgehogs died. My father made us crêpes to console us. It was the last year."

Their eyes met.

"I don't like talking about the past," she said.

"And my brother, do you remember him?"

Lili picked up her glass.

"No, he was too small, we didn't see him."

"On the day of the hedgehogs, was he there?"

"I don't know . . ."

Her voice remained suspended, for a long moment.

"He probably was, yes . . ." she said at last.

She ran a hand over her face. She said, "He was so little, your brother, your mother kept him inside all the time."

She shook her head. "That's all in the past . . . You'd do better to eat."

But he could not eat.

He left his fork in his plate, with the knife on top.

He pushed the plate to the middle of the table.

"It was your father who was keeping the light that night."

Lili sat up. "Is that why you came back? To rehash all that business?"

She had spoken loudly. She turned towards her mother, but the old woman was staring at the screen, sucking on her sponge finger, and she wasn't paying attention to them.

"We were fifteen years old, Lambert . . ."

"So?"

"I know what you think! The police carried out their investigation, they came to see my father . . . The lamp was not put out that night. They wrote it black on white at the end of the file. What more do you want?"

"Investigations get it wrong sometimes . . ."

"Not this time! Besides, my father was not alone in the lighthouse,

93

the bloke who kept it with him testified that nothing out of the ordinary happened that night."

"It wasn't his watch. At the time of the shipwreck, he was asleep."

Lili could not calm down.

"It may be hard to swallow, but it was an accident, a simple accident at sea . . ."

He got up.

"Where are you going?" she said. "And the tart? Some coffee? Won't you have a coffee?"

"No . . ."

He pushed his chair up against the table.

"Lamps don't go out when there are accidents!"

Lili slammed her hand on the table. "It did not go out!"

The noise made the old woman jump. She began moaning.

Lili groaned.

"Even my Saturdays, there's always someone who manages to spoil them for me."

"I'm sorry . . ."

"That's unlikely!"

He took his jacket from the back of the chair. "I'm going."

"That's it, go right ahead!"

He turned away from her.

He went by my table. His hand. The sleeve of his jacket.

His fingertips brushed the tablecloth.

"Is it good?" he said, pointing to the strawberry tart.

I nodded.

"I'm glad," he said.

He didn't say anything else, and he went out.

*   *   *

Théo gently pulled the door closed behind him and slipped the key behind the pot of geraniums. He paused, his hand on the railing.

From the breakwater, I could see him with my binoculars as if I were right next to him. Had he really put out the lamp? I did not believe it. He knew the dangers of the sea, and he loved the boats.

He crossed the courtyard and walked down the path. He headed in the direction of La Roche.

He was going to Nan's. For some time now she had not been well, she walked with her head down, talking to herself. You saw her going along the shore more than usual and not just on storm days. Sometimes I came across her two, three times a day. I greeted her, but she did not answer. She walked quickly, busily, as if she had someone to meet or an important task to carry out. She always ended up at the shore. The hem of her dress in the waves. Was it Lambert's presence that had troubled her in this way, his face, did she think she saw one of her own in his face? I would have liked to have known who Michel was, that man she was for ever calling for.

Théo was walking, leaning on his cane, stooped. I followed him with my gaze as far as La Roche and then I lost him when he reached the first houses.

Before, I used to follow poor people in the street, the most destitute ones, the ones on foot. I did not want to know where they were going. I just wanted to follow them. Their steps. Their shadows. They had nothing. They were cold. I took pictures. I did this for over a year. In December, snow fell. I took more pictures, those men, always from behind, their grey coats, their steps in the snow.

I took their pictures when they were sleeping on their sheets of cardboard, too.

A man's back could tell a story as well as his face might.

Some nights, just the contact of the sheet on my skin would burn me. I had to get out of bed. I would stand there, my bare feet on the floor. If that was not enough, I opened the window. My teeth chattered, my lips turned blue. Only afterwards could I lie down again and sleep.

Flowered curtains hung from my window, a plastic curtain rod. When I came here, one of the windowpanes was broken and the curtains were billowing. There was a big damp spot on the floor. For several days I wedged a piece of cardboard against the window. The cardboard got wet, I changed it and then someone came and replaced the pane.

The dark spot remained on the floor. Sometimes when the sun beat down harder than usual, it disappeared. It always came back.

The morning light seemed to rise from the sea. From my window I could see the roofs of the village all the way up the hill. To the right, the yellow lights of the handful of houses at La Roche.

Was Théo still at Nan's? Had he spent the night at her side? Old Mother must be waiting for him, her handbag on her lap. With her old woman's love oozing from her eyes. A body that did not forget. That is why she clung to her bag. What had happened between Nan and Théo? Had they loved one another? How strong was their love? I lay on the floor, my knees pulled up. My back against the radiator. Almost a year. Time passing over you. It too was eroding you. I could not stand my skin any more. My skin without your hands. My body without your weight. I rolled my jumper up against my belly. I made it into a ball. I pushed my back right up against the burning pipes of the radiator. I could feel the marks. Pipes like bars. The bars of your bed, at the end, so you would not fall.

And that other mark on my cheek, the red swelling that was gradually fading. This void in me that made me sweat and moan.

And I sweated.

I moaned, too, scratching my nails against the wall. I licked the salt to come closer to your skin.

That morning, I would have liked for time to take you further away. For it to lay waste to you. Even your face. I let out a long, silent cry, mingled with tears, my teeth sank into my arm.

You had made me swear never to speak. Never to write about

you, your bed, that place . . . The smell of the walls, the view from your window.

The last visit, the absence of sun. Because the light hurt you too much.

So, the curtain hardly open, a simple patch of grey sky in the upper pane.

*   *   *

Lili pointed to the bag.

"Could you take that to him on your way, would you mind?"

She did not say Théo. She did not say my father. She said him.

There was a silence after her words. She slipped a small bag from the pharmacy into the bag. It was from Beaumont. The prescription was inside.

"Tell him the doctor will come Monday at the end of the morning. That he'd better clean himself up."

She gave me a frank look.

"What's wrong?"

"Nothing . . ."

"I know you. That look doesn't mean nothing."

I shook my head.

"I can't tell him that . . . To clean himself up."

She shrugged, frowning, and closed the bag.

"Tell him what you like."

She put the bag on the bar.

"I like your father . . ."

It came out, in a breath.

She froze.

"You *like* him?"

"Yes."

I saw her twitch. She looked at me. She seemed about to laugh.

"You like him . . ." she said again. "You want him?"

97

"I didn't say that."

"If you like, I'll give him to you. Let's say that, right, from now on, we'll say he's yours!"

She shoved the bag into my arms, the way she had shoved the bouquet of buttercups into Lambert's jumper. The same gesture. The same strength.

"That isn't what I meant."

"Then you don't say it. You don't say anything. You pick up the bag and take it to him."

I went out.

Lambert was in the garden. He had rolled up his shirtsleeves to the elbow and he was pulling out the brambles against the wall. The windows were open. The FOR SALE sign was still hanging from the fence.

I took the path that went up to La Roche. There, the wind carried strong scents of the open sea. Spindrift that clung to my mouth. My lips now wet, now burning. Desires, here, are laid bare by the wind. It is a matter of skin, La Hague. A matter of the senses.

I stopped.

Could I love you and no longer touch you? The thought came to me, shockingly.

Could I still love you?

I was caught mid-flight.

With you, I touched the abyss. And now . . . Pain, as it receded, was digging itself inside out.

I picked up my bag.

I got to Théo's place, the cats were there, all gathered in the yard. How many were there? When I asked him, he would say, Twenty, thirty, between the ones that are born, the others that die . . .

He had a sick dog too, as old as he was, its age multiplied by seven would make the same age. But Théo no longer knew how old he was. In the village, that is what they called him, the old man. He knew they taught the children to beware of him. To be afraid of him. When he went back to the village the pebbles bounced off his back. Before, he would turn around and brandish his cane. Now, he did not care, he said the pebbles did not reach him.

I tapped on the window. I tried to see inside, but it was so dark. The grey cat was stretched its full length along the inner sill of the window. One fang slightly longer than the others emerged from its closed mouth and gave it the air of a young wildcat.

There were two other cats on the table. A bowl. Some bread.

I tapped again.

"Are you there?"

I went in.

Théo was sleeping in his armchair, his cap pulled down on his head. One hand still resting on the knotty wood of his cane, as if sleep had surprised him there, in front of the lit screen.

The little white cat was lying on his lap. Her paws gently folded back, her head heavy, she was sleeping.

The way he was sitting like that in the half-light, the room resembled Rembrandt's "Philosopher in Meditation"; for a long time I had had the reproduction pinned to the wall of my student room.

Against the wall, a stone sink, its earthenware tiles dulled by scale. A saucepan lid rested in a plastic dish rack. A plate in the basin. I put the bag on the table.

"I've brought the bread," I said.

Théo opened his eyes. He grunted. I showed him the food, the medication.

He glanced at it. His little eyes behind his glasses, the same eyes as Lili.

"The doctor will come on Monday . . ."

He shrugged. He sat up.

"And what can doctors do against old age?"

In La Hague, old people and trees look alike, equally battered and silent. Shaped by the winds. Sometimes, when you see something in the distance, it is impossible to know if it is a man or something else.

He ran his hand over the little cat's head. He said that this one was more fragile than the others, and he had to give her more love.

Was it for the same reason that he had loved Nan? Because he had felt she was more fragile?

He looked at me as if he had read my thoughts and he placed his glasses on the table. The lenses were dirty, fingerprints; they looked greasy in the light.

"I counted twelve pairs of plovers at the place you told me about."

He looked up.

"It's not enough to count them."

I let my gaze wander over the table, at everything that cluttered it, plates, newspapers, medication . . . everything he must surely push aside, at meal time, to make a bit of room.

He placed his hands together.

"The plover is a very intelligent bird, you have to observe it for a long time to understand it. When you threaten its nest, it flies away, its wings low, as if it were injured, and it lets itself fall on to the beach. It drags itself along, clumsy little hops, and it does that to become the target."

His hands were ravaged, hewn by cold, salt water, rope burns.

"It's all an act . . . It's rare and very admirable behaviour for a bird."

A furtive emotion passed over his face.

I looked out of the window.

Outside, the clouds were parting, letting a few rays of sunlight filter through. Out at sea, the sky had taken on the same grey colour as the water, as if one had poured into the other to mix this dark hue.

"Counting birds in this wind, that can't be your whole life."

"Well you did it, didn't you?"

He smiled as if to say it was not the same. He was still stroking the little white cat.

"This one never drinks with the others. When she's thirsty, she miaows and I have to turn on the tap."

The cat opened her eyes.

"She was stolen from her mother by a dog that had no puppies. The dog brought her home in its mouth. It looked after her . . ."

He caressed the cat, with the palm of his hand. "I thought of giving the kitten back to her mother, but she had seven more . . . And the dog didn't have any."

I asked him whether he thought that made it any more fair.

I saw that it bothered him. The skin on his cheeks slightly pink.

He did not answer. It was the first time that such a particular silence had fallen between us. He put his hands back in his lap, one next to the other.

"That lad who's hanging about, he's the Perack son?" He looked up at me. "What's he doing here?"

"I don't know. He wants to sell his house."

"What else do you know about him?"

"Nothing . . . I don't know him."

He picked up his glasses, adjusted them on his nose. A smile slid over his face.

"You went to the *auberge* with him, it wasn't even eleven o'clock, the other morning. You stayed almost an hour together, and when you came back out, you walked along the shore."

He pointed to the pair of binoculars on the chair by the window.

"And don't tell me it's not right to do that, because you do it too."

Now it was my turn to blush. Violently.

"Which reminds me, some day I'll have to show you the splendid view we have from the skylight."

He took the little cat's head between his hands, gently caressed it. "What did he tell you?"

I looked outside, towards the tree in the courtyard; Théo said it was so old that its roots reached down to hell. Théo said when you cut a branch off that tree, a red sap ran out that looked like blood.

He repeated his question.

I looked at him.

"Lambert thinks that it was you who was keeping the lighthouse the night his parents died."

That was not everything. He knew it. He nodded.

"You call him Lambert?"

"Lambert Perack, that's his name." He smiled.

I felt like asking him more questions.

"Can a lighthouse lamp go out at night without the keeper realizing?"

He looked up at me. "Is it you or him asking?"

"It's me."

"Well, if it's you . . . No, it's not possible."

"And if it had been him, what would you have answered?"

"If it had been him, I would not have answered." He looked away. "Don't listen to what that man says. His judgement isn't sound, he's suffering."

"You don't suffer any more, so long after."

"What would you know about it?"

I had an intuition that he was lying to me.

"Are there ever reasons that might cause a lighthouse keeper to put out his lamp?"

He chuckled.

"No reasons. It's the might of the sea that gives orders to lighthouse keepers. For the rest, nothing, no-one can oblige a keeper to turn his back on what he has to do." He said it bluntly. He was tapping his fingertips on the tabletop. "You know, when you're in the lighthouse, the only thing that matters is to illuminate the sea. So you do it. You don't think about anything else."

I was beginning to doubt. I felt the instant of it. The shadow between us.

"Lambert has lived past the age his father was when he died. He said it was for that, too, that he came back."

"He's been confiding in you . . ."

"It wasn't to me, it was to Lili. I was there, I overheard them."

"He was talking to Lili?" Théo gave a strange smile.

I saw myself, suddenly, the way a passer-by might see me through the window, at the table, beneath the lamp, gossiping with an old man.

I shook my head.

"I don't want to talk about it any more," I said.

"What are you afraid of?"

"I'm not afraid."

I was lying. I was afraid of what I was becoming. A woman without love. I wanted to know about him and Nan. I wanted to know how far they had loved, how much they had dared, and why they had not dared more.

"Tell me about her," I said abruptly.

He stiffened.

I had said Her.

I hadn't said Nan, and yet he had understood.

"What you're asking . . ."

He stayed for a moment, without saying anything. I had no father: could Théo have been my father? If he had been, I think I would have loved him unconditionally. He put the little cat down on the armchair next to him. He pressed his hand on the table and got up. He disappeared into the next room. I waited for him to come back, but he did not come back.

*   *   *

Evening fell. Behind the windows, lights came on, filtering yellow through the lace curtains.

After five o'clock, kitchen tables become places for shared secrets. Hands around cups. Heads bent, close together. Glasses left lying about, tea towels hanging from stoves.

It was the end of the day. Not yet night. But that terrible hour when shadows return. The dogs began to howl.

A first ray of light slid from the lighthouse over the surface of the water, lighting the harbour, the boats' anchorage. The beam also lit La Griffue, and then everything was once again plunged into darkness.

I walked by silhouettes, people who had become shadows, sometimes so alone that they would knock at any door to be near a gaze or a fire. The ones who had no callers would drag themselves to the bistro. Conversations were long, drawn-out. The curtain slightly closed. Even when there was no-one left to see, all it took was one shadow. And when they no longer wanted to talk about themselves, they could still talk about others. About the living, the dead.

*　　*　　*

Morgane had found work making crowns for a shop in Cherbourg. She threaded pearls on to a wire frame, and if she did not mess up, it turned into a tiara for a bride to wear. She wasn't paid much, but she said it was enough, with what she earned at the *auberge*.

She worked at the kitchen table. When I arrived, Max was looking at her. He was not allowed to touch the pearls. Or to drool, or scratch, or make noise with his teeth, he was not allowed that either. If he did any of those things, Morgane would kick him out. Without a word. A glance sufficed. It had already happened. He knew it could happen again, so he sat frozen in the chair, his hands between his thighs.

Even if he did not move, if she was fed up, she would say so, "Enough, Creature," and Max went away.

"Isn't it time for the sow?" I said when I found him there.

He shook his head. It was time for nothing. I sat down with them. A postcard lay on the table, a view of the Colosseum in Rome.

"It's from my parents, you can read it . . ." said Morgane.

A few words scribbled on the other side.

Greetings from Rome. We had a bit of rain last night, but yesterday we were able to visit St Peter's and this afternoon we're going to the Forum. We'll be back on Monday. Hugs and kisses. Papa, Maman.

Morgane shrugged.

"They travel a lot . . ."

I reread the card. Their words, strangely distant. I found it very hostile. Morgane must have realized. She threaded her pearls and looked at me from under her lashes.

"We go to see them from time to time. We leave early in the morning and come back in the evening. Last time was for Christmas. We didn't stay long."

She threaded several pearls in a row.

"Next time we go will be in July, for my thirtieth birthday."

Raphaël came out of the bedroom, his hair tousled, and he shouted because we had woken him up. He slid his hand over her shoulder, an infinitely tender gesture, and that gesture sent me back to my solitude, the enormous fault-line between your presence and absence. He saw the card. He picked it up and read it. He put it back down without making any comment.

Morgane let her head slip against her brother's side. I do not know how they ended up here, the pair of them. I know that Raphaël arrived first, and then Morgane came to join him. They were brother and sister, and they looked at each other like lovers.

That need they had to be close, to touch. Between them, always, gestures that pushed the boundaries of tenderness, and there was something extremely sensual in the way they touched, so lightly. It troubled me to look at them.

Raphaël pulled away from his sister. He opened a beer and went to drink it standing by the sink.

"You still here?" he asked, turning to Max.

Max smiled. The time he could spend looking at Morgane seemed to cancel all other time.

He said as much. "Time with Morgane, that's the temporary cancellation of all the adverse time."

Morgane shrugged.

Max looked furtively over at the dictionary. That made him dream, too, all those words locked up in so little space. When Morgane kicked him out, he took the dictionary against his chest and went to sit in the corridor.

That is what he did.

Until Morgane kicked him even further out.

The window that looked out on to the garden was wide open. The sun came in and with it, a tiny butterfly with blue wings.

"Do you think they fuck?" Max said, watching the insect flying in the light.

Raphaël turned. "Who are you talking about?"

"The butterflies."

"And why wouldn't they fuck!"

"You can see cats, dogs . . . But butterflies, you don't see them."

"They do it at night."

Max shook his head. "At night they are in the peaceful state of sleepfulness shared by all species."

"Maybe they don't fuck," Raphaël said.

"Everybody . . ."

"Not flowers, Max!"

"Not everybody," I said.

There was a silence, a few seconds.

"And fish, how do they do it then, fish?" Morgane said, dipping her hand again into the bag of pearls.

It was Raphaël who answered. "There are species where it's the male who lets go on to the eggs, once they've been laid."

"Have you studied nature?"

"A bit."

"When was that?"

"Before, when I was in love with Demi Moore, it must go back to . . . I subscribed to magazines."

"What's that got to do with it?"

"Nothing, but in those days I used to read a lot."

Max was listening to them. He was smiling. Fucking, he knew what that was. A bloke from the village took him every Thursday to see the girls in Cherbourg.

I had known, too.

The fault-line remained, a wrenching absence from my sex to my womb. There were nights when I woke up and had the impression I had been engulfed by this void. I ended up on the floor, outside my sheets, always.

That day, in the long corridor, while they were talking about you, you turned away from them. You looked at me, and you made that gesture with your hands, the way you always did when we parted, your fingers clasped in front of you. We are together, that was what the gesture meant, I'm keeping you, I'm keeping you with me. You found the strength to smile. And afterwards, yes, they took you away.

But before that, you smiled.

The doors closed.

It stank of ether in that corridor.

Max had begun to scrape his teeth over his nails.

"'Course they fuck," he said.

He looked at the three of us, one by one.

"But I wonder just how the female manages the correct positioning with her wings."

"What do you mean?"

He spat out the little piece of fingernail he had been chewing on.

"Lili says, if you touch the powder on the wings of a butterfly, it dies ... And if a butterfly beats its wings here, a thing of grave consequence can happen on the other side of the earth. Something as serious as a hurricane."

"You're getting worked up over nothing, Max! And who gives a fuck about your butterfly-fucking? It's not our species."

"Lili said ..."

"Who gives a fuck what Lili says?"

Max looked down.

Morgane smiled.

"You should go and do a bit of work . . . If you were working, you wouldn't be asking yourself all these questions," Raphaël said.

"I am working . . ."

"Working, you?"

"The sow, the boat . . . And I put the brilliance on the stained-glass windows . . ."

He scratched his head very ferociously. "I am in incessant work . . . always."

"Incessant work, yeah really, and I roam over the moor at night with a butterfly net!"

Max looked up, astonished.

"What d'you catch?"

"Stars . . ."

Raphaël put his beer down on the sink. He went over to the door. As he went by the table, Max grabbed him by the sleeve.

"Maybe we should kill them . . ."

"Kill who?"

"The butterflies, since there's so much sufficiency in the single beat of a wing?"

Raphaël looked around him, puzzled.

"Sufficiency?"

"The sufficiency of the hurricane!"

"Don't exaggerate."

"I'm not! It's true!" Max said, his forehead a network of frown lines.

"From there to killing butterflies . . ."

"Well, what shall we do?"

Raphaël opened the door. He thought for a moment.

"We don't do anything, Max . . . We look at them." And then, after a few seconds: "There's happiness to be found in looking at butterflies." He went over and placed a hand on his friend's shoulder. "We don't want to go around killing happiness, now do we, Max?"

*   *   *

I spent the day on the cliffs at Jobourg. I had my nooks in the rock, places where I could go to earth. I left my traces, handprints carving hollows. And other traces, too, piles of little pebbles. Mounds of earth. Small pyres, like Indian tepees. When I was too bored, I would set fire to them.

In the beginning, several times, I carved your name in the stone.

I had seen some chicks hatch a few days earlier. I saw them again. They had already grown. Their bodies were still covered in down, but they poked their beaks out of the nest and swallowed everything their parents gave them. The crows hovered. They were patient. The slightest error, and they would attack.

I went home at the end of the afternoon. Théo was watching for me. He gave me a little wave. The last time I had seen him, I had asked him to talk to me about Nan, and he had left the room without a word.

He was waiting for me.

He was wearing his work clothes. And a thick blue canvas jacket, closed with a single button. He made me come into the house. There was something almost impatient in his eyes. Had he been afraid I wouldn't come back? He set out two glasses on the table. Some bread, thick slices. He filled the glasses.

"It's hard on the legs, coming back, huh?"

"It is, yes . . ."

He went to fetch a plate where he had prepared some cheese. I was thirsty. My throat dry. I drank some wine. One glass. Too quickly.

A cat miaowed outside, behind the window. It had a skin disease, its fur was falling out in clumps. Théo saw it. He said that some day he would take the rifle and kill it.

The rifle was there, sitting in the corner between the cupboard and the wall. Cartridges in the drawer. Kill it before it could pass its mange on to the others. You just had to find the right day.

"I've already had to do it in the past, you know . . ."

"What would you do if you no longer had your cats?"

He thought about the question, not for long. He shrugged his shoulders.

"No doubt I'd live with the mice."

We looked at each other and began to laugh. It was so good, suddenly, this laughter between us, over nothing. It seemed to me that I was seeing Théo as he must have been long ago, the strength of his face, when he was still young and he loved Nan.

We stopped laughing, but we still had the laughter in our eyes.

On the table, his hand was trembling with an uncontrollable movement. We heard some croaking outside. It was the toad that lived near the garden pond. Théo told me that there used to be someone haunting the pond. For a long time, he would find candles burning on the flat stones, and he did not know who had lit them.

He told me other stories. The little cat was dozing, curled in a ball, on the table.

I heard the ticking of the clock.

We talked about the cormorants. Almost all the eggs had hatched, and the crows waited.

He wanted to know the colour of the chicks and the size of the nests. We talked about it for a long time. He also wanted to know if the snakes had come out.

Cheese rind was piling up on the table.

The wine had warmed me up. And the laughter. I would have liked our words to have enabled us to confide in each other. The little white cat stretched out a paw and placed it on Théo's hand. He didn't move. He was watching her.

The newspaper was on the table. On the front page, a photograph of a polluted beach north of Brest. Birds covered in oil. I pulled the paper over. I read the article.

Théo waited for me to finish.

"I used to see plenty of dead birds, when I was in the lighthouse, at night, because of the lamp . . . On stormy days, it was the wind that drove them against the glass."

He said it in a very quiet voice, as if sharing a secret.

I left my hand on the newspaper.

"At night out there, you can't imagine. It was like hell, sometimes."

He looked at my hand where it lay on the photograph in the newspaper, a dead bird, you knew it must stink.

"I remember the currents, when they turned, it made you think of snakes. The waves, yawning like mouths. When the storm was at its height, they were crashing all around you. The lighthouse would sway. How often did I think we wouldn't get out alive."

He looked up at me. He had small, deep eyes, luminous.

"When the weather was fine, we would hang coloured cloths from the window. That was our way of giving news to the people on land."

His voice trembled, as if bearing witness to the deep ties that bound an old man to his lighthouse.

"Did you stay there for long spells?"

"A week at a time, sometimes two. But I could stay longer, I always volunteered when someone was needed. Someone was often needed, particularly during the winter months."

He smoothed the table top with the palm of his hand.

His hand was in the light. Marked. It too bore witness to La Hague.

"They brought supplies over by boat. Sometimes, with the current, the chaps couldn't come alongside. We had reserves, and ship's biscuits, and barrels of water . . ."

He got up and walked over to the back of the room. There was another table there that served as a desk. He opened one of the drawers, shoved his hands into the mass of documents that had accumulated there, no doubt for years, and brought out a photograph of a mare. He told me she was called La Belle.

"This mare belonged to my grandfather's grandfather . . . He rented her out for the entire construction of the lighthouse. For months she went round in this wheel . . . The movement worked the hoists and carried up the stones."

The horse was photographed next to the lighthouse, by the wheel.

There was a man next to her, and a date, 1834.

Théo took a pencil from the table and sketched the system of hoists. He shoved the drawing over to me.

"The mare stayed out there until the end. When they no longer needed her, they brought her back to her pasture. It was too late . . ."

"Too late?"

"She'd gone mad." He nodded. "She would walk straight ahead, one step, then another, like when she was in the wheel, and she would only stop when she ran into a wall. She'd shake herself off, and then head off in the other direction. At the end, she was on her knees. They had to put her down."

He swept up the breadcrumbs scattered on the table, and made a little heap.

I did not like that story. I said, "Why did you tell me that?"

"Well, may as well . . ."

"Oh, really?"

He smiled.

I stayed for a moment with the image of the mare who had gone mad. Bumping into walls.

"And until what year did you keep the lighthouse?"

"Until 1968."

"And after that?"

"There was work on the farm, Old Mother couldn't do it all herself. Lili didn't give a damn about animals. She was already helping out at the bistro."

1968 . . . The Perack shipwreck had been the year before. Was that the reason he had stopped?

"You were young in 1968 . . ."

He slid the crumbs over to the edge of the table. Some of them fell. A cat came over to sniff them. Not hungry enough, it turned away.

"Were there other keepers after you?"

"For twenty years, yes . . . And then the lighthouse was automated and they took the men away."

I looked at him. I waited. I did not know if I could go further. If I dared.

"Did you stop because of the accident?"

He sat there for a moment staring in front of him. He got up. He went over to the window.

"There's the lighthouse. And then there are all the things around it, which are people's lives. But before anything, there's the lighthouse."

I thought he was going to add something, and that it would have something to do with the Peracks' death.

Was it too early? Was there really something to add?

All he said was, "Some mornings when I wake up and the wind is blowing very hard, it feels as if I'm still out there."

*   *   *

The weather was overcast. For three days it had been like that, space without light, heavy with a silence that made the presence of others unbearable. I was tired. I could not face any more walking. Could not face the moors.

I went to lose myself at Lili's. Not that I really wanted to. More out of habit.

When I went in, the Stork was perched on a chair and she was looking at the photographs pinned to the wall. Lili had given her a glass of grenadine syrup and milk. With her finger, the child tracing the contour of each photograph.

Lili was next to her, explaining.

"That dog was the ugliest dog of all, but the females were all in love with him. He had hundreds of puppies. All the dogs in La Hague are his children."

The waif turned to Lili. Her big astonished eyes.

"Even my dog?"

"All of them, I tell you."

The Stork looked very closely at the physiognomy of the dog with its strange ugliness. "Is he dead?"

"Dead? Why should he be dead? No . . . He's somewhere, he went off, we don't know where."

"Will he come back some day?"

"Some day . . . He might."

Lili looked at the photograph.

"And then again, he might not. Who can tell?"

The Stork nodded. She pointed her finger at another photograph.

"And this lady, here, who's this?"

"It's my mum . . . That was a long time ago."

The child turned round. Old Mother was in her armchair. She observed her for a while, just as she had observed the dog. She did not say anything about Old Mother.

"And that man, is he your dad?"

"Yes. And that's me, there."

Lili straightened up, and pointed to the glass of milk.

"You should drink it while it's still cold."

The waif stayed with her finger on the photograph.

"And who's that?"

"Who's who?"

Lili came back over to her. She leaned closer.

"A little boy who came from time to time to talk to the animals in the stable."

"Was he nice?"

"Yes . . ."

"Did he play with you?"

"No."

"Why not?"

Lili hesitated. "I was bigger than he was."

"And his mum, where was she?"

"I don't know. He didn't have a mum."

The Stork frowned. Her face suddenly grave.

114

"What was his name, that little boy?"

"I don't remember."

"He didn't have a name?"

"Yes, of course he did . . . all children have a name."

Lili moved away from the photograph. "Michel . . . His name was Michel."

She shrugged her shoulders.

"I hadn't even noticed that photograph was still there . . ."

She went back behind the bar, put a few things away, and then disappeared for a moment in the kitchen. I heard the sound of dishes.

Michel . . . I had heard that name recently. I did not need to think for long. It was the name Nan had uttered so urgently the day of the storm, when she went and stared Lambert in the face and she had thought she recognized him. That name, heard twice. Was it a coincidence? The photograph was too far away from my table for me to see the child's face.

The Stork got down off her chair, and she took a sweet wrapped in shiny paper from her pocket. She put it on the table, next to the glass of milk.

She came over to me.

"I want to do my writing . . ." she murmured, in her very particular voice, a voice heavy with restraint.

She handed me a pencil, and I drew her a model. I wrote, *Lili's dog has become a* goublin.

She copied it out. Underneath the second line. The pencil lead snapped.

"Don't press so hard . . ."

She started again.

On the third line, she made a mistake, she wrote, *Lili's* goublin *has become a dog*. She burst out laughing. I laughed with her. Lili was still in the kitchen. Old Mother turned her head.

The child and I hid our laughter behind our hands.

That is how Max found us, laughing.

"There's a wedding in the village," he said, sticking his elbows on the bar.

"So?" Lili said.

"I'm not going. It's the priest . . . Even for the arrangement of flowers, he doesn't want me there, only to sweep up after the great procession of the wedding couple, he lets me do that, and I have to go back after, when they're all gone!"

He made an odd face. "Weddings are not as sad as the holes we dig for graves, but it makes you cry just as much."

He was turning his hands, one inside the other, and looking at the three of us, Lili, the Stork and me. He looked at Old Mother, too, and then over by the pinball machine, where Morgane liked to hang out.

"I like it when the priest asks the question and then they say yes, the girl first and then it's the boy . . ."

His eyes were shining. He stood up straight, went over to Lili, and grabbed her hand.

"I'm going to marry Morgane," he said.

Lili did not bat an eyelid.

Old Mother opened her mouth a bit. Even the Stork showed her interest, turning away from her notebook to hear the rest.

"You can't marry people just like that," Lili said at last, hanging her tea towel on its nail.

She stepped closer to Max.

"First of all, they have to agree, you understand that, cousin? And you don't get angry with them if they say no."

Max folded his fingers one inside the other, almost twisting them.

"If they say no, you wait," he murmured.

"You don't wait," Lili said.

Max insisted. "You wait and you go on loving them!" He was shaking his head.

On the television screen, images flickered by. Images without sound.

Lili sighed. "No, you change your love. And you find someone who loves you back, it makes things easier."

Max looked all around, as if he were trying to read in the walls an explanation of what Lili had just said to him.

"Here, there is only Morgane to love!"

Lili did not say anything more. She returned to her work, and Max stared at her back.

He was wincing. With his teeth he bit at his hangnails, pulled at them gently.

He did that for quite a time, and then he turned away and he saw the little Stork. She had gone back to her table, with her glass of milk. He walked over, his face no longer so sad, he leaned his head to one side and held out his hand.

"Will you give it to me?" he asked, pointing to the sweet on the table.

The child looked at him, and nodded.

Max took the sweet.

Before leaving, I went over to look at the photograph. Lili in her simple dress, her hair in bunches, Théo and Old Mother. A dog on the end of a rope. The little boy she had talked about was standing slightly to the back, as if he were merely passing by, surprised by the camera lens, his hand raised as he went to stroke the dog.

"How old were you?" I asked.

Lili turned her head.

"Seventeen . . ."

"And the little boy, is that your brother?"

"I don't have a brother."

She held my gaze for a few seconds, unembarrassed.

"He's a kid from the Refuge," she blurted out, finally.

I had read something about the Refuge in a magazine I had found at Raphaël's.

I leaned against the bar. "Can you tell me about it?"

"What is there to tell? It's a place where they took in orphans, and they stayed there while they waited for someone to adopt them. It's been closed for a long time."

"Where did they come from, the kids?"

"Where do you want them to come from? From Cherbourg."

"And where was it, the Refuge?"

"At La Roche."

I thought for a moment. There were not so many buildings in La Roche that could take in children.

"You mean that big building next door to Nan's place?"

"That's exactly what I mean."

"Who used to look after them?"

"Who do you think?"

She gave me no more explanations, but I understood that she was referring to Nan.

"Those are just useless old photographs," she said, turning towards the wall. "Some day or other, I shall have to change them."

I had often gone past the Refuge on my way to the cliffs, but I had not known that it was an orphanage. I had not paid it any attention, and Théo had never said anything about it.

I stopped at the fence.

It was a long, low building on two storeys, with thick walls of grey stone. In the middle of the courtyard there was a tree. The place was maintained, and the roof seemed to be in good condition, but all the shutters were closed. Nan's house was at the end of the building, its walls the same grey colour, the same shutters, only the roof was lower.

Little blue flowers were growing on the low surrounding wall, roots that had taken hold in a tiny patch of earth. A little bit of moss. The emerald green of a few ferns. I wanted to go through the gate. To go and see Nan. To have her tell me about life at the Refuge when the children were there.

I do not know if she was there. The door to her house was closed, but I know she was in the habit of hiding, when she did not want anyone to see her. I scratched the wall with my fingers. I dug up a little bit of earth. My fingernails were black. The skin on my lips, with the wind, was like parchment.

I waited some more. Nan did not appear, and I went back to La Griffue.

*   *   *

Raphaël had been shut up in his studio for two days already. From my room, I could hear him walking. I saw the light through the cracks in the floorboards.

Morgane said he had begun his series of drawings. That was why he was shut in. She was bored without him.

She came up and knocked on my door.

She said, "When I speak to him he doesn't answer."

She paused, then said, "You want to go out and walk for a while?"

I didn't want to walk. Even a little.

"I just spent the day outside."

She collapsed on the bed.

"What did you do?"

I told her about the Refuge. I asked her if she knew anything about the place.

She did not.

Her hands behind her head, wedged against the pillow.

"You go all soft over orphans, do you?"

"I don't go soft, but at Lili's place, there's a photograph, of one of the children, he used to go and see the animals."

She shrugged. She did not care.

"That's *Oliver Twist* stuff you're on about. When was it, the boy in the photograph?"

"A long time ago, at least twenty years . . ."

"I wasn't here . . . Why are you interested in all that?"

119

I almost told her that Lili seemed upset, remembering him, and I would have liked to have known why. She pulled her hair back.

"Well, I feel like making love! Making love and getting paid. I've found an agency in Cherbourg."

I looked at her.

"You want to be a whore?"

She shook her head.

"No . . . on the telephone. There's no contact. To do it you have to have an extra phone line and Raphaël doesn't want to."

She looked straight at me. "Don't you want to?"

"Get a phone line so you can do that?"

I thought she was joking.

She insisted. "It's no more difficult than counting birds in the wind!"

She rolled on to her side. And then on to her belly, her head between her hands.

"You get the line installed, we don't say anything to Raphaël, and I'll give you a percentage."

A madam! That's the word that sprang to mind.

"We could work as a pair. It's all just pretend love-making, after all!"

Even pretend love-making, I was not very sure I was up to it.

"Well, is it yes?"

"No."

She groaned. She got up. She went over to the door, then stopped, her hand on the door handle.

"What a spoilsport! I'll give the number of the call box and do it from there. Everyone will see me. I'll make gestures, and you'll all be ashamed."

*　　*　　*

I had work to do, my drawings to finish, an entire file to fill with conclusions about the decline of migrating birds in the sector of La Hague.

I spent my day working on it.

I thought about getting out. I could have gone to Saint-Malo, it was not so far, Saint-Malo, and they said it was very beautiful, the ramparts.

I went back up towards the houses. I looked at the families sitting round under their lampshades. On dinner tables, plates with little flowers, orange borders, overflowing with food. Televisions lit. Shadows. As I walked past the stable, I heard the sound of chains. I went through the village.

The last street-lamp. After that, it was dark. That is where I ran into Lambert, in that borderline between shadow and light. His face hardly visible. From a distance, you would have said a wolf cut off from his pack. A beast alone.

We looked at each other. I wondered what he was doing there.

"It's a lovely night."

It was too dark a night.

I could not see his face.

We had met there as if we had planned it. We might have said, just as night falls, just past the last street-lamp. A vague area to wait. An old pylon by the side of the road.

We took a few steps along the road and then he went on and I could not. Because of the night. That darkness, like a pit. He disappeared into the trees, as if the road had swallowed him.

I heard his voice. "Ten steps further and you'll see the light . . ."

What light was he talking about? I took a step. I held out my hand.

"It's just darkness," he said.

I held my hand out further. Suddenly, I felt his fingers, his hand grasping mine, pulling me forward. The cold surface of his jacket greeted me like a slap. It did not last, an instant, a few seconds, I swallowed the smell of it.

We stepped apart cautiously. Without looking at each other. The wind was blowing round us, causing the grass to sway. The air was full of pepper. It was in the earth, little white flowers that opened at night and released this heady perfume.

The scent mingled with the leather.

"Your teeth are chattering."

I clenched my jaws. He turned away. The stars were pinned above us, billions of little lights.

"Normandy is a beautiful place . . ." he said.

"This is La Hague."

"La Hague isn't part of Normandy?"

"La Hague is La Hague."

He walked on a few steps.

"Your teeth – is it because you're cold?"

He untied the scarf around his neck and came back over to me.

"Do you think there's still somewhere open where we could get a coffee?"

"Lili's place."

"And other than Lili's?"

"At this time, it's Lili's or nothing."

He tied the scarf round my neck.

I asked him if he had been in love with Lili when he was an adolescent. I think he smiled.

He did not answer.

A night bird flew by, beating its wings. I heard the rustling of its feathers. When nests are no longer occupied, they can be taken . . . I had more than thirty of them. Thirty in six months. I put them in boxes. Sometimes I took them out and looked at them.

The sea was too far. Too dark. We were too alone, as well. We came back towards the houses. At a window, a curtain was drawn, then fell back too quickly for me to see a face. The shadow stayed behind the curtain. Everything that went on in the street was seen. Anything that might make a story. Gossip. No-one escaped it.

The Audi was parked a bit higher up. He opened the door. We looked at each other.

"I've heard that in Port-Racine, there are people who bathe all year round."

He climbed into the car. I heard the dull sound of the car door as he pulled it to. It was a soft sound, muffled. I thought about the person who had invented that sound.

Lambert switched on the ignition. He waited, his hands on the steering wheel.

He drove with one hand, the other on the armrest of the door. I did not know where he was going. I did not ask him.

He was driving. I was with him.

It was a strange night.

"Have you sold your house?"

"Not yet."

He drove on for another kilometre and we went through the village of Saint-Germain. At one point, he turned to me.

"My mother used to say that I was a child of love. In French, *l'amour* and *la mort* sound the same if you don't articulate properly."

He looked at the road again. "It's hard to hear you, when you speak." He switched off the headlamps, then switched them on again. He did that several times. When the lamps were off, he drove into the darkness. He seemed to like it.

"Everything seems disjointed tonight," I murmured.

He smiled.

He had the slow gestures of someone who has all the time in the world. He did not seem to be in a hurry to sell his house or to leave. No rush. He had come here on a day of storm, and he had said, I'll stay a day or two, and he was still here. Passing through.

There are birds that behave that way.

He slowed down.

He pointed.

"Look!"

The cove at Saint-Martin sparkled in the very dark night, a particular light, coming from the water. In this night emptied of people, the sea suddenly seemed to belong to us. Lambert let the

123

car roll slowly down the winding road.

He parked on the flat.

He did not get out at once. He looked through the windscreen at the beach, the sea. The beach, like a breakwater. And then he opened the door.

"Are you coming?"

I nodded.

We were outside again. For a moment, next to each other. His arms folded across his chest.

He smiled faintly.

"You should stop your teeth chattering, you're going to damage them."

He threw himself into the water like an angry beast. I could not see him at all, but I heard him, his breathing, struggling against the cold, and the powerful thrashing of his arms breaking through the water. Was he naked? He had turned round and said, Aren't you coming?

No-one ever bathed here. Except in the summertime, a few regulars.

His man's body melted into the night. Taken by the sea.

His living man's body.

He disappeared. I waited for him to come back, my knees in my hands. Then pebbles beneath my fingers.

I looked at the stars.

He swam some more. The water was cold here, much colder than elsewhere.

Had he been to visit Théo? He had told me that he wanted to speak to him, but had he done it? Why was he waiting?

He came over to me, his shirt rolled up in his hands. The charcoal grey jumper against his skin.

"You swam a long way out . . ."

I could feel his gaze in the night.

In the car, he put the heating on full blast. His hair was wet,

"I was afraid you wouldn't come back."

He spread his fingers. He closed them again. He made this gesture several times.

"I had to swim . . ."

He lit the headlamps and looked at the sea. This patch of night, illuminated. He let his head roll to the side.

And then he looked at me, as if to keep from seeing the sea.

He had a room at the Irishwoman's in La Rogue. When we got there, a little lantern was lit by the entrance.

The door was open. I followed him down a narrow hallway papered in red velvet. At the very end, there was a big room cluttered with armchairs. Heavy curtains hung at the windows.

A woman was stretched out on the sofa among big velvet cushions. She was watching television, a popular series filmed in a big American hospital. There was a glass on the table. A handbag in white imitation leather. The room stank of perfume.

"No women here," she said when I came through the door.

She did not turn round.

Lambert took off his jacket.

"She's not coming up," he said, tossing the jacket on to the cushions.

He pointed to the sofa.

The woman's name was Betty. They exchanged a few words in a very rapid English.

"May we taste your whisky?"

She held a limp hand out towards Lambert's leg and let it slide along his thigh. A sensual caress.

"You are at home here, darling." She had the husky voice of a heavy smoker.

A smile crossed Lambert's lips. He went to fetch a bottle and two glasses. He filled the glasses.

A lamp was hanging above the table, a large globe of orange paper with Chinese characters. The characters had been traced in black.

He handed me the glass.

"You're cold . . ."

Because I had shivered.

Glenfarclas. You used to drink it too, sometimes. I liked the smell of it in your mouth.

I settled back into the armchair and closed my eyes. I drank slowly, looking at the light shining through the thin paper. A strange round ball that looked like a sun.

We drank.

He talked to me about his mother.

I did not tell him about you. He took a photograph from his wallet and showed it to me. His mother was indeed very beautiful. His father, small eyeglasses, a moustache, fairly tall.

"They were very much in love . . ."

We drank some more.

Betty went off to bed.

He put the photograph back in his wallet.

"I have a few memories, details . . . the smack she gave me one day, when I answered her back."

He smiled.

"But I cannot remember the colour of her hair, though I know I loved to touch it. She let me brush it. Very soft hair."

He looked at his hands.

"I've even forgotten their voices. Before, when I looked at the photographs, I could remember. I saw them the way they were, when they were alive. Now, I can no longer see them, it's as if they had died for a second time."

He sat there for a moment, his gaze lost in his glass.

"My brother is still in the water."

He pressed his glass against his mouth.

"When I think about him . . . He would be forty years old now."

He took a gulp of whisky.

"In the years that followed, I imagined everything, that he had

126

clung to a rock, that a boat had picked him up. He was too small to say his name. I thought I would get a letter some day, and that I'd find him again. I was sure of it, but at night, in my dreams, I saw him in the water, drowning."

He looked up at me.

"The lifeboats found my father, the empty sailing boat, they kept looking and then went back. For a long time I was angry that they had not searched for longer."

"It was night time . . ."

He shook his head several times.

"When they drowned, I was asleep."

Did he feel guilty that he had not gone with them? That he had not died with them? Could he feel that?

"Have you been to see Théo?"

"Not yet . . . But I will."

He filled his glass and emptied it without blinking.

It was a little after midnight when he drove me back. He left me by the gate.

Morgane was waiting for me at the door.

"Did you sleep with him?"

Not even a good evening. That was all she said. She followed me down the corridor, came right up against me to sniff my skin.

"Go on, tell me!"

I shook my head.

"No."

"I don't believe you! You stink of alcohol!"

I placed my hand on the banister. "I have to get some sleep . . ."

"Where were you? At his place?"

"No."

"At the Irishwoman's?"

She kept walking round me. I was sleepy. She would not let me go.

"He brought you back, he dropped you off there, outside the door . . . And you didn't sleep with him?"

"No."

"What did he say to you?"

"Nothing."

"It can't be! He must have said something before he left you?"

"He said goodnight."

*   *   *

I woke up with a headache. I drank some hot milk, my eyelashes in the steam.

The weather was fine.

Lambert and I had agreed to meet the next day at ten o'clock, to go to the caves. A quick arrangement, just as he was dropping me off at the gate. It must have been close to ten.

I went over to the window. He was sitting on the terrace at the *auberge*, the same table as on the first day. I did not feel like going out. Space changes, when there are two of you. Silence is no longer silence, even if the other person says nothing.

I took a shower. I put on a jumper.

When I came to his table, he pointed to the quay.

"From this table, you can see exactly where my father used to anchor his boat."

The sun was shining. It was not warm, but we had a few hours ahead with what looked like calm weather. To go to the caves you had to walk a long way.

He smiled at me, as if he could read my thoughts.

"Don't worry, I can be quiet to the point of being mute."

We left by the path along the sea, side by side, we hardly said a thing all the way to the first houses at La Roche. Then we walked one behind the other, along the footpath. Sometimes he walked in front. Other times, I did. The landscape was beautiful. The sea luminous.

From time to time he stopped and looked. He didn't speak. When he stopped, I stopped too. We kept going and I got used to walking with him. At the cove at Établette, we looked at each other.

He said, "Everything O.K.?"

I hesitated and said, "Yes, everything's O.K."

The caves were just below us.

He recalled having taken this walk often with his parents, but he had never gone down to the caves. It was too dangerous. The path was too rough. We left the footpath and headed down a little track the goats had made that wove in and out among the bramble bushes. It was a narrow track, very slippery, and at the very bottom it came out at the sea. In places we had to cling to the branches and slide on our feet.

We jumped down to the beach. A dead gull was floating on the water, its white wings bobbing on the waves. Black seaweed, rising on the waves, too. It was a moving world, not exactly the world of water any more, but not that of land either. Somewhere in between.

The caves were there, the Grande and the Petite Église, and the Lion. The earliest legends of La Hague were born in these caves. Legends mingling animals and men.

The entrance was a bit further along.

We walked along the cliff.

A deep fissure disappeared into the side of the cliff. It was a narrow breach that opened out again beneath the church at Jobourg.

We went into the cave and walked for several metres. We came to a place where we had to hunch over to keep going.

Beneath my fingers I could feel the dampness of the walls. Animal skulls were embedded in the rock, I ran my hand over them. Birds' skeletons. The wind had smoothed them. I scratched at one until a fragment of bone came away. The taste was salty in my mouth. The bone brittle beneath my teeth.

We went deeper into the wall then came back to the entrance.

I said, "Let's make a fire."

There was some old wood. Dry branches. He took out his matches. I tore a few pages from my notebook. The wood caught. We sat round the fire, our arms curled round our knees, and we looked at the flames. Our shadows danced against the wall of the cave.

"Do you feel better now?"

He was looking at me.

I did not understand.

"My presence – can you stand it?"

"Yes . . ."

He smiled.

He lit a cigarette. He smoked it down to the filter, without saying anything.

I watched him, his hands stretched towards the fire. I thought of the hermit M. Anselme had told me about. A man who had lived for several years in this cave. He drank rainwater, and someone brought him bread. To sleep, he had a mat made of gorse branches. A few animal skins to cover him. Years without seeing a soul. Without speaking. Looking out on the sea. And one day he got up and went out. Peasants who were working in the fields saw a man go by, his beard and hair so long they touched the ground. By the time they had straightened up, the man had vanished.

Lambert crushed his cigarette on a stone. I went on poking the fire. A few cinders escaped, flew up and eventually vanished, swallowed by the darkness.

I told him the story about the hermit. When I had finished, he looked doubtful.

"Your taciturn bloke must have said a few words to the man who brought him his bread, no?"

"No . . . The bread was put in a bucket and the bucket was tied to a rope. They didn't see each other."

He nodded.

"And how long did it last?"

"Several years. Almost ten, I think."

I dug in the ground with the tip of my stick. I took away a clump of brown earth. I held it in my fingers. It smelled good.

"What I'd like to know is, why he ever left his cave."

I looked up at Lambert. He was watching me.

"He had been here for years, and one day, he got up and he left! Don't you find that astonishing?"

"I'd rather know why he went *into* the cave . . ."

"There are always lots of reasons to lock yourself away. Going back out again is much more difficult."

He picked up some tiny pebbles that were there in the cave, on the ground. He kept them in his hands. He was shifting them from one hand to the other.

"I talked to you about my brother the other evening . . . For a long time, I didn't want to believe in his death. It felt as if I was betraying him."

The branches continued to burn before us.

"The notary said that the house ought to sell within the next three months. You wouldn't know anyone who could help me clean up the garden?"

"Max could do that."

"Max, yes . . ." He rubbed his lips with his thumb.

"Don't do that . . ."

He looked at me. I did not explain.

He set the little pebbles down in a pile next to the fire.

Max was making the most of the dull weather to go and fish on the rocks. It was a place where you could catch bass. He was wearing his yellow oilskin. His bucket was blue. We could see him from far away.

When we went past on the path, he called out to us and showed us his bucket. There were no bass, only a few mackerel, some sea bream, and a fine herring. He joined us for the walk back. As a rule, anyone who wanted to buy some fish would be there, waiting by the stern of the boats. There was no-one.

Lambert asked Max if he would agree to help him clean his garden. Max did not answer.

He sat down at the edge of the quay, and he cleaned his fish, emptying them into the waters of the harbour. The scales, anything he could scrape out of the guts. Children were watching him.

Seagulls circled above the bucket.

Max cut off the herring's head. The head floated for a moment between two hulls, its round eye staring at the sky.

It is said that the herring has a soul, and that whoever meets that soul can question it, the way one questions a wise man.

And the soul replies. It is also said that a sea bream will change colour seven times before dying.

I looked at Lambert's face against the sunlight. The deep shadows in the hollow of his cheeks.

Max's dream was to go to sea and bring back a porbeagle. To do that he had to finish fixing up his boat. He said that once the boat was repaired, he would know the great bedazzlement of the sea.

"A porbeagle can weigh over a hundred kilos!" he said, scraping the scales with his knife.

"And what would you do with a hundred kilos of porbeagle?" I said.

"I'd drive a hard bargain at the fish market in Cherbourg and with the money I'd buy petrol and I'd come back."

"So you're going to be rich?"

He laughed. He turned towards the house. Ever since we had talked about butterflies, he had been capturing them. He shut them away in a cage. He wanted to wait until the cage was full to release the butterflies all round Morgane's face.

After a few days in the cage, the butterflies died.

A seagull dived in front of us, and came back up with a herring head in its beak. Lambert followed it with his gaze.

He turned round to look at Théo's house on the side of the hill.

"Will you come with me afterwards?"

I followed his gaze.

"No . . ."

He nodded.

Max smiled. "For the garden cleaning, it's agreed, I come!"

That is what he said, I come.

Lambert said he had things to do and he left. He took his car and drove up the hill. I do not know if he was going to Théo's place.

On the shore, a seagull cried.

"I'll buy your little fish from you," I said. "For Théo's cats."

Max slid the still squirming small fry into a plastic bag. He closed the bag. I took some money from my pocket, but he did not want to accept it.

"It's agreed with him, in trust," he said.

"What do you mean by that?"

He rubbed his hands on his trousers and shining scales clung to the cloth.

"It's agreed," he repeated, pointing to Théo's house.

He took his bucket and went to see if the *patron* of the *auberge* wanted his fish.

*   *   *

I went through the door.

"I've brought you some fish . . ."

Théo was at the end of the corridor, emptying out the basins he used to collect the water leaking from the roof. There were several of them. He had to empty them often.

"The tiles need changing . . ." he tried to explain, pointing to the roof.

He was calm. His eyes, his hands. I immediately understood that Lambert had not come. I had been afraid I might find him there. What other option did he have? The past haunted him. He had an intuition about the truth, and he needed to hear it.

Théo turned to me.

133

"What's the matter? Is something wrong?"

"No, everything's fine . . ."

When the yellow cat saw me, it came out of the kitchen, went along the wall, and came up to rub against me.

"This one likes you a lot . . . You see, as soon as it hears you, it comes out."

The cat could smell the fish inside the bag. Théo looked at the fish.

"You can just put all that in the sink . . ."

There were other basins higher up, on the steps. He told me he had to go and get them, to empty them, too.

I went into the kitchen. The little white cat was lying on the table. This was her place, her protected spot. The other cats knew it. It wasn't hatred, among them. It was something else. Mistrust. Jealousy, too.

I left the bag in the sink.

There was an envelope on the table. Théo's name and address written in pen. Large, sloping handwriting. The ink was blue. The postmark was Grenoble.

I turned the envelope over. There was no name on the back.

There were other envelopes on the desk, all covered with the same handwriting. These envelopes were gathered together in a cardboard box. The box was open. There were dozens of them, perhaps a hundred.

I lifted the flap of one of the envelopes. Without taking the letter out, I read the beginning, the opening words. *Dear Théo, It snowed this morning. I was able to go out and I went* . . . The rest was hidden. I slipped my finger inside. I read, *Thank you for your long letter. I am glad to hear that you are better, and thank you for your packages. With the brothers, we shared* . . .

I lifted the flap on other envelopes. Behind one of them, there was a name, Michel Lepage, followed by an address:

Monastery of La Grande Chartreuse, Saint-Pierre.

I put the letter back in its place.

Beyond the window, it had begun to rain.

Théo came back.

"I put the fish in the sink," I said, stepping away from the desk.

He saw I was near the letters. He probably realized I had touched them.

I showed him the bag.

"Max caught them. For payment, he said —"

"I know what he said."

He gauged the quantity of fish in the bag and pulled a note from his pocket. He put it down next to the bag. He went round the table and put the lid back on the box containing the letters.

In the silence, I could hear the rain falling. I thought I should go. I took the note, and went to the door.

Théo had pulled his cap down to his eyes. He added some wood to the stove. I could see him, his back, his narrow shoulders in his dressing gown.

The letter was still on the table. Raindrops were running down the wallpaper, behind the bed. Floorcloths were spread along the base of the wall. A drop fell. The cats looked at each other. Théo opened an umbrella and placed it on the bed.

"Rain from the south," he said. "Not the coldest, but it gets in under the tiles."

Now the drops were falling on the umbrella, sliding on to the floor then along to disappear in the barrage of floorcloths.

Théo moved the little clock. Every hour, the needles got stuck, and it lost two minutes.

"You hear that? Two minutes an hour, that's what it loses. Some little defect in the system, I should have got it fixed."

He shook his head.

"It's turned into something like an appointment between me and the clock, just that moment when the two minutes get lost."

He looked up, and stared hard at me for a long time.

"Some day I will tell you about those letters."

He was about to add something when the door opened. It banged. The cats looked up. It was Nan, wearing her long black dress, her hair dripping. The water seemed dirty and dark. Over her dress she was wearing a large hand-knitted woollen shawl.

She made as if to come in, then she saw me and stayed on the threshold, one hand clutching her throat. Her other hand was curled around something she held tight against her.

Strange priestess, fish-woman: she seemed to have come out of the water or some other subterranean world, and on her face she wore the terrifying mask of a Gorgon.

"I was just leaving . . ." I said.

She pressed back against the wall. As I went by, I could smell her strong odour of sweat and peat.

I did not see what she was hiding in her hand.

*   *   *

Lambert had talked to me for a long time about the disappeared, the bodiless dead who could not be buried. We were together in the cave. The fire was burning. He said, they are dead without proof.

The dead the sea has kept, with whom there is no farewell.

The darkness around us had added meaning to his words. Words that I had heard, remembered, and that came back to me.

He had said, My brother's disappearance has made me a person without balance. He had tried to smile. I thought about you. I had seen you, dead, but dead long before your heart gave way. The work of the shadow, day after day. The cry of a madwoman, afterwards, but I had been able to cry for you, to become a dead woman myself.

How could I have cried for you, if you had disappeared?

It was already drizzling when I arrived at the farm. The sow was in the yard, her trotters in the mud. The moment she saw me, she came over. I put my face right up against her damp gaze. Her nice flat head between my hands.

"You're all dirty, you pretty thing . . ."

Her eyes were soft, swollen with tears, but the tears did not flow.

The little Stork was inside the house. She saw me and tapped on the windowpane. I looked at her. The Stork was the biggest of the children, but I do not think she was also the eldest. I had often seen their father hitting them, smacks he gave them with the flat of his hand. The two eldest resisted. The little ones went flying. They would grow up. They would leave.

The father had given them their nicknames, Eldest, Snotty-nosed, the littlest one was Pisser. There was also the Willow. He had strange eyes. He didn't go to school. The cows, too, had names, Marguerite, Rose . . . When the father looked at their calves, he saw meat. The price they would fetch per kilo on the butcher's slab. I do not know what he saw when he looked at his kids.

In the midst of all that, the mother was a timid shadow; sometimes I caught a glimpse of her in the yard.

I went on my way.

It was the slack hour at Lili's. The light above the bar was lit. I went up to the door. About to put my hand on the latch. Through the window, the drawn curtain, I saw Lili. She was sitting at one of the tables. She was talking to Lambert. I saw their profiles. There were glasses between them.

*   *   *

Raphaël was on his knees, his cheek against the plaster womb. He said he could think for hours about a gesture that would take a few seconds.

"I'll stop for now," he said, wedging a cigarette between his lips.

He dipped his hands into a bowl full of grey water. Drops fell on the floor. With his hands still wet, he smoothed the flat of the hips, the fragile hollow of the groin that he worked with his thumb, and then he stood up. He took a few steps to the side and then back, revealing the still imprecise body of a sculpture, a hollowed-out womb expressing the violence of childbirth. Her mouth was closed. Mute. Her breasts stretched. There was almost no face. Her ravaged flesh expressed what mattered. The wire framework he had used as an armature was still visible here and there on the womb.

He stood further back.

"What do you think?"

He took my hand and led me over to the womb.

"You feel that? She's imploring."

All around, the studio looked like a vast field of ruins, Raphaël the sole survivor.

He let go of my hand and lit another cigarette from the burning butt of the first one.

"Ten years I've been trying to sculpt desire! Ten years I've been getting it wrong, and today, look, I've managed."

I walked around the sculpture. Long thin legs met under a mass of moist flesh, seeming to radiate all the energy.

All the rest of the body – head, torso, limbs, even her breasts – were only there to exacerbate still further the force of desire.

"Morgane told me you were making drawings . . ."

He raised his hand as if he were brushing away an annoying insect.

"Later! Later!"

He sat on the steps, his body broken with fatigue. His neck bent.

I filled two cups with the hot coffee he had made a short while earlier. I put one by his hand. He had dry plaster on his face. His hair dishevelled. His mouth twisted. He looked at the cup.

A sudden beauty had come over him, to be that close to madness.

The cup was an additional weight, something impossible to lift. I saw his hand, his fingers round it, hardly closed. The cup slipped and the coffee spilled.

The dark stain, immediately swallowed by the dust.

"It doesn't matter," he said.

I picked up the cup.

The studio had been invaded by an oppressive, mute crowd, hounded by the blinding light of the halogen lamps. The last sculpture reigned over the others, their sister, testifying to the same obsession, to make justice from injustice, to make passion from poverty.

And to make desire from absence.

That was the furrow Raphaël was ploughing.

"You look like your sculptures."

He lifted his head.

In his gaze there was a mixture of tenderness and pain, a light that is peculiar to those who live their lives with infinitely greater intensity than others. It hurt to look at him.

I turned my head away.

Raphaël closed his eyes.

"I'm not to blame . . ."

I wondered if he meant his sculptures, or what his face had become.

Raphaël slept for an hour, his back against the wall. The hour after that, he made us *beignets*.

An old table was set up in the garden, in the sun. I brought down some wine.

The *beignets* were good, gorged with jam. You bit into them and they exploded in your mouth. Max came and joined us. He was happy. He had got hold of an old fishing net at the fish market in Cherbourg. The net was spread out across the middle of the garden. He had to mend a few holes. When that was done, he could hang the net from the stern of his boat. In the meantime, he spent hours caulking the planks on the hull with a sort of thick, tar-smelling paste he spread with a spatula.

Max explained that when everything was done, he would still have to fill the hold with water to make sure the boat was watertight.

After that, he fell silent, and stared at the traces of sugar on Morgane's lips.

The sun warmed our backs. There were a few strollers on the quay. I wondered whether it was Sunday.

We talked about Lambert. Morgane said she had seen him at Lili's, at the beginning of the afternoon, when she was on her way to Beaumont. She went in just long enough to buy a loaf of bread. He was there.

"Did he know Lili, before?"

"Why do you ask?"

She held her *beignet* between two fingers. A little jam dribbled down the side.

"They must have known each other, since he spent his holidays here."

After that, the jam ran down her fingers.

Raphaël looked at us, rocking on his chair.

"The way you behave . . . Morgane speaks to you, you hardly answer. Are you always like that?" he said.

"It's atavistic," I said.

"Ata what?"

"Atavistic. Hereditary. In my family we're all taciturn."

Morgane did not like it when we argued. She said as much, "Stop arguing!" and gave her brother a resounding kiss on the cheek.

She put her arms around his neck and cuddled against him for a moment.

"The day you're fed up being a sculptor you can become a *pâtissier*."

She raised her head.

"Look, we've got a visitor!"

It was the little Stork, she was at the gate. Raphaël watched as she came over. He pulled a notebook from his pocket. He drew the waif, her figure, in a few quick strokes.

On the wall, above him, rosebuds that had been closed for a long time had opened in the sun. There were a dozen or so already, clinging firmly to the branch, braving the wind.

The child came over to us.

When she saw the drawing, she looked at Raphaël as if he were a god.

"Some day I will sculpt you," he said, putting the notebook away in his pocket.

The Stork dipped her hand into the basket, took a *beignet*, and went to share it with her dog.

"Do you know someone called Michel?" I said.

Morgane and Raphaël looked at each other.

"Michel what?"

"Lepage."

Raphaël shook his head. He turned to his sister.

"Does that ring a bell with you?"

"No. Who is it?"

"That's why, I have no idea."

I hesitated. I was not sure I felt like talking to them about all that, Théo, the letters.

I just described the strange encounter that had taken place between Nan and Lambert on the morning of the storm. I also told them about the photograph pinned to the wall at Lili's place.

"You could see Lili with her parents, and just behind them, a little boy that Lili called Michel."

Raphaël took a long swallow of beer. He looked at me, with a mocking smile on his lips.

"You must really be bloody bored . . ."

"I'm not bored."

"Well then, what else is it?" he said, rolling his eyes to the sky.

After that, he and Morgane looked at each other, and it made them laugh.

Max went to sit on the ground, by his net, and began to mend the holes in the weave. To stitch them, he used thick nylon thread.

"Tom Thumb."

That is what he said.

The first time I heard it, I did not pay much attention. That is what he did, come out with words one after the other, just like that, several times in a row, not really knowing why he chose one word rather than another. We began to clear away the plates.

Max still had his head bent over his net, his legs spread, and he said the name again, Tom Thumb, with rather wearying regularity.

"Can't you say something else?" I said when I passed him, the plates in my hands.

He looked up at me, his fingers lost in his stitches. He was wearing a dark sailor's jumper, and a kerchief round his neck. He smiled. "Michel, that's Tom Thumb!"

I put down the plates.

"You know someone who's called Michel?"

He said yes, nodding his head, and bent over his net.

"Who is it?" I asked.

He shrugged his shoulders. Not looking at me. He did not know.

"You mean you know him, but you don't know who he is?"

Again he shrugged.

"Do you know if that's who Nan is looking for when she's on the beach?"

Max did not reply. Raphaël was listening to us.

"Why are you interested in all that?" he said, crushing his beer can between his fingers.

Questions, answers, a complicated knit of lies and truths. Things said out of synch, things said only in part, things that never would be said. All the shades of something you could only see staring into the sun.

I had learned that with the cormorants.

When a cormorant swallows a fish, it is always head first. The stomach digests in stages. One day, I found a dead cormorant, I gutted it, and inside its stomach, half of the fish it had just swallowed was still intact whereas everything else was in a pulp.

I tried to explain this to Raphaël.

"When you stop asking yourself questions, you die . . ."

He shrugged his shoulders.

"Too cerebral . . ."

Morgane was laughing, her back to the sun.

Max got up.

"He was of extreme littleness," he said, taking the last *beignet* from the plate.

He looked at it, he looked at Raphael, he put the *beignet* in his pocket and he rubbed his hands.

"That's what I always said, Hello Tom Thumb! Afterwards, he did manage to grow up to be a normal altitude, but I went on saying, Hello Tom Thumb."

He dragged his net into the sun.

"It's a continuation of the name, even when things change, you have to respect it."

"Where did he live, this Tom Thumb?" I asked.

He pointed over towards the houses at La Roche. Raphaël shrugged.

Max sat down at the table.

"We had the same positioning at the school, his elbow here and mine just next to it."

He grabbed me by the sleeve and made me sit down next to him, to show me how they were, two schoolboys side by side.

"We shared the same observance of sayings and of the great knowledge."

He laughed quietly, behind his hand, his fingers spread.

"Tom Thumb had greater capacity," he said, banging his hand against his skull. "He said my capacity was not as vast, but just as deserving."

I looked at him. The memory seemed to make him happy.

"Tom Thumb was right," I said. "Your capacity is very deserving."

He blushed, confused.

I asked him if he knew where he was and whether his parents still lived here, but to all that he replied that he did not know.

"His surname, do you know that? Could it be, Lepage?"

He looked at me.

"Max doesn't know such things."

*

143

Max immersed himself in his fishing net, and I took in the glasses that had remained on the table.

"I used to be a hairdresser, before," Raphaël said, slipping his fingers into my hair.

In six months my hair had grown, rebellious. I did not comb it.

"Were you really a hairdresser?"

"Ask Morgane."

"No need . . ."

He went to get his box. He had everything he needed in it, scissors, razors, an electric shaver. "If you want me to cut it for you, you have either to come with your hair wet, or I'll cut it dry."

"I don't like to have it cut dry."

He spread his hands. I went back up into my bedroom. My face in the mirror. I ran the water. I washed my hair in the sink, killing my back. I stood up, my neck burning. I wrapped a towel around my neck and went back down. Raphaël was waiting for me.

In the yard it stank of tar from the product that Max was using on the hull of his boat. The tin was there, a few metres away, and the brushes.

Raphaël shouted.

"Can't you put your bloody stuff elsewhere!"

He made me sit down on the box.

"Haven't you got something rougher?" he said, when he touched the towel.

I had my back against his belly, his hands on my neck. Contact.

"Relax," he said.

He untangled my hair with a long-toothed comb.

"What did you wash it with?"

"I'm out of shampoo."

"What did you wash it with?" he insisted, pulling my head back to oblige me to answer.

"Soap . . ."

He let me go.

"You didn't rinse it properly," he said.

"It's not easy in the sink."

I let my head go. The cold blade against my skin, I heard the biting sound of the scissors. I closed my eyes. Locks fell.

"Not too short, alright?"

"Not to worry."

He cut the sides.

The Stork came crawling under the table, between my feet, she gathered up my hair.

"I used to have a poodle," said Raphaël, pointing to the Stork's dog that was staring at us with his submissive eyes.

Raphaël went on cutting, not speaking. I thought about what Max had said. Michel and Max must be about the same age, forty years old, perhaps a bit more. Was he the one who was writing to Théo? That large, careful handwriting.

Raphaël ran his fingers through my hair.

"How's that?"

"Don't you have a mirror?"

I ran my hand over my hair. It was no better. No worse. He did not have a hair-dryer, either. He rubbed it with the towel.

"You've cut it rather short, haven't you?"

"It's the fashion, Princess, the fashion."

I ran my hand over it again. "Didn't you miss bits on the side?"

"That's the fashion, too," Raphaël said.

He smiled.

The Stork came over to look.

"What happened to your poodle?" I said, as I got up.

"It was the illegal immigrants in Cherbourg, they ate it."

"Why did they do that?"

"Must be they were hungry."

"To eat a dog, that's disgusting."

Raphaël laughed. So did the Stork. And even Soft Spot began to yap, running around the courtyard with her belly to the ground.

145

I laughed along with them. Afterwards, I sat for a long time outside, on the bench, my head in the sun.

In the evening, in the courtyard, the light of the stars, caught in the waves. Trembling lights. As if drowning.

The mist was coming in from the sea. It had set sailors off course, sunk boats. Ships' captains gone mad with the inability to see.

A cargo ship in the distance, headed for England. The foghorn sounded at regular intervals, like a phantom bell chiming. I could no longer see anything of the houses at La Roche. Nothing of the beach. Even the birds had fallen silent. Only the lights of that cargo ship far offshore, and in the sky, a few night birds flying over La Hague like shadowgraphs. They were migrating birds. For several days now they had been arriving in their dozens, their flight impeded by the fog. Why were they flying like this, so close to the house? The birds did not stop, they continued south, towards the Camargue in all likelihood, and Africa, perhaps. They were headed for my former countries.

A wing brushed my window. The bird shook itself, a moment of intoxication in the cruelty of its own fear. Was it my light that was drawing them? It was only a faintly luminous point, but in this thickness of fog it must have given them the illusion of a beacon.

Hundreds of birds died in lights. Birds like giant insects, crushed. I switched off my light. I looked through the window.

Théo had said, You ought to go and spend a night out there, get someone to drop you off.

Out there, the lighthouse.

I put my face right up to the windowpane. The lighthouse was circled with darkness, defying the waves and the night.

Birds' behaviour changed when there was fog. It changed when there were storms. The behaviour of men changed, too.

Had Théo put out the lamp the night of the shipwreck? A lighthouse pulses with flashes from a lantern as strong as a heart. A heavy, throbbing pulsation.

That lamp, like a multitude of halogen lamps gathered into one single beam, where the sailors relentlessly turn their gaze.

*   *   *

The Stork had crept all the way into the back of the henhouse, into the dark place of nests where the hens lay their eggs. She waved to me. I went through the gate and followed her. There was a smell of feathers. In the half-light my fingers grazed straw, droppings, on the wooden bars of the perches.

The Stork was rummaging in the bottom of the boxes, bringing up eggs that looked white to me.

She laid the eggs in her basket.

I watched her. Stork, such a strange name for a little girl, and no-one could tell me why she was called that. Who had called her that so persistently that everyone had forgotten her real name? And from that day on, deep inside her, it had become impossible for her to call herself anything else.

Lili said that she was like a rag-doll. She also said that smiling was what the waif did best. That, and tracing lines carefully across the pages of her notebook.

We went back out. A sort of brutal passage, from darkness to light.

Lambert was over by the road, leaning on the fence. He called to the Stork.

"I'll buy half a dozen!"

She held out her hands and exchanged the eggs for a few coins.

Lambert turned to me. He pointed to the eggs.

"Shall we make an omelette?"

I was not too keen on omelettes.

He took a few steps. I remembered a song by Mouloudji, I hummed it, softly, *One day, you'll see, we'll meet somewhere, anywhere . . .*

I used to like to listen to Mouloudji, with you.

*

Old Nan was going up the street, on the same pavement, ahead of us. This was not her usual time, but for some days now you could see her everywhere, her forehead low, talking to herself. Old Mother was watching for her from behind the window, her hunched shadow over her walking frame. When Nan reached the terrace, Old Mother came out. They looked at each other, two old women like two hatreds. They did not say anything. Old Mother let out a long hiss, and Nan spat.

Lambert and I looked at each other and kept walking along the wall. We went over to his house. Snails as tiny as pinheads were stuck by the dozen on the stones around the door.

The key was in the lock.

The kitchen was low-ceilinged with dark beams and a farmhouse table down the middle. He put the eggs on the table.

He rummaged in the cupboards.

He eventually brought out a frying pan. A bottle of oil from the cardboard box on a low chest next to the sink. Some shopping he had done in Beaumont.

He told me that the house had been rented for two months the previous summer and also for the holiday at All Saints.

He broke an egg, a firm knock on the edge of the sink.

"In 2000, I even managed to rent the house for the entire year, to a writer from Paris."

Hot embers were still shimmering in the hearth. There was firewood in a crate next to it. I added a few logs, some paper, and the flames took again. A heavy dark beam served as a mantelpiece. Remnants of red paint clung to the wood. There was a date carved, 1823, the year of the twenty-seven shipwrecks. Many of the village roof structures had been made with wood from the ships that had run aground that year.

I went over to the window. Spiders with long thin legs had woven webs in the wooden frame. Bees with heavy bellies were trapped in the webs. They had been dead for a long time, and were dried out.

I looked up. Old Nan was in the street. Her hands clinging to the fence, she was looking at the house. A moment later, she had vanished.

I put two plates down on the table.

"M. Anselme says that this dresser is from a shipwreck."

Lambert nodded.

"I've heard him talk about it. It belonged to a Sir somebody or other . . ."

"Sir John Kepper."

He turned off the fire under the frying pan.

"We ought to have some bread, but we don't. We don't have any wine, either!"

He glanced outdoors, at Lili's terrace.

"Could you go over and ask for two glasses?"

"I could, yes . . ."

"But you won't?"

I shook my head. "No, I won't."

It made him laugh.

He slid the eggs on to the plates. He rummaged in his cardboard box looking for something to replace the bread, and brought out a packet of biscuits. He looked at me, questioningly. They were fig rolls.

We preferred to eat the eggs on their own, never mind about the bread.

He pointed round the room.

Two little red porcelain swans, set on the table. Their backs formed a hollow, full of salt.

"There are things that have disappeared . . . plates from the dresser, and the things that disappeared were replaced by other things. But these two swans were already here in my parents' day."

We ate the eggs, looking at the porcelain figurines.

"Next time, I'll make you some abalone, that will be better."

He told me that he used to live in Paris with his parents. They had a Renault 4L, and when they came here, his father attached the cases to the roof. They always stopped in Jumièges, winter and summer alike, and they would walk for an hour in the ruins and then set off again. In winter, the site was closed, but they walked around anyway.

"I liked coming on holiday here. We'd arrive, open the shutters, and go down to see the sea."

He smiled at the memory of it.

"They were endless holidays, especially the summer ones, we were here for two months, we never thought about the end ... until the day we saw my mother bring the cases out and then it was as if something heavy was falling upon us. We had to put everything away, take the sheets off the beds, and my father would close the shutters. On the way home, we didn't sing, and we didn't go through Jumièges."

He pointed to a box on the floor against the wall.

"Look what I found!"

It was drawings.

"My mother had us do them when it was raining. It rained a lot, so that made a lot of drawings."

He said nothing for a long while, and then, "I remember the way she would lean over the table and draw for us."

I went to pick up the box, and as I came back to the table I saw Nan's face at the window. She was here again.

I set the box on the table, and took out a few drawings. Lambert was right, there were a lot of them.

"I found them just like that, in the box, at the back of the cupboard."

He pointed to the cupboard behind him.

Most of them were children's drawings, but some had been done by an adult.

"Lili's mother said she saw lights here, some nights."

"It's possible ... The road mender was keeping an eye on the place, but he couldn't do everything. A family of dormice nested in the room next door ... Over where you live, you're almost in the sea, right?"

How to explain it? La Griffue is like an island, but more constricted, because it is tied to the land and cannot be what it really is.

"Yes, almost . . ." I answered.

I looked at other drawings. I showed him that, at the foot of some of them, you could read his first name.

He nodded.

"The flowered curtains upstairs, is that you?"

"They were already there, before . . ."

I put the drawings I had looked at on the table. I picked up others. The paper had yellowed with time, but the colours were still there.

"Why are they buried here, your parents? You were living in Paris."

He shook his head.

"It was one of my aunts who took care of all that. I suppose she thought they would have wanted to stay where Paul was."

I looked at him, with a drawing in my hand.

Who had helped him to grow up? How many cries and tears had it taken before he could move on from the pain and make his life bearable at last? I looked at him again, and there was a split-second of intimacy where he stopped being a stranger. I was afraid of it. A potent fear. I thought, I must get away from this.

"Last night the sky was so dark that the stars seemed to bang against my window. If I had held out my hand, I could have touched them."

I thought of you.

Our eyes met.

I did not look away.

Most of the drawings were his, but on other sheets there were the messy scribblings of the kind only very young children make.

Each drawing had a date.

"You still don't want to come with me to see old Théo?"

"This is an obsession with you."

He smiled.

"Théo's not an easy person, you can't walk into his place just like that."

"But you walked in, didn't you?"

"I'm doing the bird research."

"So?"

"He did that too, before, so it gave us something to talk about."

He took my plate, and put it on top of his.

"It's not the same topic, but I also have something we could talk about."

"Go there on your own."

He took the plates over to the sink.

"No doubt I will. I want him to tell me that he put out the light."

"What purpose would that serve?"

He stood leaning against the sink. His arms folded. "Are you protecting him?"

"That's not the issue . . ."

He smiled faintly.

"I also have a problem with Max." He said the words in the same tranquil tone of voice.

"Nobody has a problem with Max . . ."

He nodded. "But I do."

"Is it because of your buttercups? Max always takes flowers and he'll go on taking them. Everyone knows it here, it's not an issue."

"It's not because of the buttercups . . ."

"What is it because of, then?"

He came back over to the table and lit a cigarette.

"My brother's medallion that was on the gravestone . . . it has disappeared."

He tossed the match into the flames. I could not let him believe that.

"Max takes flowers, he doesn't take anything else!"

He hesitated for a moment, and he said, "I would just like to find the photograph again . . ."

His face, just then. I would have liked to have seen it in the light. I said, "Your face . . ."

He wiped his hand over his face to chase away the shadows. His hand on his slow-lipped mouth.

*

152

Surely Lambert had seen Nan's face up against the windowpane. I saw him go tense.

"Excuse me."

He went out. He came back a moment later, holding Nan by the arm. He pulled out a chair and made her sit down.

"I'm making coffee, would you like some?"

That is what he said. Nan smiled. She placed her hands, one after the other, against her bosom, and she sat there, her eyes never leaving Lambert. His movements, that is what she was following. It was astonishing to see her do this.

She seemed calm, too.

"Drink it while it's hot." He put the cup down in front of her.

She looked at the cup, the steaming coffee.

He sat down opposite her.

"I am not the man you are looking for . . ."

He explained to her for a long time who he was, and why he was there.

Nan was attentive, to his lips, to the sound of his voice, but she wasn't listening to him. He must have realized, because he stopped talking.

In the silence, Nan smiled.

"Michel . . ." she said.

He looked round, disoriented. He turned to me. "You tell her!"

"What do you want me to tell her? That you are not the man she is looking for? You can see she doesn't want to hear . . ."

"But wait! Perhaps this Michel was on the boat?"

"I really don't know . . ."

I looked at him.

"Maybe he was there, or maybe he's someone else . . ."

Lambert shook his head.

"But I am not the man she is looking for . . . We can't let her go on thinking that."

He turned again to Nan and told her. Nan was rubbing her hands together. She suddenly seemed very agitated. She could not hear what he was saying, she did not want to, so, as he went on repeating that he was not Michel, she put her hands over her ears and pressed very hard.

There was a tension in the room around her, now, a terrible confusion in her gaze, I thought she was going to cry out.

He realized as well. He reached towards her arm with his hand, he did not touch her. She looked at his hand, his gesture.

She got up and walked over to the door. Before opening it, she turned round and looked at Lambert. It was as if she had just understood something, the meaning she might be able to give that gesture. She smiled, and her smile gave me a shiver.

After that, she went out.

Lambert and I looked at each other. We wanted to drink our coffee, but it had gone cold.

"Shall we make another?"

I nodded.

He emptied the cups into the sink. Nan's visit had disturbed him. He did not want to show it, but his gestures were more nervous, betrayed him.

"I can't hold it against her . . . When people disappear, for a long time those who loved them believe that they managed not to die. I don't know if that helps in some way."

He came back with two full cups. He put them down on the table.

"The sea ought to give back its corpses. So that people can touch them, see them! Does it disgust you, what I'm saying?"

"No."

He sat back down across from me. I wanted to explain to him.

"I think that with him it might be something else . . ."

He looked at me.

"What are you thinking?"

"That he was someone she knew, someone who went away. And she's waiting for him to come back."

I looked up.

"Someone who's alive . . . A boy that Max calls Tom Thumb."

He thought about it.

A moment later, a car pulled up and stopped outside the house, and three people got out. It was the notary from Beaumont, bringing visitors.

*　　　*　　　*

Lambert and I met again at the end of the day, by the rocks in front of the great cross for the *Vendémiaire*. He was walking about. I was there.

Max was far away in the distance, on the breakwater. With my gaze I followed his tall, unsteady figure as he staggered towards the coast-guard station.

Lambert came up to me. I pointed to Morgane, stretched out in the sun, below us. Max must have looked at her, for a long time no doubt, too long, and when he could no longer bear to look at her, he did what he had to do.

He fled.

He would go and hide beyond the coastguard station, in the hollow spots in the earth that looked like caves.

Lambert pressed my binoculars to his eyes. He looked at Max. He was staring at the sea, too, towards the islands.

We talked about this place.

"And have you sold your house?" I asked him, because of the visitors that morning.

"I don't know . . ."

His tone was indifferent. "Just now, do you have anything you need to do?"

I did.

I was even running late. That was what I told him.

There were birds that used to migrate that were no longer migrating. Others who used to follow their route, merely flying over La

Hague, and who now were stopping here. We wanted to understand why there had been such changes. I had gone looking for their locations. It was not enough. I had to do more, and record everything properly. I was three days behind. After that, we would ring the birds.

Lambert listened to me, staring through the binoculars at the lighthouse. Examining it with an infinite attention.

"What I meant was, we could go and have dinner together . . . There's a restaurant in Jobourg, Les Bruyères. Apparently you eat well there."

I looked at him.

"It's going to rain," I said, pointing to the sky.

He aimed the binoculars towards the coastguard station. Max was far away, almost invisible on the path. He smiled.

"My mother used to say that too, it's going to rain, when she didn't want to go where my father was going. I don't know if she really believed it was going to rain, or if it was just that she needed to be alone."

He handed me the binoculars.

We began walking.

"Since I've been here, I've been remembering more things about her. When my little brother was born . . . She said he was more fragile than other children. I don't know if it was true."

"Théo has a cat like that."

"What do you mean?"

"More fragile than others. He said that this one needs more love than the others."

He nodded.

"I think my mother loved Paul that way . . . as if she sensed he wasn't going to grow up. What a stupid thing I've just said . . ."

"Do you think she loved him more than she loved you?"

He thought.

"I was already grown when he was born."

He took off his jacket. Just like that, all of a sudden, without warning. The air was bracing. He took a few breaths, long inhalations.

"We lived in a quiet neighbourhood in Paris. There was a toy shop not far from where we lived, Le Pain d'Épice, it was called. My mother worked there. It was a very old shop . . . in a covered arcade, passage Jouffroy . . . and a lot of our toys came from that shop. In the evening, with my father, we went there to wait for my mother. There was a place we used to go to eat cakes . . . A sort of tea room . . . I remember the women, their nice smell . . ."

He stood gazing at the sea, his jacket on his shoulder.

"When my brother was born, my mother stopped working, but we still had our walks there. I wonder if the shop still exists . . ."

He spoke about his mother's hands.

I looked at his. It would have taken ten of his hands to make just one of yours. I had loved your hands, even before I knew them. It was enough just to see them. Right to the end, the very end, the last times, when you no longer had the strength to love me. Or the will. I would wait for you to fall asleep. I would circle round your bed. It was an animal need. The palm of your hand right against my face, and I would breathe, there. Your skin had become dry. Salty. It smelled of medication. I closed my eyes. I heard myself moan. I breathed some more. I would have liked to die, to suffocate and be buried with you.

Lambert pulled me by the arm. He was giving me a strange look. What had I said? What had he understood?

He was smiling peacefully.

He pulled out his packet of cigarettes.

We went as far as the stones by the breakwater.

Afterwards, the sun was hidden and it began to get cold. Morgane came back from the beach. When she got to the cross, she saw us, and gave us a big wave, from a distance, but she did not come over.

"Whoever did your hair? You have holes . . . here and then here . . ."

He said that without looking at me. Afterwards we each went our own way.

We did not go to the restaurant that evening.

*

157

I stayed alone for a moment on the beach. Between some rocks I found a marble. I slipped it into my pocket.

The next day, when I ran into the little Stork, I gave it to her.

She looked at my face through the marble, and then at the courtyard, the trees, she looked at the dog.

She spent the morning playing with it, and when I saw her again that afternoon, she told me she had lost it.

She remembered very well the moment when she had had it and then the moment afterwards when she no longer had it. And yet it was a pretty marble. She had never had one like that. We looked everywhere for it, in the yard, in her boots.

We turned over the crate full of seashells to see if the marble had fallen to the bottom. We found snail's shells, and beetles' carapaces. We listened to the sea pounding in the shells. We sang for a bit and we forgot about the marble.

I don't know why I mentioned the marble to Théo, but when I did, his eyes lit up.

"Follow me."

He led me down the hall. He began to climb the steps of the wobbly staircase where a series of basins had been set out. He went up slowly, one hand holding to the railing. On the first landing, he stopped to catch his breath.

"From up here, you can see the sea . . ."

The little white cat went a few steps ahead of us. We came up under the roof, into a sort of huge attic cluttered with old furniture and boxes.

"Mind your head!"

The beams were very low. The floorboards were in a terrible condition. In the angle of the roof, under the skylight, there was a little pile of white bones that Théo shoved to one side with his foot.

"It's the owls," he said. "They make their nests, you can't stop them."

The bones were white, so fine they looked like needles. Next to the bones, there was a skull. A rat? Field mouse? A little wooden stepladder had been placed under the skylight.

"From here, when the weather is clear, you can see all the sea ... You can see the lighthouse, too."

He climbed up on the stepladder and raised the window. He stayed for a moment up there, his head in the wind, his eyes in the sky. His legs were trembling because of the effort required to stand there without moving.

I looked around me. Lost, forgotten objects, uncomfortable chairs, parasols from another era ... All around there was an accumulation of things that were strange to each other, and yet connected by a sort of emotional complicity. What was in all those boxes? What secrets? What mysteries? Perhaps nothing but old clothes. The clutter of attics sometimes resembles that of memories.

"Your turn now ..."

Théo climbed down, and I took his place, my hands against the tiles, my head in the roof.

I could see the pastures and the sea, the sea everywhere, massive, powerful. The low sky gave it a metallic hue. Fécamp was just there beyond that estuary. And England opposite ... To the left, the houses of La Roche. I could see the roof of the Refuge among the others, it was longer. The light tiles next to it, Nan's house. I looked. The wind was drying my eyes. La Hague is not a land like others. Few people live here, it is hostile to humans. I was learning from this land every day, the way I had learned from you. With the same sense of urgency.

I finally closed the skylight. Théo was waiting for me, sitting on a box.

He watched me come over.

"In the beginning, I spent hours here. I even forgot to eat. On my feet, behind that skylight, as if I were in my lighthouse."

He got up.

"The sea is a sickness, you know ..."

His slippers shuffled against the floor. He opened the door to a cupboard, then a drawer, and he took out a little leather case.

"This case comes from Holland, it belonged to a ship's captain, his name is written here, look. Sir John Kepper . . . His boat sank."

The lid was held to the sides with two little silver clasps. He opened them. The marbles were inside, in velvet niches. One of the niches was empty.

"The marble you found might be the one that is missing . . ."

He put the box down on the crate.

"If you found it once, you'll find it again."

He held an agate up to the light. "Sometimes, objects survive and it's men who die."

"Sir John Kepper? Isn't he the one who haunts the house across the street from Lili's?"

"Rubbish, all that! Ships sink, and their captains with them . . ."

"Lili said that . . ."

"To hell with what Lili said!"

He put the agate back in its place, and took out another marble that he rolled in his palm. It was a wooden marble, very light. There were also bone marbles and others in porcelain.

A second tray was hidden under the first one.

"These ones are actual marble, the two you see there are terracotta, and this one, the most precious, is a real agate from Venice."

He placed it in my hand. The marble was soft, almost warm. The light from the era had been caught in the varnish.

"An antique dealer in Cherbourg explained all that to me. He wanted to buy the box. I could never bring myself to sell it, perhaps because of that missing marble . . ."

He put the box back in its place. "If you find the marble, the box will be yours."

He closed the door to the big wardrobe.

"You know where it is. If I'm no longer here, all you have to do is come and get it . . . Now, let's go down, it's cold up here."

The little white cat came out from behind an old pram, looking sheepish. Spiders' webs clung to her whiskers. She came down with us. She jumped from one step to the next. When she got too far ahead of us, she stopped to wait for Théo.

He put his hand on the railing. The last step.

"You ran into Florelle the other day here, as you were leaving. It was raining."

He took his cane and went down the hall. He opened the door that led into the kitchen. He collapsed on a chair. The long walk had tired him.

He sorted through the boxes of medicine that were on the table. Chose a transparent flask that contained little blue capsules.

"She's the one I should've married. Why don't we do what we ought? What are we afraid of? At the age of ten I was already in love with her."

He swallowed a capsule with some water and left his chair to go and sit in the armchair.

"You know what they call her here? The Survivor! Simply because she didn't die with the others."

The little cat came to rub up against him. The other cats watched, their eyes half-closed, indifferent to the extra attention she received.

He winced.

"They made her grow up in the shadow of all her dead. At the age of ten she was already going down the road to sweep their graves. She was at every mass, every prayer. I never saw her wear anything but those black dresses."

He talked to me about her for a long time.

Nan had had the same destiny as the vestal virgins, condemned by the community to be the guardian of her dead. The vestal virgins were chaste. Had Nan been? I looked at Théo's hands. The hands of an old man; hands that had once been young. Could one love without caressing? Without that desire?

"From the skylight I could see the roof of her house, I could see her yard. Her light, in the evening, I knew whether she was still up."

I nodded.

"You loved Nan and you married someone else."

He smiled.

"Old Mother was pregnant."

He looked up at me.

"I didn't love her. I haven't loved Lili, either."

He said it without emphasis, but his voice broke, as if hindered by some remnant of anger.

"So many times I thought of leaving them. I would have had to leave La Hague, too, and the lighthouse. I was a coward ... That's what you think, isn't it? I was a coward, and now I'm going to die."

His hand was trembling on the armrest. He looked at it as if it did not belong to him.

"Nan never married?"

"Never."

He picked up the little cat and put her on the floor. He disappeared into the next room. The cat watched as he moved away. She went cautiously up to the wood stove. Underneath, between the iron legs, there was an old woollen jumper. The little cat went up to it, sniffed it. Then she lay down on it, her paws tucked under her chest. When Théo came back, she was like that, eyes half-closed, enjoying the heat of the stove.

Théo sat back down across from me. He had brought back an album; now he placed it on the table and turned the first pages. He pointed to a photograph.

"That's Florelle, outside the Refuge ..."

You could see the building, the large windows wide open to let in the sunlight. By the door, four children were holding hands. A young woman was standing next to them. She wasn't looking at the lens, she was looking at the children.

She was young, thirty years old, beautiful, but her expression was solemn. Was Nan so beautiful because Théo loved her? To one side, slightly further back, another woman in an overall was holding a basin in her arms.

"That's Ursula, she did the cooking at the Refuge."

A shadow on the ground, that of the tree in the courtyard. Above the door, in the niche in the wall, the stone Virgin seemed to be watching over them.

Théo turned the pages. He showed me other photographs of Nan. He talked about life at the Refuge, how cold it was in the winter. Only one room was heated, the big common room, the rest of the time the children would go back to their beds holding a stone wrapped in a cloth against their bellies, a stone that they had heated in the fire.

There was a very fine photograph of the common room, with the children at their tables and Nan among them.

Théo told me that the Refuge had been closed for nearly twenty years now, but when I asked him why it had closed, he looked at me, and did not reply.

When I left, he was still looking at the photograph.

*   *   *

I went to Lili's to fill in my charts. It did not take very long to do, but it was boring. Usually I would do it on rainy days. I was already behind, I could not wait any longer. I sat down in my usual place, and immediately saw that there was a photograph missing from the back wall. The one where you could see Lili and her parents, and the child she had called Michel. She had not replaced the photograph with another one, and there was a square of wallpaper that was lighter. Dirty grey around it. The mark of the four drawing pins.

Lili followed my gaze. She did not say anything. I did not ask her anything.

The Stork was there, playing at blowing against the window, her hot breath, and in the condensation she wrote her name, the Stork, and above it, a line, and another line, and a circle, another line

163

connected to the circle, and that name was hers, too, her first name, the one she had been given when she was born, Ila.

The name disappeared. She blew again, and in the place of letters, she drew suns.

M. Anselme had explained to me that Ila was the name of a virgin warrior, the daughter of the god Odin, one of the most famous gods in Norse mythology.

The Stork liked it when you told her the story of her name.

She came to stand across from me. What was I like at her age? Was I just as silent?

"Two crows lived perched on the shoulders of the god Odin," I said, pulling her close. "On this shoulder, there was the crow of memory and . . ." I touched her left shoulder, ". . . on that one, there was the crow of thought."

The child shivered.

I put my hands together to mime the bird's flight.

"The crows flew off every morning to visit the world. At night, when they came back, they told the god Odin about everything they had seen and heard."

With her gaze the Stork followed my hands as they flew above her. She waited, both happy and impatient, for me to tell her what happened next, right up to the last sentence, the very last of the story, when I told her that the god's daughter had her name.

To keep her waiting in suspense, I let a long silence settle over us.

"And the god's daughter was called Ila."

She smiled, and in her eyes was the image of herself, the daughter of a god. She blew on the window and I wrote the name of Odin there for her.

She looked at the name. With her finger, she went back over the letters.

"And you, shouldn't you be at school, now?"

She shook her head.

"It's Saturday . . ." she said.

"You have a lot of Saturdays in your week . . ."

Her strange face . . . Her cheeks were round and soft. Her ravaged mouth made her even more beautiful to me, like her skin steeped in the smell of earth.

No doubt she sensed that no day in her life would ever be powerful enough to make the daughter of a god out of her. And yet. What was inside her? What treasures in her destiny?

I slipped a coin into her hand.

"Go and buy some sweets."

She went to cling to the bar, and I went on filling in my charts.

Lambert crossed the road. When she saw him, the Stork went over to the window. She crushed her hand, her face, against the glass. He saw her, too. He placed his finger on the other side of the window.

He blew and wrote his name in the condensation, Lambert, but he wrote it backwards so that the Stork could read it.

She blew again too. She thought, then wrote, Stork.

Lambert shook his head. He wrote, Ila. She pointed to the dog and wrote, Soft Spot. He looked up at me, nodded, and wrote, Blue.

Lili shouted at us, because, after all, she was the one who had to wash the windows.

M. Anselme arrived while she was still shouting. Lambert came in with him. He apologized for the window. He ordered a glass of wine and some peanuts. Lili pointed to the dispenser.

"Self-service for the peanuts."

He filled a saucer with peanuts. He put his glass on the table and sat down opposite me, next to M. Anselme. He pushed the saucer into the middle of the table.

He looked at my charts.

"What's new up on your cliffs?"

"I found eggs, three white eggs striped with blue veins . . . That was yesterday, just before the Nez de Jobourg. I also saw a superb bird that I'm not familiar with. I drew it. I also did a plate, just the three eggs."

He nodded.

"What's this chart?" he said, pointing at one of the reports.

"It's for the cormorants, a report about the time they spend fishing and the time they spend resting."

Entire afternoons, glued to the chronometer.

I dabbed my finger in the salt in the saucer. Behind the bar, Lili was looking at us. I do not know if she was listening.

When Morgane arrived, we were still looking at my graphs. She walked across the room and went to lean against the pinball machine, without saying hello to anyone. The pinball machine was out of order. She put on some music, and danced in front of the jukebox.

Lambert was watching her. M. Anselme, too. Lili brought M. Anselme's tea. She put it on the table.

He said, "I remember your mother. I sometimes shared a few words with her, here, by the roadside, and on the quay, too, when she watched your father setting out."

He took a swallow of tea.

He talked about the power of men.

And the power of women.

Lambert turned to me. There were pale glints in his eyes, like little crushed stars.

"And what do you think?"

"I think that . . . it's the power they have to give birth that makes women stronger."

He took a sip of wine.

"Did you get a good mark in philosophy at the *baccalauréat*?"

"I think I did . . ."

"You think, or you're sure?"

"I'm sure."

"I didn't even get a mark . . . not even nought. I was off the subject."

He smiled.

His father had already been dead for a long time when he took his *baccalauréat* exam. I thought about that and felt myself blushing. When

166

I blush I get red patches on my neck. I feel it burning. That makes me blush even more.

He put his fingers on the rim of his glass. He was still smiling, faintly.

"My father, I don't know if he was ever off the subject . . . Oh, he must have been, yes . . . Like everyone."

"What did he do, your father?" I said.

"Philosophy teacher."

He emptied the peanuts into the palm of his hand.

"Always in his books. I don't remember much about him."

Morgane came to join us.

"I'm interrupting a conversation!"

Lambert nodded, and M. Anselme moved over to make room for her.

"Everything's fine," I said.

She looked through the drawer in the table, pulled out a wooden case with a set of little plastic horses, and shoved it over to Lambert.

"Unless you'd rather play snakes and ladders?"

We looked at each other. We would rather do nothing at all. She started a game of patience, paying no attention to us, four rows of seven, turning the cards over one after the other. She lost the first round.

M. Anselme looked longingly at her. He ordered four glasses of wine, so he could stay and look at her.

With his finger Lambert stopped the drops of cold condensation that were running down his glass. Morgane glanced at him.

"So we're not so badly off here, then?"

He did not answer.

"If there were four of us we could play a *tarot* . . ." she said. "You know how to play!"

"Memories from the *lycée* . . ."

She handed out the cards. She asked him if he minded if she said *tu* to him, and he said no, he didn't mind.

She went on talking to him as they played.

"Lambert . . . Wasn't there one in the Bible with that name . . . *The child went before and the dog followed* . . . Lambert of Assisi?"

Lambert smiled.

"It's Francis, Saint Francis of Assisi."

"Saint Francis, yes, I suppose . . ."

"Don't suppose, it's a fact."

He put the two little horses on the game board and threw the dice.

"Are you a teacher?"

"You don't have to be a teacher to know that."

She gave a little pout.

He moved his horse and handed me the dice. I threw it. The dice stopped against the ashtray. Somewhere between one and six.

I threw again.

"If the dice comes up six, you start over and you're not allowed to stop a rolling dice," Morgane said without looking up.

M. Anselme got up. This was our game. He no longer belonged. He said goodbye.

"Chelone, you see . . ."

He had not drunk his wine.

Morgane shrugged. She made two piles of cards, put them down opposite each other, and shuffled them. She formed the deck again, tapping the edges on the table.

"So, do you feel like a *tarot*? Raphaël's good at it. Raphaël is my brother," she said, turning to Lambert. "He's a very great sculptor."

She put the cards back in the drawer. She got up and put on her jacket.

"Shall we go?"

Morgane opened the car door, leapt into the front seat of the Audi. She bent down to rummage in the glove compartment, going through the C.D.s, Lavilliers, Beatles, Julios Bocarne . . .

"Who is Bocarne?"

She slotted in the C.D. After the first notes, she made a face. She put on Lavilliers, full blast. Night was falling. There was a moon. Rays of light on the sea. At midnight, you could see as if it were broad daylight. It is said that a moonlit night works on a woman's body. Opens it. Empties it from inside. I had known that, with you. I looked at them. I should have let them go off, the two of them. Let them have their moon. I looked up. I met his gaze, briefly, in the rear-view mirror.

His jacket was next to me on the seat. I ran my hand over the collar. I do not know if he saw my gesture.

It did not take long to reach the harbour. He drove slowly. Morgane jumped out before he had even finished parking the car. She ran on ahead. She wanted to tell Raphaël.

It began to rain.

The headlamps lit up the streaks of rain. There was a light on in Raphaël's kitchen. In the pasture behind the *auberge*, the cows were preparing to spend the night outside. I said something about it, I cannot remember what.

Lambert stopped the C.D. and put it back in the case.

"Shall we go?"

"Let's go," I said.

A pipistrelle bashed against the car, disoriented. I wondered why.

We spent part of the night playing *tarot* in Raphaël's kitchen. We ate sandwiches. We drank wine.

We smoked, too.

In the morning, Lambert left.

Morgane said that before leaving, he went into Raphaël's studio, and stayed for a long time in there, all alone. When he came back out, he did not say anything. He drank a last coffee and went home.

The next morning I took Raphaël's car and went to Cherbourg. I bought two litres of green paint in a hardware shop. They had to mix up three other greens to get the colour I wanted, a Hopper green. I had shown them the postcard. I also bought a bottle of white spirit to clean the brushes.

I withdrew some money from a cashpoint and did my shopping at the supermarket.

When I got back, I started painting, from the right angle of the window.

I covered an entire wall. To paint the top of the wall, I had to stand on a chair.

That was what I did, climb up, get down, climb up again and move the chair any number of times.

While I was spreading the paint, drops splashed on to the newspapers. When I got down off the chair, I walked in the splashes. Afterwards I saw I had left traces on the steps.

Hopper-green footprints.

I left the brush on the newspaper. The paint dried. I kept the paper. I reckoned I would go on painting the other walls.

*   *   *

That evening it was Max's birthday. Lili had said, any time after six, the door will be open to everyone, and there will be music. When I got there, there were already records playing on the turntable, old singles, Claude François, Stone and Charden, Sheila.

Lili had made biscuits. There were sandwiches on the tables. She had set out flowered tablecloths, and bouquets of flowers, and stuck candles in the ashtrays. Max was wearing a suit and tie that had belonged to Lili's husband. The suit was much too big for him, he seemed a bit lost in it. He did not care. He watched all of us as we came in, one after the other, the postman, the priest, the neighbours, he did not want to miss anyone. Morgane was there. Even the young teenagers from the neighbourhood. We had all clubbed together and Lili had bought a transistor so that he could listen to music on his boat.

M. Anselme was wearing his linen suit. Lambert was by the door. He had not known about Max's birthday. He apologized, he wanted to leave, but Morgane took him by the hand.

The little red pebble I had found on the shore was in my pocket. I toyed with it in my fingers.

"It's a lovely evening, isn't it?"

M. Anselme sent Lili a little wave.

"How did your little evening end?" he asked, when he saw Lambert was there.

"We went to play *tarot* at Raphaël's place."

He nodded.

People were telling jokes, left and right, and after the jokes we all raised our glasses to Max's health. M. Anselme leaned against me.

"Did you know I proposed to Morgane? . . . She didn't say anything to you?"

"What should she have said?"

He went on observing the people in the room.

"I thought she would have said something . . . I want to marry her."

"You're not serious?"

He was eating her up with his gaze. "Why not?"

"She's not even thirty!"

"She'll be thirty in July."

I glanced over at Morgane. She was still talking to Lambert.

She was wearing pink fishnet stockings; the reinforced heel showed above her shoe. From her ankle, a snagged thread in the weave rose behind her thigh and disappeared beneath the black cloth of her skirt.

M. Anselme leaned over to me.

"You see the ladder she's got? Just imagine if she says yes."

A neighbour who had come to give a hand was passing out glasses of sparkling wine that she exaggeratedly referred to as champagne. I took a glass.

He could not have asked Morgane any such thing.

"One hundred and twenty-nine days exactly, in other words slightly more than three thousand hours, three thousand and ninety-six to be exact."

He glanced at his watch.

"A bit less, because it was at five o'clock . . . Why are you looking at me like that?"

"No reason."

Morgane was still talking to Lambert.

He emptied his glass.

"Surprising, the taste!" he said, making a face behind his hand.

Someone turned up the volume. Deep in her armchair, Old Mother began to clap her hands. How long had it been since she had had a bit of fun? She tried to sing, it made her drool a little, her jaw askew. Almost unrecognizable, she was.

M. Anselme turned round to put his glass on the table behind him.

"I've heard that when Lili was born, Théo was on watch at the light. Apparently he finished his fortnight as if nothing had happened. Some say he'd have come back for the birth of a calf, but not for his own child."

He smiled at the postman's wife, he smiled at all the women.

"That Lambert, be careful not to love him too soon . . . Desire, you see, the need we have to assuage it, and the regret, once we have . . ."

He looked at me questioningly. "What do you see in him? He's common . . ."

His tone, almost jealous, made me laugh.

A moment later, there was a murmuring around the room and everyone applauded. It was Max's present, little Stork was carrying it, but the package was much too big for her and she disappeared behind it. Max blushed, he hopped from one foot to the other, looking all round, he would have liked to kiss everyone. Finally he took the Stork in his arms and squeezed her very tight.

"This is the big emotional squeezing . . ." he confessed, rubbing his eyes.

"You can open it," Lili said, pushing the package towards him.

"Apparently his mother gave birth in a field. With a cow. There was a full moon. The cow was birthing her calf."

M. Anselme said that, looking at Max.

"That's how she did it, her woman's eyes staring right into the cow's eyes. The vet that came to help the cow also helped his mother. The two at the same time. He went from one belly to the other. Apparently at one point he no longer knew whose belly he was delving into."

I shrugged. In her armchair, Old Mother stuffed herself with everything they put before her.

Max tore off the wrapping paper and pulled out the transistor. The children whistled. Lili opened more bottles. M. Anselme went on talking.

"Max was born first. After that, the vet went back between the cow's legs and brought out the calf."

Morgane went over to Max. She lifted her hand to his face.

"This is your present," she said.

Max smiled.

A caress.

He closed his eyes.

"I'll bring you some flowers," he said suddenly.

We saw him shiver, as if there were hope. He lifted his hand towards her breasts. Everyone was waiting. Lili stepped forward and pushed him aside.

"It's your birthday, not hers."

Max shook his head. He wanted to go for the flowers right away. He said as much, "The cemetery is right next door."

"It can wait until tomorrow," Lili said, pointing to the darkness on the other side of the window.

Max closed his mouth. Tomorrow was a long way away.

Lili pulled him by the sleeve back over to the transistor. The postman had found the radio waves. It was still crackling, but eventually they found some songs. Morgane went back and leaned against the wall.

Some neighbours left.

M. Anselme talked to me about a tree that was growing on the footpath beyond the coastguard station. He wanted us to go and see it together. It was a tree that was growing above the sea, a tree that Prévert had loved. Prévert had telephoned him a few weeks before he died, to find out whether the tree was still going to bloom. His breathing was already horrible to listen to. He died in the spring of that year, and the tree bloomed and still blooms.

The cake arrived, three tiers covered with pink cream. There were candles stuck in the cream. Max's name had been written in chocolate. When she saw the cake, Old Mother got up, and skewered herself to her walking frame. She moved forward, staring at the cake. It was not every day that she could stuff herself. Max blew out the candles and everybody applauded. You could not hear the radio any more, but the Stork went on dancing.

Lili sliced up the cake.

Lambert left.

Old Mother was almost up against the cake. Her mouth open. Inside, her teeth were coming loose. She held out her hand.

Lili shrugged. "Tomorrow, you're getting leek broth!" she said.

Everyone laughed.

And suddenly, the door opened. In the middle of the laughter. At the same time. The two together, the laughter and the sound of the door. Heads turned and everyone who was speaking fell silent. The ones who were laughing. Because Nan was there. In her black dress. She had left her hair loose on her shoulders as if it were a storm day.

She did not say anything.

She came forward. Her face somewhat frozen. Her white hair falling all round her. Someone stopped the music.

M. Anselme took me gently by the elbow.

"At last a little bit of excitement . . ."

She was holding a little package in her hands.

"This is for you," she said, going up to Max.

174

The package was wrapped in blue paper.

Max smiled. He looked at all of us, and showed us the package.

He held Nan against him, his large arms folded round her, and he kissed her. Only then did he open the package.

Inside, there was a woollen cap with Max's name embroidered in red letters, and an anchor.

"A fisherman's cap," he said, showing the knit anchor.

He was happy. He was laughing. He put the cap on his head, and went to see his face in the mirror.

"This is a very fine present."

His eyes were wide open, and he looked all around him for a plate for a slice of cake. A glass of wine, too. He had to give everything to Nan, give Nan as much as the others. More, perhaps. While he was filling her plate, Old Mother came forward. The two women looked at each other.

M. Anselme leaned over to my ear without taking his eyes off them.

"Between the two, the legitimate and the mistress, which one would you rather have been?"

"And in your opinion?"

He thought, and went on staring at the old women.

"To be honest, I can't see you as the legitimate. But I can't see you as the mistress either . . . no doubt these established norms are just as inhospitable to you as they are to me."

He laid his hand on my arm. "We are obliged to swim in troubled waters . . ."

The old women stood facing each other. They looked like two monsters who had risen out of the water and landed there, ready to fight. Two madwomen, fuelled by hatred. All around, there was silence. No-one moved.

Finally Old Mother hissed, "When you're dead, I will go and dance."

They were too old to hit each other. But not too old to hate.

Nan shrugged her shoulders. She turned away, slowly.

"You won't be able to . . ."

A smile lingered on her lips. She looked at Old Mother.

"You won't be able to, because you're going to die before me."

The shadow of her smile. Or something that had been her smile.

She went out.

Her silhouette, for a moment, on the terrace.

Lili took the plate from Max's hand. She removed the cap from his head, too.

"You're not on your boat," she said.

Someone started the music again.

"To friendship!" Lili shouted, raising her glass very high.

Glasses were filled. Others were emptied.

"M. Anselme . . ." I said. "Your hand on my arm . . . You're hurting me."

He removed his hand. "Oh yes, forgive me . . ."

Old Mother's head was nodding up and down. The postman helped her to sit down. He brought her the big flower made of almond paste that had been on the top of the cake. She looked at it. She was trembling, her eyes still in chaos. Her face paler than usual.

Max demanded a moment of great silence to thank everyone.

This is what he said: "I proclaim a generous thanks to all."

He explained that his boat was nearly finished, and that he was going to go fishing for the porbeagle. Everyone turned to look at Max. I went up to Old Mother. I sat down next to her. I took her hand. It was cold, repulsive.

At my touch, Old Mother raised her head. Her eyes were bloodshot, her pupils burning. As if everything living in her had collected there, in that very fragile space.

"She's a thief . . . that's why she went in the house."

I let go of her hand, but she took it again, roughly. She pointed to the house across the street, on the other side of the road.

Old Mother, her head leaning over me.

"She went there, at night . . . She stole all the toys."

"Are you talking about Nan?"

"But nobody knows what she did! Nobody . . . I saw her, the toys in her arms, I saw her take them away, she held them like this."

She showed me, her arms folded.

An unpleasant wheezing was coming from her chest.

"What did she want to do with them?" I said.

"She stole from the house of the dead, after the accident, when the boat capsized. She came here."

Her voice had become a hoarse murmur. She was talking quickly, I could not understand everything she was saying. If Nan had come to get the toys, perhaps it was to give them to the children at the Refuge.

I told her that.

She frowned. She was scratching with her fingernail on the wood of the table, and shaking her head.

"That's something else . . ."

She ran her hand over her forehead, several times, as if she were trying to remember this thing she was trying to find. This thing that had got away from her. Relentlessly. As soon as she seemed about to find it, the image shied away. She fretted over it for a while.

Lili realized. She came over to us.

"What's going on?"

She looked at her mother's face. Her expression, almost vacant. She was muttering incoherent things. She was trying to hold on, to find the memory of that thing that she absolutely must find and that she had forgotten. I do not know what Lili understood, but judging from her expression as she looked at me, I could sense she was reproaching me. I apologized. I went back to M. Anselme.

"A problem?" he asked.

I said, "No, nothing, everything is fine."

Behind me, Max was continuing his speech. His words reached me, from a distance. I was thinking back over what Old Mother had said.

Max was saying that for the colour of the cabin, he was still hesitating between blue and white, but the boat already had a name, *La*

Marie-Salope. That was its Christian name. Max said it was a fine name, and he did not want to change any of it. He also said that he would give us each a tooth, a tooth from the first shark that he killed.

He promised.

When I left, Lili was still with her mother. I turned my head, and I saw that she was looking at me.

*   *   *

The little donkeys always came back with the fine weather. No-one knew when or how they would arrive, but we knew they would be coming.

Nan was waiting for them. There, like every afternoon, sitting on a stone by the side of the crossroads. Her hair was held back in a heavy plait, tied at the bottom with a black velvet ribbon. You might have said that the stone she was sitting on was a part of her. That it was her base.

When I arrived, little Stork was next to her, playing a few notes on a cardboard drum. The drum was torn. She played all the same. It was the first time I had seen her do that.

The donkeys came along a footpath from inland. Some people said they went along the coast after the Pointe du Rozel, that they had been seen going through the village of Sotteville and then seen again a long time afterwards, above the high dunes at Biville. They had spent a few days in the marshland, and now they were here.

Old Nan had sensed their presence. Before she saw them. The smell in the air, their coats, that sweat. She heard the hoofbeats on the earth like a distant rumbling, and the rumbling came closer.

She got up. She went along the road. A few steps. The Stork abandoned her drum in the grass by the roadside. She set off at a run, all the way to the end of the big pasture.

The donkeys were there. One in the lead, the others following.

Other children showed up, and with them the people from the village. They brought water in buckets. Some meal, and hay.

There was a horse with the donkeys. He was limping. An injury to his hindleg.

When he came close, Nan placed her hands in the rough thickness of his mane. The horse was very beautiful. I wondered how he had managed to come all this way without anyone catching him.

Nan said that sometimes horses felt this need to travel. She looked at me.

"This horse might belong to the fairies . . ."

Had she really committed the theft Old Mother accused her of? And did it really matter?

Old women's quarrels, village quarrels. Women who had loved the same man.

She slipped her fingers into the thick horsehair.

"The fairies are so small that to ride they cling to the mane and make their stirrups by tying together a few hairs from the mane."

She took my hand so I too could touch the horse. "You never see fairies during the day, only at night."

"Where are they during the day?" I said.

She smiled.

"Who knows . . ."

She stroked his chest. She held the horse's head between her hands and scratched off the crusts of dried tears sticking to the corners of its eyes.

I had read stories about the fairies in a magazine I found at La Griffue. It was said that the fairies took babies from their cradles, and exchanged them for one of their own.

I asked Nan if this were true.

She nodded.

"No-one knows why they do that, but these things do happen."

She smiled, an infinitely sweet smile.

"Fairies' children are very special, they need a lot of food, but their bodies don't grow. They're called pixies."

She turned to me again.

"It's bad luck to have a pixie grow up in your house, and that's why people who have them don't show them."

"What do they do with them?"

"They hide them. I know someone who killed their pixie . . ."

She said that gruffly and then she went away. The horse was staring at the sea. I stayed by him. Long shivers ran through his breast. He probably had a fever. Two tears of fatigue wept from his eyes.

"Those are moon pearls."

I felt Lambert's breath against my neck. I recognized his body without seeing him.

"Moon pearls . . . that's what they call the tears of horses."

His smell of leather mingled with that of the animals. I did not turn round.

Nan saw him.

Slowly she came over to him.

She smiled at him. It was an exceptional moment, with all the donkeys round us and the children feeding them, and as far as the eye could see, the moor, the heather, and the sea.

Nan stood very close to Lambert.

"Do you remember, when you were little, we came to wait for them."

These were terrible words. I saw his face go tense.

Nan sighed softly.

"It's good, that you've come back."

She said this in the same even tone.

Lambert shook his head, a slow movement, but he did not go away.

"I'm not the person you are looking for."

That is what he said.

After a long while, he turned to her.

"Who is it, who are you looking for?"

She did not answer. She was humming, a gentle tune without words.

He looked at me and then he looked at her again. He touched her arm to make her stop her song.

"Who do you think I am?"

Nan smiled at him.

"You are Michel."

"But who is Michel?"

Then her gaze slid over his face. Lost for a moment.

In the grass by the side of the road was the little drum that the Stork was playing when I arrived. She had left it there, with the two wooden drumsticks. Lambert saw it. He went over, and picked it up.

It was a little cardboard toy, its colours faded with time. A clown with a blue nose was painted on the stretched skin. The paint had peeled in places. There were slight traces of colour.

Lambert ran his finger over the skin of the drum.

"This blue clown ..."

He was turning the drum over and over in his hands.

"Is something wrong?" I asked.

He turned the drum, thoughtfully, almost cautiously.

"That toy shop where my mother worked ... The arcade in Paris ..."

He was looking for something. He looked underneath the drum and then on the sides, and between the wooden drumsticks that served as a support for the drum. Then he stopped and put a finger between one of the drumstick lozenges. In a space as big as two postage stamps, there was an old label.

He showed it to me.

I read, "*Pain d'Épice, Toys, passage Jouffroy, Paris.*"

"That is the shop I was telling you about ..."

Suddenly the memory came back. I saw that moment, in his eyes, and I knew he had just found his past.

"This was Paul's drum!"

He held it against his chest. His hand was rubbing the cardboard. He was breathing in the smell. That object, more than any landscape, more, even, than the house, seemed to restore his childhood to him. What images? What memories? He was upset.

"Are you alright?" I said.

"I'm alright," he said.

He smiled a little, faintly, as if he did not dare.

Nan stood by the donkeys. She was stroking them. From time to time, she turned around and smiled at Lambert.

He was looking elsewhere, into the empty space above the sea, that space that was not the sky, but was not the water, either.

He went on sitting by the side of the road looking at the donkeys, with the drum on his lap.

Was he wondering how the toy had come to be there?

I went home.

I was cold. I needed a coffee. I ran into Morgane in the garden, she was on her way out, with a towel wrapped around her shoulders. She was going for a swim, not just anywhere, but opposite the lighthouse. She did that sometimes. She said it was no more dangerous to bathe there than anywhere else. That it was no colder, either, and besides she did not know where else to go.

"Just don't tell Raphaël, O.K.?"

She laid her towel out in the sun. She was wearing her black swimsuit. She walked up to the waves, then with her feet in the first waves, she scooped water up in her hand and wet her neck. The drops fell down her back, like black streams. She did that several times, then went further in again, and dived in. She swam, powerful strokes in the cold water. She swam quickly, she was a good swimmer. She continued straight ahead, as if she had decided to go somewhere, by sea. I sat on the rocks, next to her towel. I waited for her.

I drew a drum in the wet sand with my finger. Above it, I traced the shape of the sun. I would have liked to have known whether there were other toys, somewhere, at Nan's or at the Refuge, toys that had belonged to Paul or to Lambert. I thought again about Lambert, the odd look on his face, when he realized that the drum had been his brother's.

I stopped thinking because Max appeared by my side. He was afraid for Morgane's sake, and the fear made him agitated. He could not sit down, and he paced back and forth, striking the ground with his feet. He was angry with her. In the end he destroyed my drawing in the sand. Yet it was not the first time he had seen Morgane swim out towards the currents.

Morgane eventually came out of the water. She was bleeding, a scratch on her knee from the rocks, and there was that other blood flowing from her, from inside her thigh. Max stared at the red streak, the winding path on the milky whiteness of her skin.

Morgane came to sit down by me. The cold had left her breathless, she was gasping.

"I know the depths here by heart . . . I could swim blindfold if I had to."

Her skin was blue, she was so cold. She showed me her hands.

"I touch the currents. I can feel the moment where I'm brushing by them. It's like a great wall of ice across the sea."

Her lips, too, were blue. She paid no attention to Max. From up on the breakwater, the fishermen were looking at her. She knew it. She did not care. She knew the sea as well as they did. Better than they did. She knew it from within.

"What happens if you go through the wall?"

She did not answer.

She smiled and lowered her head between her arms. Her body was trembling under the towel. She looked at the sea, her chin in her hands.

"I lived with a guy for seven years. It was good . . . I remember one day, he wrote his name on my back, between my shoulder blades. His name, with his tongue."

She let her towel slip down as if the trace might still be there.

She wanted to show me.

"Touch my back . . ."

I touched it.

"I miss his desire."

"Why did you split up?"

"No particular reason . . . One day, we looked at each other, and we were no longer in love."

She sat up and began to untangle her hair with her fingers.

"Seven years, that's already not bad . . ." she said.

Her hair was soaked. It was dripping down her back. She turned round.

"Have you noticed, you find the number seven everywhere! The seven deadly sins, the seven wonders of the world, Snow White and the Seven Dwarfs . . ."

"The seven hills of Rome."

"The seven-year itch."

She thought for a moment, staring up at the sky.

"Seven years of bad luck! Sail the seven seas!"

"Seven-league boots . . ."

"Seven days a week!"

"Seventh heaven. Sevenoaks."

"What's that?"

"A town near London."

She took some sand in her hand and rubbed the soles of her feet. She said it was good for her skin.

She showed me the sand.

"Will you rub my back?"

She bent over, her head between her hands.

"What about you, with guys, how long does it usually last?" she asked, laughing.

"The last one, three years . . ."

She thought for a moment.

"Can't think of much with the number three."

"Three little pigs?" I said.

"Yeah . . . three little pigs. Bluebeard's three wives, too."

"Bluebeard had three wives?"

"I think . . . I don't remember. Maybe he had seven . . ."

She burst out laughing. I laughed with her. After that we tried to find others, with three, but we could not find any more.

She turned her head.

"And why did it end, you and him? You didn't love each other any more?"

I looked at the sea.

Yes, we did still love each other.

We found the horse in the garden. His wound was open, no-one knew how he had got it. Sometimes wild dogs attacked horses. Sometimes, too, the horses got their legs caught in barbed wire and hurt themselves badly trying to break free.

Morgane walked with him into the sea. She guided him, holding him by the mane. The wound was immersed in water. She went with him from one end of the beach to the other and when she got to the far end she turned round and came back.

I was waiting for her.

"The bloke . . . the one you stayed with for three years, did you leave or did he?" she asked, as if she'd been thinking about it all through her walk.

"He did."

"Want to tell?"

"No."

"Why not?"

I bent down to look at the wound. Salt had eaten into the edges and the inside of the wound.

"Do you think when his leg gets better you'll be able to swim with him?" I asked, so that I would not have to answer her question.

She stroked the horse's thigh with the palm of her hand, the wide muscle, that of a young animal who has walked a long way.

"I don't know . . ."

She turned away. She looked at the sea.

"Perhaps when he's better, I won't be here any more."

"Not here? Why, are you thinking of leaving?"

"Perhaps . . ."

"But where would you go? Who with? To do what?"

She looked at me.

"Sooner or later I shall have to leave . . ."

"And Raphaël, will he go with you?"

She looked down.

The following night the horse stayed in the pasture in front of the house. The pasture had no fence. He could have left if he had wanted to.

He did not.

When the rain fell, he left the field and went to shelter by the boat. Morgane fed him some meal and hay.

She dressed his wound with bandages she had made, cutting up old sheets that Lili had given her.

She said that when his wound was healed he would leave, and that was why she did not want to give him a name.

*　　*　　*

Dozens of wild geese had stopped off at the end of the morning on the Pointes Rocheuses. Magnificent geese, with ash-coloured plumage.

I drew them.

The necks of some of them, close together. Coiled. They knew I was watching them.

I also drew a few terns and a pair of swifts.

Lambert came to find me. I saw him coming from a long way off. He hesitated, pointed to the rock next to mine, and asked if he would be bothering me if he sat there, that he felt like watching the geese, too. I told him he would not be bothering me.

He sat down, looked at the geese, and he wanted to see my drawings.

186

"Is it to put with your charts?"

"No . . ."

I told him about the plates.

"I fill in the drawings with watercolour. Then I show them to Théo, and if they're good, I send them to Caen. Someone else will take care of the text, and someone else again for the cards . . . Théo said that the plates I've done so far are good quality. They should make a very fine book."

He nodded.

"Théo knows everything."

"Théo does know a lot about birds."

A smile crossed his lips. He took my notebook and turned the pages. He paused at certain drawings. The weave of the paper was thick, he rubbed it with his thumb.

"I thought that drawings couldn't be either good or bad . . . A teacher told me that."

"With this type of drawing, they can. The colour of the feathers, the shape of the beaks . . . There are very precise nuances to respect, shapes. I sometimes overindulge in the pleasure of drawing . . ."

"Good thing there's Théo."

His tone was ironic, and I felt myself blushing. Pointlessly. The attack was not against me.

"How many of these drawings will you need to make your encyclopaedia?"

"A lot . . ."

I pointed to the sky.

"You cannot imagine how many species of birds there are, between the ones that live here and never leave, and the ones that migrate, that just stop here to reproduce or spend the winter, and the ones that should have left and don't leave . . ."

He nodded.

"I can't imagine, no . . . and you, why did you come here? Are you like them, are you migrating?"

"You could say so. Above all, I was tired of talking all day long. When I found out that the Centre ornithologique in Caen was looking for someone, I applied, and . . ."

He turned other pages, and stopped at the drawing of a pair of young cormorants that I had studied a few days ago, across from the lighthouse. Their plumage was magnificent, and that way they had of never leaving each other. He looked at the drawing. He turned to another. I would have liked to have talked about something else besides birds. To ask him if he had taken the drum with him.

"Do you always draw both of them, the male and female?"

"When possible, yes . . . I draw eggs, too, and nests."

"And this, what's this?"

At the end of the notebook, he pointed to the drawing of a toad.

"Are you going to put him in the bird encyclopaedia, too?"

"No, but this toad is very special. He massages the belly of his female to make her lay her eggs, and then he takes the eggs on his back and he's the one who looks after them. I found him rather nice."

"So if you draw the things you find nice, I'm in with a chance, then . . ."

He closed the notebook and held it for a moment in his hands. He was rubbing the leather binding, looking at the sea.

Gulls flew overhead on their way to the harbour. We were expecting rain by evening.

"So, you're here today, and when you've finished your drawings, will you go elsewhere . . . ? I've got my house in Le Morvan, stone walls as wide as this. After I've been away, I always go back there. I don't go away often. I don't like to."

He turned his face to me. He stared at me for a moment.

"You do sometimes get attached, don't you?"

Get attached? It was not something I wanted. Not too soon. I said it softly, between my teeth. "I don't want to get attached. It's become a sickness. When I was little, I was already agoraphobic. I liked being that way, because of the name. That's what I said to my girlfriends, *agora*. It sounds good, don't you think? After that I was allergic to cats.

188

Apparently if you keep on loving them, the allergy will disappear. It's force of habit. Now, it's a fear of attachment, I don't know if there's a name for it."

The principle of reality, you talked to me about that, before you left. You said, I want to confront it with you, without pain. But you knew nothing but pain, the last two months. Curled up on your bed, you no longer even knew that it was called pain.

Lambert tossed a stick, far out.

"And does it happen often, that the birds that were thinking of migrating change their minds?"

"It happens . . ."

He lit a cigarette, his face bent over his hands.

"Let's say *tu* to each other, it would be simpler, don't you think?" he said, blowing on his smoke.

"Simpler?" I shook my head. "No, let's not say *tu*."

He remained silent for a moment. The geese flew away together, a beautiful chevron flight. They disappeared inland.

We went on sitting, as if the geese were still there.

"Just now, when you said, 'I applied and' . . . you didn't finish your sentence."

"Nothing . . . I was accepted, and I left."

And you left. I didn't tell him that.

"You should always finish your sentences . . . At school, when I told the girls I had no parents, they felt sorry for me. There were some who even thought it was love. Doesn't that happen with you?"

"Does what happen?"

"To have these waves of pity for someone?"

"No, not with me . . ."

He raised his eyebrows.

"I suspected as much."

He threw some more sticks; they floated on the water. A few metres from us, a sandpiper was walking on the shore, its feet sinking into the soft sand.

It was looking for sand fleas.

A curlew on the rocks.

The black shadow of an eider.

"And did you find out how the drum ended up on the road?"

"No, I don't know."

He smiled.

He told me that a little girl had gone away with it, following the donkeys, banging on it with the drumsticks, and he had listened to the sound for a long while.

"Max came to help me clear the brambles. He gives flowers to Morgane and to Lili. Does he give you flowers?"

"Me? No . . ."

"Why not?"

"I don't know . . . He's not in love with me."

"He's not in love with Lili, either . . ."

He blew on his cigarette smoke.

"So, the drum, who had taken it?"

"It was Nan," I answered. "She went into your house and stole it."

I just repeated everything Old Mother had told me, using her very words, not adding a thing. He listened to me. Afterwards, he took a final puff on his cigarette and turned to look at Théo's house.

We got up off the rocks and went back on to the road.

"You still haven't been to see him?" I said, because he was looking over in the direction of Théo's house.

"No . . . But I will."

He took a few steps.

"I know he's to blame, even if sometimes I'd like to believe that it was the sea. That the sea alone took them. That would look better, wouldn't it? Whereas that old madman . . ."

He stuffed his hands deep in his pockets. A few days of La Hague had been enough to burnish his face.

"It's like a man who climbs mountains, if the mountain kills him, it's better than if he's victim of a team-mate who lets go of him during a tricky manoeuvre . . ."

"Is that why you haven't been to Théo's? Are you afraid it might involve a tricky manoeuvre?"

He chuckled. He looked at me.

"I went to see Théo, a long time ago. I wanted to talk to him, I wanted to kill him, too. The house is isolated, no-one would have seen me, the perfect murder, it would have looked as if a prowler did it."

"There's no such thing as a perfect murder."

"There is, believe me, and that would have been one."

"You would have been arrested, sent to prison."

"I was still under age."

"Why didn't you do it, then?"

"Because it subsided . . . the anger . . . the terrible anger . . . You need hatred in order to kill, or you need madness . . . You can't understand . . ."

I clenched my fists. Understand what? That one day you wake up and you do not cry any more? How many nights had I spent with my teeth in the pillow – I wanted my tears, pain, I wanted to go on moaning. I liked it better that way. I wanted to die, afterwards, when the pain invaded my body. I had become an absence, a series of sleepless nights, that is what I was, a stomach sick with its own self, I thought I would die from it, but when the pain receded, it was something else I experienced. And it was not any better.

It was the void.

Lambert was still looking over towards Théo's house. Did he feel guilty for being alive? Guilty that he had not gone with them that day? He told me he had come back here by train, a long time ago. Alone. He had wanted to see the sea again, the place where his parents had died.

"The day you came back, did you talk to Théo?"

"I went by his house. He was in the yard. He looked at me. He couldn't know who I was. There was this little boy with him, leading

191

a calf on the end of a rope . . . The calf was no bigger than he was. He came over to me, and Théo called him back. He came to see what I wanted. When I told him who I was, he didn't want to talk to me. He said he had nothing to say to me, that it was an accident. That there were accidents at sea, it was something that happened. And I had heard one of the firemen say it was the lantern. I asked him if that was possible. He wouldn't talk about it. I left again that evening."

"Why would he have done such a thing?"

"I have no idea."

"Do you have any proof?"

He shook his head. He said you had to beware of proof, that if you have a strong hunch about something, it must be for a reason.

We went down to the quay. Max was by his boat. When he saw us, he ran over, caught Lambert's hand and squeezed it very tight. His hand, and then my own.

"We already saw you this morning," I said.

He knew that. He did not care. He dragged us over to his boat. The work was nearly finished. He said, "In a few days . . ." Unable to finish his sentence. Above us, the seagulls were crying, a rustling of wings, clacking of beaks, bird bodies brushing together. It was the tide coming in that made them like that. The birds were waiting for the fishermen to return.

Max was annoyed by all their shrieking.

"Boom!" he said raising his head.

"What do you mean, boom!" asked Lambert.

Max disappeared into the cabin and came back out with a rifle that he loaded as he was walking. He aimed into the flock and fired.

A seagull fell. The others flew away. He came back over to us, calmly, his tall figure swaying, and in his hand, the rifle.

"That's it, boom!" he said.

Lambert and I looked at each other.

"It is deliverance from the infernal," Max said, squinting.

We nodded.

We went to sit on the terrace, a table in the sun, and ordered two glasses of wine.

Lambert had mentioned a child in Théo's yard. A child leading a calf.

Could it be it was the same little boy I had seen in the photograph at Lili's?

If it was, could it be the same Michel that Nan was looking for?

"The little boy leading the calf – what was he like?"

Lambert looked at me, astonished by my question.

"I don't know . . . he was a kid. Why do you ask?"

"You don't remember anything more?"

"I hardly looked at him. I was there for Théo."

"And yet, you remembered him. Because he was leading the calf?"

He thought for a moment. The sun made him wince, like on the day I first saw him, in the wind, during the storm.

"I didn't know that Lili had a little brother, that's what surprised me . . ." he said in the end.

For a long time he did not say anything, then eventually he shuddered, as if he could not change his thoughts.

"And your cliff with the cormorants, I don't suppose you could show it to me instead?"

"Instead of what?"

He got up.

"Instead of nothing."

That was why we went off to the cliffs. We left the car in the car park at Écalgrain and continued on foot. We had decided to go and eat at La Bruyère afterwards.

Lambert was walking quickly, his feet firmly on the ground. Like someone who is used to it.

When we came to the great cliff, we left the footpath and headed through the ferns, narrow passages with brambles on either side. Squat bushes for a few metres, and then the brambles gave way to low grasses singed by the winds. A dizzying drop. The sea far below.

I had often come here, to forget.

We stopped at the very top of the cliff, almost at the edge, two solitudes facing the sea, come again to the origins of the world. The sea ebbed, flowed, trees grew and children were born and died.

Other children replaced them.

And the sea, always there.

A movement that needed no words. Stronger than anything. For months I had been losing myself in this landscape with the slowness of a hibernating animal. I slept. I ate. I walked. I wept. Perhaps that is why my presence here was possible. That it was acceptable. Because of my silence.

"It's here, the cormorants' cliff," I said.

He walked ahead.

I let him go. You had to be alone, the first time, to see it.

He stood there, his arms by his body, facing the wind. Not moving. What was he thinking about? What scores had he come to settle?

I sat down on a rock, a short way back. I would have liked to have had that photograph of the child in the yard, to show it to him. To ask him if he recognized the boy. But Lili had removed the photograph.

Lambert turned round. He looked at me. With my hands I stroked a low wall of stones, the leaves of the ferns, their grainy spores crunching beneath my fingernails. Along these walls you could find a strange squat little plant that is called the bad-weed. Legend says that if you walk on the bad-weed, you will get lost on the moor, and wander for the rest of your days, unable to find your way back.

You were my bad-weed.

"The cormorants' nests are against the cliff," I said, pointing to the spot.

I handed him my binoculars.

The nests were poised on the rocks. As if hanging. Wild goats wandered among the brambles, grazing, their bellies in the ferns.

There were many pairs of cormorants. I had numbered a dozen on this cliff and two more in the rocks a bit further along. Forty-two in all, including the ones I had found in the cove at Les Moulinets. Forty-two was a lot, but there had been more, before.

This cliff was an important breeding site. Fishermen came there with their boats, cast their nets, and the birds got caught in them. We found their bodies, floating.

The waves were breaking just below. The cliff trembled from the shock of them.

"Silence doesn't bother you?"

He asked it without turning round. Because I had not said anything for a while, and because he must have spoken to me.

I shook my head.

I thought back on the first time I had seen him. He had just arrived. Lots of people go through here, some would like to stay, but La Hague spits them back out. Others, La Hague will keep. Years later they are still here, unable to explain why.

Silence is part of the moor.

And I was part of the moor. It had healed my wounds.

Healed me of you.

How many times had I come here to scream, standing on the edge of the cliff? Had Lambert understood the meaning of my silence? He examined me with his gaze, overwhelmed me, forcefully. A brutal contact. I did not move.

It was pounding down there. The sea coming in. Its blows made the cliff vibrate from within. A strange pulsing.

"If you lie with your stomach right against the earth, you will feel the sea pounding."

"You want me to lie down there?"

"I don't want anything."

He smiled. He stretched out. "I can't hear anything."

"It's organic, you ought to be able to hear it."

He did not say anything.

I got up. I went over to the edge of the cliff. The sea was covering the rocks. Stirring up the seaweed. Would I be able to stay here much longer? Morgane wanted to leave.

On one of the rocks, two cormorants were beating their wings in the sun. Their plumage was an oily green, almost black. These two birds had been living as a pair for a few weeks. They did not have any eggs to watch yet; they were fishing together.

I turned round. Lambert was still stretched out on the ground.

"You're seized up, if you're seized up you can't feel it."

"I'm not seized up . . ."

He sat up. An earwig was clinging to the collar of his jacket.

"Apparently male cormorants love their female for life," I said.

He brushed off the soil that had stuck to his knees.

"They don't live as long as men, it's easier for them. Do you spend your time here?"

"Here, and a bit further along."

"And you get paid for it?"

It made me laugh.

"I get paid, and I get a place to live."

He nodded. The earwig was still on his collar. Shepherds had gone mad because of earwigs, the beasts went into their skull while they were sleeping in the shade of a tree.

"Once they're inside, they nibble at your brain, and come out the other side . . ."

"What are you talking about?"

I pointed to the earwig.

"There is a hospital in Cherbourg that is looking after them, very nicely . . . What did you think, that day, when you saw Théo again, in the yard?"

"I thought about hitting him. And then I thought about my mother . . . I thought that she would be sad if I did that, and afterwards, I remembered that my mother was dead."

A black shadow plunged a few feet from us, and slipped beneath the surface of the water, quick and precise. It was a cormorant. Its black body mingled in the grey shimmer of the waves, millions of little incandescent lights. Usually they would stay underwater for a minute. The hardest thing was to find them again when they surfaced.

"You're not listening . . ."

"I am listening . . . You were thinking about your mother, and you remembered that your mother was dead."

I looked at him. His grey eyes had become darker.

He was hurting, somewhere.

As I was hurting.

"We've all had the roof cave in on us . . ." I said. "I have, so have you. We all have. Even cormorants, they —"

"Some roofs are bigger than others."

I looked at him. His high, almost stubborn forehead.

"A roof is a roof."

I snatched at the air. Dogs sweat through their tongue. And cats, how do cats sweat?

I asked him, "Do you have any idea how cats sweat?"

He did not know. Neither did I. One day, I counted the same bird diving over three hundred times in a row. Dives that lasted one minute and thirty seconds.

I told him that. I was tired.

It was getting tense between us. Too complicated.

He looked over at the lighthouse.

"Nothing has changed, the houses are the same, the moor . . . Sons resemble fathers, everything is the same, and yet . . . I would like to hate Théo, and yet I can't any more." —

"Is that what hurts so much?"

No more of this unbearable suffering. The injustice of living when the others have died, the injustice of surviving.

Still surviving. In spite of everything.

In the face of death.

And to find oneself laughing one day.

197

A seagull flew over and the bird's shadow slipped over Lambert's face.

"There was a time when I had to scream . . ."

I looked down.

I had screamed, too.

I turned away from him. When you play Ludo, if you throw a six, you play again, if the dice falls on the ground, you say it is broken and you have to throw again. I have thought about that. And if the dice rolls on the edge of the board, you say it is broken and so there too you have to play again.

In life, you do not get to play again.

Before, I used to recite poetry to myself. I know Aragon by heart, and whole pages of Rilke.

"That night, he put out the light. But I still don't know why."

He was on about it again. As if stuck in his tunnel. Banging against it. I remembered the pipistrelle that came to bang against the walls, and I could not understand why. What torment was it caught up in? And there was the mare that went mad and banged against her walls, too.

I was banging against walls, like her. I was afraid of loving. That is what your death had left me.

"There isn't always a reason why . . ." I said.

"And sometimes reasons are disappointing. I know, that's what I've been told a thousand times . . ."

He took a long puff on his cigarette, the red ash burned down to the filter and went out.

"My father knew the passes, he knew his sailing boat. He liked to sail at night, he wouldn't have taken unnecessary risks, particularly not with Paul on board."

He said that. Not with Paul on board.

He walked a short way along the footpath, his hands in his pockets. He was turning over the memory in his mind. Hunting for the detail. The footpath was narrow. Just here, the ferns vanished, giving way to scrawny little trees with black branches corroded by salt.

"When they left, I stayed on the quay with Lili. We watched them sail out. They were headed for Alderney. Alderney is right there . . . I remember, my mother leaned over, made great gestures with her hat . . . It was a canvas hat with a red ribbon. That's the last image I have of her: her hand and that hat."

He stopped and looked at the sea, its contours drowned in mist, the island of Alderney, so near.

"We spent the day with Lili, in the rocks. Her mother had made us some biscuits."

We took the footpath, and retraced our steps. He was walking ahead of me. Suddenly, he stopped, almost brutally. I do not know why he did that.

I bumped into his back.

"Don't stop like that," I murmured, my hand against his jacket, the chill of the leather beneath my palm.

I breathed in the smell of his jacket, the presence of a man. It was violent. I could have wrapped my arms around him, stayed there pressing against his back, offering him my skin as a possible answer to all his questions.

I was not a possible answer.

I moved away slowly.

I took my hand away from the leather.

I breathed in the air.

He spoke, without turning round. "Do you know why we do that . . . ? Taking deep breaths, the way you just have."

I did not know.

"It's our cells," he said. "They need to recharge their oxygen. We often do it after an emotion."

He turned round. He looked at me. What must I look like at that moment? What face did he see?

He placed his hand on my cheek and I felt like biting him.

*   *   *

Lambert dropped me off on the square. He was waiting for some visitors for his house. The baker had made the most of the sunny day, going round in her van to sell springtime croissants. A way of celebrating the arrival of the fine weather.

She was parked outside the church.

They were very special croissants, with a taste of orange. M. Anselme did not like them, he said the springtime croissants were surely delicious, but they did not have the taste you had the right to expect when you asked for a croissant.

I bought several. I needed sugar. I wanted to take some to Morgane and Raphaël, too. I ate one on my way.

Outside the gate to old Nan's house there was a metal basin full of bits of stale bread, and peelings, and carrot tops. It was for the donkeys. There were a lot of basins like that here and there in the village. When I went by, Nan was at her door. She could have run away, to hide. She had loosened her hair, and she was brushing it in the sun.

I showed her the bag, the croissants. She motioned for me to come in.

The bench where she was sitting was made of a board set on stones.

She looked at the bag.

"These are springtime croissants," I said, opening it to show her.

She put down her brush, and slipped her hand into the bag.

She began to eat, staring at the ground between her feet. When she had finished, she looked up at me and told me that the croissant was very good.

She took another.

I looked over at the Refuge. All the windows were closed. It did not seem so dreary, now that there was sunlight.

"Théo showed me a photograph of you, by the tree, with the children . . ."

She shook her head.

"You were young . . . There was Ursula, too."

She smiled.

I looked at her, and this face crisscrossed with wrinkles was superimposed upon the other face, so infinitely smooth and sweet, that I had seen on the photograph.

The woman Théo had loved.

I looked up.

The little stone Virgin was still there above the door, in the niche in the wall.

"Can we go in?"

Nan took a handkerchief from her pocket, and wiped her hands, for a long time.

"There's nothing left in there, just dead rats and memories."

"I like memories."

I waited, then said, "Théo told me that that photograph had been taken right at the beginning, when you had just opened the Refuge."

"They were barns, before. Stables. My parents kept their animals in there . . . The walls, the rooms, we had to clean everything, empty out the hay loft to make bedrooms."

She rubbed her dress to get rid of the crumbs. Some of them stayed in the folds.

"Do you remember the first child who arrived?"

She nodded.

"I remember all the children . . . The first one, they brought him to me, his mother didn't want him any more . . . five years old he was. I'd never heard a child moan like that. He stayed six months, and then a family adopted him, a couple in Nantes. They came to get him by car . . . He wrote to me every year, at Christmas, he seemed to be doing fine, and then one Christmas I didn't get any more letters, he'd hanged himself."

She took another croissant from the bag. "Why do you want to go in there?"

"To have a look . . ."

"There's nothing to see. It's been closed for twenty years ... At night, there are stone martens running about. It must stink."

"I like smells."

She raised her eyebrows.

"Smells like that ..."

She sat for a while without speaking. I thought I ought to leave. I looked at her. I would have liked her to tell me who Michel was. I did not dare ask. Would she have answered?

Suddenly, she raised her hand and pointed towards the Refuge.

"There's a passage all the way at the back, the last window before the barn. To get in all you have to do is push it open."

She held me by the arm.

"If there are beasts in there, don't go complaining ..."

"I won't complain."

I crossed the courtyard to the place she had told me about. The window was loose. All I had to do was push it. I climbed over the sill. I found myself in a dark empty room. I had to wait for a moment for my eyes to get used to the darkness and I saw that this room led to another.

In the other room there were tables. Nan was right, it stank – pongs of dead rat and dried droppings. I went over to the tables. In the wood there were knife marks. There were lines on the wall, too, clusters of five, crossed through, like in prisons.

Flies had come to die there, under the window, hundreds of them, deprived of light, they must have banged against the shutter and died.

A little light filtered through the openings in the shutters. At the very back of the building, a stone stairway led upstairs. The steps were covered in dust. Pieces of plaster that had come loose from the ceiling littered the floor in places. The stairway came out on to a long dark corridor. There were rooms on either side. The old hay lofts that Nan had talked about. I opened a door. The room was cluttered with iron beds. On one of the beds was a pile of old brown woollen blankets. I went over to the window. Through the gap, I could see the courtyard, the tree, old Nan sitting on her bench. The sea in the distance. The pastures. There had been life, and children, here; only silence remained.

It is said that water remembers. And what about walls?

I went back to the door.

Before going out, I turned my head, and my gaze was drawn by something lighter in the darkness. It was a bed that was still covered in a sheet. The sheet was no longer white but it was light. I had not seen it on coming in. There was a toy there, on the floor, by the bed. I bent down.

It was a little bear on four wheels, with close-cropped fur so worn in places that there was nothing left but the threadbare cloth. The axis of the wheels was rusty. One of the bear's ears had been torn by teeth – a child or a rat? A little bit of horsehair stuffing was leaking out. There was nothing else in the room, only the little beds and this toy. How many children had come, one after the other, through this room, the ones arriving envying those who were leaving? What had become of all of them?

I put the toy back on the bed. I had no right to keep it, and yet I found it hard to leave it there. I picked it up again. I turned it over. The wheels were set in a wooden board. I went back over to the window. The paint was gone. Where there were still traces, it was flaking. Under the board, between the wheels, was a label. The label was glued, partly torn, but legible, I turned the toy to the light. It was the same label as the one glued to the drum: *Pain d'Épice, Toys, passage Jouffroy, Paris.*

I went back by Lambert's place. I wanted to tell him about the little bear. Tell him that I had not taken it, but that it was there, in one of the upstairs rooms. I could not do that, be a thief as well.

I walked through the garden. The key was in the door. I wanted to see the drawings again. All those rainy day drawings that I had gone through so quickly the day we ate the eggs. There was one I wanted to see again.

It was dark inside. I switched on the light. The drawings were still in the box, and the box was at the end of the table. There was also a bowl, and a few books. A jumper over a chair. Lambert had made a fire. There were still some red embers. I placed some wood on the embers, and a sheet of newspaper rolled in a ball. All it took was a match.

The drawing I was looking for was mixed in with the others. A drawing in grey pencil with just a touch of colour, I had seen it that day, hardly noticed, but enough to remember, a little bear mounted on four wheels, his leather bridle coloured red.

I looked, and eventually I found it.

It was the little bear I had seen at the Refuge. It was drawn on a sheet of thickly grained paper. The lines were neat and straight. It was not a child's drawing, it had to have been Lambert's mother. Next to the drawing were a few angry strokes, a sort of incoherent scribbling.

I looked at the table. I tried to imagine the mother and child, close together, the scratching of the pencil, the rubber, the child watching, then trying in turn to make a clumsy drawing, and all the while, on the table before them, standing proudly, the little bear stuffed with horse-hair.

All the way at the bottom of the sheet, like on most of the other drawings, there was a date, 28 August, 1967. They are still together, a mother and her son. They are drawing.

Hardly two months left to live. They do not know it.

Time for a few more drawings. A few more rainy days. I sat for a long time looking at that drawing. This story was touching on my own, causing everything with feeling to vibrate. In the end I put the drawings back in place, the way I had found them, one on top of the other in the box. I looked around. On the table, the ashtray was overflowing with cigarette butts. A forgotten match.

Lambert's jumper on the chair. I picked it up, held it. My face buried in its smell. Looking for another smell, another skin: yours.

*   *   *

The weather had turned almost summery, with mild afternoons where you could stay strolling outside. The horse was better. Max was still working on his boat. He did not seem to be in any hurry to finish it. He went on catching butterflies and putting them in a cage, waiting for the chance to let them all fly out around Morgane. How was he going to choose the day?

Morgane spent her days making her tiaras. She was fed up with it. She was also fed up with being a waitress at the *auberge*.

She had had a fight with Raphaël.

"What sort of desires do you have, then?" she asked, moving over slightly so that I could sit down next to her on the bench.

"My desires . . . I don't know . . . they're not the same every day."

She nodded.

"And today, what are your desires today?"

I thought about you again. It came back to me quite suddenly, desire, the last time. I also remembered the white walls. The nurse's voice, He's feeling better today. Because you had got up. Your hands, placed on the table top. All is well, you murmured. Your expression was calm. I took your hand, and I licked the skin inside, that's all. The nurse saw us, she smiled.

I would have made love to your dead body when they took it away.

"Your bloke, before, why didn't it work out?"

"It's not that it didn't work out."

"What happened, then?"

"Nothing . . . It's just a story."

"Give me the title. The title, that's not the story."

"Later . . ."

"I don't want it later. Look at this, black lace from Chanterelle . . ."

She showed me the dark trim on the underwear she had under her skirt.

Raphaël came to join us. He sat with his back against the wall. In his blue pea jacket he looked like a gypsy. He was staring at Morgane. I do not know why they had argued.

She had been on edge for some time.

"Stop doing that!"

"Doing what?"

"Your skirt, when Max is around! I've already told you dozens of times."

Morgane shrugged.

The sun was still shining, but above the sea the sky was black. A few broad swathes, getting ready. There was no wind, only a tension in the air. The clouds passed in front of the sun. Morgane moaned. Raphaël went back inside the house.

We sat on a bit longer.

"Was he a good fuck, the bloke you stayed with for three years?"

"He was, yes."

She nodded. I turned away.

"What's good, for you?" she asked.

I could not answer.

I went back up to my room. I looked outside.

Between the clouds, in the places where they had been torn: that stretch of sky and light – some people say you should never look there, for fear of seeing the Virgin's face. They say there are women who saw her face and became wanderers. Doomed to go as far as the swamps, and they never came back. Raphaël had sculpted them.

With the storm, the power went out. Raphaël was working by the light of candelabras, an entire box of thick candles he had found in one of the rooms on the first floor.

The candle flames lit up the walls, the earthen statues. I saw him through the crack. I could also see my reflection in the mirror.

I avoided my eyes.

I went down to see Raphaël. The studio door was open. A little clay tightrope walker stood proudly on the wooden steps.

He was working on another one that was placed on a base, covered with a damp cloth.

I liked to watch him working. His damp fingers in the clay.

"Have you been crying?" he asked.

"No."

"What's that, then, if it's not tears?"

"It's raindrops, Raphaël, all the rain on the window panes . . . or perhaps it's the candles . . . the smoke hurts my eyes."

He wiped his hands on a rag. He picked up his jacket and rummaged in his pockets. He pulled out a little tin box. Inside, there were black pastilles, they looked like coffee beans. He handed me one.

"Here, take this."

"What is it?"

"Temesta."

"I know Temesta, this isn't Temesta."

"Just pretend that it is. Or Valium. You want to pretend it's some Valium?"

He slipped the pastille into my mouth. It was hard. His fingers were dry.

Outside, night had fallen. In the silence which followed, I heard a ship's horn.

"Don't bite it," he said, putting the box back in his pocket.

"What happens if I bite it?"

"Don't bite it," he repeated.

On contact with my saliva, the pastille went soft. It gave off a strong smell of sap. Prévert used to swallow pellets of hash, and he would drink a cup of coffee on top of it. Very strong coffee. He would let a little while go by, then he would take another half a pellet with half a cup of coffee as well. M. Anselme told me all that.

"Your dead people . . ." I said.

"What dead people?"

"Those ones!"

I pointed to his sculptures.

"They're not dead people," he said.

"That man nailed to his wooden post, he frightens me."

"He's an Ephemera."

He picked up the tools that were lying about on the floor.

"Where is Lambert?"

"I don't know . . ."

He turned to me.

"He's a decent bloke," he said.

"I don't want to carry anything any more," I eventually said.

"Who's talking about carrying anything?"

"The minute you love someone, you carry them."

"What rubbish! When you love, you love!"

"Rilke said that . . ."

"Who gives a toss what Rilke said!"

Morgane came in.

"No more television!" she said.

She saw us.

"Am I disturbing you?"

Because we were next to each other. She smiled sweetly.

She was wearing a striped jumper that she had knitted during the winter with plastic needles. The jumper was very big. She wore it with yellow stockings. She collapsed in the armchair. Her legs tucked underneath her. She leaned over her stockings to scratch at the dirt that had stuck to her ankle. Her red nails in the mesh.

She looked up at me.

"You and Lambert were together at the cliffs . . . I saw you. Did he tell you what he's doing here?"

"He's selling his house."

She went on scratching the dirt in the mesh.

"Well he's not just a bloke selling his house," she said, spitting on her stocking. "That's not all of it."

Raphaël came over to the table. He removed the damp cloth that was protecting the little clay sculpture.

"Rilke said a funny thing about that . . ."

"Who is this Rilke?" she asked.

Raphaël chuckled.

Morgane turned to me.

"Will you tell me?"

"He's a poet, he wrote very beautiful things about life, desire, love . . ."

"What sort of beautiful things?"

"Things . . . He also said it's impossible to live under the weight of another life."

Morgane adjusted her stocking.

"Well, you'll get nowhere if you start off like that!"

Before going to sleep, I replayed all our nights, all of them, again and again.

*　　　*　　　*

By early morning, the donkeys had gathered in the meadow along the little path that leads to La Roche. In the near darkness, they were like shadows. The horse was with them, not among them but in the same meadow.

A faint wind brought odours of earth and moss. The little village streets were deserted. It was low tide. I had left the lamp on in my room.

In the darkness, I could see the yellow cut-out of light.

The Audi came down the village road. It slowed. It went by me and stopped a few metres further along.

The window was rolled down.

"Want to get in?"

Drops of dew shone on the roof. I put my hand there, it left a mark. My five fingers in the moisture.

I got in.

Lambert was staring at the road, at the darkness on the other side of the windscreen. He did not look at me.

He stank of alcohol.

"Did you come to my place?"

"Yes. I wanted to see the drawings . . . I didn't touch anything."

He switched off the engine.

"The drawings . . ."

He laughed. "In that case . . ."

"I found another toy at Nan's, with the same label as the one that is on the drum . . . A little bear on wheels . . . I found the drawing."

He laughed again.

"You're having fun! And what does that prove?"

He was right, it did not prove a thing, except that Nan had gone into his house to take the toys, and that Lili's mother was not so crazy.

He leaned back against the headrest.

"You know what I did, while you were playing with your cuddly toys? I went to see the old man."

He pointed, in the darkness, towards the place on the hill where Théo's house was.

"He greeted me with a gun. He didn't want me to come in."

"The whisky, was that before or after?"

He chuckled.

"After."

He was staring at the place on the hill.

"I shook him a little bit . . . Not hard, but he went on insisting he hadn't put out that bloody light!"

"Shook him in what way?"

"Not as hard as I would have liked to, when I left he was still on his feet."

"And what if he was telling the truth?"

"The truth! He stinks of lies when he talks about that night . . . He oozes them. It's a smell I recognize."

"The smell of lies?"

He turned to me, and gave a nasty laugh.

"I used to be a policeman."

He rammed his head back against the headrest.

"I know, it always has this effect . . . I should say anything but, undertaker, tax collector! Even a killer on the run would sound better."

He leaned towards me. His face a few centimetres from mine.

He pulled me towards him, immobilized my head, my face between his hands, like a vice. He made me look at him.

Just look at him.

And then he opened the car door, on the passenger side.

* * *

I went up to see Théo. There had been a catfight in the yard. When I got there, they were still growling. I saw yellow eyes, defiant in the dark.

It was late. This was not my usual time.

"I was going by . . ." I said.

Théo looked at his watch.

"You were going by . . ."

He switched off the television.

"Today is my day for visits."

He walked over to the window. The two tomcats who had been fighting were there. One of them was a squat grey animal. The other one, who seemed wilder, had a bit of his ear torn off. The female they had been fighting over was lying stretched out on top of the wardrobe. Indifferent.

Théo turned away. "Was he worried?"

"Yes, a bit."

He opened a bottle of wine that was on the table. He filled his glass. He put his hands around the glass and looked at the wine inside.

"He says you put out the light on the night of the wreck."

"I know what he says!"

He grumbled, a string of inaudible words. A bare bulb hung from the ceiling. Connected to a wire, it lit the table but showed nothing of his face. There was dust around the wire and on the glass of the bulb.

"You're on his side . . ."

"I'm not on anyone's side . . ."

He rubbed his face, several times, with his hands.

"He just turned up here, mad as a hatter . . . started asking me the same questions, all the time! What does he expect me to say? The lamp was lit, that's what I told him, the truth. He grabbed me by the collar . . ."

"He says you aimed your rifle at him."

"A man's got to defend himself . . ."

The rifle was there, in the corner, propped between the wall and the buffet.

Théo's hands were in the light, joined together.

"What happened to him is a great misfortune, but there have been other misfortunes . . . What more do you want me to tell him? It's never a good thing to stir up the past."

A yellow cat came to miaow outside the window. It was a cat with strange eyes. Théo got up, opened the window, and the cat jumped inside.

Théo remained standing.

"Those nights in the lighthouse, no-one can understand . . . I remember one young lad they sent out there with me. He hadn't asked to come, it's just someone was needed and it landed on him . . . He was a little fellow, he was afraid of the sea. For days he stayed crouching like an animal between the bed and the wall. Not even on the bed . . . All scrunched up on the floor, with the sweat freezing his back . . . Pale as death. He was just a kid. I thought he'd get over his fear. I took his watches. I didn't sleep. Neither did he. When I saw that the fear wasn't leaving, I told them ashore. They didn't come and get him. The kid threw himself into the sea on Christmas Day, when I wasn't watching."

His hands closed over each other. The darker gnarls of his veins. Their shadow on the expanse of the table.

"There are lots of stories about lighthouses, stories about men ... I could tell them to you. Two mates who died because of a gale that went on too long, they died of hunger. They'd boiled the soles of their shoes trying to survive until the others came out to relieve them ... Only they never came."

The little white cat rubbed against him. She jumped up on his lap.

"Right after the war, there was one bloke, he'd got the gas at Verdun, he only had a scrap of lung left. What was missing, he'd already spat out up there in the trenches ... The rest, he finally coughed it away out there, with all those steps to climb."

That evening, for the first time, he talked to me about the lighthouse, that secret, unimaginable life. He told me about the women who got themselves taken out with the supplies, and the fishermen would fetch them in the morning.

He smiled.

It was already late at night, and he was still talking.

Had Nan ever gone out there to join him? Their love, far from anyone, in the middle of the sea.

He said he had had a cat out there. But there are always cats in lighthouses. He remembered the first female, very well. She had had a litter, five kittens. In the bed, they looked like rats.

At the end, when he walked with me to the door, he said, "Your Lambert needs someone to blame, so he won't give up. The best thing would be for him to go away from here."

*   *   *

It was late when I got back to La Griffue.

I was tired.

I had been cold on the walk back, even walking quickly, my arms folded. I sat for a moment on the floor with my back to the radiator. My knees up against me. My arms around them. I felt the heat penetrating the weave of my jumper.

I closed my eyes.

One day, you said to me, You're going to have to forget me . . . and you made love to me with your voice. No, first of all you made love to me with your voice and afterwards you said, You're going to have to forget me. You have to start now, while I'm still alive, that's what else you said.

That it would be easier, afterwards.

I found myself outside.

You were inside. Behind your walls. I screamed. In my bedroom, that night, I bit my hand so hard it bled, I wanted to stifle the cry. Another night. A night without you.

I slept there, rolled in a ball against the radiator, my hands over my belly. I woke up early.

It was raining.

I worked on my plates, my drawings of pipistrelles, scoters, the watercolour of the big owl I had started more than ten times.

I worked doggedly. The format of the sheets, always the same. I drank litres of coffee. At noon, Morgane came and knocked on the door. I did not answer. I did not want to see anyone. That's what I shouted. She didn't persist.

She went back downstairs.

I heard her talking to Raphaël, later, about me.

*   *   *

At the end of the day, I went out. I went back up to Lili's. It was not raining any more but it was too late to go to the cliffs. I was still cold. I needed to see some faces. To hear some voices.

Lambert was there, sitting with M. Anselme. And Morgane. When she saw me, she looked away. There were some men at the bar, a few fishermen.

I took off my jacket.

I sat at their table.

M. Anselme was asking Lambert whether he knew how to suppose. I knew what this was. An absurd tirade from Prévert's "Adventures of the Stool".

I put my jacket on the back of the chair. M. Anselme took my hand and kissed my fingertips. He looked at my face, his forehead worried. Yet I had put on some make-up, a little bit of sand-coloured powder and some gloss on my lips.

He turned again to Lambert.

"You still haven't answered me, do you know how to suppose?"

"Yes, no . . . maybe . . ."

I struck a match. I held it between my fingers, as long as I could, until the flame licked my skin. I blew it out.

"Tell him you know how to suppose, he will go on all by himself . . ."

Lambert looked puzzled.

"Yes, I know how to suppose . . ."

That was all that M. Anselme wanted. He rubbed his hands, pleased.

Their voices came to me from a distance.

I listened to them and went on burning my matches.

"Well, suppose I'm in the street instead of being here, and follow my reasoning. Do you follow?"

"I follow."

"So I'm in the street, sitting on a bench, a woman walks by, I get up and I follow her. Are you still following me?"

"Yes."

"Good! Now. In French, we would say, rather, Prévert did say, *Je suis donc un homme qui suit une femme. Si je suis une femme, je ne suis pas un homme, puisque c'est une femme que je suis.*"

It made me smile, I knew it by heart. Ever since I had known M. Anselme. I struck another match.

Lambert turned to me.

"Is this Prévert again?" he said.

"It is."

I looked at him.

"You were a policeman before, but you aren't any more?"

"No."

"Why?"

"Why was I a policeman before, or why am I not one any more?"

"Both."

"I did it for thirty years. I learned to run fast. And to make people confess. And then one morning, I'd had enough . . . but I was good."

He looked at me, his smile faintly mocking.

"You don't like the fact I was a policeman, do you?"

"I didn't say that."

"You didn't say it, but you don't like it."

He leaned over. I remembered his hands holding my face in a vice-like grip.

"The only one I didn't manage to get a confession out of is old Théo . . . but I haven't said I was giving up. Why are you looking at me like that?"

"When you force someone to confess, it's not always a confession."

He nodded.

M. Anselme was talking about a drive he went on with Prévert.

"One day, we went to get carrot tops at the covered market at Cherbourg. For his guinea pig . . . All four of us, Prévert, Trauner, my father and I. It was winter. There was snow . . ."

"Isn't that rather far to go, Cherbourg, for a few carrot tops?" Morgane said, looking up from her crossword puzzle.

M. Anselme smiled.

Lambert turned to me.

"I've been thinking about your business with the cormorants," he said in a low voice. "The fact that there are fewer than before . . . The reprocessing plant isn't very far from here, is it? Could there be a connection?"

"There could be, yes, but there have been measures. There are fewer emissions."

"If there are fewer emissions, there should be more birds?"

I sipped my chocolate.

M. Anselme glanced at the clock. It was his time. He got up. He left three euros on the table. Three euros for the coffee, that's the way it was. At that rate, it's more expensive than Paris, Lili would say.

He put his coat on over his jacket.

Morgane went over to the pinball machine and we were alone.

"Are you feeling better?" I said, referring to the alcohol he had put away the night before.

Purple shadows under his eyes.

He shook his head.

"No. Did you go to see him?"

"Yes."

"And?"

"And, nothing . . . He's fine."

"What did he tell you?"

"What do you want him to tell me? The same thing he told you, nothing more."

"And you believed him?"

"I don't know . . ."

I looked up at him. He was looking at me, too. I thought about the man that Nan was looking for. I don't know what it was that intrigued me about that story. It was an obsession, the way I went after it.

Lili had removed the photograph, as if she were afraid of something.

"The child who was leading the calf . . . you said that Théo had called out to him. You don't remember his name?"

He looked at me, flabbergasted.

"That was forty years ago!"

"Yes, of course . . . but there used to be a photograph there, behind you, where that light spot is."

He turned round.

"You could see Lili with her parents, and a little boy. His name was Michel, he was a child from the Refuge. I think he is the one that Nan is waiting for."

"So?"

"So, nothing . . ."

"Could it be their child, Nan and Théo's?"

I shook my head. "Nan doesn't have a child."

He listened to me. Without laughing. Without even smiling. I talked to him about the letters.

"Envelopes addressed with a pen, lots of them . . . They were all handwritten by someone whose name is Michel Lepage."

He put his head in his hands.

"What exactly are you getting at?"

I looked deep into his eyes.

"I think that the child in the photograph and the one you saw are the same child. I also think that Théo knows where to find the man that Nan is looking for. They've been writing to each other for more than twenty years."

*   *   *

The female cat that the two tomcats had been fighting over died. Théo found her, stiff, in the ditch just below his house. When I got there, he was standing over her. Her flank was hollow, already gutted by death. A little patch of pink tongue emerged from between her teeth.

Théo lifted her up.

"Poison! That's what some people do."

Her mouth was open. A bit of drool there, transformed into a yellow crust at the corner of her mouth. One eye staring at a spot in the courtyard.

Théo took the animal behind the house, to the end of the pasture, where he had buried all the other cats. A shady spot beneath tall trees. A place of moss and ferns.

The two males followed him. They were walking side by side, almost touching.

I followed them. Théo put the cat down in the grass and rolled up his sleeves.

"I've buried a few, in my time . . ."

He dug. Under the grass the earth was dark, almost black. Crumbly. A moist earth.

The two toms sat next to each other, very straight, at an equal distance from the female. They followed the movement of the pickaxe with their eyes, the little pile of earth that grew by the old man's feet.

When the hole was deep enough, Théo looked at them. He said a few words in a rough patois, picked up the female, and threw her into the hole. He filled the hole with earth. A little mound that he flattened with the pickaxe. The entire time, the tomcats did not move. They stayed next to the hole.

Théo and I went back to the house. To the kitchen. He stuffed the wood stove with the logs that were next to it. His movements were slow.

A pad of letter paper lay open on the table, with a pen on it. The page was partly covered in a fine script.

Next to it was a letter Théo was answering. The letter was open, the envelope beside it.

Théo came back to the table. He shoved the letter to the end of the table and we talked about the cats.

We drank some wine.

I asked him if he remembered someone called Tom Thumb. "A friend of Max's, they were at school together."

He shook his head. He said he did not remember.

He was lying.

We talked about other things.

When I went back out, the two cats were still beside the hole. They did not turn their heads, even when Théo called to them, showing them their bowls.

*　　*　　*

219

Monsieur Anselme was listening to me, his elbows on the table, his head between his hands.

"And then what did you do?"

"I went to the cliffs."

He smiled at me.

"God must be surprised to find you there so often."

He leaned over, parted the curtain, and looked outside. A clear sky, without a cloud, he said it would be a good day to go to the coast-guard station. That's what he said, "Why don't we go to see Prévert's tree? It's such a special tree! Jacques liked it very much. He would be pleased to know that someone still visits it."

I agreed.

We went out. He took my arm.

By the path, three little girls were inventing a circle game. They had put their dolls in the middle of the circle. They went round and round, quick little steps, first one way, then the other.

We stopped to look at them.

"Prévert liked children very much. Personally, I find them a bit too noisy."

The little girls continued to go round.

Turn, turn, little girls
Turn around the factories
Soon you'll be inside
To live unhappily ever after
And have lots of children.

It was a poem by Prévert.

We crossed the road.

Lambert's shutters were open. The Audi was parked a bit farther along. M. Anselme followed my gaze.

"He's a strange one, that Lambert, isn't he? He was supposed to leave, and he isn't leaving. Lili refuses to talk about him. What do you think of him?"

"I hardly know him . . ."

He squeezed my arm.

"That's very good. It's never a good thing to get to know someone too well."

We went on walking.

"My neighbour in Omonville, who is well acquainted with the notary in Beaumont, said that he's asking a very tidy sum for his house. Incidentally, you can understand, the dwelling is a few steps from the sea, and even if the roof needs repairing, people from Paris are prepared to pay anything for that sort of place. What does he do in life?"

"I have no idea."

M. Anselme stopped.

He looked at me, hesitated for a moment, then went on walking.

"You were seen going about with him, and I heard you were at the cliffs together. Does he make you laugh, at least?"

He thrust the tip of his cane far ahead of him.

"Because a man who cannot make a woman laugh . . . and your game of Ludo, how did it end? Did he let you win?"

"We didn't finish the game."

He thought about what I had just said.

"There are times, you see, when I find it infinitely difficult to grasp the discrepancy in sensitivity between our two generations."

We turned off to the right, the road leading to the coastguard station. There were no more houses, only pastures. A few cows were enjoying the sun, their heads turned towards the sea. You could feel the breeze growing stronger the closer you got to the sea.

"The man is boring and yet you find him attractive . . ."

"I didn't say that."

He squeezed my arm.

"No, indeed, you did not say it, but the fact remains."

When we got to the coastguard station, we took a little dirt footpath that went along the coast.

"Incidentally, don't blame yourself, where attraction is concerned, we don't choose. Look! Here we are! This tree is Prévert's tree."

He pointed to a sad little tree, so scraggy that it did not seem to have a trunk.

M. Anselme was proud.

"Well, what do you think? Isn't it lovely?"

I walked up to the tree. It had been bent over by the wind. The leaves on the windward side seemed to have been sacrificed so that the others could live, the leaves clinging painfully to the branches on the leeward side.

"You're right," I murmured, "where attraction is concerned, we don't choose."

He took me by the hand and made me touch the trunk. The tree was skeletal. He pointed to the leaves, the buds.

He placed his hands firmly against the bark.

"Trees die, others grow, some stay as they are."

He listened to the tree's heartbeat.

We eventually sat down on a rock, our backs to the tree. We were in the sun, with the sea before us. A lizard was warming itself on a stone. Right next to it, a little blue butterfly was gathering nectar in a cluster of flowers. Its dark proboscis sank into the petals like a blade. The lizard looked at it. The flowers were a very pale yellow.

M. Anselme looked first at the lizard and then the butterfly.

"I had dinner recently at the home of Ursula Dimetri . . . She is a very dear old friend who lives in a charming house on the hills after the cove at Saint-Martin."

"Is she the one who used to cook at the Refuge?"

"Do you know her?"

"I saw a photograph of her at Théo's place."

He nodded.

"One thing leading to another, you know what conversations are like, we began to talk about you. Ursula said she had seen you in the yard, at Nan's, near the bench . . ."

He breathed in the sea air, several times, deeply.

"Although Nan is not her real name . . . She's called Florelle, but you must know that, too . . . No matter. So, we were talking in a friendly way when, one thing leading to another, we began to talk about that old person as well."

The lizard had gone closer to the butterfly. Moving very slowly, it raised one leg and then the other, its colour mingling with that of the rock. It kept its eyes fixed on its prey.

What happened next was predictable.

I did not take my eyes from the butterfly.

M. Anselme sighed. "All it would take would be a gesture on our part . . . a simple movement . . . for that poor butterfly to fly away, and its life would be saved."

He picked a little flower from among the ones that grew at the foot of the tree.

Nature has no qualms about things, that is a major difference between us and nature. That was what I was thinking. M. Anselme twirled the flower in his fingers.

"Man does things and often, afterwards, he regrets them. This flower for example, I shouldn't have picked it . . . There are no pots or vases for flowers this size . . . and even with a vase, one shouldn't put a flower all by itself."

He looked at the flower. In the next instant, the lizard pounced. Its mouth wide open, it caught the butterfly and chewed it. The blue wings outside its mouth, still fluttering.

We watched the lizard until it had swallowed everything.

"You were talking to me about Nan . . ."

"Nan, yes, indeed . . ."

He put the flower on the spot where, a moment earlier, the butterfly had been.

"I have been told . . . but this may be mere gossip . . . Well, in any event, there is always a grain of truth in the stories that people tell you."

He was looking at the palms of his hands, as if he would find there the best way to tell me what it was he had to tell me.

"The orphanage in Cherbourg sent children to Nan, and she would look after them for varying lengths of time, orphans or a few children whose parents didn't want them any more . . . Did you know that?"

"Yes, I knew."

"Then you must also know that these children stayed at the Refuge the time it took to find them a family, which could mean several weeks to several months."

He crushed a bit of earth between his fingers. It was a loamy, white earth, impregnated with salt.

"What were you doing that day, on the bench, with her?"

His question surprised me.

"I was just passing by . . ."

"You took her croissants?"

"I had them with me . . ."

He smiled.

"Springtime croissants! And what did you want her to tell you, that you were giving her such a treat?"

I didn't like his question, what he was insinuating. I stood up, abruptly, but he held on to my hand.

"Such impatience! You can't bear the slightest remark. Utterly typical of solitaries, you want to be careful, it can also be a failing."

He kept my hand in his, obliging me to sit down again.

"Look at that lizard, rather . . ."

On the rock, the creature went on chewing, staring into space. A little bit of blue wing was still stuck between its jaws.

Do lizards digest butterfly wings? Maybe they spit them back out? This one seemed to want to swallow them.

I wondered if there was blood in butterfly wings.

M. Anselme waited for me to sit down before going on.

"Ursula said that Nan keeps photographs in her house of all the children she took in at the Refuge. Every afternoon, weather permitting, she would walk on the beach with some of those poor wretches clinging to her dress . . ."

I forgot my anger.

I listened to him.

He let go of my hand, he knew I would not leave now. As long as he was talking.

"Ursula told me that one day, a new boarder arrived, a skinny little thing like half a bird. They had found him in Rouen, in a place that, according to her, had been used as a mass grave during the great plague epidemics. His mother had gone to give birth there, on the ground, and she had abandoned him. He was three years old when he came to the Refuge. He was too small, and not very nice looking, and nobody wanted him. Ursula said that Nan got more attached to him than to the others. She also said that the child used to run away, but they always found him in the same spot, all alone, sitting on a rock by the sea. When they asked him what he was thinking, he said that he didn't know."

M. Anselme talked for a while longer about this child with his gentle nature, who always came back without putting up any resistance.

And yet he would leave again.

The tide was coming in. Below us, the waves were lapping at the shore.

"The most astonishing thing in this story is that Nan adopted the child."

I turned to look at him.

"Nan has a child?"

"As I explained. She sent him to school, first here then afterwards in Cherbourg. According to Ursula, he was a very good student."

"But . . . where is he?"

"I asked Ursula the same question, and she replied that she didn't know."

With the sea rising, the wind grew colder. A damp breeze came to sweep over the coastline, from east to west. M. Anselme glanced at his watch. He adjusted his scarf and stood up.

I followed him.

"What happened to the child?"

"He grew up, and one day, he left, and no-one knew why. He was seen for the last time on the road beyond Beaumont, with a suitcase in his hand. No-one knows where he went. He was seventeen."

"He left just like that?"

"Yes."

"Did he know that Nan was not his real mother?"

"Of course he knew."

He rubbed his trousers, and straightened the folds of his jacket. I could not understand. Why do we always cause so much hurt to those who love us the most?

M. Anselme bent over to wipe off the sand clinging to his shoes. When he stood up, he looked at me and said, "His name was Michel." He said it the way you end a conversation. In a quiet tone of voice, almost playfully. Michel . . .

He waited for me a few yards or so further along the path.

"What's the matter? You look quite strange."

"At the café, there was a photograph of that child you just told me about. He was at the farm."

M. Anselme nodded.

"Nan's child at Théo's place – nothing terribly surprising about that. After all, the Refuge and the farm are not very far apart . . . And besides, children are always drawn to animals, and orphans probably a bit more than the others. Let's go back now, if you don't mind, the weather is deteriorating."

I walked next to him.

"The boy left, and you say he never came back?"

"I didn't say it, it was Ursula. She also said that the Refuge closed a few months after the boy left. Apparently, Nan changed a great deal, from being a lively, cheerful woman, she became . . . the woman we know."

The wind was biting, now. We hurried our steps.

All along the path, we talked about the child, inventing a thousand different fates for him. His mother had abandoned him in rags still full of blood. Had he left to go and look for her?

When we came to the first houses, M. Anselme took me by the arm.

"And by the way, that day when you shared your croissants with Nan, you went into the Refuge. What did you think you might find there?"

"Nothing . . . There's something about closed buildings. I like to visit the inside."

He cocked his head to one side.

"Is that so . . ."

*   *   *

I found Max on the deck of his boat. He was feeding the butterflies, pushing flowers coated in honey through the bars of the cage. The butterflies were dying one by one. It made him sad. He captured others. That way, he had always twenty or so in the cage.

During the night the donkeys had come to wander round the yard, they had left their hoof prints outside the door. They had drunk from the buckets, eaten some hard bread and the gruel that Morgane had put out for the horse.

Lambert was sitting in the sun, his back against the breakwater. I was not surprised to see him there. His house had still not sold. He did not seem to be in a hurry to leave. I knew you could stay like that for a long time, with your gaze on the sea, not noticing anyone. Not speaking. Not even thinking. When that had happened, the sea poured something into you that made you stronger. As if it were making you a part of it. Many people who experienced this did not leave again.

I did not know whether Lambert was going to leave.

I did not know whether I wanted him to stay.

I left him there. For two weeks I had been watching three cormorant eggs: the parents took turns sitting on them. They were going to hatch, it was a matter of hours. Two days at the most. Sometimes the hatchlings were not quick enough to break their shell and they died inside. I had already seen this, on rare occasions, a ruthless law, and yet the parents seemed to remain indifferent.

When I got there, the male was fishing in the rocks. The female was on the nest. I waited.

I saw a few gannets fly overhead, on their way from Alderney.

The employees from the Centre ornithologique had parked their four-wheel drive by the side of the road. I knew they would be there. They came to take samples from the nests. One of them abseiled down the cliff face. He took two nests and three eggs. You could hear the birds' cries, the sharp clackings of their beaks echoing against the cliff.

A lot of the eggs were dying and no-one understood why. At the Centre they said there were parasites inside. They wanted to check the level of radiation. Last year's samples had not yielded any results.

"Hikers go through here," I said.

"There are fences."

"That doesn't stop them."

I had a reputation for being taciturn. At the Centre they did not mind, they said I did a good job, and I was not being paid to make speeches.

The director took note of the problem with the hikers in his notebook. He said he would send a guard for the summer season.

"How's Théo doing?"

"Alright . . ."

"Still have all his cats?"

"Still does."

The wind was veering, bringing clouds. Rain was forecast for evening, but it would be here sooner. With the wind, it would be here in less than an hour.

"Need a lift?" he said, pointing to the sky.

Above the sea was the entire range of greys, to the darkest mass of the storm gathering out to sea.

I thought about the eggs. The shells were cracked. The birds might be born in this rain.

We climbed into the car. The first drops splattered against the windscreen. The director drove with one hand. He liked me. He was always patient with me. He told me they were looking for someone in Caen who could work on the data. He explained the job, his eyes on the road all the while. It was a steady job, and interesting.

"You can't stay here for ever . . ."

He looked at me.

He was not wearing a wedding ring, but there was the trace of a white mark across the suntan.

Lambert did not have a wedding ring, either.

He had no trace.

A first thunderclap broke above the sea. A red light rolled over the crest of the waves.

"If the issue is housing, there's a studio free in the Caen Centre."

"I like it better here."

He shrugged.

"As you please."

We came to the first houses. He turned to me again.

"A team will be coming by boat in the next few days. They'll count the nests, from the sea. After that they'll adjust the figures together with yours."

Another raindrop, and another. The windscreen wipers began to thump.

"Where shall I drop you?"

"At the bottom."

He did not say anything more until we reached La Griffue. He did not switch off the engine, but he took a notebook out of his pocket and wrote down his phone number. He tore out the page.

"Call me whenever you feel like it."

He smiled.

"If you change your mind about Caen . . ,"

"I won't."

He nodded.

"You never know . . ."

Five minutes later, I pushed the door open. It was pouring.

The walls of my room were moving, it was like the pitching movement in Venice or on the deck of an unseaworthy ship. It came and went.

"It's seasickness," Raphaël said, when he saw me come back down.

He laughed.

He reached into his cupboard and took out an old wooden pipe that he stuffed with grass. He struck a match. The grass flared. It burned for a moment and then the flame went out. The wisps curled in the bowl.

He pointed to the sofa. I lay down and stretched out. There were bread crumbs on the blanket. A remnant of a biscuit in its wrapping.

"Have a draw, you'll feel better."

The bowl was warm. There was a smell of burned vanilla.

"I might be going to Caen," I said.

He made a gesture with his chin.

"Smoke, we'll talk afterwards."

I inhaled one puff, then another. I was not used to this tobacco. It made me cough. Raphaël put his matches back in his pocket.

"What would you do in Caen?"

"I'd work. There's this guy, I think he's in love with me. Maybe I could love him . . ."

He raised his eyebrows, sceptical.

"For a day or two . . . and then what?"

"After that, I don't know."

The room was still pitching.

I looked at him. His fingers were dry, whitened by the clay. The halogen lamp projected our shadows on to the wall.

"You worked all night long . . . I heard you, you were walking."

"I can't sleep, so I may as well work."

"Why can't you sleep?"

"Can you sleep?"

I closed my eyes.

He left me alone for a moment, and then he came and sat down next to me.

"What are you thinking about?" he said.

"I had a house, before, where I was born . . . A house in a real village . . ."

"And what happened to your house?"

"Nothing . . . Every autumn, they organize a car race on the hill. It makes a hell of a noise. They are also destroying the old walls, and building zones, and they say it's for business . . ."

Raphaël nodded.

"Good taste is not something you can decide to have."

I smiled.

He placed a finger on my lips.

"Be quiet now."

He could have run his hand over my belly if he had wanted, I would not have struggled.

"I wouldn't have struggled, you know."

"Why are you saying that?"

"No reason . . ."

I was not a woman any more. Nor was I a mother. I could not remember having been a girl. Still less a sister. Unable to be a spouse. Unable to belong. To depend on a man or an affair. There were men who had loved me. I had always loved the ones who did not love me.

Until you.

"I love you, Raphaël . . ."

"I love you too, Princess . . ."

"But you and I will never sleep together?"

He looked at me, amused.

"Never, Princess."

I took another puff. He put some music on. After a while, it felt like it was snowing in my head. It was snowing and the sun was shining through the snowflakes. One sun per snowflake. I had not seen snow in a long time. I liked it.

"From the top of the Nez de Voidries, on a clear day you can see the Channel Islands . . ."

"Be quiet . . ."

He took a blanket from the cupboard and came to spread it over me.

The suns of snow went on shining behind my eyelids.

"When the snow falls, it will be beautiful . . ." I heard myself murmur.

*   *   *

Lili said the donkeys would stay all summer, then one day they would leave again. Without warning.

Just like birds, then, the donkeys.

Just like the child that Nan had loved and who had gone away.

There was a full moon. I could not sleep. I went out. The sea was as bright as in the middle of the day. I walked along the beach.

I was bleeding. For some time, I had not bled. For months. And now I was bleeding. Oddly, this blood flowing out of me was soothing. I went to sit on a rock and watched the blood drip on to the sand. Seeping.

This blood coming back, it meant forgetting you, I was not sure it was something I wanted.

Your face, your smell, everything had gone inside me, from your skin to my pores. When I sweat, it is still your sweat. When I cry. And when I desire?

I got undressed and slipped into the water. In the darkness, the sea was black. The moon, glinting on the water. A cold water.

Nobody knew that I was there.

That anyone was there.

Even the ships passing with all their lights. I swam. A wave of salt water came into my mouth. I spat it out. I could have swallowed it. And kept swallowing until I joined you. They would not have found me. Or only after a very long time, my body unrecognizable, a handful of bones. Some clothes.

The silence at La Griffue. For several days now, I could not even get the radio.

*   *   *

The female had been dead for days, and the two tomcats stayed by the hole. Théo said they slept there, and neither was willing to give up his place to the other.

He called them. He took them food so that they would not die.

He put the plate down between them and the female. The cats would not touch the food. They would not even sniff it. For days.

"They are even fighting over their time of mourning."

"You should go and get them . . ."

"It would serve no purpose."

"We could shut them in?" I said. "For a while . . . separate them. In Venice, they shut the cats in the cellars so that they'll kill the rats."

Théo turned away.

"We're not in Venice here . . ."

He walked towards the house. He went round the growling cats' bowls. His leg was trembling. It had been like that since his fall, his body more fragile.

"I brought you some bread, milk and ham. Some soup, too. Lili says you have to heat it up on the gas."

He held on to the iron railing and went up the steps. He stopped on the landing to catch his breath and look at the sky.

Night was falling, long before it was time.

He looked out towards the lighthouse. For a long time. I looked with him.

"Did you put it out?" I said, and I saw his hand tighten around the railing.

He turned away slowly. His face in the shadow.

He pointed to the yard, the gate. "I'm not keeping you here." He opened the door and disappeared into the house. I went in behind him, put the bag on the table.

If I left, I would not come back.

He had his back to me. He was checking the fire in the stove. I sat down at the table.

"There are fewer nests over by Jobourg," I said.

He lifted up the cast-iron lid and dropped in a log. He stuffed the remaining space with newspaper, and struck a match. He waited for the fire to catch.

"Fewer nests and fewer chicks in the nests . . . They're going elsewhere to breed," he said, poking at the fire with a long iron bar.

Another team had located some cormorants in the bay at Cherbourg. They had come from La Hague and found refuge in the rubble of the forts, sheltered from the currents.

I talked about the cormorants with him, gave him details.

When I had finished, he turned to me.

"How can you be sure that they are cormorants from La Hague?"

"We're not sure about anything . . . Except with the ones who've been ringed. But not all of them have been."

"It will have to be done . . ."

"We're planning to."

The fire was burning.

He put the iron lid back and pushed aside the cats that had gathered round him. He filled their bowls. Then he took off his jacket, and hung it on the coat rack. He put his dressing gown on over his clothes; the wool was threadbare, and he kept it closed with a belt.

When he walked, I could hear his soles scraping against the floor.

"Last time, you talked to me about the fishing zones . . ."

"There's nothing very precise about that either . . . Cormorants fish anywhere, wherever they feel like it, depending on the wind or their inclination."

"Have you been able to follow them?"

"In Jobourg it was impossible, there were too many currents, you never know where they'll come back up. But in Écalgrain, yes."

Théo nodded.

"What else?"

"They have work for me in Caen."

He went to rub his hands above the stove. The room was not cold, but the air was damp. He had to breathe it, all the time.

The bag was on the table. He had not touched it. Hardly looked at it.

"You ought to put the ham in the fridge," I said.

He shrugged.

He went over to the window.

"Have you noticed, there is someone lurking about."

He stood aside to let me see. I could not see anything except the shadows of the growling cats.

"It's not the first time. Already yesterday and the previous evenings."

He sat down again at the table.

"He thinks I can't see him."

He raised his head and our eyes met. There were just those few seconds where I thought about the lighthouse that night, and he thought about it, too.

"Théo . . ."

I did not need to ask the question again. He had understood. He pressed his lips together. I think he had wanted to smile. There was a moment of hesitation, between a laugh and a wince, and finally he grunted.

"Go away." In a very low voice, and he repeated it.

I got up. I pushed the chair back.

I went over to the door.

I had my hand on the latch. It was freezing; or was it my skin?

I heard his voice.

"Sometimes at night I would wake to the heavy thud of birds crashing against the glass of the light."

His words, caught in that voice from the back of his throat.

"Magnificent birds ... They threw themselves blindly into the light."

I turned round.

Théo was sitting down. He was looking at me.

After a very long time he said, "You would have done it, too, you would have put out the light."

He said that, then pointed to the chair across from him. I came back and sat down.

None of the cats was moving. There was an odd silence in the room. As after a loud scream. Waiting for the echo.

Théo emptied his glass. He scratched at the table top with the point of his knife.

"I remember the day I did it for the first time."

He smiled faintly.

"I put it out for a few minutes ... Afterwards, I got into the habit. I did it when I was alone. The moment I lit the lamp again, more birds crashed into the glass."

The tip of the knife left marks in the wood. I could hear the sound of the blade sinking in.

"I didn't see the birds that I saved, only the ones that died ..."

He raised his eyes to look at me.

"The storm panes were double. I could see – the bodies, the feathers, the blood – I could see all that, but there was no sound."

He tried to smile again.

"It was like being in a silent film. The birds were drawn by the light, blinded. Their flight had death for an ending. They'd appear suddenly out of the night, beating their wings, looking for a space. The luckiest ones smashed against the window and didn't know what hit them."

Théo fell silent. He got up to fill his glass at the sink.

He checked the fire. I heard the ticking of the clock.

"I remember the first bird that crashed that evening, the night of the shipwreck. It was a goose, flying with others."

He was not looking at me now; he was staring at the wall behind me, at a spot just above my shoulder.

"I put the lantern out. Not for long . . ."

He jerked his head, as if trying to get away from the grip the image had over him. A stubborn memory. His eyes stayed glued to the wall.

"Time is so long, at sea . . ."

He said that and wiped his hand over his face, over the new traces his confession had left.

"Nowadays, the birds still crash into the light, but no-one is there to see them any more."

He took a swallow of water.

"The passes are narrow . . . In places, the rocks show on the surface . . . you have to know them. That night, the weather was not as bad as all that. How could I know there would be that sailing boat?"

He looked over at the door as if someone were there.

There was no-one, only memories.

"It was Captain Gweener who led the search. They found the man's body some hours later. The woman they found the next day, the currents had brought her back, on the beach."

He was rolling his glass between his hands. I could see the sea in his eyes, the sailing boat, I saw everything he had seen, it was spilling out of him.

A confession, in a hushed voice.

"You should have told Lambert. You owed him the truth, it was his due."

He winced. The little white cat padded across the room with her swaying gait and went to lie on the jumper, between the feet of the stove.

He waited for her to settle, her paws tucked beneath her.

"I went on keeping the light for one more year. Never once did I put out the lantern again. At night, when the birds crashed, I looked at them. I never looked down. Never looked away. I forced myself to see them to the end, their bodies bursting. I felt as if I were paying. There were so many that crashed into the light that last year."

"Why didn't you tell the truth?"

He laughed.

"Out of cowardice, no doubt."

"Lambert thought of coming to kill you."

"I waited for him for a long time. One day, a few years after the accident, he came, he spoke to me at the gate, I thought he was going to come again the following night to kill me. I stayed up very late that night."

"Would you have defended yourself?"

He shook his head.

"I had left the door open. Old Mother was upstairs, with Lili, they were asleep. I waited for him."

He looked at his hands for a long while, and said nothing more.

*   *   *

I went past the house perhaps a dozen times. There was a light on in the kitchen. I did not dare go in, perhaps because it was night-time. Or because of what I had to tell him. He was there, and it was so late.

I went through the gate and looked in the window. I saw him sitting by the fireplace. Looking at the fire. He was wearing a thick jumper of light-coloured wool, like a ski sweater.

He was just looking at the fire. And I was looking at him, and I understood that I had no choice but to go in.

I had to do it.

I would want him to do it for me.

I opened the door.

He hardly looked up. The only light in the room was from the flames. I saw his hands in the glow, his face. A smile passed over his lips, and I could not have said whether it was joy or sadness, most probably a mixture of the two, but it may also have been something less definable.

I closed the door behind me.

It was warm in the room.

I took off my jacket. I brought a chair, to sit next to him.

There was a bottle of some alcohol on the floor, by his feet. He bent down, filled his glass, and handed it to me.

I took the glass in my hand.

He knew that I had come from there. The prowler that Théo had seen, that was him.

I drank, a sharp swallow that turned my stomach. My eyes burning, welling with tears. I waited for it to pass. I stared at the flames. He was in no hurry, neither was I. I took another swallow. My eyes were used to it now, the alcohol did me good.

I told him everything that Théo had told me, everything, the night, the sea, the light. I told him about the death of the birds.

I told him about the other nights. The birds bursting out of the night, born of it.

He took the glass from my hands. He filled it. We drank some more.

It was a strong alcohol, I felt myself sweating. His jaw was clenched.

I kept strictly to what Théo had told me. Nothing else.

"The night of the wreck, he saw a flock of birds coming, migrating, a magnificent formation. They began to crash into the light, by the dozen."

I told him about the lighthouse lamp reflected in the birds' eyes, and the immense pity that overcame him, because he saw them flying towards him with so much trust.

"He said there shouldn't have been anybody on the sea that night. And he said that he couldn't bear to watch all those birds dying."

"And an entire family that dies, that's nothing to him?"

I did not answer. I waited for him to calm down, and I told him the story again. I do not know how long it lasted. A long time. There were moments when I was silent, I looked at the flames.

"Ten or fifteen of them crashed into the light, that night."

Lambert stood up. He walked behind me, somewhere in the room.

"Théo was on the other side of the glass, he could feel the thud. When he opened his eyes, he saw the blood."

I heard the sound of the glass breaking violently against the wall. I looked at him. His hand against his thigh, trembling.

"At what point did he say to himself, I'm going to put out the lamp and never mind if there are boats?"

"I don't know if he thought about that."

I added some wood to the fire. I stayed for a moment on my knees, staring at the flames.

"Théo realized that something had happened when he heard the sirens. He saw the lights on the quay, and the doors wide open, and a lifeboat going out. When the lifeboat reached the place of the wreck, there was no-one left on board the sailing boat. They searched the sea. It was night-time. They had lamps, but the waves were strong."

"They didn't search hard enough . . ."

"Théo said that they could not have searched any more."

Lambert shook his head.

I finished my glass.

That truth was something that he had wanted to hear. There was another long pause. I had told him everything. To tell him more would have been cheating with memory, accusing or forgiving. I did not want that.

Or to invent any memories.

It was his story.

"And my brother, the sea kept him. The sea took its due, as they say round here."

"Yes, that's what they say."

"And that doesn't bother you?"

He walked over to the door. He went out. I thought he was going to leave but he stayed there outside, in the garden. It was cold. It was dark. He was clutching his arms with his hands, as if they were fastened there. The door had stayed open wide. Nocturnal insects gleamed in the dew. I could hear them. I followed him.

"In the morning, they came here . . . I was asleep. That's what my mother had said before she left, If we're late, go to bed . . ."

He turned to me.

"When they died, I was asleep."

I could not see his face, only his eyes.

"I woke up, I heard people talking in the kitchen, I thought it was my father. I went down. Two firemen were there, with the mayor . . . I looked at them. I think I understood straight away. I turned, I wanted to go back to bed, back to my blankets, not to hear what they had to tell me . . ."

He looked down, and stared at the ground between his feet.

"I was ashamed, ashamed I hadn't gone with them. That I hadn't died, too."

He looked up.

"The day of the funeral, the entire village came. We went to throw flowers on the sea. Lili was crying. Everybody was crying. It was towards the end that I heard a bloke say that perhaps the light had been put out again."

He smiled at me.

He handed me his cigarette, we smoked it and we lit another.

"As for Paul . . . the sea kept him. He has no earth, no place . . . That is the hardest thing to accept."

He turned away, gruffly, as if he wanted to involve the heavens as his witness.

"For forty years I've had it in for the sea, and for that crazy old man! Forty years!"

He went into the house. He came back out with his jacket. The car keys in his hand.

"I want to hear it from him!"

He left.

I went back into the house, I tossed logs on the fire, I pulled over an armchair, stretched out my legs, and waited for him to come back.

I woke up, the fire had gone out. It was dark. Lambert had still not returned. I had no idea what time it could be, midnight, or a bit later, no doubt. I made some coffee, I waited some more, then I went back down to La Griffue.

From my room, I looked out of the window, towards land. The hill, in the night. The sky was black.

There was no light in Théo's house.

The next morning, I woke up much later than usual. I had had trouble falling asleep. I could see the waves, the sea, it was pounding into my eyes and then I wondered what Lambert had done at Théo's place. Several times I had thought of getting out of bed to go and see. Eventually I had dozed off, in the early morning. A dreamless sleep.

In the morning, my face in the mirror, a battered expression.

I drank coffee, very hot and strong.

Théo was waiting for me at his gate. He did not talk to me about Lambert. Not a word about his visit. He did not talk to me about the birds or the cliffs.

I thought that Lambert had not gone in. That he had stayed on the road, in the car, looking at Théo's shadow in the kitchen. That he had stayed there until the light went out. He must have left after that.

That is what I thought and I looked at Théo.

Something was different from usual. His eyes were avoiding me.

"I've heard Florelle is not doing too well just now."

That is what he said, those exact words.

"I've heard she's taken to running along the shore again, shouting out her speeches."

His hands were trembling.

"I'd like to see her. Could you tell her that, on your way by, that I want to see her?"

"I'll tell her."

He did not say anything else.

"Everything alright, Théo?" I said.

He gave me a strange smile. He turned away without answering, went up the front steps and disappeared inside the house.

*　　*　　*

Nan was sitting on a chair by the window, embroidering the dark cloth of a shroud. All I had to do was open the door.

Raphaël had sculpted her like that, the seamstress of the dead, a figure bent over her work, with her madwoman's locks.

This was the first time I had come into her house. The room where she lived adjoined the large deserted rooms in the Refuge. I stayed by the door.

"Nan?"

She looked up from her work. In her lap she had a large pair of scissors, and a ball of cloth stuck with a multitude of pins with coloured heads.

"It's Théo. He wants to see you," I said.

She gave a sort of low growl, like that of an animal that has been disturbed, and she went on working. I went closer. The needle pierced the cloth, I heard the sound of the thread pulling and the old woman's tranquil breathing. The rustling of the shroud when she lifted the length of cloth over her thighs.

243

She was using very fine, close stitches. There was a tin box on the windowsill, containing coloured spools. The cloth of the shroud shone in the light.

Nan was tracing the letters of the name.

"It's mine, my death cloak," she said, pointing to the shroud.

Embroidered on the grey cloth was her name, Florelle.

She had not embroidered Nan.

Nan was the name the living gave her.

The cloth was cold.

"Blue-grey, the colour of the sea on days when the sea takes the living."

She looked deep into my eyes, her gaze uncomfortable, going through me without seeing me.

"What does he want, Théo?"

"I don't know . . . To see you."

I stepped back.

A painting was hanging above the fireplace. In tones of blue and green, too naïve, depicting the Refuge in summer. On the shelf there was a large clock, and photographs of children, dozens of them. Some were simply balanced against the wall. Some were bigger than others, and there were still others behind, that you could not see.

"Are these all children of the Refuge?"

She did not answer. The photographs were grimy, covered in finger-prints and traces of soot.

"Are you the one who took them?"

"I am."

She gathered up the shroud and put it on the back of the chair. She got up and went over to the photographs.

"Some of them still write to me, for my birthday, at Christmas . . . The ones who went bad don't write to me."

She took one photograph in her hands, that of a child alone, stand-ing in the courtyard, his arms held out from his body. He was wearing baggy shorts.

"This one was the son of some fairground folk. His father had a bear, he would walk it through the villages, just like that, at the end of a rope. They put their caravan in a field above Jobourg. They stayed for a few days. They left and they forgot the lad. When they realized, it was too late, they were far away. They picked him up again the following year."

She sorted through the other photographs.

"I remember every face . . ."

She showed me another photograph, with a scalloped edge.

"This one stayed six years with us. We tried to find him a home, no-one wanted him! Such an angelic face, though . . . A terror inside. Ursula and I said, finally, he'll end up killing someone! It took him fifteen years, but he did."

She picked up another photograph, a little girl dangling a teddy bear by its leg. Her forehead low, a timid upward gaze.

"She was a miserable little girl . . . Always wet, with rain, tears, piss . . . And filthy to boot! She infested the whole dormitory with her lice, even though we shaved her."

She put the photograph back in its place.

"A hopeless case, that child . . ."

She turned her head and looked at me, an even, very open gaze.

"Why doesn't Théo come here?"

"The doctor doesn't want him to go out."

She gave an odd laugh.

"Since when does Théo listen to doctors?"

She turned away from the photographs.

There was a large wardrobe against the wall. Two doors in walnut. She turned the key, opened one side.

"I sewed the names of all those children on my dresses."

She showed me. In the wardrobe, on hangers, there must have been fifty or more heavy black dresses, all the same. These were the dresses she wore to brave the storms. She ran her hand over them. She took one dress out and carried it over to the table, to the light.

She took my hand, I felt the thickness of the cloth, the raised bump of the thread, the letters traced in grey against the black background of the dress.

Names. Words.

Her eyes were a few inches from the letters. There were sentences. The cloth smelled musty. She took out other dresses.

"I wrote the whole story."

I do not know what story she was talking about. Was it her love for Théo, or the story of these children? I had counted more than fifty photographs, and some were hidden behind others, and some were so small you could hardly see them. And on some of the photographs there were several children.

"And that child you loved so much . . ."

She frowned.

"Michel?"

"Michel, yes . . ."

She smiled and looked through her dresses. Her gestures feverish. She showed me the writing of the thread in the cloth, *Today, Michel turned eight.* Other things were written. She read them. *Michel had fever all night long. We had to send for the doctor.* There were things on other dresses, *Michel started at the lycée,* the words sewn in large irregular stitches, *Two years now Michel has been gone.*

Nan raised her head.

"Has Michel come back?"

"I didn't say that."

With an abrupt gesture, she picked up the dresses and shoved them into the wardrobe. She pushed them in, without hanging them up, and she closed the door. She came back to the photographs. She searched through them. Her hands were agitated, her face nervous. Some of the prints fell on the floor. As they fell, the glass from a frame broke. She finally found what she was looking for, a photograph of a child, and she held it against her chest, her hands crossed over it.

"Michel . . ."

She repeated his name and began to laugh.

"The sea gave him to me!" is what she said.

The photograph was partly hidden by her hands. Only the lower half was visible. The child's legs, his feet in a pair of lace-up boots, and next to them a little wooden train that you could tell he was holding by a string.

Nan swayed back and forth with the photograph, rocking. She went on laughing. I tried to talk to her, but she did not hear me. I picked up the photographs that had fallen. The pieces of glass from the frame. I looked for a rubbish bin to throw the shards away. I could not find one. I kept the glass in my hand and put the frame back where it belonged.

"I'm going to go now . . ." I said.

The frame without its glass. It was a medallion. I looked at the photograph, the little polo shirt with the boats . . . The child's smile. I had seen that face somewhere. It took me a while. The face, the polo shirt, that angelic smile . . .

The medallion was the one that Lambert had put on the grave. The one that had disappeared. Lambert assumed that Max had taken it.

What was that picture doing here?

Nan still held her hands crossed over her heart, swaying with the photograph.

She had certainly stolen the toys. Why steal the photograph of a child, when she had so many already?

She went over to the window.

From the back, I saw her heavy plait. I imagined her hands, folded. She was humming as if she were alone.

"You won't forget to go and see Théo?"

She did not reply.

I looked at her one more time before going out. I slipped the medallion into my pocket, and closed the door behind me.

*　　*　　*

The donkeys had gathered further down, in the little street near the wash-house. They were eating what the children had left for them outside the door.

They say here that if you disturb a donkey you will die of solitude.

I went along the footpath by the sea. With the shards in my hand. The photograph in my pocket. I knew this path by heart. I walked over slabs of stone, occasionally treacherous, and slippery soil, and the soft springy carpet of moss. I had the sea in my eyes. The dazzling light. I sat on a rock. I took the photograph from my pocket. The child had his eyes wide open.

By stealing this photograph, had Nan wanted to add yet another face to her long collection? To take another child into a house that no longer took children in, as if the story of the Refuge should continue? Was that it?

I slipped the photograph into my pocket, without really knowing whether I should give it to Lambert, or put it back on the grave and say nothing.

I took the footpath as far as the beach at Écalgrain. A snake had come to die between two rocks. A long column of red ants was patiently gutting it.

An egret plunged, breaking the water. It surfaced a moment later with a little silvery fish in its beak.

Morgane was on the beach with a boy. They were walking together, their arms round each other. They stumbled into each other, from holding so close.

Morgane was wearing her pink woollen jumper. I do not know who the boy was. I had never seen him before. They kissed.

I looked at them through my binoculars. A kiss right on the mouth, unrestrained, and already their hands were searching, eager, asking for more. They were standing, facing the sea. They fell on to their knees. They went on kissing. Hardly hidden.

Max was there too, concealed in the shadow. He was there, as if it were impossible for him to be anywhere else. He was speaking, words coming out of him.

"Where Morgane goes, I go."

He was hardly moving his lips. He scratched his cheeks with his fingernails. An unpleasant grating.

"The insides of her thighs, it's like velvety, it's like snow, when the snow has just fallen."

He was taking great strides towards the path, I thought he was leaving.

He went back.

"Morgane smells like chalk. When she washes, the water slides down her back, it makes traces of sunlight, like snail drool across the back of the rocks."

He spoke hurriedly, as if to get rid of his words. Then he too was on his knees, digging in the red earth, moist soil that he scratched up with his long fingers. He rubbed his lips with the earth. He was moaning.

I would have liked to do what he was doing, to be capable of it. I squeezed my hands, and I felt the shards of glass in my palm.

"You have to get up . . ."

My hands were bleeding.

His eyes.

"One day, I will tear the men away from Morgane's belly . . . Morgane will be mine. One day . . . It won't take long."

He got up. He stepped back. He did not understand.

"Some day, when she sees, she'll have no other choice . . ."

I threw my shards of glass into the hole he had dug.

"You have to leave," I said.

I touched his hand.

"It's weather for going to bars . . ."

He looked at me and looked at the sky. His lip hanging.

"It's weather for nothing," he said.

He looked again over towards the rocks, where Morgane had disappeared.

"Come on now, Max, let's get going."

He was right, it was no weather for going to bars. It was weather for nothing. I left him by his boat and I went back up to the village. Lambert was not at home. The house was closed, shuttered.

Had he gone to Théo's place?

The FOR SALE sign was still hanging from the fence.

The sky was white, with darker streaks above the sea. Streaks that were becoming blacker and blacker. It would end up being weather for rain.

The next day, Max set all his butterflies free. All the butterflies he had been keeping for Morgane.

He went to the top of the field overlooking the sea. He opened the cage. He let the butterflies go.

The next day, I was supposed to meet the people from the Centre up on the cliffs. When I got there, they had already started removing egg samples. They had taken several, from various nests, and put decoys in their place. I was there to record the birds' behaviour, and keep track of their movements with the stopwatch. The birds were all screaming, the ones they had taken the eggs from, and the others. Below us the sea was rising, heavy rollers of white spume. The gulls flew low, skimming the cliff. It filled them with rage to have human hands on their nests. Two cormorants that they had taken an egg from flew away. I clocked sixteen minutes before the first one came back. He went to his place. The egg had been replaced by a decoy. He did not realize. I clocked nine more minutes before he sat on the egg again.

The second bird came back three minutes after the first.

I filled in my charts. The wind was blowing. I had special clips to hold the paper.

Twenty-five minutes later another bird arrived. Rage in his eyes. His beak open. He began to walk on his nest, on the edges and then in the middle, he ransacked everything. The eggs that were still in the nest fell out on to the beach.

Only afterwards did the bird calm down, settling on a nearby rock to preen his feathers.

The men from the Centre stayed a little longer. I waited for calm to return over the cliff.

An albino sparrow came and landed near me. I gave him a few biscuit crumbs. It was the first albino I had seen. I should have drawn it. I didn't feel like it.

*   *   *

Lambert had still not come back. The house had been shut up for several days now. I went past it in the morning, and also on my way back from the cliffs.

Morgane did not know where he was. Nor did M. Anselme. Even Lili didn't know anything. When I asked her, she shrugged.

I decided to go and see Théo.

I took the long way round on my way back down to La Griffue.

He was reading his newspaper. When I went in, he did not get up, but he jabbed his finger at an article.

That night, a wild dog had attacked one of the goats . . . It had dragged it to a customs sentry box. The coastguard had found the animal by the side of the path, its head sticking out of the sentry box.

Théo slammed his hand on to the newspaper.

"Bloody dog!"

I took off my jacket.

The room was small, the stove was going full blast; it was always too warm in there.

Théo talked some more about the goat and all the other animals that had been devoured on the moor. It was so that he would not have to talk about Lambert. The visit Lambert must have paid him. I looked round, as if I might find a trace of his passage. Théo went on talking. I am sure he was thinking about Lambert, too.

At one point he folded the newspaper, his hands crossed on it. His head down.

"Lambert came to see you the other night, didn't he."

He nodded.

"What happened?"

"What do you want to have happened? He wanted me to talk about that night, I told him what I told you, nothing more."

Théo grumbled a few words between his teeth. He refolded the newspaper in half and then in quarters, smoothing the folds.

"He came, we talked, he went away."

"Where did he go?"

"How am I supposed to know? I asked you to go by Florelle's place: did you?"

I hesitated before answering.

"I told her that you wanted to see her but I don't know if she's going to come."

"How was she?"

"When I got there, she was sewing."

"And when you left?"

I looked at Théo.

"She was holding a photograph against her chest, cradling it. It was a photograph of Michel."

He did not bat an eyelid. He only remained silent for a moment, and then he nodded.

"I'm sorry things happened the way they did ... To save a few birds, those people dying ... I wanted him to believe it was the sea, and only the sea that was to blame, it would have been easier for him."

He had changed the subject, going back to Lambert as if to avoid still more difficult words.

"Easier for him to blame the sea?" I said.

"Yes ... We forgive the sea more easily than we forgive men ... I told him everything about that night . . . It's what he wanted. At one point, he went outside to sit on the steps, among the cats' bowls. I thought he had left. He was smoking. After that, he came back. He wanted me to tell him more, from the start, everything . . . He asked the same questions."

He raised his hand, fatalistic.

"I don't know where he went."

He gave a half-hearted smile. He was tired. The sombre face of someone who has slept badly, or not enough. Was it remorse? No doubt my presence was making his fatigue worse.

Lambert had needed to hear the truth. Was that also why Théo had agreed to tell him? So that he would not go to his grave with his miserable secret? I wanted to ask him if he knew why Nan had stolen the photograph from the Perack grave. I thought that probably it was not very important.

The cat began to purr.

Théo got up. He went to the desk, lifted up some papers, put them down again, he was looking for something in his inextricable mess.

"From time to time, Florelle would spend the night with me, at the lighthouse . . ."

That is what he said. Wooden crates were piled on top of each other, as shelves. Inside, there were a few books, their blue covers reminding me of old schoolbooks. At the very top of the crates were dusty knick-knacks, and an old wireless radio.

Another more modern radio was on the windowsill.

"There was a fisherman who brought her over. He liked us . . . The sea had to be calm and he had to come at night. He would pick Florelle up again in the morning, when he went home."

He had found what he was looking for.

He said, "On those nights, Ursula slept at the Refuge."

That was what he said.

He put a sheet of paper on the table. A4 format. Folded.

"You give this to him . . ."

He left the room. I could hear him going down the hall and then nothing more. I do not know where he went. Perhaps he went up to the attic, to the skylight where he could see the sea, the lighthouse, and Nan's house.

I unfolded the paper. It was a typewritten document, with the stamp of the harbourmaster's office in the upper left-hand corner.

I read it.

Report of the wreck of the Sphyrène *in the sector of the Cape of La Hague, dated 19 October, 1967.*
Place of the accident: le Raz Blanchard
Type of Vessel: sailing boat.
Nationality: French.
Number of occupants: three.
Number saved: none.

As reported by Captain Cristian Gweener

On 19 October, 1967, at 23.07, the coastguard station at La Hague received an S.O.S. coming from a sailing boat that had just struck a rock in the middle of the Raz. We were informed that there were three occupants on board. Westerly wind. At 23.30, the lifeboat was launched. Poor visibility. Strong seas, with an ebb tide running against the current.

At 23.40, we entered the search zone, three nautical miles to the north-east of La Hague. At 23.55 we sighted the sailing boat Sphyrène. *The jib and mainsail were torn. We came alongside with great difficulty. There was no-one on board. Wind from the west force seven, gusting. The sailing boat was drifting rapidly, driven by the wind and tide. We concentrated our search in the zone, and then further west. At 00.30, the body of one of the sailing boat's occupants was found. It was a man of 40 years or more, life-less. Our inflatable dinghy took him back to Goury. We stayed in the zone to try to find the two other members of the crew. The sea was still rough*

with strong winds and poor visibility. After long hours of fruitless search-
ing, we decided to go back. We were able to tow the sailing boat, but
halfway there, the boat began taking on water and sank deeper and deeper.
We were obliged to cut the tow line. A quarter of an hour later, the sailing
boat disappeared into the water. At 4.10, we were back on land, exhausted
by the long night searching.

The lifeboat was back in its shelter at 4.30.

A second lifeless body, that of a woman, was found the next morning
on the beach known as Écalgrain.

To this day, the body of the third occupant has not been found.

*   *   *

Raphaël had begun to sculpt a figure who resembled the Stork.

"What do you think?" he said, leading me into the studio.

The body was waiflike, the legs disproportionately long. The Stork
in her cape. Raphaël had gouged with his thumbs, to hollow out her
belly, to make it a void. All the rest, her head, her arms, seemed to
vanish in comparison to the strength of her belly.

He sat down on the sofa, his knees folded in front of him.

"Aren't you going to say anything about it?"

"No."

He smiled.

"That means it can't be all that bad, then . . ."

He stuck a cigarette between his lips. Everything he used to make
his sculptures was spread around on the floor, bits of wood, wire mesh
. . . He did not throw anything away, he liked the mess, he said the bits
of wood were the traces of his work.

"I'll call her 'Dying of Hunger'."

I curled up next to him on the sofa.

"When I see you with your eyes like that, I reckon I ought to sculpt
you. You look as if you'd swum to get here."

"On a raft," I said, "with two oars."

My neck was burning.

"Oars are what make the difference, especially if you've got two of them," I said, running my hand over the back of my neck.

"What happens if you've only got one?"

"You go round and round, Raphaël, round and round."

He rubbed his hands together and placed his palms against the back of my neck.

"You're not exactly tense, are you?" he said.

He massaged my neck, a regular back and forth motion. I tried to resist, then I closed my eyes. I thought of you. Your smile came back to me. You had said, We'll part on an odd-numbered day, for a laugh, that is what you said.

"Your muscles are like cables."

"Be quiet."

"Did you have an accident?"

"Of a kind."

"What do you mean, of a kind?"

"Two months spent wandering about with loonies."

"On the medical staff side?"

"No, the patient side."

His fingers stopped moving. "You're pulling my leg, aren't you?"

"No."

"Loonies – truly insane people?"

"Truly insane."

"With straitjackets?"

"Chemical straitjackets. Don't stop."

I had a nerve somewhere that was trapped, blocking the back of my neck. The pain ran all the way along my arm, to the tips of my fingers, I could feel the bar of fire. At night it woke me up.

"And you got free doses so that you could get high?"

"Free doses . . . Pretty good doses, too . . ."

"What's that got to do with your neck?"

"I don't know, but it's since that time."

He went on massaging, not speaking.

"You're good at it . . ." I said.

It made him laugh. He readjusted my collar. He stretched out, both his hands behind his head. He looked at me. He reached out a hand.

"You coming?"

He insisted, a quick jerk of his head.

"Come on . . ."

I stretched out, five centimetres between his body and mine. His hand closed again.

"Relax . . ."

There was no more space between us. My head was against his shoulder. I could hear his heart beating. Or perhaps it was mine.

"Raphaël?"

"Mmm?"

"You're not in love, are you?"

I could sense he was smiling.

"No. And you?"

"I'm not either."

He put his lips against my forehead.

"That's all right then. No need to worry."

*   *   *

M. Anselme had been away for a few days, he had gone to Paris. When I got to Lili's, he was waiting for me, with a book about Prévert.

"To be handled with extreme care . . ."

I leafed through a few pages. My thoughts were elsewhere. He showed me the letters, photographs, a drawing by Picasso dedicated to Prévert, a postcard from Miró, Prévert with Janine, Prévert with André Breton, Prévert in Saint-Paul-de-Vence.

He was boring me. It was the first time I had felt it so strongly. I saw myself, at this table, with this ageing, obsessive man.

"The first time I met him was at La Colombe d'Or . . . That same day, he dived fully clothed into a sort of pool that was on the terrace."

"A *fountain*, M. Anselme . . . You usually call it a *fountain* . . ."

I was annoyed with myself for being unpleasant. I turned my head. Lambert's house was still closed. His car was no longer outside the house. It was no longer by the quay. The garden had been cleared of its brambles, but Max said that behind the house there was still plenty of work to do.

The FOR SALE sign was still on the fence.

"A *fountain*, yes, you're right . . . You must come and see me in Omonville. I'll show you the house at Le Val, the house where Prévert decided to spend the last years of his life. You will like the place, I'm sure of it!"

He turned to Lili, and ordered two strong liqueurs from a bottle without a label. He rolled the glass between his hands. It was a transparent liqueur with a good taste of plums. He took a swallow.

"It's a stiff concoction," he said, gasping with surprise. "But sometimes we need it."

He looked at me.

"Am I boring you? My daughter tells me that sometimes, that I'm boring."

He closed the book and put it to one side of the table.

"What is it that is troubling you so today?"

"Did you know that Théo loved Nan?"

He looked at me, apparently somewhat surprised by the question.

"Of course I knew. Everyone knows that here . . ."

"And that sometimes she joined him when he was out at the lighthouse?"

He pointed to Lili and Old Mother.

"I've heard such things said, but . . . perhaps this is not the best place to speak about them."

He put his hands together, his lips against his fingers. His smile, amused. He leaned towards me.

"You know, the emotions of love . . . What is it that makes us fall, just like that, at first sight, when we've never seen each other before? Sometimes an encounter takes place, then there are all the others that we miss, we are so inattentive . . . Sometimes, we come upon someone, all we need is to exchange a few words, and we know we are going to experience something vital together. But it wouldn't take much for these things not to happen at all, and for each of us to go on our way all alone. So, if those two fell in love . . ."

He had been speaking in a hushed voice, glancing hastily at Lili.

"Théo gets letters," I said.

"What sort of letters?"

"I don't know . . . There are lots of them . . . Envelopes all with the same handwriting, in purple ink."

"And what is in them?"

"I don't know. I didn't read them . . . They come from a monastery near Grenoble."

"Might Théo have family among the monks? I've never heard that he does."

He settled back into his chair.

"We could ask Lili, but something tells me that to ask her anything about her father is not exactly wise."

He thought for a moment. "Do you have a good rapport with Théo? The simplest thing would be just to ask him. Or, you find a discreet way to borrow one of those letters, you read it, and put it back in its place."

"I can't do that."

"In that case, let's talk about something else . . . Promise me you'll come and see me in Omonville. Could we agree on tomorrow? No, tomorrow is Friday, my children come on Fridays . . . They need fresh air. Although they do arrive rather late in the evening. If you come at the beginning of the afternoon, we might be able to arrange it . . . Or perhaps Monday, on Monday they'll be gone."

"M. Anselme?"

"Yes?"

I looked at him.

"You told me that Nan had adopted a child, isn't that right? And that his name was Michel?"

"That is so."

"What was his surname?"

He opened his eyes wide.

"I don't know that! I'm not sure anyone ever told me."

He thought for a few moments.

"If you are really that interested, I could ask Ursula."

"Does the name Lepage mean anything to you?"

"Lepage? . . . No, I don't think so."

"Or Tom Thumb?"

"Tom Thumb? Gracious me, where on earth are you taking me? Forgive me . . . No, Tom Thumb doesn't mean anything to me . . . Perhaps you could explain?"

I said, "Tomorrow we'll visit Prévert's house and you'll find the little boy's surname for me."

I went to Omonville along the footpath by the sea. M. Anselme had described his house to me, a garden, a low wooden fence at the front. I had no difficulty recognizing it. When I arrived, he was perched on top of a stepladder, cutting the dead heads from a climbing rose that clung to the façade.

"It's a 'Pierre de Ronsard'," he said, coming down the stepladder.

He took off his apron. "Did you come on foot?"

"Yes."

He rubbed his hands.

"I've made you some orangeade, one of my grandmother's recipes!" he said, hurrying into the house.

He came back out with a carafe. We drank a glass, talking about the garden. Flower beds full of irises bloomed all along the wall. Daisies. A large jasmine.

He exchanged his gardening clogs for a pair of cream-coloured shoes, and a little silk handkerchief which he pressed down into the breast pocket of his jacket.

"Shall we go?"

He held my arm, proudly, as if we were being seen, observed, spied upon.

"There are shadows everywhere, behind every door, every curtain. Don't tell me you haven't noticed them? You, for example, everything people say about you, you cannot imagine . . . The fact that you were seen having lunch the other day in the *auberge* with that Lambert fellow . . . All it takes is one person! I don't know what you see in him either, he dresses badly, he doesn't comb his hair, and that jacket he wears has no shape! Moreover, he has a very common way of walking."

He turned to me. "By the way, has he turned up again?"

"No, he hasn't, not yet."

The cemetery where Prévert was buried was very near. We planned to stop there and then go on to the house at Le Val.

M. Anselme was smiling.

"It's really very nice that you are here . . ."

He was making plans for another outing. He wanted us to go to Cherbourg to buy apple tarts.

"At 5, place de la Fontaine! Prévert went all that way for that very purpose, every Wednesday! His tartan cap on his head. The *patronne* didn't know who he was. When he died, she recognized him on the television. On the evening news. That's my little Wednesday customer! she said."

He turned to me.

"We shall go there, shan't we?"

"I don't know."

That did not stop him from smiling.

"If you don't come, I'll go alone and I'll bring the tarts back."

It was a beautiful sunny day. People were out in their gardens, on their doorsteps. Washing was drying on the lines.

My thoughts were elsewhere, he must have realized, because at one point he asked me to tell him what was worrying me.

I told him everything, about the photograph at Lili's, the medallion I had found at Nan's, the truth about the shipwreck. He listened attentively.

"And now it's been three days since Lambert disappeared, since his argument with Théo."

He thought about what I had said.

"I'd heard he was boarding with the Irishwoman at La Rogue?"

"Yes . . . but I don't know if he's still there."

"There must be a telephone there . . . why don't you call?"

He said, "The death of the Peracks, therefore, was the unforeseeable consequence of an act of love, a lighthouse keeper's passion for his birds."

He said it again, the unforeseeable consequence.

As for Michel, however, he knew nothing. He would have to speak to Ursula.

We went into the cemetery. Prévert's grave was close to the fence, a tall stone on which little pebbles from the beach had been laid. The pebbles formed a fragile pyramid that was collapsing under its own weight. M. Anselme caressed the stone.

"The only time that these great men belong to us, in a way, is once they are dead. We can invite ourselves to visit without going through some great useless formality."

He laid the creamy-white flower he had taken from his rosebush on the grave.

"Prévert himself chose this spot near the rubbish bins. He knew, and he didn't care."

The two graves next to his, Janine's and Minette's. And behind, in the shadow of the wall, was the grave of his friend Trauner.

"He died in April, on Easter Monday. Two days earlier, journalists had begun to camp outside his house. Janine cried a great deal. She threw her bouquet on to the coffin. It was such a lovely bouquet! We all threw flowers."

Ivy had taken root in the earth. I dug in my pockets. I brought out a smooth red stone and placed it with the others.

M. Anselme took my arm. His step, in time with mine. We continued along the path. Large flowers grew among the brambles, giant fuchsias spreading their blooms all the way into the bushes. The flowers were seeking the light. The ones that could not break through the bushes were crawling along the earth.

"Is it because he was abandoned that you are interested in that child? Or because he was adopted by Nan? Don't tell me, let's sum it up, rather . . . You saw the child in a photograph at Lili's, a photo that Lili then removed. The same child that Lambert saw in the yard at Théo's, walking a young calf. Is that correct?"

"That's it. But we can't be sure it was the same child."

"Not sure, but you believe it to have been the same. And the child that Nan adopted went away. And you would like to know why."

A child born in a doorway, in a place that was a mass grave during the epidemics of the plague. How could you stand something like that, survive it?

"I think that the person who is writing letters to Théo must be this same child."

He rubbed his hands.

"If we can prove that the surname of the child is Lepage, then we may conclude that the person who writes to Théo and the child that Nan adopted are one and the same individual."

"Yes."

We had come to Prévert's house among the trees, surrounded by a garden. We went through the gate. The vegetation was luxurious, the rosebushes, the sunflowers in bloom, plants with giant leaves and names that were impossible to pronounce. A little stream ran through the garden and under the little bridge by the entrance.

"The plants you can see there, behind those high plumes, are called gynerium. And over there, you have gunneras."

A flagstone path led to the house. We went along the wall, looking at the garden. M. Anselme was thinking.

He turned to face me, quite suddenly.

"If it's the same person, we still need to find out why Théo hasn't told Nan where the person she's looking for can be found."

He paused a bit longer to think, looking at the house.

"The fact that Lili took away the photograph, that you can understand . . . If it was Nan's adopted child . . . But you are right, there's something strange about this story . . ."

I still had the medallion in my pocket. I showed it to him.

"This is Paul Perack, Lambert's brother. Nan stole this photograph . . ."

"So, that's him . . . Poor child . . . Did you say Nan stole this photograph?"

He handed it back to me.

"Are you afraid of death?" he said.

"Not death . . . But the idea of growing old . . . Becoming ugly and dirty and not being able to walk on my own – that, yes, that frightens me."

I put the photograph in my pocket. I wanted to give it back to Lambert as soon as possible, along with the official report of the shipwreck.

"You can get old, you know, get so old that even dogs can no longer stand your caresses."

M. Anselme nodded.

"If you look at it like that, indeed . . ."

*   *   *

I found Lambert's scarf on the bench in his garden. He must have left it there. Forgotten it. It had slid between the bench and the wall. The wool was damp. It smelled of earth. It smelled of water and sunlight.

It smelled of the man and his sweat. A few hairs were caught in the wool. I left the scarf on the bench.

I went behind the house. Max was right, the garden was overrun, there was still plenty of work to do.

Two days went by. The scarf was still on the bench. On the third day, the wind lifted it up and flattened it against the wall. The sun dried it. I picked it up. I tied it around my neck.

The following night, it rained.

I remember that night. The first night on which I stopped thinking about you.

Because of him.

That first night I dreamt about him. Where I got lost, in a dream, with someone else.

You had said, Forget me. You had made me swear to love again. My mouth, inside yours. You're going to have to forget, that's what you said, forget or forget me, I don't remember which, you never took your lips from mine, you spilled that into me. You are going to have to live without me, swear to me . . .

I swore.

My fingers crossed. Behind your back. You were still standing. So tall. I put my hand on your shoulder.

How can I love after you?

*   *   *

In the morning, the beach was covered with dark seaweed.

"Who was that bloke?" I asked Lili, referring to a strange fellow who had bumped into me on the terrace before I came in.

"A son of a bitch," she said, as she went on putting her bottles on the shelves.

Then she put her hands flat on the bar.

"I'm not joking, he really is a son of a bitch."

I could not find out anything more.

It was Sunday. Teenage boys were gathered on the terrace. They wanted Lili to buy a football table. There was no room, she would have to do away with a few tables. Or the jukebox. Or use some of the kitchen space, but the kitchen was Lili's private domain, she did not want anyone to touch it.

"Go to Mass, that will keep you busy!" she told them when she saw how idle they were. "Go and do some charity work!"

That just made the boys laugh. Eventually they went away.

Lili turned to me, as if I were her witness.

"They'd like nothing better, the old folk around here, and God knows there are enough of them, just a visit from time to time."

I looked outside.

"He still hasn't come back?" I said, pointing to Lambert's house.

Lili looked up.

"Haven't seen him."

"He didn't say anything to you?"

"What should he say to me?"

I let go of the curtain.

"Do you know where he went?"

"I know what I see," she said, "and I see that the shutters are closed. More than that, it's his life."

I saw that she had pinned up another photograph to replace the one where you could see her with little Michel.

"Where did you put the photograph that used to be here?"

She glanced over at the wall.

"In a box with the others, why?"

"I'd like to see it again . . ."

She shrugged.

"I'll have to go and look for it."

I did not insist.

Judging by her tone, I was sure she would not do it.

"Théo's acting very strange these days," I said.

"He's always been strange!"

266

"I don't think he's feeling very well."

She plunged her hands into the sink. She put the clean glasses upside down on a cloth. One of them cracked when she banged it against the edge of the sink. She swore. And yet it was not the first time she had broken a glass.

"Do you all have it in for me today, or what?"

She stood for a moment behind the bar, bitching.

"What the hell are you on about, anyway!" she said gruffly, looking at me.

"Nothing . . ."

"It's not nothing. I can see it in your eyes!"

I looked down.

"Is it because of my father? Have you got a problem? Don't I look after him properly?"

"That's not what I mean . . ."

"Well, if you don't know what you mean, keep quiet! Drink your coffee, fill in your charts, then get out of here!"

I folded the newspaper. I picked up my things. "You will weep when he's dead."

"I won't weep. Not a single tear, d'you hear me!"

She stood up straight, the cake slice in her hand.

"He gave me nothing but grief, and her too, you can't imagine."

"That was a long time ago."

"That changes nothing, whether it was a long time ago."

She turned towards her mother.

"She put up with everything . . . Everything! So that he wouldn't leave! And I grew up with a father who went away at night to sleep with another woman. Shall I tell you how I spent my Christmases? Everyone round here knows. My mother cried so much that she cried for her life and mine as well. What drives me crazy is that she's prepared to go back there."

"But she did end up leaving," I said.

"She did end up leaving, yes, but it took her long enough."

"Why are you shouting?" groaned Old Mother from the depths of her armchair.

"We're not shouting!"

"You're talking about the old man. What's he done, the old man?"

"He hasn't done anything," Lili said.

Old Mother shook her head. Her eyes welled with tears. All her tears ravaged her face, bloating her skin, puffy purple bags under her eyes.

I looked at her. Beneath the lamp, completely motionless, she looked like a dead woman breathing.

The boys were still outside, revving the motors on their mopeds. All they were waiting for was to be old enough to get a car, so they could go further away, to Cherbourg or Valognes.

It was always like this on Sundays, mopeds making the neighbours complain, the same ones who complained about the old men who went outside to piss. The same ones who complained about everything, anyway. The next day the kids were at school, during the week there was no engine noise.

*   *   *

Raphaël had shut himself in the studio with the red stone outside the door. He was working, listening to Callas.

It had just turned late afternoon. It was still daylight. I lay down. I pulled the blanket over my eyes, I did not want to see the light. I rolled the pillow against my stomach. The music came through the floor, it lulled me.

I slept.

When I awoke, it was dark. There was still light in the studio. The light came through the cracks, printing very fine streaks on the ceiling.

I put my nose against the windowpane. The sea was calm.

It was still very early in the morning. The Stork's dog was waiting on the stone outside the house. The stable gave on to the street. I could

268

hear the cows. I went through the door. The cows turned their heads. It was dark, almost night. There was a smell of straw, and milk dripping from udders. Heavy chains hobbled the cows by the neck. Chains scraping against the walls. I slid my hand over their soft bellies, their warm necks. There was hay in the mangers, and mash in the buckets.

The Stork's father was there, standing by the calves. Between shadow and light. Nearer the light. A pitchfork in his hand. No doubt he was already there when I came in. He was looking at me. A somewhat brutal smile.

He rammed his pitchfork into a bale of hay.

"Not good to go hanging about stables," he said.

He said it again in a duller voice.

"Not good."

I took Raphaël's car and I went to see the Irishwoman. I had Paul's photograph, and the report about the shipwreck. I parked in the courtyard, outside the door. I went into the hall. I found Betty just as she had been that first time, lying on her sofa in front of the television.

She did not get up.

She told me that Lambert had left. That he had been gone several days already. That he came home late during the night on Tuesday. He had taken his things and gone.

"He didn't tell you where he was going?"

"No . . . and I didn't ask."

"How was he?"

"What do you mean, how was he? No more smiles than usual, no chattier, either. Just his usual self, so to speak."

"If you see him again, could you tell him that I have . . . a photograph to give him?"

"I'll tell him."

She turned back to the screen, staring at the credits for a film that was starting. She paid no attention to me after that.

I could have sat down. Watched the film with her.

I went on to Cherbourg.

The train station. I wandered all around. Trains that arrived here and went no further. End of the line, rails suddenly stopping not far from the sea. I thought of buying a ticket, going elsewhere. From here, every elsewhere is possible. Even going without a ticket. If they checked, I would pay a supplement. I did not care.

A woman was waiting, hunched over on a bench, her bags gathered all around her.

There was wind. Clouds piling up. I went back out. I found a dreary little street in a dark neighbourhood. A café. The *patron* pointed to the poster above the bar.

"No smoking here!"

I smoked anyway. He did not want to make a fuss and besides, there was no-one, just him and me. A match on television.

The toilets, a door at the back of the room. A hole in the door. If you put your eye up to the hole from outside, you could see what was going on inside. And the opposite, too, from the inside, you could see out.

"Are you the one who made the hole?"

"What hole?"

I pointed. He shrugged. He went on cleaning his tables, watching the match.

On my way out, I stopped off at the *pâtisserie* on 5, place de la Fontaine, and I bought the apple tarts that M. Anselme had told me about.

*   *   *

I found Morgane in the kitchen, finishing a bride's tiara. It was a magnificent diadem that she had put together, with pearls shaped like fake diamonds.

It was beautiful. It shone.

The rat was sleeping curled up in its box in the middle of all the pearls. I touched its stomach. It rolled on its back, paws spread, and I went on stroking it.

Morgane looked up at me. "He still hasn't come back?"

"No."

"He could have said goodbye."

"He could have, yes."

She went back to her work. "I'm sure he's going to come back, actually."

We talked about him, about love, about desire. We talked about him again and about the men that Morgane had loved. Raphaël heard us. He came to drink a beer, standing by the window.

"Where've you been, Princess?"

I showed him the cake box, the tarts inside.

He came over to the table.

"Lambert has left," Morgane said, her nose in the pearls.

He looked at me, frowning. He took my hand and breathed on the inside of my palm.

"And yet you stink of man . . ."

Morgane tied the thread on her crown, held it up to check the overall effect, and placed it on her head. She was magnificent.

She pushed the box to the end of the table. "You want to tell us about it?"

"There's nothing to tell."

"Who was it?"

"I don't know, a bloke in a café."

"That's how you find the blokes you sleep with?"

"I didn't sleep with him."

Raphaël sat down next to Morgane. I looked at them. Their hands, their skin . . . They were brother and sister and they loved each other. In what way, I was not sure. I did not know if they touched. I had often seen Raphaël's hand lingering on his sister's neck. The disturbing way they had of smiling, of looking at each other.

"Who's the bloke who got you into this state?"

"There is no bloke."

"That's a good one."

I looked away.

"There is no bloke, I'm telling you."

She raised her eyebrows.

"Have a good fuck, you'll feel better afterwards."

"I don't want to feel better."

She handed me her cigarette. "Take a puff, then."

I looked outside.

From the window, you could see the sea.

We ate the tarts.

Raphaël called Max. He told him that there were tarts, but Max was sawing planks for his boat. He didn't want to come. The Stork was there, with both her feet in saddlebags. It was Max who had given them to her, when he changed them on his old bike. She didn't want to come, either. We put two tarts aside.

Morgane took out the rat and closed the box. We talked about Lambert again.

Morgane wondered what he would do with all the money when he sold his house.

We talked about his parents' death and the disappearance of his brother.

The Stork came to join us. She sat on a chair and began to pick at a bit of dried scab that was peeling off her knee. She was bending over it.

"It will leave a scar . . ." I said.

She didn't care. She pulled carefully until she had got the entire crust.

Max appeared a moment later.

"I'm lapidated!" he said.

"What do you mean by that, Max?"

He bit into his slice of tart.

"I don't mean."

"Lapidate . . . That means when you throw stones at someone."

"I'm lapidated in a different way . . . without the stones."

"Without the stones!"

"Yes . . . Lapidated . . . Annoyed, that is."

"Then say annoyed, it's simpler."

The child was staring at him. Max was all that interested her. The gestures he made. What he was building, a marvellous boat.

"Annoyed, it's not as strong on the scale . . ." he said.

I smiled.

"You're right . . . You are lapidated . . . Why not, after all?"

And when I asked him why he was lapidated to such a degree, he did not know. He said he had forgotten.

In the evening, a white mist caught on the masts of the boats. Over the harbour, the phantom murmuring of the chains restraining the hulls.

A small black boat was gliding over the water, heading away out towards the pass. A man was standing in the prow. A night-time fisherman. He was wearing a big black garment that looked like a cape. The boat seemed to glide across the water.

I heard the lapping sound of the oar. I thought of the bodies the sea took and did not give back. The bodies imprisoned by the water.

Tossed about, buoyed. The endless nightmares. I thought of Lambert's little brother.

La Hague is a country of legends, a place of beliefs. It is said that some of the disappeared come back at night, incapable of leaving this land behind. Of parting from it.

I walked along the quay. The seagulls had gathered on the breakwater. Some of them were already sleeping, their beaks tucked under their wings. The mist absorbed the sound of my footsteps, of my own breathing. The church tower in the distance.

It is said that on nights of a full moon you can see a man riding over the moor on a tall horse. The women dream of meeting him. They go out at night and leave their homes. They follow one of the very narrow footpaths that lead deep into the moor. They come back in the morning, and no-one can say what they have done.

A sudden sharp cry, and then nothing. Silence again. A rabbit bolted down the path ahead of me. I walked. Walked again tonight, as on the first nights, when I wanted to leave you behind. I walked and walked, to exhaust my body. And even when it was exhausted, I still walked.

That is what I did.

And tonight, once again.

I slept badly, tangled in my sheets. Or in my dreams.

I struggled.

The next morning, I found Raphaël sitting on the bench in the hall. His back to the wall. There were cigarette butts on the floor, and others that he had stubbed out on the bench.

"You'll set everything on fire," I said.

He looked up. He had been drinking. Or smoking. Or both at the same time. Unless it was the extreme fatigue that came over him after hours of work.

I picked up the cigarette butts, and tossed them outside.

"It's cold, you shouldn't stay there . . ."

He did not answer.

He pointed to the studio, the door wide open.

"Have a look . . ."

I went in. It was the smell that surprised me, whiffs of a wild beast, the impression I had of going into a cavern.

The floor was littered with drawing paper, from the door the sheets looked blank, but when I went closer, darker lines appeared and I saw they were all covered with drawings. They were everywhere. I walked around the room. Some of the drawings were hidden by others. I moved them. There were some on the table, on the steps, too, some that Raphaël had done on his knees, an old man sitting on a base, abandoned in a torpor close to death. Half-naked souls, dressed in rags, ready to be submerged and yet saved. As if they had been spared.

Everything was in shades of black and grey, an impression of dilution. In places, dust had stuck to the charcoal, you could see traces of it.

I went from one drawing to the next.

Everywhere, the same frail shoulders. The same dislocated limbs. A few rare landscapes.

I counted over a hundred drawings.

"One hundred and seventeen, to be exact . . ."

Raphaël was holding to the wall in the door frame, transfixed, a lost look on his face.

"Why did you make so many!"

"I don't know. I just did."

He raised his hand, it seemed heavy. His eyes looked as though they were bleeding.

"Hermann is going to come and fetch them, he's also going to take those sculptures . . ."

I gathered up some of the drawings and took them over to the light. It had taken him only a few days, a few nights to do them, but what he had captured was excruciating.

"No-one will forgive you for this."

"Some people will understand!"

"Yes, of course, some will . . ."

All around, the strange crowd of plaster continued to murmur, beggars with black shadows, women whose hollow bellies opened on to raw flesh, twisted limbs, disproportionate, imperfect bodies.

A carnage, that was the word that came to me. I told him so, "It's a veritable carnage," and he smiled.

He sorted through the drawings, the ones he was going to give to Hermann, and the others, the most unbearable ones, he put to one side.

When Morgane came to join us, she saw how exhausted he was. She put her face up to his. She looked at him, so close. She seemed to be breathing his breath.

So fearful for him.

So proud, too.

She murmured something and moved away, and came over to me.

She led me over to the stove, so that I would sit next to her on the old sofa.

She seemed sad. Something had changed in her over the last few days.

"What's wrong?" I said.

She hesitated. She tucked her legs under her, without answering. Raphaël went on sorting his drawings.

Morgane let her head drop against my shoulder. She looked at her brother.

"What is there, between Lambert and you?"

"There's nothing. We just met . . ."

"That's already something," she said.

"It should have been somewhere else, later, another place . . ."

She said she would like to meet someone, not a casual encounter, but someone absolutely necessary to her life.

An encounter that would change her, utterly and completely.

I told her about you.

In a hushed voice, almost a whisper.

The words. It took time.

At one point, Raphaël raised his eyes, looked at us.

When I had finished telling her the story, Morgane took my hand and placed it against her face.

"You've got to fuck now . . . Even if you fuck without love, but you've got to fuck."

She murmured it in my ear, never taking her eyes off Raphaël. I could feel the warmth of her breath on my skin.

*   *   *

Outside, it was slack water. The sea at its calmest. The motionless moment, when the shore is bare. Odours of sludge rising from between the rocks, a sour stench. On the damp sand there were paw prints. Rotting seaweed.

It was as I was on my way up to Lili's that I saw the Audi parked outside the house. The gate was ajar.

I walked past it a first time and then I came back. I hesitated, then I went through the gate. Lambert was by the fireplace, a log in his hands, lighting a fire. He turned his head. He did not say anything. He did not smile.

He put wood in the flames and stood up straight. We looked at each other.

I was angry with him. For leaving like that. For not saying anything.

"You're back . . ."

That is what I said. In a strangled, swallowed voice.

He came over to me.

"Forgive me."

I wanted to hit him. With my fists. To be violent with him. I turned away. I was suffocating. I looked towards the door.

He said it again, Forgive me, and I shook my head.

I could not.

"Forgive me . . ."

He repeated it for the third time. He pulled me close to him, his hand a vice behind my head. He forced me to look at him. It lasted a short moment, and then he moved his hand, just his fingers, curled them around the scarf.

"This is mine . . ."

I backed away from him. Infinitely slowly. One arm, then the other, my torso, and then my entire self. I untied the scarf.

"It's not what you think."

He smiled.

"I don't think anything."

He went back over to the fire and put a log on top of the one already burning.

He took his packet of cigarettes from his pocket. He tore the paper. He lit his cigarette.

"I wanted to get away. I went as far as Saint-Lô. I walked."

That is what he said.

I knew about walking. You do not walk for eight days.

"What is there in Saint-Lô?"

"Nothing, that's the whole point. Afterwards, I went home."

He inhaled his cigarette.

"I needed to think about all that."

He sat down by the fire. Reached his hands out to the flames.

I went to sit next to him. Like him, I looked at the flames. I could still feel the force of his hand on my neck. I wanted to ask him why he had come back.

"What happened with Théo?"

"Nothing . . . We talked."

"You talked . . . And then you left immediately afterwards, in the middle of the night."

"In the middle of the night, yes."

He rubbed his hands in front of the fire. He had his eyes on the flames, with something very particular in his voice.

"I remember when my mother asked me if I wanted a little brother. We were here, in front of this fireplace, sitting like this . . . I was thirteen years old, I had my habits. I said yes, to please her . . ."

He fell silent.

I slipped my hand into my pocket. I pulled out the photograph of his brother. I handed it to him.

He took the photograph in his hands.

"You found it again . . . Where was it?"

"At Nan's . . . With other photographs of children. You mustn't be angry with her."

"I'm not angry with her . . . Do you know why she did it?"

I said I did not know.

He went on looking at the photograph.

"He took my fingers, like this, and played with them. I liked his hair."

I listened to him talk about his brother, my face in his scarf. The

278

steam that came from my mouth clung to the woollen strands. The wool became damp. I breathed in the smell.

"In my dreams, I have drowned so often, and I'm still drowning . . ."

He gave a faint smile and then his expression vanished. He sat for a very long time with the photograph in his hands, poring over it.

I gave him the report on the shipwreck, the carefully folded A4 sheet. He read it. When he had finished, he folded the sheet again, and put it together with the photograph.

"Do you know why I came back?"

He was turning the photograph and the folded paper in his hands.

"There's something that doesn't fit . . . I don't know what, but there's something . . ."

He turned his head away, his gaze suddenly impregnable. As if the fact that he was here frightened him. What he still had to do. To learn, perhaps.

"I became a policeman so that I could get to the bottom of this sort of thing."

He said nothing more.

I sat for a moment longer, then I got up. Before going out, I looked back.

He was still gazing at the fire.

I looked at him again, through the window. He had not moved. The same worry lines across his forehead.

I went back down to La Griffue. He had held me close to him. An instant. A need of skin. That strength in his hands. You embrace stones when you have nothing left, I had known that.

I did not want to think about him.

I went into the yard. The man from the foundry was there, with his minivan. It did me good to see someone. He was delivering two sculptures cast in bronze, "The Sitting Thinker" and "The Wandering Woman of the Slums". They set the sculptures in the studio.

Hermann was there too. He had come on purpose. This was the

first time I had met him. The bronzes were superb. He was walking around them. These were not the first sculptures Raphaël had had cast, but they were the biggest.

Hermann said he would come back for the sculptures at the end of the week. He took the drawings with him.

I went up to the emaciated face of "The Wandering Woman", as if she were a sister in misery, her open sex, her wound. This immodesty . . . How did Raphaël dare? I do not know where he drew his strength from, what obscure part of himself fed this need to dig ever deeper. Uncompromisingly. I should have liked to have been able to live the way he sculpted. Of blood and flesh?

Dare to be what I was.

They left, the man from the foundry, Hermann. I stayed alone in the studio, I put my hands on the bronze hands, "The Wandering Woman", whose hollowed cheeks and empty lips reminded me of the emptiness of my own womb. Of my nights. With you gone, the emptiness.

This woman had carried her child in her arms. She had walked with him. She had nursed him, until someone tore the infant away. A shred of flesh. An arm. The way they had torn you from me. What do I still have of you? In the end, I could not cry any more. They made me sleep. For hours. For days. One morning, they opened the door. There was sunlight. They told me I was better.

I asked for you. In churches, on my knees, although I believed in nothing. They had to lock me up again. Until you became a silence. An eternal shadow beneath my skin.

I raised my head, slowly. There before me, "The Wandering Woman" seemed to be smiling to me. It must have been a trick of the light in the folds of her face. Where did she go, after they tore her child away from her? Was she able to love again?

There were tears on my cheeks. I had not realized that I was crying.

And yet I was: tears so salty that they made me feel sick to my stomach.

*   *   *

Max was resting, sitting in the sun, his back against a cross. With his finger he was tracing the shadows of birds over the stone. He watched as I approached.

"The roots must be able to have adequate breathing," he said, indicating the ground he had turned up at the base of the flowers.

The soil of the dead. How many nights did I wake up with its taste in my mouth? Where were my friends? My telephone, somewhere at the bottom of a handbag, unplugged for months. There were some whom I should call.

Max pulled me by the sleeve.

"Raphaël said that some day, there will be no more sun, we will get up, it will be morning and then it will be noon, and it will be dark."

He spat.

"He said the flowers are going to die."

He took a piece of bread from inside his pocket, and began to gnaw at it.

"Do you think that some day, when my boat goes to sea, Morgane will live with love for me?"

He was staring at me, his head to one side, his gaze somewhat grim. "Raphaël says the thing is not possible, but Raphaël is not Morgane and he does not have all the knowledge."

He waited for me to reply. He was still scraping his teeth against the hard crust of bread. He could scrape like that for a long time.

"I don't have all the knowledge either, Max . . . but I think that this thing you want is not possible."

He nodded. A brief instant, his eyes were all white, as if rolled up inside his skull. I knew he was taking medication to deal with these absences.

I put my hand on his arm.

"Max?"

It took him some time, several long seconds, before he came round. He rubbed his eyes, he put all his belongings in his bag, and he led me into the church. He wanted to show me two engravings, the one of the

281

ship, the *Vendémiaire*, and the other of the submarine that had sunk it. He'd been talking about it already for several days. An accident that happened in 1912. The cross of the *Vendémiaire* that was located next to La Griffue was in homage to the sailors who had died that day. Max knew the story by heart.

Nan came when we were still inside the church. We saw her when we came out, she was on her knees on the big square tomb. She was removing the withered flowers from the pots of begonias. She had done this every day from the time she was seven. She had grown up, grown old, bent over the dead. Where was the child that she had taken in?

Max was looking at her, too.

What was he thinking about? What did he know about the child who had abandoned her?

I picked up some gravel and poured it back and forth from one hand to the other.

"Do you remember the day you told me about your friend . . . ?"

He smiled and nodded, a vigorous nodding of his head.

"Do you remember the day he left?"

"Yes . . . Max was very sad."

"And what about *him*, was he sad?"

"I don't know. He was leaving."

"Did he tell you why he was leaving?"

"No. He was leaving . . ."

Nan went on rubbing the slab, she paid no attention to us.

"And your friend, did he have other friends?"

"No, he was Max's friend."

He frowned, as if he had suddenly recalled something.

"One day, he cried. After that, he left."

I looked at him.

"Why did he cry?"

He went on following every one of Nan's gestures, the slowness of her steps.

"Who made your friend cry?" I said.

"Lili."

"Lili? Do you know why?"

He shook his head.

He pointed at Nan.

"She has made her hair loose-hanging, but today is not a shipwreck day."

I looked and saw that Nan's hair was flying behind her, as on the day of a great storm.

It was on leaving the cemetery that I noticed them, Lambert and Lili, they were in the yard to the rear of the bistro.

I do not know what they said to each other. It looked as if they were arguing. They stayed for a moment longer, outside, and then afterwards, Lambert left.

M. Anselme drew up alongside and stopped the car. He rolled the window down.

"I have very little time, but I wanted to tell you ... My friend Ursula is coming for tea at my home on Saturday. Would you care to join us? Ursula is an excellent *pâtissière*, she always brings very good cakes."

He smiled at me with a knowing gaze.

"We could meet early in the afternoon? She will tell you about the Refuge. Well, what do you think?"

I told him I accepted his invitation. If the weather was fine, I would come on foot along the shore.

He drove on for a few yards then stopped again.

"By the way, why are you so very interested in the history of that Refuge? It's only an old building! And those children, how could their fate possibly ... ?"

I tried to make my smile as luminous as his own.

"I am like them ... My mother gave me up at birth."

I would have liked my tone to be lighter, almost affectionate. My words sounded leaden. I felt myself blush.

M. Anselme reached his hand out to my arm.

"You don't need to ..."

What did he mean? That I did not need to be ashamed? Of course not. Who would be ashamed of that?

Old Mother peered through the strips of the plastic curtain. She watched me come in, her fingers fiddling with the plastic strips. They were sticky. Impregnated with everything that left the kitchen in the form of a vapour.

She took a few steps and came up to me, her eyelids heavy.

She was clutching her handbag.

I sat down at the table.

She took the chair opposite me. She was poised, her eyes down, slowly rubbing her hands one against the other. Waiting. Not speaking.

Lili was not there, she was still in the yard. At the back of the garden. After her argument with Lambert, a need to walk.

"What do you want?" I said to Old Mother.

She did not answer.

I talked to her about the farm. About Théo, a few sentences, and then about the yard, the house. She slowly sat up. Attentive to my every word. She made no sound, even with her teeth. I described our moments together at the table, and Théo's steps when he went with me to the footpath. I did not say anything about the skylight, or about taking the detour to go by Nan's place.

She opened her bag and took out her wedding photograph. She showed it to me as if it were the first time.

And I looked at it as if she had never showed it to me.

Her eyes began to fill with tears. Thick tears, spilling only slightly. In the end, her eyes were like huge pools.

To me it was beautiful.

She took out another photograph and pushed it over to me. It was the one that Lili had taken down.

I just had time to glance at it, the child standing slightly to the rear, little Michel, when we heard the door to the kitchen open and shut again with a slam.

Chairs scraping. Old Mother put the photograph in her bag. Lili had come back. I could see her from behind, through the strips of curtain, slightly more stooped than usual.

It was rare to see her like that.

Then she saw us.

"What are you two plotting?" she asked, going behind the bar.

We did not answer.

Old Mother went back to her place.

Lili picked up the post and threw it on the table next to her catalogues. She would look at all that later. She wiped her glasses. Glasses that were already clean. She also wiped the counter.

She was waiting for customers. She wanted the place to fill up.

She said as much: "What are they doing, why aren't they here today?"

*   *   *

A collector from Dinard stopped at the studio and bought two bronzes from Raphaël, "Christ on the Cross" and also a "Beggar". He said he was going to put the "Beggar" in his garden.

Raphaël had already sold bronzes, but for works that size this was the first time. And two at once!

With the money he would be able to cast other sculptures. Later, as soon as he could, he would cast "The Pleading Women".

"The Pleading Women" were his dream. For months they had had pride of place in the studio, three women joined together at their wombs, their hands raised, fingers spread, all the upper part of their bodies opened out. Their ascetic faces seemed to have been ravaged from within. They were imploring. Raphaël had fettered them, their bare feet held tight in the base as if, for some obscure reason, he refused to let them go.

He ran his hand over the plaster.

"All I need to do is sign them."

He took a nail from his pocket. He found a modest spot at the bottom of the base.

He spat on the head of the nail and dug out the first letter, the R of Raphaël. R. Delmate. He blew on the dust. The print went deeper.

This was the first time I had ever seen him signing his work. He explained that some artists sign directly in the bronze, they do it with a drill, a tool that looks like a dentist's instruments He did not like that.

I watched until he had written the last letter of his name.

"How does it feel, to carve your name on your work?" I asked when he had finished.

"I don't bloody care about my name!"

He put the date, the month and year. He rubbed the spot with his hand.

"I have to do it. I try to be as discreet as possible."

He got up.

"If I sell 'Virtue', I'll cast 'The Seamstress of the Dead'."

He leaned his head to one side.

His car was in the yard, the boot open wide, filled with blankets and cardboard sheeting. He called Max, and together they loaded the plasters.

After that, Max went back to his boat. He was putting a final coat on the bottom of the hull, a very dark green, almost black.

"You should wear a mask . . ." I told him.

Everyone told him so. Raphaël too.

He did not wear one.

At the end of the afternoon Max turned up in the kitchen, holding his head between his hands. He sat down at the table. Morgane dissolved two tablets in a glass of water.

"We told you to wear a mask . . ."

She stirred with a spoon, the water whirling the particles.

"Drink it!" she said, because he was looking at her, not drinking, and the particles of aspirin were already sinking to the bottom of the glass.

She had to stir it again.

"This time you swallow it!"

The next morning, Max finished painting the hull. He still had to varnish the cabin door and repaint the letters of *La Marie-Salope*. When he had done all that, he could set sail.

He was practically weeping with joy. He had had the motor checked, and all the boat's equipment. An official paper certified that *La Marie-Salope* was indeed seaworthy and could brave the tides.

He kept the paper on him, always.

He was still hesitating over what colour to use to repaint the name. He wanted a colour that looked good against the sea.

He asked me what colour the sea was and I told him that sometimes the sea was blue. That very often it was brown. But that it could also be black or metallic, or take on the colour of the sky, and then you could not really tell what colour it was.

Max decided to paint the letters green, because green went well with all the colours I had just mentioned, even the indefinable colours of the sky.

He asked us our opinion. Raphaël gave him a tube of paint and a brush and Max went back over the letters without trembling.

That was also the day, or maybe it was the day after, that the Stork turned eight. Raphaël gave her a big box filled with pencils, felt-tips and pastels. When she saw it, she sat down with the box open on her lap, and she did not dare touch anything.

After a short while, she opened a first felt-tip and sniffed the tip. She made a few tests on the smooth wood of the bench, and a few lines on the back of her hand. After that she spilled the box, and put the pencils and the rubber and the chalk into her pockets. She held the sketchbook that was inside close to her, and the little notebook, too, and she hugged Raphaël and left without saying where she was going.

The next day, the Stork was there again, in the hall. Where she had sprung from, who knows, and she was again wearing the garment that was too big, but it had pockets to contain her treasure.

Her hair tangled, one arm down at her side, she began to draw on the wall. A black streak that unfurled like Ariadne's thread, a dark shaky line that the child drew and which went round the latch then outside to streak the white shutter. Then the black turned brown when the child changed her pastel. The little papers covering the coloured sticks drifted into the brambles and caught on the thorns.

The print of the soles of her shoes in the crumbly earth.

Little grassy plants grew along the wall, heart-shaped, and their leaves secreted a fine layer of poison. All around, beneath the leaves, there were the cadavers of flies and bees and butterflies. Dozens of them lay there, curled up where death had caught them by surprise. Some were already decomposing. No-one had ever been able to tell me the name of that plant, but I knew that from the humus of its victims it drew the energy to strengthen its roots.

The Stork also drew on the hull of the boat, flowers in the shape of a heart or a sun. I wondered what Max would say when he saw the drawing.

I also wondered what would happen to the drawing when the boat went to sea. The child had abandoned her felt-tips all round the boat, the pencils with their leads crushed, and caps scattered here and there.

Did she know that those heart-shaped plants secreted death in order to live?

The Stork's empty box stayed on the bench. The plastic display case. The hollows where pencils could nest.

And then one morning, everything had disappeared.

*   *   *

On Saturday I went to Omonville. It was raining. I left Raphaël's car in the car park next to the church. M. Anselme was waiting for me with Ursula, the two of them sitting in the conservatory.

He was happy to see me. He took my hand.

"We've been hoping you'd come."

Ursula had very short hair, extraordinarily black. Sparkling eyes. She held me close, infinitely affectionate.

M. Anselme poured orangeade into the glasses, and cut three slices of cake. Figs were set in the dough, they looked preserved.

"Do you like it?"

The sweet seeds crunched beneath my teeth. I smiled. It was delicious. We ate slowly as we talked about the garden and the very pleasant life in Omonville, where the climate was so special that apparently no flowers ever froze. The village seemed to be an oasis of peace, far enough away from the fury of the sea, yet close enough to receive its energy.

Ursula was discreet.

M. Anselme was smiling.

Ursula said a few words about the past there in Omonville, and also about the Refuge. She described the life of the children there.

"You know, it was a special time, and things were simpler than they are today."

She had a large ring on one of her fingers, an enormous stone, and she played with it while she spoke.

She looked at M. Anselme and me.

"I've never known anyone to love children the way Nan loved them. She was often criticized, but she was the one who started the Refuge. She fought for it. The kids who turned up there were all miserable, each one more than the last. With the scant means she had at her disposal, she managed to make a nest for them."

"And Théo?"

"Théo would come, then he didn't come . . . He had the lighthouse to keep. And then, Old Mother was not easy to deal with. She didn't like him visiting the Refuge."

"Which you can understand," I said.

"Why? That's all bloody choirboy morality, a cheap way to feel good about oneself! There was some truly disgusting gossip going round about Nan. And there still is. You mustn't listen to it. They would have worked well together as a pair, if they'd been left alone."

She had spoken heatedly. After that, she did not mention Théo. I was the one who insisted.

"Why didn't he just leave everything behind if he loved her so much?"

She gave a short laugh.

"They would have made their life impossible, that's why! Old Mother was born here, her family have lived here for generations. Nan bears the cross for her loved ones, she sews shrouds. She's between two worlds, and some people say she has the evil eye . . ."

Ursula ran her hand through her hair.

M. Anselme did not say anything. His chair slightly further back from the table, he sat listening.

"Nan knew that she would not have children of her own, so when Michel came along, how to explain it . . . That kid was like a grub, just impossible to pep him up! No matter what you fed him, the best you had . . . The moment you let go of his hand, he headed straight for the sea. Who knows why? In the end, we let him. I always found him in the same spot, sitting on a rock. I don't know if he was sad when I came to get him. We can't be sure either what he would have done if I hadn't gone to get him."

She rubbed a few strands of hair between her fingers.

"One year, there was snow, and ice on the windows. The littlest children wet their beds, and it froze in the sheets."

She talked about that terrible winter, and how there was not enough food, the hot soups, the cold rooms. The smell of cooked cabbage that lingered everywhere in the corridors, as if it had impregnated the walls.

"Do you remember when Michel arrived?"

She shook her head.

"No . . . I had just given birth to my youngest daughter. When I started work again, he had already been there a week, perhaps two."

She thought for a moment. The images were coming to her as she spoke.

"The first time I saw him, he was in the courtyard, sitting in the sun. We knew nothing about him, just that he had been found in Rouen, on a pile of rags. Not even a name . . ."

She took a swallow of orangeade, then put her glass down.

I looked at her.

"People say that Nan stole toys from the Perack house."

She laughed, but made no attempt to lie. She could have kept silent.

Instead, she looked at me, her gaze very open.

"And so what? Where is the harm in that? Who was going to use those toys, anyway? The children had to play with something."

"Why did she take the toys at night?"

"Everything happens at night here, that's the way it is. Did you go inside the Refuge?"

"Yes."

She looked at M. Anselme and me.

"Why are you looking for that child?"

"I'm not looking for him . . ."

I had known refuges too, and they were all just like that one, with other smells, of damp laundry, dirty nappies. The stifling promiscuity that had made me so desperate for solitude.

"It's just that I was born like that, too . . ."

That is what I said, like that, without parents, without anybody. She looked at me. I tried to smile. She nodded. There was a silence. She understood. That is what she said in the end, I understand.

She told us some more.

"Nan had prepared a room next to her own, in her house, but he always preferred to sleep with the others. He would get up during the night, and go barefoot back into the dormitory."

M. Anselme filled our glasses again.

I listened to Ursula. I liked the precise way she had of telling the story, as if she wanted us to see it. The fragile silhouette of the child walking along the corridor, his feet in the dust, and Nan's sad eyes in the morning when she found the empty bed. The door he had to push open.

"Max was his friend, wasn't he?"

Ursula nodded.

"Yes . . . particularly when they were little, but even afterwards, when Michel went to the lycée, they stayed in touch."

"And you don't know where he went when he left?"

"No . . . it was a few weeks after he turned seventeen."

She fiddled with the ring on her finger.

"Most likely, he went to Rouen . . . and then after that, elsewhere. He must have been looking for his family, at least that's what we supposed. There were not many places he could look."

She pressed her hands together.

"I was angry with him . . . Not for leaving, no, that I could understand, but for leaving us the way he did, without news."

Her voice trembled. You could sense her emotion stirring.

"It's been at least twenty years now . . . Nan kept his clothes in a little box, the clothes he was wearing when they found him . . . The last time I went to her place, she showed them to me again."

She looked at me for a long time.

She said, "Those children are more difficult to understand than the others, they come here and they leave again in the same way, we don't know why or where they came from. You just have to take them in."

Are those children more fearful than others? My throat was tight. I could no longer speak. M. Anselme put his hand on his friend's arm.

"And Théo, how did he get along with that child?"

"They got along well. Even very well, I'd say. He may have been adopted, but he was Nan's child . . . There was something very strong between them. When Théo wasn't at the lighthouse, Michel spent his days with him at the farm. He wasn't allowed inside the house, but he could go into the stables."

She turned her head and looked outside, her eyes lost for a moment in the flowers that grew in beds along the side of the conservatory.

"Say what you like, but it's with Nan that he should have had children."

She turned to us once again.

"After Michel left, everything changed. Nan was no longer interested in the children. She had them placed with families, all of them, one after the other. The beds emptying, it was heartbreaking . . . One morning, the last child left, and she closed the shutters of the Refuge."

"And you?"

"I . . ."

It had begun to rain, steady drops on the roof of the conservatory. Ursula looked at her watch. It was late. We had talked for a long time.

We all got up at the same time.

Ursula's car was parked nearby. I walked with her to the car. When she sat down behind the wheel, I asked her if she remembered the child's surname.

She looked at me, she did not need to think, no doubt she had known I would ask her this question. She was ready.

"His name was Lepage, Michel Lepage."

I watched the car pull away.

The rain was falling on my back.

It seemed to me that all was well.

*   *   *

293

Thus I had not asked my questions in vain. The Michel who was writing to Théo was indeed the child that Nan had taken in. A child who had grown up. How old would he be now? Forty?

Max had been one of Michel's refuges.

The way you had been mine. All the time that I knew you. Loved you.

I watched the windscreen-wipers beating. And then, when the rain stopped falling, I watched the sea, beyond the windscreen. I stayed there.

The letters I had seen at Théo's had been written by that child, grown up. A monastery, the ultimate refuge?

The child who had grown up, had he become a monk? He was writing to Théo, and yet Nan did not seem to know where he was.

I went back to the village.

The road was blocked off. There were posters stuck up here and there, on doors, letters bright with colour to say there was a village fête that evening. I left Raphaël's car by the side of the road, near the wash-house.

*   *   *

For days the sheep had been waiting for death, in a little pen, staring at the ground. I was there when they brought it up to the square. I saw the children clamber on to the walls. The dogs were howling.

They killed it. An hour later, its skin was drying on the fence, and that evening Max turned the spit. He had spent the week cleaning the stained-glass windows, but you could not see them because of the dark. They would have had to have put lights on inside the church.

A little group of musicians had set up on a podium. The children were dancing. A few couples. The Stork was off to one side with two other girls, showing each other what they had in their pockets. I walked round among all these people I did not know. I brushed against them. They were talking to each other. They had a shared history.

I thought of going back down to La Griffue.

Lambert came out of his house. He walked along the dance floor and disappeared for a moment behind the dancers. He went by a first time, very close to me, almost touching me. He was looking elsewhere. He did not see me.

I could have made a sign, he would have turned round. Perhaps. I hugged the wall even closer. I was one of those people you do not see. Not beautiful enough. Not ugly enough either, probably. Somewhere in between. Already as an adolescent, when I went to parties, it was the others who danced.

He went by a second time.

I bought a raffle ticket. A sugared waffle. I slipped the ticket in my pocket. And then he came over. From the side.

"Have you been here for long?"

I said no, that I had just arrived. He told me he had changed the glass on the frame and put the medallion back on the grave.

He went to buy a waffle, he wanted one after seeing mine. Morgane was there, on the dance floor, she was dancing with a young man. She was wearing a black sleeveless top, her shoulders bare despite the chill, the rat curled against her neck.

I looked at them.

Lambert was looking at them, too.

"People who desire each other are always more beautiful. It's enough to make you want to desire, just to be beautiful like that."

That is what he said. He went on eating his waffle. At one point, he asked if I wanted to dance, there was almost no-one on the floor. I said no, it was not my thing, and he said it was not his thing either, but after all, it was a dance.

He finished his waffle, took my arm, and led me on to the dance floor. He held me close to him. It was a slow dance.

"Lili knew . . ." he murmured into my ear.

"Lili knew what?"

"About her father, that he'd put out the light."

I felt his hands against my back. I did not know where to put mine.

"Relax, everyone is looking at us."

He said it without taking his eyes from the dance floor. He was a good dancer, I am sure he was lying when he said it was not his thing. Other couples joined us.

"Is that why you were arguing?" I said.

"Did you see us?"

"From the street, yes . . ."

Morgane had stopped dancing, and she disappeared down a side street with the boy. She waved to me.

Everywhere we looked, the girls were beautiful. They had fastened crêpe-paper flowers to their hair.

"Do you know the story about the two goldfish that go round and round together in their bowl?"

I shook my head.

"Well, they go round, and round . . . and after a while one of them stops and asks the other one, What are you doing on Sunday?"

It made him laugh.

At the time, I thought it was stupid, but afterwards, I laughed, too. I was still in his arms. Around us, boys were looking for girls, and girls were waiting for boys. Sixteen-year-old boys holding fifteen-year-old girls, swearing to love each other for life. They swore it with their eyes closed.

I envied them.

The music stopped.

We left the dance floor. Lambert lit a cigarette.

Morgane had disappeared with the boy hanging on to her.

"I'm going home," I said.

He held me back by the arm.

"I told you there was something that didn't match up . . . The last time I danced here, I was thirteen, it was in summer."

"Is that what doesn't fit?"

"No, that's not it. But that summer, my mother was wearing a white

296

dress, and my father was dancing with her. I remember my mother's white dress, but not her face. I've forgotten her voice . . . Sometimes, at night, I dream about her, and I see her again. I see her the way she was before, as if death did not exist."

I stayed beside him. He was smoking, looking at a couple kissing.

"The place where I used to work, before, there was a girl, she always said yes when you asked her for a kiss. It was nice."

That is what he said.

After talking about his mother.

The music stopped again and everything froze, suddenly, on the dance floor. Someone asked for silence, because the raffle-drawing was about to start. It was the priest who won the sheepskin, he went up on the podium to get it. He said he was going to put it at the foot of his bed. That was the first prize.

There were other prizes after that one.

I won a hand-knitted cardigan. I did not go to fetch it. I was holding the crumpled ticket between my fingers. They repeated the number several times, through the loudspeaker, looking at all the people in the crowd. Then they went on to the following prize. The cardigan stayed on the podium. I opened my fingers and the ticket fell on the ground.

Lambert leaned over to me.

"Her name was Nicole, the girl who kissed me. It's not a very nice name, is it, Nicole? And she wasn't very pretty either, so I suppose her name suited her."

He said that, and stepped on the ticket.

The music started again. Children ran in front of us. There were a lot of people, suddenly too many people.

He pointed to his house.

"From the dormer window up there, you can see the sea."

That was what he said. From the dormer window, up there.

We looked at each other. Five minutes later, we were in the garden, and went into the house. We did not even turn on the lights.

The door leading upstairs creaked. Lambert went first. I followed him. You could not see a thing. We banged our feet against the steps. It made us laugh.

We laughed quietly.

It was fun to go up like that, unable to see anything. The sounds from outdoors came through the walls, firecrackers so loud you might think they had been set off in the courtyard, just there, below the windows.

We went into a room. He bumped into something and swore. He went on, one hand ahead of him, and pushed open the wooden shutter protecting the dormer window. The light from outside lit up his face. I said, "At Théo's place there's a skylight like this one". The air was damp. We leaned out and looked at the street, just below us, the dancers, the musicians, and the sea in the distance.

The beam from the lighthouse.

And the dancers again.

It felt good up here. High up. It was very tempting to think that up here you could be better or freer than elsewhere. Stronger, too.

"You know, that man that Nan mistakes you for . . ."

"Later . . ."

"No, now."

He stepped back. He looked at me.

"Now? Alright."

He went to sit at the back of the room. I heard a mattress creak. I stayed by the window.

"About the man, I know where he is."

I told him about my meeting with Ursula. About the Refuge, the letters Théo received from the monastery. The child who left, and no-one could say why.

I was talking, and I could not see him. At one point, I saw the red burst of a flame when he lit a cigarette, and then the flame went out.

I waited for him to say something, but he did not say anything.

I too fell silent.

He got up and closed the shutter. I heard the sound, the little iron hook, and the rustling of his jacket.

We found ourselves in the dark again. Our eyes got used to it. We could see each other faintly, the outline of our faces.

He stayed like that for a while, next to me, not moving, then he said, "I think maybe that story is none of our business."

He did not say anything else. We went back downstairs.

He went with me to the door.

There was no more music. No more dancers. People were all headed down to the harbour, to see the fireworks they were going to set off above the sea. We stayed there, on the doorstep, watching people go by.

"Aren't you coming . . ."

He shook his head.

He was going to sleep here, in one of the rooms, in the new sheets he had bought in Cherbourg.

When I got to the gate, he called me back.

"That photograph you talked about, the one that was pinned up in the room, you said Lili was going to get it for you?"

"Yes."

"But she hasn't, yet?"

I looked at him.

"No . . ." I answered.

I took three steps.

"It's in Old Mother's bag."

"And you haven't tried to get it?"

"No. Why, should I have?"

He nodded, and I went off towards the harbour.

I followed the people walking along the road. Most of them were families, with children. A noisy, happy little crowd.

I stopped outside the farm so I would not be caught among them. A sick ewe was stretched out in front of the barn door. The Stork's father had separated her from the others. For two days, she had been tied with a rope to a nail. Almost outside. The cats were circling around her.

The sow went nowhere near her. She could smell death. She didn't like it.

At midnight, they set off the fireworks. Young men climbed on to boats and tossed flowers on to the water. The waves buoyed the flowers. Projectors lit them. The air was mild. I was not sure whether I felt good.

I think I was feeling the need to be with someone. I wandered round on the quay for a moment.

I went back up into my room. Late in the night, I heard an accordion, dance music from the square had started up again, and I thought that Lambert would probably not be able to sleep.

*　　*　　*

La Hague, a few hours before the rain. Stormy weather. My skin can sense the smell of sulphur. It always could. It can sense the lightning coming, hours before the first flashes.

That is the way it is with skin.

Some skin.

I got up late. It felt too good in the sheets. I could not tear myself away.

Max was beneath the shelter, by his boat. He was ready to go to sea, that is what he said, just a matter of choosing the right day.

"Will you take me as far as the lighthouse?" I asked him, leaning out of my window.

He looked up.

"The currents have the dangerousness of the breaking waves. No-one can go."

"But people used to go, before?"

He scratched his chin and looked at the lighthouse. The currents were black, as if they had been spewed out by the night.

"I have to ask Raphaël."

When I went up to him, he was frowning. He was putting his tools away.

"I always ask Raphaël, for everything."

I did not insist.

I went down to the shore. A little bird with a yellow beak was pecking at sand fleas.

The solitary imprint of my soles.

My shadow, insignificant, on the road.

Morgane came up to meet me.

"Why don't you move on?" she said at last.

I hesitated before replying.

"I feel good here . . . These few square miles are enough for me."

I was lying. They were not enough. They were no longer enough.

"And you?"

"I'll never leave without Raphaël."

"And the boy I saw you with at the fête?"

"That was nothing. He's from Beaumont."

We came back along the quay. The sea was coming. We could hear the water lapping.

"The fellow who gives me work said that later, if I like, I can buy a moped and come and sell dresses in his boutique in Cherbourg."

"Haven't you got your licence?"

"No, but I do know how to drive."

I looked at her. The wind was blowing her hair on to her face. A little bubble of saliva was trapped in the fold of her lip. She was beautiful. I did not feel jealous. At another time, no doubt, her youth would have been unbearable.

"Are you looking at me?"

"You're beautiful."

"I'm getting old," she said, making a face.

"Certainly you are!"

"I'm going to be thirty, do you realize!"

It made me laugh. She cocked her head to one side.

"Still, I think I ought to lose weight . . . Don't you think?"

"I don't know . . ."

"Neither do I, that's why I don't, as long as I don't know."

"It's going to rain," I said.

She looked out towards the lighthouse. We went through the garden and into the house.

She took the rat out of her pocket and put it on the sofa. She went over to the window. "It's not raining . . ."

"It's just that the sky is so grey."

"Grey, that doesn't mean rain."

She sat down at the table, looked over her latest crown, adjusting what was not right. She did not feel like working. She said, "I'm fed up with doing this!"

She went and stood next to the window.

The rat climbed on to the table, and went into its box. I picked up a pearl. The rat showed its teeth.

"Now it's raining," she said.

She turned to me. "You were with him yesterday . . ."

"Yes."

She picked up her crown.

"What did you do?"

"Nothing."

She cut the thread with her teeth. She threaded several pearls one after the other, tying knots in between them. Strands of hair swept across her face. She tucked them back, but they were rebellious strands, and they fell forward again. I liked watching her, her hands around the pearls.

She eventually put the diadem down. She looked down at her hands. Her nails, the skin gnawed.

"Sometimes, I think I should get away from here."

Her eyes filled with tears. Drowning for an instant, and then the tears spilled over. She crushed them with the back of her sleeve. It happened so suddenly. There were tears on the table, too.

She tried to erase it all with a smile. She spread her hands.

"I can't do a thing without him."

What could I say to her? I wanted to put my hand on hers. She withdrew. She did not want me to touch her. That is what we all believe, that we will never be able to manage without the other person. And then the other person leaves, and we discover that we can do masses of things that we had not even imagined. Different things, and it will never be the way it was. I tried to explain all of that to her.

That you can go on, after all.

She was sniffling.

I talked to her about you.

Like a thorn thrust deep in my flesh. Sometimes I forget you. And then all it takes is a gesture, the wrong movement, and the pain returns, absolutely alive.

Sometimes, too, the pain is not there and I am the one who goes looking for it. I find it, I awaken you.

Familiar pain.

We seek consolation with tears too.

Morgane dried her tears. She tried to smile.

The door opened, it was the little Stork. She had been caught in the rain. She had found Raphaël's jumper in the corridor and she put it on. It was far too big for her. It reached down to her calves. Her head was hidden in the collar. She came up to us, swaying from one foot to the other, her arms spread wide. I could hear her breathing through the weave of the jumper.

Morgane took a packet of biscuits from the cupboard. She called Raphaël. He did not want to talk about his work. He did not want to tell us anything about what he was doing. He was working.

He put his hands on the Stork's head. "What are you doing in my jumper, then?"

He told us that in two days' time a journalist from *Beaux-Arts* would be coming to take a look at his work.

*   *   *

In the afternoon, they launched Max's boat. First on to the rails, and then they let it slip slowly.

When it reached the water, the boat heeled over. We were afraid.

And then it was afloat.

It is not every day that a boat is put back in the water, so people from the village had come down to see. There were other people there too, that we did not know.

The *patron* of the *auberge* grilled some baby shrimps. Lili brought sandwiches. She served sparkling wine in plastic glasses. She had changed the colour of her hair, a red that was slightly too red, and there were streaks of it on her neck.

Standing on the quay, we all toasted fair winds to *La Marie-Salope*.

Morgane took a photograph of Max with the fishermen and another one of him standing on the deck of the boat. The brand-new paint job sparkled in the sun.

Lambert was there, too.

He was looking for a rubbish bin, a bag, somewhere to throw his glass. He could not find anything. He kept the glass in his hand.

He came over to me.

We did not look at each other. We were looking at the boat.

We were looking at Max, at the sea. The breakwater, like a rampart keeping out the storms. Old Mother was there too, she had come down by car, she needed to lean on things, she was wobbly. She hesitated between sitting down and holding on. Her eyes were wide open, it was not every day that she could see the sea.

Lili was handing out mulled wine. Pieces of orange floated on the surface. Slices of lemon. She filled our glasses, first mine, then Lambert's.

Lambert held her by the arm.

"There was a picture at your place, on the wall."

She looked up. "What are you talking about?"

"Apparently you took it down. I'd like to see it."

Lili looked at him abruptly, almost brutally. And then she looked at me.

I turned my head. I lowered my eyes.

Old Mother was next to us. You might have thought she was smiling, but it was the light.

Lambert and I went to drink our wine over by the boats.

Max thanked everybody for their *indulgence*, and for other things, too.

We eventually found a rubbish bin and threw away our glasses.

Before leaving me, Lambert said, "I think I've found someone for the house."

In the evening I painted the door to my room with what was left of the Hopper green. I left the window open to let the smell out.

I went out.

There was no-one on the path. Just a longclaw observing the moor.

I sat there until the space swallowed me. Made me into a mineral being contemplating the world.

* * *

The journalist who wanted to write an article about Raphaël came the next day, at ten o'clock. He brought several issues of *Beaux-Arts* to show him.

Raphaël prepared some coffee. He put biscuits on the table. He wanted me to stay there, with Morgane. We leafed through the magazines. The rat was in its box. The journalist asked Raphaël if it was important for him to work in a place like La Hague. Raphaël said that he did not know, that no doubt he could work elsewhere, but he liked being here.

He poured the coffee. He gave some biscuit crumbs to the rat. He said that if he did not sculpt, he would be terribly bored, and he would undoubtedly have to do something else. Gardening, or fishing. Or he would do like Morgane, make crowns for the dead.

The journalist nodded. He asked other questions and Raphaël answered. When he did not know, he said, I don't know.

The journalist did not press him. He drank his coffee. We had time, with Morgane, to leaf through all the magazines.

Afterwards, the journalist glanced at his watch. He wanted to visit the studio, and take a few photographs. Raphaël slumped in his chair. This was a difficult moment for him, the moment where he had to show his work.

"Let's get going," he said in a lifeless voice.

He drank some more coffee.

Then he stood up.

He went out into the hallway. The stone was outside the door. He did not explain why it was there.

He opened the door and stood to one side. The journalist stood still.

It was always like that, people who came into the studio stood there speechless.

I was like that myself, the first time. Motionless, with a desire to flee.

Raphaël waved his hand, it was all there, the essence of what he could say.

The journalist walked in among the sculptures. The light falling through the windows enhanced the red patina. The sculptures seemed to vibrate. The man walked close to the wombs, not daring to touch them. The broken limbs that lay about in boxes, the heads with mouths like cries.

Raphaël let him walk where he liked. He went to sit down at his table.

The bronzes captured the light, absorbed it. And this captured light became another light. A very long time went by. Eventually, the man pulled out his camera and took a few photographs of the bronzes, "Silence" and "The Pleading Women", "The Seated Women", a few sculptures without titles.

He took a photograph of the signature on the base.

He came back over to Raphaël.

"I would like to take a picture of your hands."

A close-up, with a little bit of the wire mesh that Raphaël was fiddling with in his fingers.

He also made two portraits of him.

"I'm going to get you a two-page spread."

Raphaël did not reply.

Before going out, the journalist turned round.

"That would be good, you know, a two-page spread in *Beaux-Arts*."

*   *   *

The sick ewe died. When I went past, she was still there, but she was no longer attached by a collar. Her head had rolled to one side. Her belly was open, and three famished cats were tearing up her guts. Her eyes were wide open, and she still seemed to be looking over towards the sheep-pens.

A first shiver of the coming storm over the slack sea, and then it rained. The Stork came back up the path with her dog and the entire herd. In near darkness, along the road. The weak beam of her torch pierced a hole in the rain. It was like the light of a firefly.

The sow was waiting for the herd in the shelter of the big chestnut tree, in the courtyard.

Lili said there were men who had hanged themselves from the branches of that tree. The women did not go near it. On days of wind, you could hear a low wailing, but nobody could say whether it came from the tree or elsewhere.

*

I stopped off at Théo's. I had to knock several times before he answered.

He scarcely looked at me.

"Is it your leg? Is it hurting?"

He gestured no with his hand.

I spoke to him about the birds, I told him that I had seen a kestrel and a meadow pipit. I showed him the drawings I had made in my notebook. I described the place to him.

"The druids put up their menhirs at that place you're talking about. They also sacrificed children."

He said it in a dull voice.

He sat up. The little white cat was on the bed. She stretched.

"Am I tiring you?" I said, because I could see that he was not his usual self.

He nodded. He said, "I think I've been tired for a very long time."

The following night, I dreamt of chains, of doors. I heard the sound of keys. It was the wind, outside, and the boats' moorings, creaking.

I woke up in a sweat.

*   *   *

The envelope arrived the following week. A large brown envelope that the postman left on the table. Raphaël called us over.

It was a heavy envelope, with three cancelled stamps, a tribute to Vauban. The magazine was inside, with its glossy cover, a photograph of the Fondation Maeght.

Morgane was stamping her feet with impatience.

"Well, are you going to open it or not?"

He leafed through the magazine, backwards, then went back to the beginning.

Morgane was furious.

"Why did he send you the magazine if you're not in it?"

She grabbed it out of his hands.

"He said a two-page spread! You should see it, a two-page spread!"

She also started at the back. She leafed through it, but more slowly. The rat had come out of its box and it stood before her on its hind paws.

Morgane went through everything, even the tiniest articles at the bottom of the page.

"What the fuck has he done to us!"

She was about to start over from the beginning when suddenly she stopped, her mouth open. It was there, a large title, "A Sculptor at the Gates of Hell". There was the article, the photographs, and it continued on to the following page.

We looked at each other. Not one, but two two-page spreads. It was incredible! We stood close together, shoulder to shoulder, with the magazine wide open between us. First the photographs, then we read the article.

The first words, on Raphaël's work, *The obsessive torment of a man forging his path with strength and talent.*

Morgane slammed her hands on the table. She pulled her brother close to her, she kissed him.

She was trembling.

She went on reading, out loud.

". . . *Everywhere, the same message, an authentic testimony.*"

She repeated it, *an authentic testimony.*

Raphaël raised his head slightly.

Morgane was laughing.

"How many copies does a magazine like this sell?"

They did not know.

She went on reading.

There were a few comments at the end, on "The Seamstress of the Dead", *the apotheosis, in this old face, summing up all on its own the artist's infinite compassion for the misery of his fellow creatures.*

"That's really good, Raphaël, isn't it, don't you think?"

Raphaël nodded his head. He gave a faint smile.

"You're going to have to install a telephone now!" I said, laughing. I was happy for his sake.

We reread the article. The rat ran in and out among our glasses. We were laughing when Lambert came through the door. He looked at us.

"I saw the light . . ." he said.

Morgane waved the magazine at him, "Come and have a look!"

We made room for him. We let him read. His eyes skimmed over the paper. He read everything, attentively. He took his time. When he had finished, he closed the magazine, and looked up at Raphaël.

"You're going to have to put in a telephone, now."

We all burst out laughing, and Morgane explained why.

*   *   *

Nan died the next day. Her body was found, in the morning, on the beach. A shell-seeker. He said he saw a shadow curled on the beach. He went closer. He thought it was a seal that had beached there, it was not rare to see them at this time of year, creatures that had come down from Scotland or the coasts of Ireland.

It was not a seal. It was a woman. The gendarmes said that Nan had taken a boat as far as the Île de Bas. She must have rowed herself, the way she had done so often. The way from the shore to the island. Poor madwoman . . . Once too often. She sometimes went there, it was on the shore of that island that her family had died. She needed to row, to row above the waters.

What had possessed her? Before, she was young, she was up to it! At Lili's café, everywhere, in the street, behind the curtains, that was all anyone was talking about. A death in a village with so few souls.

Sitting at her table, Old Mother listened. She had not understood yet. No-one had explained to her.

She just sensed something.

"Who is it that's died?" she said, her hand on the table top.

Not loud enough for anyone to hear.

"What's going on?" she said, because she knew perfectly well that something had happened.

Something that was out of the ordinary.

The veins on her temples were covered with a purplish skin. Her heart pounding underneath. Was it hatred that gave such a colour, almost livid, to her blood? Or the pleasure of learning that it was the other woman, the one everyone was talking about, who was the dead woman.

"She finally died," blurted Lili.

Old Mother grabbed her dress. She wanted her to say it again. I heard her nails scraping against the cloth, the cheap nylon.

Lili stepped back, to get away from her hand.

"Isn't that what you wanted?"

"Who died?"

Old Mother groaned when she asked. There was terror in her eyes.

"The old woman! You should be happy!"

Old Mother went from moaning to tears.

"The old man . . ." she mumbled.

"What d'you mean, the old man? He's not the one who died! It's the old woman, I tell you!"

It mattered little who had died, it made you shudder, death striking.

Old Mother was weeping her fear.

"You'd better make up your mind what you want!" said Lili.

She brought her a glass of water with some tablets. She put it all down on the table. She waited next to her, her arms folded. Old Mother reached out her hand, it was trembling, her fingers were unsure, but she managed all the same to put the tablets into her palm, and she swallowed them.

Théo knew the breathing of the sea. He said, "I woke up and I knew that the sea had just taken someone."

That it was Florelle.

He said he knew long before the cars came along the shore – the doctor's, the gendarmes', and then other cars, and the neighbours'.

They found the boat a few hours later, brought back in by the waves, too. As if the sea had decided it had had enough of the whole business.

The gendarmes calculated the moment when the body must have drowned. They said the body, not old Nan, or Florelle.

They said, "It must have been midnight, perhaps shortly after." Théo said, "It was just before ten o'clock." He did not say anything else.

He turned away.

I heard a bird shrieking in a tree behind me. The presence of donkeys in the distance. I walked in their tracks. My soles in the mud.

The mark of their hooves.

And more smells, elusive.

Women from the village had gathered on the bench outside Nan's house. The bench where she had tasted the croissants. I went over to them. The women did not say anything to me, hardly nodded their heads, I walked past them.

I went through the door.

That is what you do, here, you say farewell to the dead. You go into their houses, the door is open. They are there. On the table there is sugar, there are cups. They are waiting for us, for a last conversation.

At Nan's there was the stuffy smell of houses that have not been aired in a long time, for fear of the cold or an evil passer-by or some other obscure reason. Nan was laid out on her bed, dressed in black.

The women had taken care of her body. The intimate preparation, they had washed her and combed her, and dressed her in her final dress.

They had made coffee, too, which they had kept hot in a coffee pot, for visits. Reheated, you could not really say when. Cups next to the pot, upside down, on a chequered tea towel.

I looked at Nan. Her face already betrayed. What need did she have to row all that way?

My fingertips brushed the cloth of her dress. A story told and written in tight little stitches. The black of the thread only slightly shinier than the black of the cloth. Indecipherable embroidery. An old woman sewing, that was what I often thought when I saw her bent over behind her window. An old woman darning. A madwoman.

At her waist, wedged in her folded hands, was the wooden crucifix. I had often seen her with it, exhorting the sea to bring back her dead.

The sea had brought nothing back to her, on the contrary, it had taken her too, now.

Her hair had been carefully brushed, and it seemed even whiter, as if the sea had taken it too, the brilliant light of her hair. It is said that hair continues to grow long after death.

The shroud was on the chair. On the windowsill everything was just as Nan had left it: the sewing box, her shawl over the back of the chair, a large pair of scissors. Her slippers by the entrance. Her brush on the table. An old umbrella. The photographs, on the shelf above the fireplace. The bread, a tea towel hanging from a nail, a plate in the sink. A knife, a glass. Everything seemed frozen. Would someone be told to open the cupboards, the closets, and make everything that was piled up in there disappear? Which one of those women?

Unless everything was left just as it was, to be mummified by time, buried beneath the dust.

Her dead woman's head resting on the white pillow. The hollow imprint when Nan would no longer be there. How long would it take for the imprint to disappear? How many days?

Objects outlive us. They wait for a hand to take them away, to be given new life.

Ursula arrived, I was still in the house. She exchanged a few words, outside, with the old women.

She was not surprised to find me there.

"You shouldn't stand here rotting so long all alone with a dead woman," was all she said, coming over to the bed. "No, you shouldn't."

"I'm not rotting . . ."

It made her laugh.

Laughter at the bedside of a dead woman.

"Your eyes, I can tell you've been chewing over too much trouble, that's not good."

She pulled me by the arm and led me into the kitchen.

"The old women said you've been here for nearly an hour."

She set two cups down on the table.

"We'll have some coffee, and then after that, you'll go."

She filled the cups.

A little coffee spilled on to the tablecloth.

I drank. With the second sip, the coffee turned my stomach. The smell, too, sickening, indistinct, the smell of coffee and another smell, the one coming from the dead woman's body. The smell you had to breathe.

Ursula took my hand.

"Are you alright?"

I nodded.

On the table was a basket with some apples. An open newspaper.

Ursula looked round.

"I haven't been here for a very long time."

She walked over to Nan.

"You don't go out rowing at your age. Sooner or later, that had to end, too."

She turned away. She had tears in her eyes. Her gaze glanced over me, over the room.

She pointed to the photographs.

"We should try to find all these kids. Tell them . . ."

With her finger, she touched a few of the faces.

"A lot of them wouldn't make it, but I'm sure some of them would come all this way."

She chose a few photographs at random, trying to remember their names.

"As soon as they got here, she made them stand over there, outside, by the door, and she took their portrait. She said that the light gave them beautiful faces. She pinned the photographs up next to their beds. The little ones liked that, the photograph by the bed. They were all orphans, motherless children, so a face, even their own, made them feel less alone."

A minute or two went by, a time when she said nothing.

"When they left, she kept the photographs."

She looked at other pictures, going from one to the next.

"This was him, little Michel . . ."

She handed me the photograph. It was the one that Nan had pressed against her chest so tightly the day I came to tell her that Théo was waiting for her. I recognized the little lace-up boots, and the train at the end of the string.

The child with blond curls. His clear gaze. An acid taste of coffee suddenly rose in my throat. I felt that I was going to be sick.

I went over to the window. My hand on my throat. I opened the window. I took a breath, close to vomiting. Just breathing.

Ursula was concerned.

"Is something wrong?"

I said that everything was fine. I leaned on both hands. I was having cold sweats. I closed my eyes and waited for it to pass.

I still had the photograph in my hand.

The child: it was the same face, the same curls, the same look and the same polo shirt with three little boats. I turned the photo over, there was a date written at the back, November '67.

Lambert's parents had died in October that same year.

I went to lean against the wall. The child was Paul, Lambert's little brother. I looked at Ursula. She was standing next to the dead woman. Leaning over her. She had taken her hand, she seem to be talking to her.

I waited.

When she looked up, I showed her the photograph.

"Are you sure this child is Michel?"

She looked at me.

She nodded her head, and said that she was sure.

"Why are you asking me that?"

"No reason . . ."

I slid the photograph into my pocket and went out. The old women watched me go by.

Outside, on the line, sheets were flapping in the wind.

*　　*　　*

I had to see Lambert, but when I went back up to the village, the house was closed. He was not at home.

I went to wait for him at the café. His brother might be alive. It was Nan who had raised him, who had brought him up. How could I tell him that? From the window, I could see his gate.

The Stork was there, tracing her letters. Lili was sweeping under the tables. The broom banging into things. Old Mother deep in her armchair, her expression somewhat agitated, lost, now that Nan was dead. Nan, the other woman, the rival.

She knew it, but had she understood? Had Nan died accidentally, or had she let herself be carried away? Everyone said that she was used to going out in the rowing boat. I took the photograph from my pocket. And what if I were wrong? I began to have my doubts. The child was wearing the same polo shirt with little boats, but sometimes there are coincidences. And the resemblance, so disturbing.

The Stork was pressing too hard. The letters made an imprint on the page underneath. And when she made a mistake, she rubbed it out. Too hard, as well, the rubber making a hole in the paper. She picked up the little shreds of paper, put them in her palm, and then in her pocket.

"Why are you rubbing that out – it's correct."

I ran my fingertip over the place on the paper. She frowned.

"It's important to learn to erase," I said.

I glanced into the street. I brought my chair closer. I showed her how.

Old Mother began calling for Théo. She was shouting. Lili said that it was because of her dentures, that she did not shout as loud when she was not wearing them.

"You only have to rub out what is wrong," I tried to explain to the child, but she was not listening.

Later, Max arrived, he was carrying a rabbit. He had been poaching. It was for Lili.

He had been poaching for years. With the money she gave him, he bought jerry cans of petrol to fill the tank on his boat. He also bought some fishing line, and boxes of hooks. He kept all his money in a little tin box somewhere at the back of a cupboard at Lili's place.

"Have you seen Lambert?" I said.

He nodded.

"He went to Alderney."

"What's he doing there?"

He shrugged, as if to say he had not a clue.

He went over to the Stork, and leaned over to see what she had written, her notebook with its mysterious tracings.

He always watched her write with infinite quantities of envy.

"I am going to dig the hole for the entombment of the body," he said.

He talked quietly. He did not want Old Mother to hear.

The child went on tracing her letters.

Max looked one last time at her notebook and went to get his money box. He sat down, alone at a table. He did not know how to write, but he could count. His tongue between his teeth, he did his calculations with a lead pencil scarcely three centimetres long, held between his fingertips.

Lili came over to me.

"You look really out of it today . . ."

She had blood on her hands, the rabbit's blood.

"You should get out, go to Cherbourg . . ."

She went behind the bar to rinse off the blood.

"There are cinemas in Cherbourg, places where you can dance . . . I'd go and have a good time myself if I didn't have this bloody bistro."

"And couldn't Morgane keep it for you?"

"Morgane? Leave her the bistro for an hour, perhaps, but any more than that and she'll turn it into a brothel."

Lili had prepared a *daube* for lunch. She said, "A *daube* takes time, nearly the whole morning on a low flame."

In the room, there was a smell of carrots, meat and sauce.

She filled a plastic box for Théo.

"Can you take it to him?"

She did not talk about Nan. She did not say a word. And yet Nan was there, everywhere, in every thought.

She put the bag on the table and came to lean against the window.

The FOR SALE sign was gone from the fence. She did not talk about that either.

"I went to Cherbourg, and a seagull shat on me. I had to go in and buy a top at the Prisunic. It was too small, but I managed. They charged ten euros! Ten euros for a synthetic top. The saleswoman made fun of me . . ."

The postman came in. He was wearing low boots that laced up. He left streaks of mud on the floor. Lili fussed. She went back behind the bar, took a wet rag and mopped up the streaks.

M. Anselme arrived immediately afterwards.

"I was looking for you," he said when he saw me.

He wiped his feet for a long time on the doormat. He pulled out a chair.

"Nan has died . . ."

He said it the moment he sat down. He removed his scarf.

318

"Ursula called me to let me know. She also said she had seen you there, with the dead woman, and that you seemed – how did she put it? – evaporated, that's the word she used."

We talked about Nan.

Lili went on mopping the floor. M. Anselme kept giving rapid glances her way, he was trying to attract her attention so that he could order.

"I went by your house ... Your friend, the sculptor, he doesn't seem well at the moment. He didn't want me to go up and knock on your door. He put some sort of huge rock in the way ..."

He turned round again, but Lili was still not paying any attention to him.

"He told me that the presence of that rock alone should prevent me going past. He looked me up and down the way a beggar would."

"Beggars don't look people up and down."

"Oh, but you're very much mistaken, some of them do!"

He looked at me.

"Is there anything else? What's going on?"

And he put his hand on mine.

"You seem to be ... elsewhere. It can't be the death of an old lady that is making you so sad?"

I wasn't sad, I was simply beginning to understand that Lambert's brother had not disappeared at sea.

Was Théo in on the secret?

Monsieur Anselme turned round, and managed at last to catch Lili's eye.

He asked for a small glass of white wine, well chilled.

Lili tossed the floor cloth near the table. The wet fabric snapped like a slap. M. Anselme leaned towards me, in a low voice, over the table, "Is it just my impression, or is the mood a bit tense here?"

We spoke some more about Nan.

I did not share with him what I thought I had understood. And besides, had I really understood?

*

Monsieur Anselme was still waiting for his glass when Théo came through the door.

To see him there: an unusual silence fell upon the place. Lili made him a coffee, as usual. She did not ask him anything. Not a word about Nan.

He seemed tired. Aged.

Lili put the cup in the saucer, and the saucer on the counter.

Old Mother could sense the old man was there. She raised her head. When she understood he really was there, she grabbed hold of her bag. Théo paid no attention to her. He drank his coffee. The time it took for her to get up, walk all the way round the table to reach him, he had already put his cup back down.

As a rule, he would drink his coffee, pick up his bag, and leave.

He drank his coffee, but he did not look at the bag. He did not leave, either. His hand was on the bar. M. Anselme and I looked at each other. I saw his hand. Lili saw it, too. Old Mother moved forward with her walker, her bag squeezed against her waist, she had almost reached him. He did not turn his head. He did not say anything to her.

He just asked Lili for a phone card. That was what he said.

Lili did not move, as if she had not understood, so he said it again, the same few words, the same request, articulating carefully. Lili finally opened the drawer, pulled out a card, and shoved it over to her father the same way she had shoved the cup of coffee.

Théo laid a note down next to the cup. He took the card and put it in his pocket.

He turned round. Old Mother was there, her hand outstretched; it was an entreaty, those old woman's eyes trembling, her open bag slowly spilling because she was not holding it properly.

Théo stopped. He looked at her. I did not see his expression just then, but I could read it on Old Mother's face. Her outstretched hand fell back down. The photograph slipped from her bag, the one where you could see both of them standing side by side on the threshold, you might have thought they were happy if you did not know the story.

Théo looked at the photo.

Old Mother stood there without moving, her feet frozen.

*　　*　　*

Max dug Nan's grave the way he had for all the other dead. There were not many of the living in the village, so he did not have a lot of dead. A few in the course of a year, all the same. In the months of bitter cold, there might be several.

Max could also go months without digging. When it rained, the earth turned to mud, it was filthy work.

The day he dug for Nan, it was sunny. A plot of earth facing south, sheltered from the wind. He took off his jacket. The earth he dug up was dark. Almost brown.

"The digging must be masterly, and as close as possible to her loved ones."

That is what he said, showing me the grave. The church bell began to toll. It would toll several times during the day, and the following day.

I walked among the graves. I went past the Peracks'.

Lambert had put his brother's photograph back, in a new frame, the frame on the slab. Another bouquet of flowers. I took the photograph out of my pocket. The smile, the eyes. The two faces were identical. It was the same child.

I watched for the return of the Alderney boat, but Lambert was not on board. It was his second night on the island.

In my room, I went over to the sink. I looked at my face. I ran some water. There was some soap in a dish. It was a little white soap, rectangular, Ph neutral. It was not a proper soap dish, some water was stagnating at the bottom. The soap had sat in it. It was soft. When I picked it up, I kept it in my hand. Impossible to put it back.

Morgane found me like that.

"Is something wrong?" she said.

321

I showed her the soap.

"It looks like a drowned bird."

"A drowned bird?"

She looked at my eyes, into them, the way you look through a window when it is too dark out.

"You'll be alright . . ." she said.

She took the soap and threw it into the sink. She wiped the inside of my hand with the towel. She rummaged in my clothes.

She finally collapsed on the bed.

"Who is that?" she said, when she saw the photograph.

"Just a photograph . . . I found it at Nan's."

"You steal from the dead, do you?"

"I didn't steal it . . . It's just that I wanted a memory of her."

She examined the photograph more closely.

"Who is this kid? One of the ones she took in?"

"One of them, yes."

"I don't like kids much. There are some good ones, you'll tell me . . . but it's more in general that I don't like them. Why did you want a memory of her?"

"I don't know . . ."

She put the photograph back down on the bed.

"Wasn't there anything more . . . personal?"

"Nothing, no."

She looked at me.

"What's going on with you?"

I shook my head.

"Nothing . . ."

*   *   *

The first sounds of the bell began to toll, slowly and sadly, muffled in the mist.

There were already a few people on the side of the road. When the procession went by, I followed. A procession without family. There were not many of us.

Without too much sadness. From the house to the cemetery, only the hill to climb. We left La Roche behind. Someone near me said, I was afraid it would rain.

The hearse took the road that went in front of Théo's house. It was driving slowly. They could have taken a different route, through the harbour or behind La Roche, but they had chosen that route, no doubt because Nan often went that way, and also because that was the route that went by Théo's house.

Outside the gate, the hearse slowed. It did not stop, but at one point it was moving so slowly that you might have thought it had stopped. I saw Théo's shadow behind the window. Immobile. A shadow like a stone.

The hearse waited, one minute, perhaps two. He did not come out. Old Nan was leaving. She was leaving him. His Florelle.

The hearse went on its way.

The priest was waiting outside the church, in his cassock. He did not like the idea of that death in a rowing boat. Disapproval was written all over his face. Impatience in his gaze.

We gathered by the gate. People came out of their houses and moved closer in mute little groups.

Those who did speak kept their voices low. When the coffin arrived, even the most talkative people fell silent. Death, asserting itself.

A taxi pulled up once we were all there. A man got out. People looked round. Afterwards, there were other cars. Ursula arrived in turn. When she saw me, she motioned to me. She crossed the road.

"All the people who didn't give a damn about her when she was alive, you'd think men have no recollection and women even less!"

She pointed with her chin towards a group of women.

The men carried the coffin to the entrance and the priest stepped aside. He said his mass, rapid prayers. He spoke about the dead that

Nan would be joining, the dead who would die for a second time because there was no-one left to remember them the way she had remembered them. He spoke about sin, about the evil that is within each of us. He spoke about forgiveness, too. His voice echoed. Everyone listened, heads bowed.

I looked round for Lili. She was not there.

Max stayed outside during the mass, off to one side, with his shovel. His boots were too dirty.

When we were coming back out of the church, everyone looked over towards the bistro. Tongues began to wag. Lili had been there to bury all the others, was what people were saying. Here we bury even the people we do not like.

Death, like a truce.

The priest moved ahead, he looked at the condition of the grave. The man who had got out of the taxi passed in front of me. I noticed him because he was different from the others, taller, more handsome too, perhaps. He was wearing a long coat.

He went to stand slightly to one side. He spoke to no-one.

The men lowered the coffin into the pit. I heard the sound of the wood scraping against the earth. The sound of the ropes.

They gathered up the ropes.

Nan stayed all alone at the bottom.

Alone in the earth, with her secret.

People waited patiently in a line. The priest looked at his watch and hurried things along. Bending down, he picked up a handful of earth and tossed it in the hole. That was the example to follow. The line followed suit. Gazes lingered. There were a few flowers, a bouquet of lilacs, some irises in a pot. Not much. The man with the long coat threw a bit of earth, too, and went to join the others. Suddenly, a murmur ran through the crowd. A whispering, like the rustling of wings.

And then all of a sudden, there was nothing more, silence fell. I looked round.

Old Mother was there, by the fence, still far away, she was moving forward, heaving herself painfully, her entire body leaning on her walker. The metal feet sank into the gravel. She was dragging herself more than she was walking. Everyone was looking at her. No-one did anything to help her. She eventually stopped by a cross, slightly to one side. She looked at the hole from a distance, the dark gaping of it, the coffin you knew was at the bottom, already in the dark, in the cold, and it was for the pleasure of seeing it that she had gone to all this trouble.

Her chest was heaving uncontrollably. You could hear her lungs wheezing.

Someone said, She's going to snuff it.

Everyone waited. For her to die or to leave. The priest tucked his hands back inside his sleeves.

Old Mother gathered her strength like an animal that has to go right to the end, her hands gripping the frame, her forehead low, she staggered forward. Everyone moved aside to let her go by. She was smiling. Not really mad, Old Mother, just full of hatred, she moved on to the edge of the hole.

There was a murmuring when she leaned forward. An old woman in black, sweating. One female who had come to bury the other, the rival.

Not the oldest one, but the one who was already dead.

Old Mother leaned still further, we thought she was going to pitch forward, a woman cried, Watch out!

Old Mother did not step back.

The wind blew her dress against her thighs. She was standing before the grave, with that smile on her lips, a smile that showed her teeth, and suddenly she stood up straight, both hands gripping tight on her frame, trembling slightly, and she spat.

Someone said, She spat!

There came a murmuring, that old woman spitting on the grave of a dead woman.

*

The bells rang. First the ones in Auderville, a few notes, and then immediately afterwards the ones in Saint-Germain. The ones in Auderville were deeper and slower than the ones in Saint-Germain.

I went through the door.

Théo was not asleep. He was staring at the wall.

The cats were dozing as if it were night. Or as if they were keeping watch over him.

He was slumped in his chair, one arm folded on the table.

"You need some light," I said.

On his head was his wool cap, rammed down to his eyes. His cheeks were hollow. Nan's death had withered him.

He had let the fire die. Perhaps he wanted to let himself die, too. I tossed a log into the stove. Newspaper in a ball. I hunted for matches. It took me a long time to do each of these things. The little white cat was sleeping, curled up in a hollow in the sheets. When she heard the fire crackling again, she opened her eyes.

There was some coffee left in a saucepan. I heated up two cups. I put one down in front of Théo.

I pulled up a chair and sat down.

He looked up at me. His eyes were red. With pockets of tears.

"How was it?"

What could I say? I saw the black hole again. The hole in broad daylight, and black all the same.

I talked about the people who had been at the church and the ones outside. I did not say anything about Old Mother appearing, nor about Lili's absence. I pushed the cup closer to him.

"There were flowers," I said.

I took my cup. I lifted it to my lips. The reheated beverage was vile. I drank it anyway.

"Max said the grave is well located, and he'll plant some irises in the soil."

He looked at me. It was devouring him, his need to know. To hurt himself, exhaust himself. I lowered my head. I wanted to talk about

326

something else. His gaze kept bringing me back. Like an obsession, his need to hold tight to the other person.

Even when that other person has been buried, we would like to be able to go with them. The last time I saw you, your last morning, in that room where you could no longer see any light. That day, I looked at you, for a long time. The doctor said, He won't come back. I did not understand. He explained. He was an old doctor. He let me look at you.

I pointed to the coffee.

"Drink . . ."

He took a sip. He could not swallow it. He clenched his fists.

"That bloody rowing boat! I knew it ought to be burned . . ."

Two tears ran down his cheeks. They were fat tears, heavy and round.

"You don't burn rowing boats . . ."

I wanted to talk to him about Michel, but I no longer had the will.

I looked away.

"I'll go now."

*   *   *

Raphaël sold "Virtue" to a collector in Saint-Malo.

"'Virtue'! Can you imagine?"

The bronze would be collected during the week. He led me all the way to the back of the studio to show it to me. Next to it, "The Seamstress of the Dead" seemed to be waiting.

"I'm going to cast her, too."

"If you cast her, you won't want to sell her. She'll be too beautiful."

"I'll cast her, I'll sell her, and I'll make others!"

He led me to other sculptures. He wanted to work on his idea of the great tightrope walker. Morgane was listening to him. She had wrapped a scarf around her forehead. She was looking at her brother

327

as if something were taking over, inside her. Something she had not chosen, that she had to submit to all the same.

She turned to me.

"I saw Lambert again, he was in the harbour . . . He'd just got back from Alderney. I think he was looking for you."

I did not answer.

She did not insist.

She stayed silent for a long time.

"That bloke . . . Your bloke . . . You can't spend your life —"

"Be quiet."

She said nothing more. For a moment, not long.

"You know what? It's your clothes. You'll never find a guy wearing clothes like that."

"I never said I wanted to find one."

She shrugged.

"No-one can see your breasts under your jumpers. I could lend you some tops that are a bit more . . . Huh, Raphaël, don't you think she dresses like a tramp?"

"Leave her alone . . ."

She clicked her tongue against her palate.

"You see, if I were you, I —"

"You aren't me."

She smiled.

"Yes, but if I were you . . ."

I went by the farm. I saw the Stork's father loading manure into a wheelbarrow. The wheelbarrow was heavy. He pushed it and went to empty it on to a big pile that was in the middle of the yard. The sow followed him.

One of his kids was crawling around the sow. In the pastures, the cows had their hooves in mud. At one point, the father raised his head. He looked at me. His gaze did not bother me.

The child went on crawling in and out between the sow's legs. He had empty eyes, slow gestures. He climbed on to the sow's back and fell off on the other side.

A child who was growing up like a cat.

The Audi was parked a bit further up the street. I thought I might find Lambert at home. The door was open.

I called out.

I went in.

He had a fire going. I waited for him by the fire, sprawled in one of the armchairs. I must have fallen asleep. When I opened my eyes, it was dark. He was sitting at the table. He was looking at me.

"That way you have of sleeping . . ."

No doubt because I had dozed off, or perhaps he had spoken to me without my hearing.

"Was it nice, Alderney?" I said.

"How did you know that?"

"Everyone knows everything here."

He went to fetch his packet of cigarettes from the pocket of his jacket. His matches. He pulled up a chair and came to sit beside me.

"It was nice, yes."

He took off his shoes, his feet on the stone. He lit his cigarette.

"I wanted to eat some sea bream, but I couldn't find any."

"Is that why you spent two days there?"

"Not that, no."

He talked about Alderney, he told me that his parents used to go there often. That they had had friends there.

He turned to me.

"Sea bream . . . Doesn't that tempt you?"

I shook my head. "I have something to tell you . . ."

He waved his hand.

"Later . . ."

"No, not later."

He tossed his cigarette into the fire.

"Yes, later."

He settled into his chair, his neck against the back of the chair, his legs stretched out. He closed his eyes.

"I have to steal a cigarette from you."

He waved, pointed to his jacket.

I got up. I went over to the jacket. I touched the leather. I took out the packet.

In the same pocket there was a photograph. I took it over to the light. It was the photograph that had stayed pinned to the wall at Lili's for so long, the black-and-white photograph, you could see Lili and her parents, and little Michel in the background.

This photograph had been in Old Mother's handbag. I don't know how he had managed to get her to give it to him. Nor why he had done it.

I put it back in its place.

Lambert still had his eyes closed. It looked as if he were sleeping. Perhaps he was pretending.

I went out to smoke on the steps. It was drizzling over Alderney way and drizzling on the sea, too. Between the islands and the lighthouse. The sun slipped in and out of the clouds, a few rays scratching the surface of the sea, you could see them again in the pastures, lighting the tree trunks. Everywhere, the tall grasses vibrated with red hues. For a moment, on the steeper slope of the hill, it looked as if the ferns were on fire.

And then the shadow took over. In the distance, in a single movement, the sky spewed a long flow of black ink on to the line of the horizon, and the sun disappeared.

Lambert slept for an hour and then he woke up.

"I was promising you sea bream, wasn't I, or was I dreaming?"

"You weren't dreaming."

He got to his feet.

"Will you wait here?"

He went out.

He came back a quarter of an hour later with two magnificent sea bream.

"Don't move."

He cooked them with herbs. I could hear the butter sizzling in the frying pan.

At one point, he turned his head, and looked at me over his shoulder.

"Did you have something to tell me?"

"No, nothing . . . Nothing important."

He nodded.

He slid the spatula under the fish, lifted them gently and turned them. He added some lemon juice.

He let it cook some more without taking his eyes from the fish and then he turned off the flame.

He slid the sea bream on to the plates. He told me that it was Max who had caught them. With the tip of a knife, he cut into the flesh, and removed the bones.

"Next time, I'll invite you," I said.

He raised his eyebrows.

"Do you cook?"

I shook my head.

". . . But it's good at the *auberge*."

"The *auberge* can't be as good as at home."

That is obvious, I thought.

He gnawed at the lemon, right down to the skin. It gave me an acid taste in my mouth. He went over to his jacket, took out the photograph, and came back and put it down in front of me, on the table.

He pointed with his finger.

"You must recognize this photograph, it's the one that was at Lili's. And this is the child that Nan adopted. The same Michel she thought was me."

I looked up at him. What had he understood?

He began to eat his sea bream.

"Don't you like it?" he said, because I had not touched mine.

"Yes . . ."

"What's wrong then?"

I hesitated to reply.

He looked at me. I turned my head away.

I do not know what he had sensed, but he would have to go to the depths of the truth all by himself. The way I had done.

How far had he got?

Had he spoken to Nan?

Now Nan was dead, who would he have to turn to?

He pointed to the sea bream.

"You ought to try to eat it before it gets cold."

A sharp pain, at the back of my neck.

When I left him, the mist had parted. The sky was clearing, brighter. And then the light departed. Perhaps that is what drove people mad here, this absence of light. Gloom, long before and long after the night.

And the space of the sea, without limits.

*   *   *

Hermann came to get "Virtue". He took two other little plaster statues, Raphaël called them "Solitude". Hermann wanted to try to get him an exhibition in Paris, to show both the sculptures and the drawings. It was an ambitious project.

For a while now, Raphaël had not been sleeping much, just a few hours a night. Sometimes, he slept in the afternoon. His sleepless nights made him gaunt. Life in the outside world was no longer important to him. The space of the studio had become his life. Another life. And it seemed as if only this life mattered.

Morgane was suffering. I heard them arguing several times that week. One morning, I went down, and Morgane was crying.

Raphaël was in the studio, standing by one of the "Thinkers", and they were staring at each other. Looking at them, I wondered who was contemplating whom.

Raphaël's face was lined with fatigue. He said that even when he was sleeping he was sculpting. That the plaster was shaped in his sleep.

"*Rue de Seine*, can you imagine! I'm having an exhibition on the *rue de Seine!*"

He was happy.

He wanted to get back to work right away, to get going on new things.

"I'm in the process of understanding . . ."

He had a project for an angel with clipped wings. A stone creature, that would be both real and evanescent.

"I've been looking for it for so long . . . I think I'm getting close now."

And then the idea for the tightrope walker. He said that all the other sculptures had been created just so that he could get to that one.

He took the plaster of "The Seamstress" to Valognes. He also took one of the little tightrope walkers.

The door to the studio stayed wide open. The door without the stone. During his absence, the studio was an empty, silent temple.

I went in.

I walked through the shadows of the petrified silhouettes, their dry wombs open, without modesty. The silence of women. Those faces were anonymous and yet I seemed to know them. Their hands with stone fingers. I went up to them. Without fear. Raphaël's sculptures were my sisters, they were my pleading women.

The silence in the studio was of a piece.

There were traces of plaster on the floor, where "The Seamstress" had stood. The mark from the base. Raphaël's jumper.

*   *   *

Max burst into the studio.

"Have you seen Raphaël anywhere in the divinity?"

"In the what?"

"In the divinity!"

"Vicinity, Max, the vicinity . . . He's gone to the foundry, he took 'The Seamstress'. He told you. He waited for you, too. You had promised to go with him."

He looked round.

He rubbed his forehead with his hands.

"You have a problem?" I asked.

He did not know. It was Raphaël who knew when there were problems and when there were not.

"It's the fuel, I don't have enough for the boat!" he explained at last.

He took three steps towards the door.

"The harbourmaster said I have enough to go out to sea, but not enough to come back. He won't let me leave if I don't have fuel for the return."

"He's right."

"He took the key to the boat!"

He nodded his head several times.

"He did that, so that I wouldn't activate the ignition of the engine."

"What do you want Raphaël to do about it?"

"Raphaël is validity on earth."

"Validity on earth?"

It made me laugh. "How many litres do you need?"

He did not know that either. The harbourmaster had made a mark on the gauge and Max had to fill it up to the mark.

"It's a foamy night!" he said, pointing to the sea. "On foamy nights, there are porgies!"

I took a note out of my pocket, but it was not money that he wanted.

Eventually he left.

He went back up to the village. He went round all the houses, with a bucket and bottles. He asked for fuel for his boat. He promised fish in return, or sharks' teeth. He promised everything. Some people emptied a few litres directly into his bucket. Others did not give him anything.

Max stank.

Lili did not want him in the bistro. She did not want him to go out to sea.

She gave him some food, outside.

Max went back into the narrow streets. He knocked at other houses, went through other doors. By evening, the fuel had reached the mark.

The founder brought "The Seamstress" back the next morning. She was wrapped in a sheet. It took them some time to get her out and lift her back to the studio.

They put her on her base. I was there when they removed the sheet. The dark patina vibrated in the light. As soon as the light changed, the patina shifted to grey-brown hues, almost red. It took very little, a cloud beyond the big window that looked out to sea.

Now that she was here, it seemed impossible to part with her.

When Hermann arrived, the atmosphere became tense, Raphaël no longer wanted to sell his sculpture. Hermann needed it, however, for the posters of the exhibition.

"Your 'Seamstress' will reign over it!"

He had planned everything.

Except this.

"I won't have the exhibition without 'The Seamstress'!" he said in the end, slamming the door.

That evening, the *patron* of the *auberge* came to get Raphaël, Hermann was asking for him on the telephone, it lasted for a while. And then from the telephone box, after that, because the *patron* was fed up with their endless conversation, they spoke some more and Raphael finally capitulated. "The Seamstress of the Dead" would go to Paris, to be exhibited and sold if someone wanted her.

He shook his head.

"It's my first exhibition, I have to show the best I have. If I sell her, I can cast others."

Morgane exploded.

"You're not a beginner! He has no right to treat you like that!"

She threw a magazine across the room. The pages flew open with a loud rustle.

"I can't see why you give in so easily!"

Raphaël picked up the magazine. Since he had taken his decision, he seemed very calm, almost indifferent.

"The main thing is that she exists."

He smiled. "I have other ones inside me."

"There will never be another seamstress!"

It lasted for a while, the two of them. Morgane would not calm down.

A draught of damp air came up from the ground. On some of the older sculptures, the plaster was flaking off, all you had to do was touch it with your finger; a scarcely visible erosion and yet very persistent. The sculptures were in danger. Raphaël knew it. They would all crumble if he did not cast them.

He ran his hand over his sister's face, her anger impossible to calm.

"It's not such a big deal . . ."

Morgane stepped back, as if scorched by his hand.

"Come on . . ." He pulled her, held her against him, tight.

"You are beautiful when you get angry . . ."

He talked to her for a long time, one hand in her hair, the way you calm a young child.

Max left at the crack of dawn, I heard his engine start. By the time I got to the quay, the boat was already leaving the harbour, still on smooth water, but already in the pass. I ran to the breakwater, waving my arms. I do not know if he saw me. He was looking straight ahead, proud, he was a sailor, not a great sailor, but a man on his boat. The pass he was taking was Le Blanchard: he was going to navigate through it for the first time.

A pass like a wall.

A baptism, with the waves waiting for him. They came and were caught under the hull. Ahead of him, they rose up, several pounding assaults. Beneath the boat they made troughs of black water, roiling ferociously. *La Marie-Salope* heeled over.

Max held the wheel, heading straight for the open sea, the boat absorbed by the light, as if swallowed by it. It became a spot, hardly whiter than the crest of the waves, so far away that no matter how I squinted, I no longer knew if it were Max on his boat or a whitecap, or my eyes clouding over from staring into the light like that.

I sat down, my knees tucked up, my head on my arms. I kept watching the spot on the sea where Max had disappeared.

He had not gone out aimlessly. The fishermen had told him where he could find porbeagles. To strike them, he would need some luck. He would find his first shark just like that, and afterwards he would scour the area. There will be times when he will be exactly where he should be, and it is the sharks that will not be there. Other times, it will be the other way round. And one day they will both be in the same place and Max will get his porbeagle.

Morgane came to sit beside me. She sent pebbles skipping over the water. The pebbles jumped from wave to wave.

"At one point, I thought he was going to turn. When he was just there, in the pass."

She tossed another pebble.

"D'you think he'll get his shark?"

"We have to trust him. It's his dream, and there's not much harm that can come to people who have dreams."

"And people who don't have dreams, what harm can come to them?"

"I don't know . . . But it's not as easy for them."

She threw another pebble even further than the first one. It did not skip. It slid on to the water and disappeared.

She went on staring for a moment at the spot on the waves where her pebble had sunk.

"In the end, Max hasn't done so badly," she said finally.

I nodded. "Not badly at all, no."

Max came back at the end of the day, with small fish, the kind you could catch with a line.

As for the porgie, he said he had struck, but the line had broken.

*　　*　　*

Hermann took "The Seamstress" away. She was no longer in the studio, and yet it felt as if she were still there, you could wander round her.

Raphaël got back to work, more determined than ever, a large plaster silhouette, still a rough shape. He was sculpting something that was unfamiliar to me, that I had never learned to see, and now it demanded that I look at it. A sculpture that did not plead.

It was a tall man walking, his body in motion, leaning on a thin stick. He seemed to be climbing a slope, a mountain or a hill?

The light poured through the window from outside. On the floor, at the feet of the walking man, a well of white light penetrated the shadow, inscribing the angular shape of the window. In contrast, the shadow looked blue.

Cold.

This sculpture, still just a rough shape, had been born from the departure of "The Seamstress".

From her absence.

After a few hours' truce, the wind began to blow again. The branches tapped against the windowpanes, came to add their lament to the already keening prayers of "The Pleading Women". One of the windowpanes in the studio was cracked along its entire length, and the sea breeze found its way through, an icy wisp of wind that caused the dust to swirl.

Raphaël was on his knees, looking at his walking man. The plaster's shadow was crushed beneath him, on the floor.

"It's as if he were following his shadow."

He got to his feet, rubbed his hands on his trousers.

"I'll call him 'The Follower'."

"The Follower" found his place, assertively, forcefully, as he joined the teeming crowd in the studio.

Morgane came over. She put her arms around my neck and held me. She smelled of soap, perfume and the clay cream with which she coated her hair when she had just washed it.

"What are you thinking about?" she murmured in my ear.

"The passing of time."

"And?"

"Time's a bitch."

She gave a faint smile. She laid her head against my shoulder. She had a square of light fabric knotted around her wrist, a transparent silk that seem to be woven from her skin.

"Don't you get bored?" she said.

She was not smiling any more.

We talked about men. We talked about Lambert. And about life, also a bitch.

We talked about the south and sunshine.

I would have liked to have been able to talk about you. About your life, your death. About your life, above all.

I ran my fingertip over the silk square.

The walking man's shadow still spread across the floor. Other shadows. Other hands. Everywhere, the powerful imprint of the bases.

It still stood there majestically before us, in the middle of the space abruptly saturated with light, the remembered presence of "The Seamstress of the Dead".

The following night, I slept. Not much. Poorly. I thought I could

339

hear footsteps in the corridor. I opened the door. The stairway was grey and cold. There was no-one. I finished the night on my floor, against the radiator. Rolled up in a blanket.

Looking at the bed.

In the morning, I saw my face in the rust-speckled mirror. The reflection behind me, the shape of the empty bed.

*   *   *

The sow had got out of her enclosure, she was in the car park sniffling with her snout through the rubbish bins of the *auberge*. She had found some potato peel, some old carrots. No-one seemed surprised to see a sow on the quay, stuffing herself while she watched the boats head out.

I spent the day on the cliffs.

I saw right away that Morgane had been watching out for my return. When I got there, she threw herself into my arms. She kissed me. She was laughing, her lips against my neck, I could not figure out why she was so happy. I said as much, "What's going on?"

"I'm leaving!" she said.

Amidst her laughter, those few words, I'm leaving.

Well, well.

"What do you mean, you're leaving?"

"I'm going to Paris! It just happened, we were talking, Hermann is looking for someone for the gallery."

"But . . . You don't know how to do that!"

"Who gives a damn, I'll learn! He needs a girl . . . He's been looking for two months. He said it's the perfect job for me."

She reached for her handbag, and rummaged inside it. A single ticket, Cherbourg to Paris, she waved it under my nose.

"Saint-Lazare, that's the name of the station when you get there . . . Can you imagine, I'm going to live in Paris!"

"But where are you going to live? Paris is a big place!"

"A studio above the gallery. A shower, a bed, it's got everything, it's not big but it's in a good area. The window looks out onto a little street with real Parisian cobblestones."

"Well, in that case – real Parisian cobblestones!"

I instantly regretted speaking like that. I said to her, "Forgive me."

She did not mind. She sprawled on the sofa. She could not sit still, she got up again.

I looked at her.

She was leaving.

She was going to dare to do it.

"And Raphaël, what did he say?"

"Nothing. He's happy for me. There's a *Métro* station not far away. Hermann will take me for one month on a trial basis. If it works out, I'll stay."

"And if it doesn't work out?"

"It will!"

She took the rat out of its box and danced around with it. She was singing, snatches of hit songs, she hardly knew the words, I recognized "Les Filles de Pigalle", "Revoir Paris" . . .

Suddenly, she froze.

"The rat!"

She looked at her animal.

"I'll bet they don't like rats in Paris . . . Besides, with my work, I won't be in the studio all the time . . . And then he's so used to being here . . ."

She looked at me.

"Oh no, don't go getting ideas . . ."

"I'm not getting ideas . . . It's just that I wondered if maybe you could . . ."

I waved no with my hand.

"Ask Raphaël?"

"Raphaël! These days, all that matters is his work. He'll let it die . . ."

She looked up, her big eyes imploring.

I looked at the animal.

"All you have to do is just let him go. Rats, after all, they're used to living around boats."

She shrugged.

The rat had sensed her stress, the heat of her skin no doubt, her sweat, too. He was scampering all over her, her arms, her neck. He was looking for a place to hide, he finally slid inside her shirt, his little pink paws clinging to the delicate fabric.

"When are you leaving?" I said.

"In three days."

"Monday!"

"Yes, Monday. My train is in the morning. Can you come to the station with us? I told Raphaël I was sure you could."

She held me close, squeezed me.

"You'll come and see me in Paris, won't you, promise?"

She took my hands.

She stepped back. She looked at me, from head to toe.

"I'm going to give you some clothes."

"I don't need any clothes!"

She led me into the room right at the back, it was her bedroom. Just before we went in, "Will you think about the rat?"

"I *have* thought about him."

She opened the door.

In her haste, she made an awkward movement, and her necklace broke. The beads scattered in all directions across the floor. We had to pick them up on all fours, we put them in a box. After that, she opened her drawers, and went through her clothes. She got out for me everything she didn't want.

"I'm giving you this, it will look good on you!" It was a shirt with transparent sleeves that gave a glimpse of your skin. She shoved it into my hands.

"You mustn't close these two buttons," she said, pointing to the two snaps at the top.

She threw T-shirts on to the bed.

"From the days when I was slim . . ."

A jumper, a few scarves.

She gave me her big striped jumper. "A jumper like this in Paris," she said. "There's no way!"

She gave me some woollen tights, a few T-shirts. She made me promise to wear them.

I promised. I had to swear. She piled everything she wanted to give me into my arms.

"You are beautiful . . ." I said.

"You like women?"

I laughed.

"No, only men."

It was her turn to laugh.

I had her hair in my mouth.

"So, what are you waiting for, to love him?"

"I'm not waiting for anything."

"We're all waiting!"

"Not me."

She looked deep into my eyes.

"When you stop waiting, you die."

That is what she said.

She went over to another cupboard, and opened another door.

"What sort of stuff does he eat, your rat?" I said in the end.

Morgane filled two suitcases. The things she did not want she left in the bottom of the drawers.

When Max found out that Morgane was leaving, he went to the very end of the breakwater and wept.

She gave him the beads, all the beads from her broken necklace. With some string, he could repair it and send it to her in Paris, in an envelope, Raphaël had the address.

She gave him her big scarf.

And he was the one who agreed to take the rat. He held out his hand, I'll take care of it. Morgane looked at his hand, and hesitated.

He found a wooden crate and put an old woollen jumper at the bottom. He came back with it and he said, "Rats like to live on boats."

When she saw the crate, Morgane hesitated.

She said, "Why not, after all? . . ."

She explained to him about the food. After that, he went back out on the breakwater, but not as far as the first time, and he wept some more.

Morgane gave him the shirt from her pyjamas, which had her smell in it, her dreams too, her sweat. Max held the shirt against his chest. He looked at her, his temples were red.

The horse was in the pasture. Morgane went to give him some water. Her hands held out in front of her, forming a bowl.

She forced herself to smile. She slipped her fingers into his mane. Her hands, and his mouth.

"I've never seen such a soft tongue . . ."

This intimate mixture in her, laughter and tears.

"Is she really leaving?" Max said.

"Yes, she's leaving."

"When is she coming back?"

"I don't know . . ."

"When are you coming back?" he said, grabbing her arm.

"I don't know, Max . . ."

Her voice cracked when she said it. She had never spoken to Max like that, and he stepped back.

He looked over towards the breakwater, but he did not go.

She looked all around her, she wanted to give him something more, in addition to the rat and the shirt.

She went back into the house, and came out with the dictionary.

"Here, this is for you."

She forced it on him, because he did not want to take it. He did not dare.

"It's yours, I'm giving it to you. It's for rainy days, on your boat."

He touched the dictionary, and then he took it, and held it against his chest.

"All the words of submersible language?" was all he managed to mumble.

Morgane smiled.

"When I come back, I'll bring you another one, and it will have even more words."

"Will there always be more words?"

She nodded.

"Always, yes."

We left just before eight o'clock. Morgane sat in the back. That was the way she wanted it.

We took the road along the sea, through Saint-Germain and Port-Racine. Raphaël was driving. The suitcases were in the boot. Morgane looked at the sea, her face up against the window. I could see her profile in the rear-view mirror. Her lips slightly crushed, and that way she had of looking at the sea, as if she wanted to take it.

I said to her, "You look as if you want to take it with you."

She nodded.

That was why she wanted to sit all alone on the back seat. Raphaël was driving slowly. The train was at nine o'clock, we had time. I think he did not want to get to the station too early.

He had to circle round for a while to find a parking space. He got some drinks in the station from a vending machine, and two sandwiches wrapped in plastic. Morgane had already gone to the platform. She was waving to us, arms spread wide, because the train was there and we were not walking fast enough.

Raphaël looked at her the way she had looked at the sea. With the same infinite urgency. I think he wanted her to leave. To get it over with.

"Will you be alright?" I said.

"It's going to kill me."

He tried to smile and he went up to her. Her suitcases were already on the steps of the train, a young man had helped her to carry them. A voice in the loudspeaker, the train was called, it would be stopping at the stations of Valognes, Carentan, Bayeux, Caen, Lisieux and finally Paris.

Morgane was looking at us, the boy behind her tugged on her suitcases to put them into the compartment. She turned round and what she said to him made the boy laugh.

She came back down on to the platform to kiss Raphaël and me. "I love you," that is what she said, "I love you madly!" I smiled. I love you, that is what she had said to the horse. She had said it to the rat, too. She was laughing. She still had five minutes, but she had already left.

She talked about Max and Lambert, and the crowns of pearls that she had left behind.

"You can finish them if you want! The instructions are inside."

She said all the things you say when you leave.

"Look after yourself, wear my T-shirts . . . Take care of the horse!"

She made me promise.

"And sleep with Lambert, too . . ."

I did not promise.

She kissed me again.

Raphaël was devouring her with his eyes. She turned to him. She was frightened, frightened of the moment when they would have to part. His hands in her hair. Their eyes closed, suddenly.

I stepped back.

They were breathing each other.

Her white tennis shoes, one lace undone. The hem of her trousers was torn, dragging on the ground, catching in the heel.

They held each other, clung to each other.

I do not know what they said.

The station master walked by and Morgane pulled away, and stepped back. She was in the train, already, and Raphaël was on the platform. They were still holding each other's hands. Raphaël gave her the bag with the sandwiches and drinks.

"There's a telephone there, call when you arrive."

He said other words, Take care, look after yourself . . .

The doors closed. On her, and between them. Morgane's face, her lips twisted because she was crying, her white hands pressed up against the window.

She murmured words that he could not hear. They stayed like that until the train lurched forward, staring into space, two disoriented creatures who were going to have to learn not to live together any more.

I drove on the way back. It was raining. The windscreen-wipers creaked. Raphaël stared at the road.

I parked in the yard at La Griffue. Morgane's bowl had stayed on the table. Its round shadow on the tablecloth.

Silence.

The box of beads, an open packet of biscuits, all her presence gathered there. Her blanket by the television, rolled up, the rat's spot. Her balls of wool, the needles, a few rows of a jumper she had only just begun. Her yellow leather boots in the corridor. As if she had gone away for an hour, or a day.

Morgane would be arriving in Paris at noon. She was supposed to call as soon as she was with Hermann. We waited. Slightly before noon, we went to stand next to the telephone box. We waited some more. The sow was on the quay. When she was hungry, she behaved like a dog, eating whatever she found.

When the telephone rang, Raphaël picked up. Morgane said, "Everything's fine, I've arrived."

A few more words. Afterwards, Raphaël went back to his studio and I went to hang about on the beach.

*   *   *

The wind only whistles if it meets something in its path. An obstacle. It never whistles over the sea. The space leaves it silent.

Lambert told me that, on the evening of the fête, when we were leaning against the dormer window. He talked to me about the wind, where he lived. A never-ending whistling in the trees, that woke him and made him think about the night.

I went back to the cliffs.

Three chicks had been born in a nest in the hollow at Écalgrain. A place where the rocks were almost red. I spent an infinite amount of time looking at them. The ferocious appetite they had, barely hatched.

I did not feel like drawing them.

I did not go past Théo's place.

"The sea is making a strange sound today . . ."

Lambert had come up to me, silently. He always came up that way. Without me hearing him. The sleeve of his jacket against my arm. I touched it briefly.

He spoke very quietly. Sometimes that's just the way it was, here, it was impossible to do things any differently.

I told him that Morgane had left. He knew. She had come to say goodbye. They had talked.

The tide was rising. It was darker to the west of the lighthouse. It is in that stretch of sea that the female sharks give birth, a dark stretch beyond the bar of foam, they keep their young with them and then one day they abandon them.

I showed him what I had in my pockets, an abalone shell that Max had given me.

"The abalone are dying, it's the pollution, all the stuff that man has put in the soil to grow maize."

I told him that the shellfish were dying, too, the seaweed.

He breathed in the smell inside the shell.

"It doesn't smell."

I shrugged. He looked at the sea. Did he talk to Morgane about her brother? The boats were coming in. It had been a good day, their pots were full.

We went to walk along the edge of the quay and watched them unloading the crates.

"They say here that God made the lobster and the Devil made the crab . . ." I said, pointing to a basket of shellfish that a fisherman was taking to deliver to the *auberge*.

"Is that why you have dinner with them in the evening?"

"At the lobsters' table, with plastic flowers and a pyrex flower vase."

He lit a cigarette, and cocked his head slightly to one side.

"The vase isn't made of pyrex, it's crystal," he said, blowing smoke.

He handed me his cigarette.

We were having trouble speaking. We were sharing all the news, somewhat out of order. We left the quay and went to the hamlet of La Roche. Nan's Refuge. As we went by, he stopped. He looked at the façade, the closed shutters.

What did he know?

He said nothing.

We went as far as the houses at La Valette and then we headed back in the other direction from La Valette to La Roche, along the walls. We did not meet anyone. Strange plants were growing in a garden. Lambert said that perhaps they were butterfly plants, because of the many butterflies fluttering about. He talked to me about Le Morvan. He said, "I'll have to tell you about it."

We walked back and forth along the path several times. Until the beam of the lighthouse came on. Every time we walked by the Refuge, he turned his head and looked. The last time, it was almost dark. He pushed open the gate.

"Shall we?"

That is what he said.

He walked across the courtyard.

I followed.

He tried all the windows and eventually found the one that opened.

He climbed over the sill.

"Why are you doing this?" I said.

He did not answer. He jumped inside. He waited for me on the other side. He had a torch in his pocket. It had a powerful beam, it lit up the first room. He walked round it the way I had, taking his time. I wondered what would happen if anyone found us there.

It was cold. We went through the building, along its entire length as far as the stairway, the beam from the torch lit up the steps, the corpses of flies. On the first floor, the long corridor, the beds. He was looking. He noticed things that I had not seen, an old painting, a pair of shoes. Had he any idea that his brother had spent years of his life walking up and down this corridor, at night, barefoot, because he could not sleep anywhere else . . . ?

We went into the dormitory. I went over to the window and looked down at the courtyard. I had seen Nan down there, on the bench, she was eating a croissant.

Today, it was dark, you could not see anything and Nan was dead.

I turned my head.

The little bear was on the bed, just where I had left it. I could tell from its darker shape. The beam of light passed over it, Lambert didn't see it. He went into an adjacent room. I hesitated, I picked up the bear, and I joined him in the corridor. I did not need to say anything.

He just turned it over to read the label and he nodded.

He handed it to me so I would put it back on the bed. He seemed lost in thought.

"That doesn't mean a thing . . . And in any case, it's not enough to stand as proof," he said.

We looked at each other.

What I had understood, he had understood.

"It's not enough," I said.

We went back out and sat down, outside, on the steps. He lit a cigarette and smoked half of it without saying a word.

He was looking at the ground between his feet, a stubborn frown on his forehead.

"I spoke with Nan the day before she died. I was on the beach, she came over to me. In everything she said, there were things . . . Since then, I can't stop thinking about it . . ."

"What things?"

"A chain she was supposed to give back to me . . . A chain with a tag. She said it belonged to me. She talked to me as if she knew me."

"She was like that with everybody."

"No. Not like that . . . She asked me why I had left, and where I had been all this time. I told her about Paris, and Le Morvan, and she got annoyed because it didn't match her story."

He let out a long puff of smoke.

"Had you already been inside there?" he said, pointing to the window behind us that was still open.

"Yes."

"Why?"

I did not answer.

He did not insist.

He went on smoking.

"I too had my suspicions, so I did what I used to do when I was working, I questioned her."

His expression grew tense. His eyes squinting, almost closed, as if he were concentrating on one thing, an idea that he might lose at the slightest disturbance.

"In the end she told me about a kid they had brought to her, so sick he was almost dead, and I could see in her eyes when the two stories got mixed up. She didn't know any more. She was waving her hands, disoriented, and then suddenly she stopped walking, and stared at a spot on the beach in the rocks. She said, 'That is where you were.' After that, she left."

He lit another cigarette. In the night, the red glow made a point of light that must be visible from the path.

"It wasn't me who was down there."

For a moment he stared at the cigarette burning between his fingers. Long seconds ticking by in which he said nothing.

And then slowly.

"I believe that my brother is alive."

He looked at me, disturbed that he had to say it, had to utter it aloud.

"I think he survived the shipwreck . . . I think Nan took him in."

He got up.

"Don't ask me why or how, but I think, too, that she gave him someone else's identity."

He threw a piece of gravel far ahead of him. The gravel struck a shutter.

"Fucking intuition!"

That's what he shouted.

"I don't know how it all happened, but I'm going to find out."

He went back over to the window.

"We're going back inside."

He lit his torch again.

"We can't not find something . . ."

At the end of the second room, between the common rooms and Nan's house, there was a thick door, it was used to communicate between the two buildings. We tried to open it, but it was locked. Lambert looked all around him, until he found a piece of wire, and began to pick the lock. It made a strange scratching noise in the house of a dead woman.

"You can't do that . . ." I said.

"Why shouldn't I?"

He started over several times. Finally he had only to push the door open.

In the kitchen, everything was just as on the day when I had gone there, just after Nan's death. The cups, the coffee in the coffee pot, the newspapers.

Lambert looked round quickly, just like that, not touching anything. In the other room there was the bed, and the pillow, still hollowed out. Another room, behind, smaller, that I had not seen the first time. He looked at it all and then he started searching through everything. I do not know what he was looking for. Nor did he. He said, "There must be a trace, something! There's always something."

He opened the cupboards. He was careful not to disturb anything. He disturbed all the same. His hunt was meticulous. I shone the torch on to his hands, inside the drawers. He came upon a ledger in which Nan had written down the names of the children as they arrived. Departures in another column. He sat down at the table. It was an old notebook. He turned the pages. 1967. There was a departure on 13 September, another on 6 November. One entry, 12 October, a boy, two years old. A few other notes followed, all written on the same line, in separate boxes. An arrival date, nothing for the departure date. Right at the end of the line, a name, Michel Lepage.

The last box was empty.

"This child arrived at the Refuge and never left."

"That makes sense," I said. "She adopted him."

He nodded.

"Normal, sure . . ."

He looked closer. Something had been written in the final column and then rubbed out. He held the notebook to the light, under the lamp, but even like that it was impossible to read anything.

"Paul disappeared in October '67, on the 19th to be exact."

He reread everything written in the column.

"This child arrived a few days before. He was the same age as my brother."

He turned to me, his gaze angry, searching.

"I know, these are called coincidences! But when you're a policeman, you learn to mistrust coincidences. There are facts, and the facts either match or they don't. And in this case . . ."

"What are you thinking, exactly?"

He raised his hand to his neck.

"Paul had a pendant. The same as mine. Our four names etched on it, that's what my mother wanted . . ."

He showed me the pendant he was wearing, the other side, the four names.

"Nan said something about a pendant that she had and that belonged to me. It must be here somewhere."

"Unless Michel left with it."

"Unless, indeed . . ."

He hunted some more.

I told him about the photograph I had found here, among the others, the photograph Nan had held so tightly against her chest.

The little boy with the wooden train. A print that was forty years old.

"It could be your brother, a few days after the shipwreck."

I had left the photograph in my room.

"I'll bring it to you tomorrow."

I told him about the letters Théo was receiving, letters from the monastery. He listened attentively.

"So Paul might have become a monk . . ."

I thought about Théo. He must know the truth about the child Nan adopted. No matter which way I turned it in my mind, it was impossible for him not to know.

Lambert searched some more, everywhere, the same stubborn diligence, he wanted to find proof, his brother's trace in this house.

I left him.

When I got to the door, I turned. I looked at him. I was glad for him.

I told him so, I'm glad for you. He had opened the door to the second room. He had already disappeared inside.

He did not hear me.

*

It was dark but it was not very late. There was still a light on at Théo's place. I went back to La Griffue, took the stairs four at a time, and fetched the photograph taken at Nan's house.

I went back up to the village, and took the medallion from the grave. The two photographs in the light of a street lamp. It was the same child, taken a few days apart. Only the background of the photograph differed. On the medallion, you could see the corner of a shutter, on the other photograph, a simple door. Everything else, the same face, the same polo shirt with little boats.

In between the two there had been a shipwreck.

Théo could not lie to me. He could not deny it. I took the path to his house.

When I got there, he was watching television, curled up in his dressing gown, his cats all round him.

I went in.

He looked up. He hesitated for a moment then switched off the television.

"You're rather late today."

I went up to him. I looked at him. He seemed so alone, so tired. I pulled up a chair and sat down.

I took the photograph from my pocket, the one I had found at Nan's place. I slid it quietly over to him. He looked at me again and adjusted his glasses.

He picked up the print, and held it up to his eyes. I could hear his dry fingers rubbing against the paper. The slightly wheezing sound of his breath.

There was a bottle of ether on the table, and some cotton wool. The nurse had been. Théo never put anything away any more.

"This picture doesn't belong to you . . ."

He said nothing else, that was all, and he put the print gently down on the table.

"Théo, you have to tell me . . ."

"What do you want me to tell you?"

"Who is that child?"

He gave a resigned smile.

"It's Michel."

"I know that."

"Well, if you know, why are you asking me?"

He said it very gruffly. It was a most odd moment, when I thought he might go out of the room and leave me there. I think that was what he wanted to do.

I think too that if he did not do it, it was because he remembered that Nan was dead, and that it no longer mattered so very much. A shadow passed over his face, immensely painful. Long seconds passed before he picked up the photograph again.

Long seconds still before he spoke. And his voice was unrecognizable.

"That little wooden train he's got at the end of the string, I'm the one who made it for him." He said, "I had forgotten that Florelle had this photograph."

He spoke about the child, his words slow.

"At times it seemed to me, when I would look at them together, that Michel really was her child, her child and mine."

"Your child more than Lili was?"

He thought about it, and said, "My child, yes, more than Lili."

He bent down and took the little white cat on his lap. He was not caressing her. Just touching her lightly.

"He was a marvellous child . . . He looked at the world around him with his eyes full of wonder, and yet sometimes they could be so sad."

His hands remained motionless, curled around the soft slope of the little cat's back.

I took out the medallion. I put it next to the other photograph. The same two faces.

"You knew, didn't you?"

He looked at me. His eyes, suddenly extraordinarily clear. He could have said that it had nothing to do with me, that I had no business there. He could have shown me the door and I would have left.

He said nothing.

He got up. He went over to the window and looked outside. Since Nan's death, he seemed to have renounced any form of struggle.

"That night, the wind was blowing from the west."

He turned round. He glanced at the two photographs.

"Westerly winds often bring in the bodies."

He picked up the photographs.

"Florelle left her house when she heard the sirens. She spent the night on the beach, walking back and forth. She was waiting for her dead."

He came and sat down again at the table. Only a tiny bit of light filtered from his eyes.

"So when she found the child, in the morning . . . He was attached to a small dinghy, hardly even wet. She hid the dinghy among the rocks. I was the one who went to get it a few days later."

He folded one hand over the other.

"He was little, barely two. She hid him, she didn't know if he would survive . . . Afterwards, when she understood that he was going to live, she hid him still so that no-one would see him."

"She didn't tell anyone?"

He shook his head.

"He had been brought back by the sea, for her, you understand . . . She had been waiting for years. A child brought back alive in exchange for all those the sea had taken from her."

"But you, did you know who he was? Did you know that he had a brother?"

"Yes, I knew . . . So did she, she knew, deep inside, but she preferred to forget."

Knotty veins ran over the back of his hands. In the light of the lamp, the blood they contained looked black.

"She found Michel in the waves."

"His name is Paul."

"Paul, yes . . . All she could think of was saving him. Afterwards, there were other things . . ."

"Other things . . . ?"

"She grew to love him."

I picked up the photographs. Lambert's face, superimposed upon the two faces.

"You kept them from knowing each other! You kept them apart, and they had already lost the most important —"

"I often thought about that, yes."

Suddenly Théo disgusted me. That he was capable of such a thing.

"And when he came back, and he saw you in the yard . . . That child with you, it was his brother, and you said nothing to him!"

I got up. I suddenly felt I needed air, I had to get out.

He held out his hand.

"Don't go . . ."

I looked at him. In disgust or pity. I found myself outside. Sitting on the steps, trembling, indifferent to the cold and the growling cats.

Max said that the female porbeagle abandons her cubs after a year, and that they forget they ever had a mother. Had Paul forgotten his parents? Had he grown attached to someone else? I felt sick to my stomach. I held on to the railing. Leaning forward, my hands on my belly.

Théo was still under the lamp. In the yellow light of the bare bulb. He had not moved. He was waiting for me, as if he knew that I would come back. No doubt he would have waited for me for hours still, just like that, without making the least movement. Bent over in his woollen dressing gown. The little cat was sleeping, curled in a ball on his lap.

I sat down again.

We sat there for a long while in silence. At the end of a time span that seemed infinitely long, Théo looked at me.

"What do you want to know?"

"Paul . . . You gave him someone else's name."

"We had to."

"Who was Michel Lepage?"

"A two-year-old child. A woman entrusted him to Florelle, some sort of gipsy, she didn't want him, the child was already very sick when she brought him to her. She knew he would not live."

"I saw the ledger. He arrived a few days before the shipwreck."

"And he died a few days afterwards, from pleurisy."

I looked at him.

"That child no longer existed for anyone," he said.

"And he had a name . . ."

"Yes, he had a name . . . We buried his body behind the house."

There was a very heavy silence after he said that.

"Someone might have come to ask for him? That woman, was she his mother?"

"She left him there, she didn't want him any more."

He slid his hand over the tabletop.

"The first time I saw Paul, he was sleeping in the room with all the smallest children. Florelle said, 'It's the sea that brought him back to me.' I didn't understand right away . . . Only later, when she asked me to go and get the dinghy on the beach."

A muffled groan came out of him, like a sob.

"That dead child, you understand, there was nothing more we could do for him. Nan didn't even have the mother's address to let her know."

He seemed to slump on to the table, his upper body frailer than ever. He spread his hands as if the child were still there in front of him.

"It took Florelle only a few nights to sew his shroud, he was so little. She didn't write a name on it."

"And you buried him like that?"

"In a little wooden box, with the shroud."

"People might think that Nan killed him . . . Or that she let him die to give his name to another child."

Théo nodded. He pressed his hands together.

"I thought about that, too."

I was staring at the table. I wanted to keep hold of the words, everything he was saying to me. I wanted to keep it all.

"In the village, nobody ever suspected anything?"

He nodded.

"Old Mother worked it out very quickly, when he started coming to see the animals . . . She blackmailed me with it. She said that if I left her, she would go to the gendarmes, she would tell them everything and they would take the child away from Florelle. She said that Florelle would go to prison. There were rumours that he was our son, Florelle's and mine. Florelle was never pregnant, but she always wore such large dresses . . ."

He said, "She was a good mother, you know . . ."

"And you, were you a father to him?"

He looked distraught.

"I've never been a good father to anyone."

The smile faded, became a shadow that faded too, until there was no trace left.

He closed his eyes again.

I let him sleep. I thought about the part that chance had played. The truth might never have come out if I had not found that photograph at Nan's. And it would have been enough if Paul had been wearing a different polo shirt, not the one with the three little boats.

Did Ursula know?

No doubt she too had been in on the secret. I could hear the ticking of the clock, the cats' breathing mingled with Théo's, hoarser. Little groaning noises in sleep.

He slept for ten minutes or so. After that, he sat up. He hunted for his glasses on the table.

"Was I asleep?"

"A little while, yes."

He looked towards the window. It was dark. The little cat was curled on his lap.

He picked her up and put her down on the bed.

"Would you like a coffee?"

His gestures, with the little cat, were infinitely tender. In the space of a few days, they had become the gestures of an old man.

He heated up some coffee in an iron pot. His slippers slid over the floor, pushing aside clumps of cat hair and dust.

His shadow against the wall, the slow shadow of his arm.

"Lili worked it out, too, much later on . . . I don't know how . . . I argued so often with her mother. She must have overheard."

He poured the coffee in the cups. He came to put the cups on the table.

"She could have adopted another child, there was probably no shortage of real orphans?"

He looked at the cups set down side by side.

"But that child had been given back by the sea."

"And he had a brother!" I shouted, getting to my feet.

I could not help it. I found it all so hateful, so sordid.

He said nothing.

He sat down again. The cat came back on to his lap.

"You love that man, don't you?"

I did not answer.

"You love him. You already love him, but you don't know it."

He took a sip of coffee. He raised his eyes to look at me.

"How much could you keep silent for his sake? How far into silence could you go?"

He waited for me to answer.

I thought about you.

I would have gone far, very far, if I could have saved you. I went over to the surgeons, I lifted up my jumper, Use me, use my guts . . . I said. I wanted them to take whatever they needed to save you. They told me they could take it, but that it would not save you.

I looked out the window.

"I'm not judging you."

He closed his eyes.

"I know."

What time could it be? The night was long and it seemed as if it would never end. As if there would be no other mornings. Even the growling cats sensed that this night was not like others. They had gathered, silent, on the steps outside the house. They were not fighting.

The dampness of the night made the iron railing shine, the railing Théo clung to when he needed to get into the house.

Was Lambert still at Nan's place? Perhaps he had driven past Théo's house. He must have seen the light, but not realized I might be here. Had he found anything more, apart from the ledger?

Théo's eyes were still closed. He had fallen asleep the way cats do. Suddenly. His hands folded on his stomach.

On the dresser, the hands of the clock turned.

I went back to La Griffue. I slept a dreamless sleep.

In the morning, my head felt empty.

I drank coffee. Until I felt sick.

I waited for the sun to rise. Shut in that room facing the sea. I heard the angelus chime, three slow peals, and then again. I remembered my childhood, the wandering, from house to family, all the time spent seeking, waiting.

One day I burned my bed, because I had to live.

One day, too, I met you, an improbable meeting on a village square, one morning. It was cold. There was a fountain. It was frozen. You were there. I looked at you.

I knew that you were the one that I had to meet.

Max woke me up, tossing pebbles against my window.

He had found an injured seagull inside his boat. The bird's tongue had been split, a piece of flesh torn away by a hook. It could no longer feed itself, so Max had been fishing for it. He spoke to it the way he spoke to the rat, with his dictionary vocabulary.

The seagull listened to him.

Max said he was going to tame it. That it was easy, all you needed was fish and words.

I was not sure whether it would want to stay on the boat.

Raphaël's car was in the courtyard. Since Morgane had left, he no longer used it. He did not care if it got rusty.

*   *   *

I walked back up to the village. The Audi was parked on the pavement. The shutters of the house were closed. Lili knew, she was in on the secret. Buried. She too, like Old Mother. She had used the story in order to hate her father.

I slipped my hand along the door handle. I was afraid to go in. Afraid of the moment our eyes would meet.

I went through the door. Lambert was there. His face, crumpled. Lili looked at me. She was sitting opposite him. At the same table. There was no-one else.

I was wearing my thick rain jacket. I felt like apologizing, for being there. I said it, I think, I mumbled, Excuse me . . .

I did not say anything else. I looked at Lambert a bit longer than usual and then I put the two photographs on the table.

Lili saw them. She went pale.

Had she loved Lambert? A love made of lies and silence, things unsaid buried so deep that you could hear the wolf pack howling.

Do voices change with time? It is said that only eyes do not change. But what of eyes that close? You said, You must love, after me.

I looked at Lambert, his face, his hands.

Lili picked up the photographs.

*

"I heard them arguing so much of the time . . . Insults, all the time, over nothing. When he was fed up, he would go off down the road, he went to be with her. They never told me anything, but in the end I worked it out . . ."

Lili got up. She stood behind the table, she looked outside, through the little space of windowpane above the curtains.

"Your brother came often, to the farm . . ."

Lambert shivered. Lili went on.

"He liked the animals, he was always hugging them, caressing them. For a long time I believed he was a kid from the Refuge like the others . . . I didn't pay any attention to him. My mother didn't want him in the house. I think I knew that Nan had adopted him, long before I understood what that meant."

Lambert listened to her.

"You never asked any questions?"

"What sort of questions would I have asked? I didn't care, for me he was a tinker's kid, nothing more, except that he didn't go away again like the other ones . . ."

Lambert shuddered.

I was at the table, across from him. I could see his face, the quivering of his eyelids when the emotion took hold of him. The tiny film of sweat above his lip.

Memory is modest. I could feel it beating inside him, the images that Lili gave to him, all of them carrying that element of intimacy.

"One day, they had a fight, and it was the one fight too many, and that day, I understood he was your brother."

Lambert went pale, I thought he might go out and be sick. Lili said, "I cursed them."

He clenched his fists.

Old Mother got up from her armchair. Leaning with one hand on the table. The other on her throat. She came over. They stared at each other, the two of them, the mother, the daughter.

"And she put up with it all, without a peep!"

Lambert got up.

"You could have written to me, you could have told me!"

"There was a time when I thought I would . . . I had managed to get your address from the gardener who looked after your house."

She put the pictures down, side by side, and rubbed her face; her father had the same gestures.

"You thought about it, but you didn't do it."

"For twenty-five years I'd been living with them . . . No man in my life, no child. At least I had a secret. I had learned to keep quiet. And I could control my father with it. He knew it, he no longer talked about going away. He would be no happier than we were, that's what I reckoned, time and again! No happier . . ."

Old Mother had come right up to us, her belly against the table. I could smell her old woman's smell. Her life of silence. Lili looked at her. There was no love in her look. No pity.

"Isn't that right, Old Mother, no-one can say he's any happier than we are?"

A victory without glory. It was so sad, a victory over what? Old Mother was mumbling something.

It all seemed such a terrible waste.

Lambert rubbed his eyes.

"Why did he leave, in the end?"

Lili stood still, one hand on the bar. She gave a short laugh.

"Why does anyone leave? Or stay? Who knows . . ."

Hesitating for a moment. Her gaze suddenly confused.

She had spoken without looking at him.

She turned away.

"You think I didn't see you, when you came with your grandparents, to visit the grave? Three times a year, in the beginning. You never came to say hello. How do you think that made me feel?"

He looked at her, shocked by what she had said.

"We went down to the sea and tossed flowers! Paul was there, somewhere, alive, perhaps he was playing in your bloody yard, and you're reproaching me because I didn't come and give you a peck on the cheek?"

She shook her head.

"At the time, I didn't know . . ."

He got up and went over to her behind the bar. He took her by the arm.

"I don't believe you."

She pulled away from him. She was staring at something in front of her, in the sink. Water, or glasses. Or maybe she wasn't looking at anything.

"That's not what I'm reproaching you with," she said.

"What is it then?"

She did not reply so he said it again, louder. Finally she looked up.

"One day, you came back, you were nearly twenty. You were all alone."

Lambert thought about what she had just said. It took him a moment to understand.

"You spoke with my father."

"So you know that too . . ."

She held his gaze. For a few seconds.

"I was behind the window, I recognized you right away, I heard you talking with my father, I opened the window a little. You didn't even ask him how I was."

He was looking at her, as if he wanted to understand something, something he could not grasp. The stubborn spitefulness in Lili's eyes. In her voice. He turned away for a moment, and then looked at her face again.

"I was in love with you . . ." she said, forcing a laugh. "And I thought you would love me, too . . . I waited for you for years, and then one day I understood that you wouldn't be coming any more, so I married a . . ."

She left her sentence like that, suspended.

They looked at each other for a moment, he was disoriented. Had

Lili loved him so much that she sought to take revenge on him, too, the way she had taken revenge on her father for loving another woman? And for loving another child more than her? A child who wasn't even his own blood.

"You were in love with me . . . ?"

"We kissed a few times."

"Kissed, maybe . . ."

He went back over to her.

She had let him toss flowers upon the sea for a dead child who was not dead. She had watched him moan, weep, wait, believe.

"That kid who was with your father, that day, in the yard, holding a calf on the end of a rope, do you remember . . . ? Was that my brother? Tell me, it was him, tell me!"

"It was, but I didn't know it at the time."

"You knew!"

She shook her head.

"I knew, but much later."

Lamberts clenched his fists. I thought he was going to grab hold of her, strangle her. I think that Lili would have let him hit her, that she would have put up with anything, without trying to resist. But it was the bar counter that he hit. A hard punch. The glasses shook. And his voice, too.

"And you wanted me to come and say hello! Maybe you wanted me to marry you, too!"

He took her arm, her face between his hands, a few inches away.

"You're just like your mother, you're full of hate. Who wants to fuck a woman full of hate?"

I saw Lili's face go to pieces under the ferocity of the insult. For a moment she had to grab hold of the bar. Her lip was trembling.

He looked away. She went on staring at him, even when he turned his back to her.

He opened the door.

I saw him cross the road.

Lili went into the kitchen, behind the strips of the curtain. Her figure shrunken.

I stayed there alone with the old woman, who now looked even older, so intent, so red in the face, too. She was incapable of sitting down. Incapable of standing up.

I could not touch her. Take her by the hand, help her to sit down. I went to fetch her a glass of water, I put it down in front of her, on the table. More than that I could not do.

I remembered the night of the storm, when we all came back here, to this bistro, Lili's face when Lambert came in.

Her expression had hardened. What had she felt when she realized who it was? What fear must have gone through her?

He had not left. He had hung about. And then he had settled in the house just across the way.

"Are you going to be alright?" I said to Old Mother, going back to her.

She did not answer.

Her cheeks had lost their colour, but she seemed to be breathing more calmly.

"I'm going to leave you, now."

I went to the door. I put my hand on the latch. I turned, she was there, following right behind.

"The old man, he thinks it was me ... But it wasn't me, I didn't say anything."

She fixed her eyes on me. I could smell her heavy breath.

"It wasn't me," she said again.

She shook her head several times, as if she wanted to banish the ghosts.

She seized my arm. Her eyes were hardly open. They looked like a lizard's eyes.

"It wasn't you, what?" I said.

She was waving her hands.

"It wasn't me . . . It was her, she told Michel everything . . . And after that I had to come here."

She finished her sentence with a trickle of drool. Her chin in her neck. Her eyes desperately empty.

I looked up. Lili was there. She was staring at us. I thought she was going to come and clean her mother's face, but she walked past her without doing a thing. She went over to the window. She looked outside for a long time.

"They'd been arguing again, that day. It wasn't the first time he had made her cry, but he went to get his suitcase and said he was leaving. He was going to go and live at Nan's. He said he wanted to be happy, for a few years, that Michel was grown up now, go and tell him whatever you want to, he didn't care. He also said they didn't send people to gaol such a long time afterwards. I couldn't stand the idea that he might be happy. Even a tiny bit."

She smiled faintly.

"The next day, I went to wait for Michel outside the school. The shipwreck, his parents, I told him everything."

She turned round.

"I could tell you that I told him for his own sake, so that he'd know the truth . . . but that's not true. If I told you it was for Lambert's sake, or against him, that would be closer to the truth."

She lowered her gaze and looked over at her mother.

"I did it for her, for everything he made her endure."

"How did Michel react?"

"Well . . . He was already very . . . very mystical. I think for him that it didn't change much, whether he had been abandoned or lost at sea . . . That evening, he came to the farm. He spoke with my father. He was young, seventeen at the time. I was thirty. He asked questions about his parents, the circumstances of the accident . . . He left a few weeks later, without telling anyone."

"Did he leave because of that?"

"Because of that, or something else . . . I think he would have left no matter what, some day . . ."

She opened the door, because there was some sun.

She took her mother's arm and led her outside to a bench. I watched her walking, with her burden of an old woman leaning on her arm. More a daughter than a woman. Desperately a daughter.

Had she been able to love? Had she known how to be a woman? Such a need in her to destroy, to keep from dying from her own pain.

"Lili?"

She turned her head.

"You told him about the shipwreck, but you didn't tell him he had a brother?"

She hesitated, a few seconds, I saw that instant where she did not know what she should reply, and she shook her head.

I picked up the photographs that were still on the table. His forehead, the childlike stubbornness on his lips: did Michel look like Lambert? No doubt he did. Nan had not been so very mad to confuse the two. She knew how to recognize, in the older brother's face, the younger brother's features.

Lambert hardly turned his head when I came in. He was looking at the fire. A fire that had gone out. The grey ash made a bed for a few pieces of charred wood that the flames had licked.

I went over to him.

I would have liked to have been able to touch him, hold him, give him my warmth. My hand, a few inches from his shoulder. He suddenly seemed so far away.

"Does he know that I exist?"

That is what he asked me. Without turning his head.

I did not know what to reply.

"It was for Paul that Nan came to steal the toys . . . Because they were his toys . . . She wanted him to play with them . . ."

He looked around him, as if he were searching for Nan's presence, the traces of her passing.

"When I saw him in the yard that day, leading the calf, I didn't recognize him. How can you explain that . . ."

"You thought he was dead."

He ran his fingers through his hair.

"Yes, I did. But I should have recognized him . . . I should have looked at him! Instead, I looked at the old man. What did she say to you?" he asked, pointing to the terrace.

I repeated Lili's words to him.

"Do you think my brother came into this house, afterwards, when he found out? That's what I would have done, I would have come here."

"Lili said he went to the grave. She didn't say anything about the house."

He looked around him again.

"Tomorrow, I'm going to go back to Nan's place. Would you come with me?"

He was happy.

Tired.

He was afraid.

But he was happy.

A daughter taking revenge on her father. Revenge, because she was not the favourite . . . Because there was an absence of love. Wherever she looked. A desperate quest. I thought of Raphaël's sculptures, "The Pleading Women".

I wondered what he had understood about Lili to be able to sculpt those women. If he had understood anything or if it had come to him from elsewhere. From another story.

Stories are alike.

And there are always more stories. It does not take much, sometimes, an angelus ringing, people who meet, who are there, in the same place.

People who might never have met. Who could have walked past and never seen each other.

Walked past and never said anything.

They are there.

*   *   *

Théo took off his glasses, rubbed his eyes. I had been there for a long time, and we had already talked a great deal.

Lili had taken her mother to live with her, it was a few months after Michel left. She had taken everything away and Old Mother had followed. Théo had ended up all alone, in the big house.

"Why didn't you go and live with Florelle? There was nothing left to hold you back?"

He shook his head, slowly.

"It was too late . . . I got a first cat, a female. She had six kittens, they grew up, and then other cats."

He smiled. I think that was the last time I saw him smile.

He got up.

"Now I'm old, it doesn't matter any more."

He walked over to a door that gave on to a windowless room. He disappeared inside. I heard another door creaking. He came back a moment later, with a little wooden box.

He put the box on the table. All the letters he had received from the monastery were inside. He sat down again.

"Michel wrote me a first letter shortly after he got there. I answered. He never tried to hide his whereabouts from us, but Florelle didn't want to know. She thought he would come back by sea, like the first time."

He put his hand on the box.

"Twenty years of personal confessions . . ."

He pulled out a letter at random, and read it. He handed it to me. It was dated November of the year that had just gone by.

372

Smooth handwriting, blue ink.

My dear Théo,

It's snowing here.
The snow is falling, whipped round by the wind, and it plasters the walls of the monastery. It's very important, snow. It didn't come like the other years. Usually, it comes the way the sea rises, with an ebb and flow. It falls, it melts, it comes again, it melts a bit less, then it covers the countryside in successive layers. This year, it came and settled all at once. Yesterday, I was able to go for a walk. It's always an important date, the first time you can go out in the snow.

I hope you are well at the moment, and that it is not too cold in your house.

I am praying for you all.

Michel.

Théo folded the letter, put it back in the envelope, and then put it away with the others. He pulled out another one. Behind us, all around us, the cats were dozing. I could hear the regular ticking of the clock.

I read another letter. On some pages, at times, there were only a few words.

I went out early this morning. Only animals had taken this path before me. Many had gone past, their tracks were all mixed up. I could tell there were wild boars, and deer, or stags, hares, dogs (their tracks are enormous, a wolf?).

I read other letters. They all talked about the monastery surrounded by mountains. They did not talk about prayer, but about nature, bedrock. In one of the very first letters, Michel wrote,

This monastery that was only meant to have been a way station has become the place of arrival. I am staying here, enchanted. The happiness of walking through the mountains. The wind at times, crashing. And the stars at night. In the evening, I write to myself, in my little notebook, everything that has filled me. Everything is so present.

I cannot find the words to express it. Perhaps a profound intimacy.

Kiss Mother for me.

From the cupboard Théo took a photograph that he slid next to the letters.

"That's him . . . That's Michel."

The lamp lit the photograph, the face of a man sitting at a table. Wearing a large light habit with a hood that fell on to his back. His hands were in front of him, a book open on the table. Another book, smaller than the first one, was next to him, closed. A white bowl. He was looking down at the book. The light came in through the window, falling on the desktop, illuminating the bowl, an entire side of his face, while the other side remained in shadow. You could not make out anything else in the room except the man sitting at the window.

"You must have seen him, the day of Florelle's funeral."

I raised my head. I looked at Théo.

Suddenly, the image came back to me, a man in a long black coat. He had stayed to one side, speaking to no-one. A man with a thin face, and very light eyes. A taxi had dropped him off by the gate. Afterwards, Old Mother arrived, and I no longer paid any attention to him, but when I left the cemetery, he had vanished.

Théo nodded.

"He arrived with the noon train and left again on the evening train. He came here, after the funeral. I hadn't seen him for twenty years. We talked. The taxi waited for him on the road."

Théo touched the letters lightly with his fingers.

"How did he know about Florelle?" I said.

"I called him, and he came."

I remembered. Strangely, everything began to fall into place, to take on its true meaning.

"You called him that day you asked Lili for a telephone card, isn't that right?"

"Yes, that was the day. Nan had died the day before."

He turned his head and looked over towards the window. Night was falling. The yard was becoming a den of shadows with only the yellow eyes of the growling cats as they passed by, their bellies close to the ground.

"I didn't know whether he'd be able to come . . . When you call there, you know, it's somewhat unusual . . . You leave a message, that's all, and the monk who answers passes it on."

"Did you tell him that his brother was here?"

"Yes. He knows he has a brother, I wrote to him about it, a long time ago."

"And he never tried to meet him?"

"You'll see, he's an exceptional person."

"You didn't answer my question."

He shook his head.

"Michel has other brothers now . . . Such things don't matter to him in the same way."

"Such things?"

"Real life . . ."

"And Florelle?"

He looked up at me. His words came from the back of his throat, I could hardly hear them.

"What, Florelle?"

"Florelle, why did she look for him the way she did? Didn't she know where he was?"

"Yes, she knew . . . but she didn't want to think about him in that way. The idea that he could shut himself away voluntarily. His vow of silence, too, she never read his letters. She wanted him to come back, but I knew very well that he would not."

He looked down at the photograph.

His voice was a murmur.

"He doesn't speak, only a few hours in the entire week. He explains it in his letters, you'll read them, the moments when he is allowed to speak. He says they are rare and precious moments." He closed the box and pushed it over to me. "I have learned a lot from his letters. You'll read them, won't you, and then give them to his brother."

I picked up the box. What I had read made me want to read more.

He took off his glasses, the lenses had steamed up.

"His pendant, the clothes he was wearing when they found him, and the rope that was used to hold him to the dinghy, all of that is at Florelle's house."

"Lambert searched, he didn't find anything."

He sat staring into space.

"Behind the dresses, at the back of the wardrobe."

*   *   *

Since Morgane's departure, Raphaël no longer put the stone outside the door. You could go into his studio whenever you wanted. He saw me go by with the wooden box under my arm and he called out to me. I told him I was tired, he said that I would never be as tired as he was, he took me by the arm and led me over to the table. The ashtrays were full. The rubbish bins were overflowing.

A little clay tightrope walker stood poised above all the mess, balancing on his rope.

"Morgane sold one for me, almost the same. A bronze one! Hermann wants others, sculptures, too."

I looked at him.

That afternoon, they had put in a telephone. He showed it to me, he was so pleased with that, too, Morgane would be able to call him every evening.

He had news from her. She liked her job at the gallery, she had made a new friend, a girl her age she could go to the cinema with. She did not mention any boys. She had already sold two drawings and a bronze.

She said her room was small, but that in five minutes she could be on the banks of the Seine. She had visited the Louvre.

She did not talk about coming back.

Raphaël told me all that, out of order, and he looked at the wooden box.

"What's that?"

"It's nothing."

"Some more of your bloody nests!"

He sat back down at the table. The sleeves of his jumper were too short, I could see the thick veins running under his skin. He had knotted one of Morgane's scarves around his neck.

"Do you miss her?" I said.

He gave a faint smile that faded into a wince. His hair was flecked with grey. He said it was the plaster.

He looked up.

"And how are you?"

What could I tell him?

"The Conservatoire du littoral is offering me a two-year contract."

"To do what?"

"To monitor the shore between here and Jobourg. I would also have to go to Caen once a week."

"Will you take it?"

"I don't know."

He turned round and looked at me.

"If you say you don't know, it means you will."

He forced a laugh.

"So we'll go on seeing each other, then!"

I read the letters during the night. I read and I slept. And read some more.

The letters contained a man. Words. A voice.

Michel had left without taking anything with him, and he had walked for days. Cars stopped for him but he did not get in. He walked the entire way. He went through villages and women gave him food to eat. He slept at farms, with the animals. He arrived at the monastery in the early days of autumn. He had asked for hospitality.

And now, he was a contemplative monk.

In one of his letters, he wrote,

I always have a notebook on me, to write down my impressions when I am out walking. So that I won't forget.

Sunday afternoon, it has just rung three o'clock. It is already time to settle in for the night. The sun has disappeared behind the peaks, the temperature is well below zero. I am in my bedroom study. My lair. Yesterday I put on my snowshoes and waded through nearly a metre of powdered snow.

I thought about you, how you have never known such thick snow.

Some day, you will have to come here.

I read all the letters.

In the morning, I put the letters back in the box and went up to look for Lambert.

We went to Nan's place, entered the way we had the first time, climbing over the windowsill, and we walked the length of the Refuge to the door of the house. Without speaking. Lambert went to the wardrobe and opened it.

The dresses were all hanging one against the other, and he pushed them aside. They smelled of mothballs, and little white balls rolled out. The back of the wardrobe was cluttered with shoes, plastic bags that contained balls of wool, remnants of fabric.

The cardboard box, like a shoebox. Lambert found it. He pulled it out. He put the box on the table. We looked at each other for a moment and he lifted the lid.

The little polo shirt was there, folded on top of the rest, the blue and white stripes with the three boats. Lambert took it in his hands. He held it against his face.

It was the polo shirt Paul was wearing when he left for Alderney. The same polo shirt as when Nan took her photograph, and in the time in between he had become Michel. Why had she felt the need to make him wear the same clothes?

Perhaps she thought it would reassure the child.

Under the polo shirt there was a pair of green cotton trousers with a pirate badge sewn on the pocket. Newspaper articles. The paper had yellowed, the photographs were faded, but the text was still legible. At the very bottom of the box, there was the rope that Théo had mentioned, which had served to tie Paul to the dinghy.

There was also the chain and the tag. Lambert showed it to me, the four names engraved behind.

He clenched the tag in his fist.

I put my hand on his shoulder.

"Nan loved him . . . she brought him up."

That was all I could find to say.

He looked at me.

"She wasn't his mother."

"He knew that . . ."

I took my hand away, then I put the wooden box on the table.

Lambert looked at the letters.

"They are for you. From Théo . . ."

I went out. I saw his face through the window. He had opened the box.

I walked all round the house. Before leaving, I wanted to find that little spot of earth where Théo had buried the child. He had described the place to me. A magnificent lilac bush had taken root in the soil. Pushing aside the branches closest to the ground, I found the little white cross.

A child died, another one now bears its name. Had Michel come to meditate on this grave when he had found out his story?

What should he be called? All the letters were signed Michel.

I put my hand in my pocket. I took out a few smooth pebbles I had picked up on the beach. The two abalone shells. I left them all at the foot of the cross and carefully put back in place the one or two branches that my hands had parted.

I did not know how to pray.

At that moment I would have liked to have known how, of that I am sure.

I took my notebook out of my pocket. I reread fragments of Paul's letter that I had copied out during the night, words that had the strength of a prayer:

The noon Angelus is ringing. The same bell, three chimes, repeated three times, then another bell rings twelve times, repeated twice. A dog is barking. It is noon, but the sun is low on the horizon; from behind my back, it casts my shadow on the path.

When I left, Lambert was still at the table. Bent over the letters.

I went back to La Griffue. In the afternoon, I had to go to Caen to sign my contract. Raphaël lent me his car.

Since Morgane had left, Max was sleeping in the boat with the rat. At nightfall, he would come to La Griffue to read a few columns in his dictionary. Raphaël had told him he could go into the kitchen if he liked, but he preferred to keep to his old habits from before.

The before, when there was Morgane.

To observe what she had forbidden, too.

"I am in search of thoughts," he confessed, in the end.

He would read in the corridor, his knees tucked up under him. He turned the pages. From time to time he lifted his head, stared at the door, the white handle. The least little thing would make him jump.

That little thing might be the Stork, or it might be the wind, branches against the roof. Sometimes, he looked for Morgane. He would forget that she had gone.

And then he would remember, and his eyes suddenly became very white. There were times when he still went all the way to the end of the breakwater, to hide his sorrow there.

He would leave on the tide to go fishing. Either in the evening or the morning, and on a few rare occasions I saw him leave at night. He did not go very far.

He was learning the patience of sailors.

He fished with a line while he waited for the porbeagle to bite. Whatever he caught, he sold. With the money, he bought fuel, and went back out to sea.

III

I signed the contract, a two-year commitment, I would have to come to the centre once a week. Every Thursday. My expenses would be paid. I also agreed to give a number of lectures at the University of Cherbourg. Starting in the new academic year.

With the contract, I could keep the flat. I would have to buy a car.

I spent one night in Caen. In the evening, we went to eat all together in a restaurant in town. We laughed, we talked. They gave me books to help me prepare my classes. I slept, a room that they had reserved for me in a little hotel.

I came back in the morning.

I found a paper on my table, *Come and see me, as soon as you can.*

It was from Théo.

I do not know who had dropped the paper off, perhaps it was Max. I left my bag in the entrance and went out. The weather was mild, with a damp wind blowing in from the open sea, bringing the spray with it. I spread my arms, my hands. I was happy to be breathing the wind of La Hague again.

I found Théo at his table, holding tight to the little white cat. I immediately felt that something had changed. The way he looked at me when he raised his head. And then something else.

"I was waiting for you."

He was wearing his green woollen cardigan, the one he always wore when he had to go out. The cardigan had eight mother-of-pearl buttons. The buttons were each shaped like an anchor. One of them was broken.

I was not used to seeing him dressed like this so early in the morning.

"I was in Caen," I said.

He nodded.

His dressing gown was on the bed, folded. The cats were dozing around it. One of them, who had come in with me, jumped up on a chair and began to wash, slow, meticulous. Everything was calm, almost like usual.

And yet.

I turned my head and saw the suitcase by the wall. Théo followed my gaze.

"We still have a bit of time . . ."

That is what he said.

He got up and made some coffee.

"Where are you going?" I said.

He slid the palm of his hand along the table.

"I'm going to go to be with him . . ."

He gently stroked the little cat's head as she slept. He served the coffee.

His looked at me, calmly.

"I'm going to live in a cell a few metres square, and from my window I'll see the mountain."

He drank his coffee, standing with his back against the sink.

"I've never seen the mountains . . . Apparently, snow is something else . . ."

He put his bowl down, quietly.

"Michel is waiting for me. When he came here, we talked about my leaving."

Morgane had left, too, but Morgane was young, and Théo was so old.

I looked at his suitcase again.

"You're leaving just like that, so suddenly!"

"I'll write to you, and you'll reply, and then you'll come to see us too, Grenoble, after all, it's not that far . . ."

Would he have left had Nan not died? And had Nan died so that he *could* leave, at last? In her confusion, had she understood that he would go to join Michel once she was no longer there? That it was something he needed, the way she had needed to go to her dead?

Lambert's presence had awoken the horde of ghosts. Caused them to rise and move forward in a great mass, and Nan had followed them.

Théo was looking at me as if he understood the meaning of my silence.

"No doubt in the sea she saw . . . or thought she saw . . . She was dazzled in that way, sometimes. I wish I could have loved her more."

Always, that regret, that one did not love enough. That one stayed on the edge. Lambert would have liked to weep even more.

I had missed you, I had known that feeling. Now I no longer did. I wish I could have known it for ever. I missed missing you, but what I was missing was no longer you.

Théo slowly pushed his chair against the table. He did that, and it was the last time.

The bowls stayed on the table. The coffee, almost not drunk at all.

"I'll carry on a bit, and then, there will be my last footsteps."

That was what he said, and he leaned against the edge of the table, and looked at the cats, all of them, one after the other, giving time to each of them. An infinitely long gaze.

With his toe he pushed the rags against the wall and put the little cat down on the bed. He stayed like that for a moment, leaning over, his hands still underneath her belly, then he leaned still further down, and put his lips against the animal's forehead. The cat curled up in a ball and I heard her purring.

She closed her eyes.

Théo removed his hands.

384

He opened one of the drawers and took out a brown envelope. He told me it was money to feed the cats. That there was enough for a while.

"I thought I would ask Max, but now Max has his boat . . ."

He put the envelope on the table.

"I'll send a transfer every month, you need only ask the postman, he's been informed."

He did up the buttons of his cardigan, one after the other.

"I'll feel better like this . . . One of them might need the vet. And then the heat must be left on during the coldest months, and the window in the corridor has to stay open so that they can go in and out . . ."

He readjusted his collar.

"My pension will be enough, I don't need anything where I'm going."

He removed his slippers and put on his good shoes. I did not say anything, all that time. I could not say a single word.

"The *notaire* has been informed. When I die, the house will go to Lili."

I heard the clicking of the clock as the hands stuck, when the hour hand, as it went over the number ten, got stuck somewhere in the hidden cogs of the mechanism. We fell silent. In the time it took for the hand to come unstuck, two minutes were lost, out of time.

A cracking of time that got away from us, from him and from me.

Théo ran his fingers over the smooth edge of the table, a spot so well-worn by the rubbing of his sleeves that it was as if it had been polished. Here and there a few marks, left by his knife.

He put his slippers neatly side by side at the entrance.

He wound the clock.

"From time to time, if you remember . . . just a few turns."

He put the clock back in its place.

"You see, I think I'll be happy, there, to know that this clock is still marking time. And then my cats are used to hearing the noise. It's a bit like a heartbeat, isn't it?"

He let his gaze wander over at the furniture, the sink, the papers that covered the desk. The knife, the bread. He did not put anything away.

He said, "It's better like this, for the cats . . ."

He said, "Michel said that in winter the monastery is surrounded by snow and that you can see wolves go by."

He put on his heavy jacket.

"Do you believe in God?" I said.

"In God, I don't know, but I believe in the goodness of certain individuals."

I looked at him.

Had he told Lili that he was leaving? There were no words for her on the table. No letter.

Nothing for Old Mother.

"I'm going to be fine where I'm going."

"But you won't see the sea any more."

"Neither the sea, nor the lighthouse."

He turned away from me to look out of the window one more time, at his view outside, and then at this room where he had lived.

"Lili will be angry with me all her life for having loved a woman who was not her mother . . . and a son who is not mine."

He handed me a piece of paper, the address of the monastery.

He looked out the window again.

"I would have liked to be able to leave the way he did, on foot, taking the path, having all that time to remember, but my legs will no longer carry me. I've chosen a quicker and more comfortable means of transport."

I turned. There was a taxi by the gate. The driver was leaning against the car door, waiting.

"He's going to take me there."

"If I hadn't come, you would have gone, and I would have found the door locked."

Théo put his hand on my arm, gently.

"I wouldn't have left. I would have waited for you."

He went to the door.

"I've heard it's a lovely place for walking, there, especially at this time of year."

He looked one last time at his cats.

"Perhaps there will be one there, where I'm going . . . They always have cats in monasteries, don't they?"

He took my arm, just as he had done a moment earlier.

"Don't be sad . . ."

There was no sorrow in his voice, no regret, only the serenity of a man who has made his choice and who is leaving.

He picked up his case. The little white cat was sleeping. Théo looked at her one last time.

"You must pay special attention to her. I have loved her very much, the other cats know it, they'll want to take their revenge, they'll surely try to stop her getting near the food bowl."

"I promise . . ."

He turned away.

"I'll be at the monastery some time tonight."

He opened the door and went out.

I stayed on for a moment, sitting at the table, and then afterwards, outside, on the steps because the sun had come out and it was warm.

At noon, I ate an apple that I found in a crate.

I made some coffee.

I talked to the cats.

In the evening, Max brought back his first porbeagle. A creature that weighed eighty kilos, that he had struck out on the open sea and dragged in behind his boat. I had seen him coming from a long way away, with the seagulls above him, tracking the blood.

He gutted his shark in the waters of the harbour. He did it with a knife and his hands.

His seagull was there, perched on the cabin. It never left the boat. Max was afraid for it. That the other seagulls might kill it because it was being fed by a man.

He tore out the porgy's teeth. He gave me one. A few millimetres of light-coloured ivory, still attached to a bit of bone.

*   *   *

I found Lambert behind his house. He had lit a bonfire, where he was throwing branches, brambles, everything he had cut and that he had to burn. With a pitchfork he pushed the branches into the flames. Sparks flew out from the fire, drifting lightly up into the night.

In places, it was as if the shadow of the pasture was burning.

For a moment I looked at him, before he saw me. And then I went up to him.

"Théo has gone away," I said, as if I had to give an excuse for being there.

"I know."

With a gesture of his chin, he pointed to the road.

"He went past in a taxi, he stopped outside the bistro. He stayed for a moment, sitting in the back."

"Lili didn't come out?"

"No, but she saw him from behind the curtain, I'm sure she was there."

Tongues of fire leapt out, long red and gold flames crackling in the shadow. The fire was damp. The smoke gave off an acrid smell.

He planted the pitchfork in the earth and lit a cigarette. With his thumb he rubbed the hollow of the deep wrinkle that ran across his face.

"Do you know where he's going?"

"Yes, I know ..."

He looked at me. He had read the letters. He understood. He stayed silent for a moment, staring at the ground between his feet, and then he picked up the pitchfork. He tossed branches on to the flames.

The fire burned. The hot flames reddened our faces. Our hands.

With the next rain, the ashes would be absorbed and they would mingle with the earth and water.

He went round the fire to gather in its centre everything that could still burn. The last brambles. A few old boards. The FOR SALE sign that had hung from the fence round the house.

He left his pitchfork planted in the earth.

"I have some Bordeaux, a Cantemerle '95, how about it?"

I liked drinking with him.

"Is that yours? That top?" he said, pointing to my shirt.

"It was Morgane's . . ."

This made him laugh.

We talked about wine, all the wines that existed, and the happiness one could have drinking them. We emptied our glasses and filled them again. I do not know what we were drinking to, whether it was happiness or despair, no doubt an intimate mixture of the two.

At one point, he looked at me.

"And what if it wasn't true? If we'd been mistaken? If Théo had lied to us?"

He had known his share of coincidences, foolish mistakes, carelessness. He gave me examples from investigations, leads he had followed with his eyes closed, straight into a brick wall.

We drank some more. He was silent. Then he spoke again, and finally picked up his glass.

"But the clothing, hmm . . . the clothing, that's proof, after all, isn't it?"

He no longer knew.

The letters were on the table, in the bag. A big yellow bumblebee lay on its back, its legs in the air. It had come to die there, a long time ago, no doubt. I took it in my hand. It was so dry, I hardly touched it and it disintegrated. I closed my fingers one by one. I did not know what to do with the dust that was all that was left.

"The last time he saw me, he was two years old . . . you don't remember, at the age of two. Whereas I remember him well. How long does it take to go there?"

"Paris, Lyon . . . and Grenoble. Ten hours?"

He filled our glasses.

"Ten hours, that's all right. I'll leave tomorrow."

We drank and went back over the story, from the beginning, the photographs, the toys. The dinghy his brother had been tied to.

He took my hand, and opened my fingers.

"Why are you keeping this?"

He blew on the dust.

We had already drunk too much. For him, it was to get used to the idea that he had found his brother.

As for me . . .

I do not know.

I put my hand in my pocket. Beneath the bits of string, I felt some shells, and the shark's tooth. Down at the bottom, the smooth contact of the two bones of truth.

I pulled them out.

I showed them to him.

He held out his hand.

His palm was wide, deep. I could have buried my face in it.

I put the bones into his palm.

He tossed the bones in the air and made a wish, his eyes closed. The bones landed, both of them in the right direction.

He smiled.

He got up.

He came over to me.

"I'm going away, two, three days."

My forehead was against his chest, a few inches away. The wool of his jumper had absorbed the smell of the fire.

*

I slept there, in one of the armchairs, by the fireplace.

When I woke up, he was gone. I found his jumper next to me. I snuggled my head in it.

I slept some more.

I woke up a second time, it was dark outside. The bones of truth were on the table, next to his packet of cigarettes. The glasses. The letters.

I got the fire going again.

I reread some of the letters.

In the morning I went to see the cats. I filled their bowls. I made sure the window was still open and I wedged it with a stone so that the wind would not blow it shut.

The little white cat was not there. I looked for her everywhere, in the courtyard, in the hayloft. I called her.

I sat down on the steps.

I thought about you. I was losing you. Or you were fading. Or was it me? Not so long ago, I could put my hand on your shoulder. Your warmth. Closing my eyes, without an effort, I could still snuggle up against you.

Time was doing its dirty work. Insidiously. Already, I no longer cried.

*   *   *

I heard the sound of Lili's steps in the room above. The door of a cupboard groaned. The creaking of the floor.

Old Mother was back in her place at the table. She was moving a spoon around in a soup made with alphabet noodles. She was staring at the swirl of letters. She was chewing, swallowing indifferently.

She seemed even older now that Nan had died.

Lambert had been gone for two days. The windows, the house, the closed shutter, the road sign on the other side of the street.

Jobourg, 4.

Beaumont-Hague 10, via the D 90.

Via the D 45, Saint-Germain-de-Vaux 0.7.

Omonville-la-Petite, 5.

Cherbourg via coast road, 30.

I knew it all by heart.

"This isn't your usual time!" Lili said, on finding me there.

She went behind the bar. We looked at each other. What was there to say?

"What would you like?" she said.

"I don't know . . ."

What had she gained from telling the truth to Michel? Would things have been more difficult for her had Théo gone to live with Nan?

"Would you like some nice hot vermicelli?"

"Vermicelli?"

She pointed to the bowl, the alphabet noodles.

I nodded.

She poured a piping-hot ladleful into an earthenware bowl.

She came to me, with the bowl in her hands. She was looking at me. Scrutinizing me. She glanced outside, the closed shutters.

Her father had left.

She had been silent for years, and to go on living she would have to keep that silence.

"Did you spend the day at the cliffs?"

That is what she said.

She did not say anything about Théo. And yet it was the day when I usually took the bag of food for him.

The bag was there, hanging from a nail. Nothing in it. Would she find the strength, some day, to take it down?

"You have the eyes of the moor," she said, putting the bowl down in front of me.

Eyes of the moor, the eyes of a wanderer.

"A whole day on watch by the sea, it felt good . . ." I said eventually.

She looked at me again. She was willing to talk about birds so that she would not have to talk about her father.

"And what did you count?"

I took the notebook out of my pocket, slowly, trying to swallow my saliva that had suddenly become dry.

I opened the notebook.

I showed her.

"469 gannets, 3 common scoters, 71 terns, 2 oystercatchers, 3 gulls and 46 sandwich terns."

She stood up straight, her tea towel in her hand.

And then she put the towel over her shoulder.

"You counted all that?"

"All that."

"And what's your conclusion?"

I closed the notebook.

I looked at her. Her eyes like slits. Her father's eyes.

"That oystercatchers are rare," I said.

I got into the habit of spending an hour or two at Lambert's place, at the end of the afternoon. I lit a fire. I made coffee, too. I waited for him to come back.

I finished his bottle of whisky.

Michel's letters were on the table. I read them all again.

I do not know if the house had really been sold. There were no more visitors.

When I left, I put the key over the door.

At the end of the day, I went to Théo's place to feed the cats. I filled their bowls. I made them a fire. I put the radio on, too, so they would hear some noise.

I wound the clock and I waited, sitting at the table, until the hands got stuck, and when the moment came, those two minutes of motionless time, I thought of you.

Sometimes, one of the cats would jump on to my lap, curl up in a ball and go to sleep. I no longer dared to move. Time went by.

The little white cat that Théo loved so much had still not come back.

*   *   *

A little white hull in the distance. Max sailed for a long time along the coast as far as the cape of La Loge, between the coastguard station at Goury and Port-Racine. A few minutes longer, then the boat headed out to sea, until it was no more than a spot of light between the sky and the sea. And then it vanished. The Stork was following it with her gaze. She would have liked to have gone away with him. To go to sea, too. She watched him for so long that she was sick to her stomach. It was the sickness of those who stayed on land and watched the boats sail away.

The sickness of those who look on as others live, the same pain. The same nausea.

"Later, when you're grown up, you will go away too."

She looked at me with her big eyes. Her mouth with its crushed lip.

"When is later?" she said.

I took her by the hand.

"I don't know. Soon . . ."

Her hand was warm, curled up in mine.

"Soon, that's too far away!" she murmured.

"It will come quickly."

She ran off. She was gone, all the way to the far end of the meadow, her dog following her shadow. She went further and lay down on a patch of low grass, in the light. Her mouth open, her arms spread wide. She pulled up her jumper to bare her tummy.

Children grow more quickly in the light, like plants, flowers. I'd heard Lili say that, but she was talking about moonlight.

Moonlight or sunshine . . . The Stork had lain down to escape from her childhood, to reach tomorrow more quickly.

I followed the boat in the distance through my binoculars. Max was at the helm. The gull was on the roof. It went everywhere with him, on land as well as on the boat. He caressed it the way you caress a cat. He taught it how to speak. Simple words. He said that seagulls were capable of learning to speak. Other fishermen said so as well.

Max rarely spoke about Morgane.

Several times, Raphaël had called out him, to tell him that she was on the telephone. He had come. He had listened. He hardly said a thing. His gaze was detached, as if no longer seeing her had helped him to love her less.

Raphaël no longer called him now when Morgane was on the telephone.

The cats were getting used to Théo's absence. When I got there, they came over to me, rubbed themselves against my legs. They ate what I put in their bowls.

They allowed me to caress them.

Some of them purred.

I stayed for an hour or two.

I aired the house.

The little cat had still not come back.

I wrote a first letter to Théo, I told him that everything was fine.

*   *   *

The telephone rang, I was in the corridor, on my way back up. It was almost dark. Raphaël called out to me. I could hear Morgane's laughter at the other end of the line. She was talking fast. She seemed happy. She wanted to know how the sea was. I opened the curtain. I looked outside, towards the lighthouse.

"It's high tide."

"And the colours?"

The sky and the sea the same grey, slightly brown, it was the wind, it was blowing from the east, it stirred up the silt. The heather was already fading on the hill.

I described it all to her.

"There are seagulls flying above the beach. The lighthouse has not been lit yet. It's a matter of minutes."

"Will you look, will you tell me when the light comes on?"

I stared at the lighthouse. The weather was changing over by Alderney, there would be mist.

I told her that Max had gone fishing. That he had tamed a seagull. That the rat was fine.

I went on to the landing, I wanted her to hear the seagulls. To hear the wind, too.

"Yesterday, Max saw dolphins swimming at Le Blanchard. Raphaël saw them, too."

"Dolphins!"

Morgane could not believe it. She wanted us to take photographs, and send them to her.

I heard footsteps behind me.

"What were they doing, the dolphins?" she said.

"I don't know . . . Max said there were more than ten of them. They swam in the currents following the boat."

"Raphaël saw them, and he didn't tell me!"

"Raphaël doesn't care about dolphins."

"You say the rat is doing all right?"

"He's fine, yes . . ."

"And you, are you all right?"

The footsteps, the smell of the leather jacket. I sensed them before I saw them, a rough pounding in my heart.

"And you?" she insisted, because I had not answered.

"Me . . ."

He was there, behind me, almost against me. I could feel his breath against my neck. He wrapped his arms around me. Closed them. His hands. I could feel his heart beating in my back.

"I didn't see the dolphins," I mumbled.

Morgane's voice mingled with the throbbing of my blood, asking me if the lighthouse was lit yet. It was not.

He put his hand on my belly. His hand, all of it. And then his hand on my face. My cheek against his hand. My lips against his palm, on the inside, my entire mouth held.

I breathed in his hand.

Inside it, my lips against his dry palm. To the verge of stifling. Not saying a thing.

My neck against his shoulder. I waited for my heart to grow calm. It took me a few seconds, and then afterwards there was an infinitely gentle time where I could move again and place my hand on his arm, and then yet another moment when I could turn round and look at him. This man who had his arms around me: it was not you and yet I was in peace. I burrowed my face against him. My lips against his jumper. The warmth beneath the wool. My hand slid down, found its way to the place it so loved with you, between the jacket and the jumper, a fearful little creature, found its place, and nestled there.

"You've come back."

He held me tighter, and at last I could close my eyes.

It was dark. The sea rose, breaking against the lighthouse, bursts of short, heavy waves. The weather was stormy. The air was already electric.

In the room. My face reflected in the mirror. The wound from the piece of sheet metal had completely disappeared and yet, when I came in from the cold, you could still see the trace of it, a light mark that disappeared as soon as my skin got warm.

A transient trace.

A red shadow.

A memory.

Lambert was sleeping.

I looked at him.

And then I went out.

I went to finish the night on the sofa, in Raphaël's studio. A night of vague dreams, it seemed to me that I was calling you. I pulled the blanket over me. It had been lying about on the floor. It smelled of dust and plaster.

In the morning, Raphaël found me there. He asked no questions. He made some coffee. He just said that the weather was rainy, and that I should not have wrapped myself in such a dirty blanket.

I went to walk on the beach. A seagull was perched on the very top of the roof, staring at the sea. When it saw me, it let out a shrill cry and flew off, its wings spread, it went to graze the surface of the water almost in front of me. The cows gathered by the fence, they had spent the night there, they were ruminating, their heads turned towards the village. Humans were waking up there. The first lights.

I walked as far as the cross. A clump of little centauries had taken root at the base. You could find them in bloom here, even in winter.

It began to rain. A few drops. I looked at the sky. The rain at the end of summer is never like the autumn rains. It is fiercer, it batters the seashore, digs into the slopes with the strength of a jealous woman.

The old men are saying that this winter will be a winter for snow.

I went back to La Griffue. I looked up. There was a light on in my bedroom.

I picked up a pebble. A little pebble of black granite, on the side there was a light-coloured scratch, an impact the shape of a star. I closed my fingers around it gently, and slipped it into my pocket.

*   *   *

Lambert stayed for a week, and then he left again. He came back ten days later.

He left again.

398

On each of his trips, he went to see Michel. When he came back, he talked to me about him. About their meetings, only a few hours a day. He would have liked to have stayed longer, but the rules of the monastery would not allow it. On his last visit, he had been allowed into the cloister, the more private area, reserved for the monks. A moment of conversation in a windowless cell. They had drunk water. They had eaten a few biscuits.

They had talked.

Those visits, however brief, made him happy.

*   *   *

I knew now that I could love other hands, desire another body; that is what I had found again with him, the desire, but I also knew that I could no longer love like before.

Sharing nights.

Your death had severed me from that.

Did Lambert understand?

He watched as I left him. He did not try to keep me there.

He spoke to me several times about the house he had in Le Morvan, an old mill by a stream. He did not tell me anything more about it, simply that he would like to show me the place.

He left again.

It was good, like that. I was learning to wait for him.

There were troubling silences between us.

One day, he took a letter out of his pocket, a letter he had received from his brother. In this letter, Michel spoke at length about forgiveness. He said that forgiveness was not forgetting, that you had to know how to follow that path, and he quoted a sentence by John Paul II: *The man who forgives understands that there is a greater truth than himself.*

That night, I told him about you. We were in his car. Beyond the windscreen was the sea.

He loved me that night, afterwards. At his house. In his room, a bed

399

with white sheets. He loved me the way that you knew how to love me, that same manner, just as absolute.

In the night I got up and went to lean against the wall under the skylight. The sky was full of stars. I thought that one of the stars might be you.

Sounds in the night. Rustlings, light whisperings.

I turned round and I watched him breathing, the man who had just loved me.

I sat down, my back to the radiator. From the pocket of my jacket I took the little notebook that never leaves me. I turned the pages, I went through all the drawings up to the pages that followed, the last ones, the white pages, and I began to write our story.

The next day, Lambert told me he was going back to see his brother, and that if I wanted, I could go with him. It was the end of September. The fine days were over. The wind had begun to blow from the west, bringing moisture, banks of fog from the sea. Flakes of foam that it ripped from the waves and tossed against my windows. Even on days with sun it was cold.

* * *

We set off very early in the morning. When we left Auderville, it was already raining. There were drops clinging to the windows. We put on some music. We talked about Michel.

Shortly after Caen, I pointed to the countryside, I told him, Françoise Sagan lived somewhere over there. He did not give a damn about Sagan, but I told him about the manor house all the same.

A few years ago, I came here with you. We had ventured into the grounds. Sagan was there, in an armchair, her body protected from the cold by a blanket. And yet it was summer. She was asleep.

The following year, when we came back, she was dead.

Lambert pulled over after Dozulé and I drove.

With my hands on the wheel, I thought about Sagan and that day. Thoughts without sadness. We had not had many other holidays, after the ones spent in Normandy.

By ten o'clock the light was stronger, but the sky remained grey. We stopped, a place on the autoroute that was called Fleury-en-Bière. We drank coffee, and after that, Lambert drove.

The car lulled me. His voice. He talked to me about his brother, and the peace that he had been feeling since he had found him again.

Just beyond Bessey-en-Chaume, we stopped for lunch.

Afterwards, I took the wheel.

At one point, Lambert pointed to the forests, far in the distance, and told me that Le Morvan was there, beyond the expanse of trees.

We kept on driving.

We stopped again.

And set off again.

I fell asleep. When I opened my eyes, I saw mountains. We were very near Grenoble.

While I was asleep, Lambert had covered me with his jacket. My warmth beneath it, preserved. I looked at him. He smiled at me.

We left the autoroute.

We drank hot chocolate in a town at the foot of the mountains, just before we entered the gorges. Lambert explained that in the old days, it was from here that the monks set out, on foot, to make their solitary way to their place of withdrawal. They went all this way.

We talked about Michel, who had set off from much further away. We looked at a stream running between the houses.

We got back into the car, a very narrow road against the side of the mountain. On our right there were gorges, with a stream running at the bottom. We went through tunnels dug in the rock. There were waterfalls. There was water seeping everywhere, on the road and also against the sides of the mountain. Lambert told me that this road was called the road of Le Désert. That sometimes you could see lynxes here.

We did not see anybody.

We arrived in Saint-Pierre, it was nearly dark.

Lambert had booked two rooms in a hotel in the village, the Hôtel du Nord.

His room was number 4. I had number 16, it was not on the same floor. We had dinner in a little restaurant, we ordered ham with hay, a speciality that the waitress recommended. We drank a bottle of good wine. He told me about the pathetic investigations he had to conduct when he was in Dijon. Sordid stories. I told him I liked sordid stories, and that made him laugh.

He told me about the period in his life when he was a militant, hoping he could change the world.

Afterwards, we walked around the narrow streets, holding each other close, it was even colder than in La Hague, but here there was no wind.

I was the one who went to him that night. His door was not locked. All I had to do was open it. He was standing by the window. He did not say anything. He was waiting for me.

*   *   *

The next morning, it was late when we got up. We had a quick breakfast, in an empty dining room.

Lambert wanted to show me a little church, a place that was called Saint-Hugues, there were several paintings hanging inside, a way of the cross. The painter was called Arcabas. The colours he used, like gold.

We stopped to feel the icy water flowing from a waterfall. We saw trout.

Afterwards, we took the road to the monastery.

We left the car in a car park a bit lower down. Ours was the only car.

A path went through meadows. It was lined with very old trees, their roots broken through to the surface, sinewy across the ground. We could not see the monastery, it was at the end of the path. Surrounded by mountains. Already enclosed.

We had to walk some more.

Something mysterious emanated from the place, a particular aura, I felt it very strongly before I even saw the first roof.

The monastery came into view, almost abruptly, a vast surrounding wall standing firm in the earth, with cow pastures all around, and trees, and the blue expanse of mountains, and fir trees. We stopped. The place was isolated from everything in the same way that La Hague could be isolated. But this place was sacred. Even the trees seemed to be praying. The stones by the side of the path.

I ran my fingertips over the thick bark of a tree. The Hopi Indians say that it is enough to touch one stone on a river bed for the entire life of the river to be changed.

An encounter may suffice.

Lambert took my hand. Simply. He squeezed it and we went on. One step and then another. Without speaking. These mountains were carried by silence, impregnated with it, the slightest noise, the briefest word would have been an insult.

I looked at the walls. The roofs you could glimpse through the trees. The men who lived here had withdrawn from the world, they had renounced the sight of other humans. Renounced a life with them.

A life outside of time.

For a God.

We went up to the front door. A chain was hanging there, a heavy bell at the end. It was still too early to announce our presence.

We carried on, climbing the path that went around the monastery. The air was cold, the sun was shining and the earth smelled good.

The slate roofs shone in the sunlight. Grey walls. A figure in the distance, in what seemed to be a garden. A man bent over, carrying a spade.

Furtive shadows. Mute men. I could sense their invisible presence. I could have been like them. After you, I could have done the same, locked myself in behind walls and never left again.

At two o'clock we came back to the main door. It was Michel who opened to us. He was wearing a long habit, the cowl down his back. I looked at him, at his face. The men who live here cannot look like other men. They are inhabited by light. Michel seemed timeless.

He took my hands between his own, and then Lambert's. He told us he had two hours until Vespers. We exchanged a few words about the long road we had had to take to come this far. He explained that the longest roads were often the most necessary. To walk, to meditate. He had taken many long months to arrive here. And years after that to understand what real life was. He had touched wisdom. He had learned contemplation.

He said, "Some day, I shall carry on as far as Compostela."

From above, the sun illuminated the pastures.

Was time divided up here as it was elsewhere, into months and years? Did one year count as much for him as it did for me?

He had no watch.

What did two years, ten years represent for men who lived so withdrawn? Bells gave rhythm to the hours, the way tides marked time in La Hague.

He spoke about nature, so beautiful and strong. He smiled again. A light from within lit up his face. He seemed to have no anxieties. Yet the sea that had killed his parents lived on in him. He carried it, buried, in mute recesses. Even forgotten. The sea. A trace of it. The memory of the cold, perhaps.

Did he remember the shouts?

The currents?

He must carry the intense light of the lighthouse within him.

The two brothers set off together along the path into the forest. I watched them go, small figures, one dark and the other light. They were walking side by side and talking.

I went back to the main door. I waited for a few minutes and it opened again. Théo's face greeted me. Behind him, the thicker shadow of a passage. That was all I was able to see of the interior of the monastery.

The door closed again. A deep thud. The scraping of shoes over gravel.

Théo was wearing the same clothes as on the day he had left, the same cardigan and his little old corduroy trousers, frayed by his cats' claws.

We moved off into the trees. Little spots of light danced at our feet. There was water running, no doubt a spring, or the overflow from a recent rainfall. A few puddles.

Théo walked slowly, one hand curled around his cane. I gave him news of his cats. I told him about them, and then about La Hague, the cold weather that was settling in. I talked to him about his house, and some more about the cats.

I did not tell him that the little white cat had disappeared.

We walked as far as a wooden shed. Long tree trunks had been dragged there, waiting to be sawn into pieces, they were all marked with two lines of white paint. There were some deep tracks in the mud.

Théo had been there almost three months. He seemed to be fine. He helped with the chores in the kitchen. He peeled the vegetables and cooked them. Always in water. With a bit of salt. Insipid-tasting, nothing inventive.

He told me that sometimes he missed Lili's cooking. He smiled, I could not have said whether the smile was sad, he turned his head in the direction of the mountain where the two men had disappeared.

He was silent for a long time, his gaze slightly veiled.

"Michel is the most solitary man in the entire monastery, but when he goes out, he is also the most talkative."

Théo stooped slightly, his neck heavy. His legs no longer carried him very well.

We went to sit on a bench in the sun. Next to each other.

"Don't you miss the sea?"

"Not any more . . . but I often think of it."

"You don't get bored?"

"Get bored? There are so many things to do here . . . Just looking at the sky, you never tire of it. And I have a friend, a very old blind monk. He lives behind one of those windows. We spend many hours talking together."

"I thought the monks were not supposed to talk?"

He smiled.

"Of course, they're not supposed to, but we do anyway. Who can hear us?"

"God?"

"God . . . How much more could he punish us, he has already made us so old . . ."

"He might send you to hell!"

"Then let him."

There was amusement in his voice.

He spoke again about Michel and about the deep silence that reigned within the walls.

"Michel reads a great deal, and he writes. He receives a lot of letters you know . . . he's very surprised by the way people live. He said that some day, because of the atom, the world will explode and mankind will go back to using the flint."

Théo raised his head. He looked at the mountains for a long time, an entire area caught in shadow, almost black, whereas the other slope, facing south, was still bathed in sunlight.

"He is the one who sews the shrouds the monks are buried in. He does it, just like Florelle did."

He said her name, Florelle, a delicate memory, his eyes moist.

Tears that took him back to La Hague, to the breakers.

I let long moments go by. Did Michel feel resentful towards Théo? Had they talked about that?

When I put the question to him, Théo shook his head.

"Michel does not know how to reproach. It's not how he looks at things. It's not his way."

He spoke again at length about his life, from now on, between those walls, the walls of the monastery and those of the mountain.

The walls that they call the cloister.

"Do you know that there are very specific laws governing the life of this mountain?"

He talked about the animals that lived there in the shelter of the trees, countless animals, roe deer, lynxes, a few wolves.

He talked about the men, solitary souls in quest of the absolute, who offered up their own silence to the silence of the mountain.

Théo told me that he missed the sunsets, that here, because of the mountains, there were no sunsets.

I gave him news of Lili.

I told him that Old Mother was well.

He listened to me.

And then he was overcome by fatigue. The chill, too. The bench was in the shade now. A shiver. He wanted to go back. The infinite slowness of his steps. I went with him up to the door.

I looked at him.

He was one of those men who die without leaving a trace.

I promised him I would come back, and he said, "I know you will come back."

A moment later the bells of the monastery began to ring, one after the other, and then all together. Time was measured here in masses and prayers. The whole week looked ahead to Sunday. And all the weeks in turn looked ahead to a few precise dates, depending on the season; it could be Easter, or Christmas.

And their very lives looked ahead to death, the last appointment.

I thought of you.

The bells stopped, but they continued to echo for a long time, an echo held prisoner between the walls of the mountain.

The sky, laid bare.

Silence.

The two brothers came back. They had walked for a long time. I watched as they drew closer, one beside the other. Michel slightly taller. His habit dragging in the grass.

It had just gone four in the afternoon, time for Vespers. Michel opened the door. Two monks were hurrying along a lane, the sound of their sandals on the gravel. I could see a shadow behind one of the windows.

Michel did not ask us if we would be coming back. No doubt, he already knew that we would.

A moment later, we heard a key turning on the other side of the door, a rustling of cloth, and then nothing more.

Silence once again fell over Le Désert, engulfing it in its secrets, engulfing the solitude of the men who lived there.

Lambert took my hand. He had a big, warm, trusting hand. He murmured something infinitely tender into my ear, and together we went back into the world.